THE FIELDS OF FORTUNE

To ...ord
Cra ...gh,
see ...er
hus ...e's
run ...his
lor ...at
Nic ...the
Cra ...er
fath

Ge ...its
web ...ut
is ... is
pen ...to
sna

Inc ...rd
Cra ...of
the ...ith
the ...rie
Oli ...on
who

THE FIELDS OF FORTUNE

Jessica Sterling

WINDSOR

PARAGON

First published 2007
by
Hodder & Stoughton
This Large Print edition published 2008
by
BBC Audiobooks Ltd by arrangement with
Hodder and Stoughton Ltd

Hardcover ISBN: 978 1 405 68606 8
Softcover   ISBN: 978 1 405 68607 5

British Library Cataloguing in Publication Data available

Printed and bound in Great Britain by
Antony Rowe Ltd., Chippenham, Wiltshire

To My Long-Suffering Editor
Carolyn Caughey
(and not before time)

CONTENTS

PART ONE

The Legacy of Eve

CHAPTER ONE

It had long been a tradition in the Templeton family that marriages were arranged beneath the oak that shaded the front lawn of the house. Under its leafy boughs grandfather had asked grandmother to become his wife. Thirty years later, after grandmother had passed away, grandfather had bent the knee again with, Nicola assumed, a good deal of grunting and cracking, and had proposed to a starchy widow, who, in lieu of youthful passion, had brought to the union the best part of fifteen hundred acres of prime grazing land and an income in rents of almost six hundred pounds a year.

In that same year, 1752, Nicola's father, John James Templeton, had invited young Miss Morrison to join with him in holy matrimony and to seal the bond of love by persuading her father to sign over to Craigiehall seven farms and eight hundred acres of uncultivated ground, to which terms Daddy Morrison reluctantly agreed. And that, as far as Nicola could make out, was all that marriage had ever meant to the Templetons—a means of acquiring land.

She was not, however, prepared for what was to come when on a fine spring morning Sir Charles de Morville's carriage rolled up the driveway and Papa, dressed in a new striped waistcoat and his very best coat, hurried out to greet the gentleman and escort him to the ground floor drawing-room where they remained closeted for the best part of an hour.

The taking of a one o'clock dinner and, with the meat hardly settled in her stomach, an early tea, did not increase Nicola's apprehension, for Sir Charles and her father, Lord Craigiehall, chatted about farming and politics without once mentioning matrimony. Only when Papa, with a curiously arch little smile, suggested that she show Sir Charles the ancient oak where so many bargains had been struck did it dawn on her that she had been put upon the marriage block.

Hiding her dismay, she set off with Sir Charles, trailed by her maid Molly, Sir Charles's manservant Lassiter, and, creeping along the drive at a funereal pace, de Morville's carriage, brought up, Nicola assumed, in case an excess of emotion rendered the elderly Sir Charles incapable of walking the short distance back to the house.

In spite of his exalted position as a judge in the highest court in Scotland and one of Ayrshire's principal landowners, her father was not partial to entertaining. He hosted occasional small supper parties during court session in Edinburgh and enjoyed the hospitality of the well-to-do when he made his Circuit journeys but, as a rule, chose not to sup with his neighbours.

Sir Charles had not been a frequent visitor to Craigiehall. There had been no regular courtship, no exchange of *billets doux* and emphatically no hint of indiscretion on Sir Charles's part. He was a gentleman of the old school—the very old school—who firmly believed that billing and cooing were much less important than settling terms.

Nicola reckoned that words of love did not come easily to the lips of a man who had buried two wives, fathered three sons and had grandchildren almost as old as she was. Sir Charles's conversation was vague and halting, unlike the almost brutal directness of Grant Peters, her sister Charlotte's husband, who had thwarted all Papa's attempts to end his whirlwind courtship of Charlotte by invoking the word 'love' with a vehemence usually reserved for advocates pleading capital charges.

If she had been in Charlotte's shoes Nicola too might have surrendered everything to Grant Peters for he was handsome in a burly sort of way, with coal black eyes that sized you up in an instant and a shock of dark curly hair that could not properly be contained by a wig. He had rushed Charlotte to the matrimonial oak under cover of darkness and had framed the vital question with such rhetorical vigour that Charlotte did not quite know whether she was saying yes or no, and had merely managed to nod which, it seemed, had been agreement enough for the impatient young lawyer.

Three weeks later they had been married with a minimum of fuss in the crumbling little church at Kirkton and had returned at once to Edinburgh. Papa had stubbornly refused to attend the wedding and for almost a year now had spoken not a single word to Charlotte and addressed Grant Peters only when the business of the court demanded it.

'Nicola—may I call you Nicola?' Sir Charles enquired.

'Why, of course,' Nicola answered politely.

'I do not wish to appear too—ah—pressing but time is not on my side.' She had already noticed that Sir Charles rarely quoted Latin authors and never dropped French phrases into the conversation like her father's Edinburgh friends.

'Miss Templeton—Nicola—it behoves me to declare that you—you look particularly ravishing this evening.'

'Ravishing?' Nicola said. 'Really?'

'Filled with—with spring sap.'

'Sap? I see,' said Nicola. 'Why, thank you, Sir Charles.'

'Charles—Charles will do. In the light of what's between us you are not obliged to address me by my title.'

'What's between us?' said Nicola. 'What *is* between us, sir?'

'Oh, nothing indelicate, I assure you. Have I presumed too much?'

Sir Charles de Morville might be the wealthiest man in North Ayrshire but his kidskin breeches did not quite cover his bony knees and no amount of tailoring could hide his wobbling little paunch.

Nicola would have liked him better if he had been a bluff artisan in search of a young wife to warm his bed or even a wizened Edinburgh rake scheming for a wealthy bride to pay off his debts. As it was, Sir Charles appeared to have no interest in her virtues and the prospect of cohabiting with the diffident old gentleman, whose mental competence was, or soon would be, less than intact, filled her with revulsion.

She stopped in her tracks and glanced back at Molly who raised both hands helplessly. Lassiter, the manservant, stopped too, and the carriage ground to a halt.

'What is it, my dear?' Sir Charles asked. 'I trust I have not said something to offend you?'

'No,' Nicola said, 'but I fear that you are about to.'

'What do you mean?'

'I mean I've no intention of marrying you, no matter what sort of accommodation you may have reached with my father.'

'I haven't asked you to marry me.'

'Are you not primed to propose as soon as we reach the oak?'

'Well—well, yes. I mean, I am.'

'No,' she snapped. 'No, no, no.'

'Lord Craigiehall, your father, assured me—'

'He may assure you all he likes, sir; I will not marry you,' Nicola said, 'not even to appease my father.'

Her mother had died soon after Nicola was born and some years later her brother Jamie had been brought down by a wasting of the lungs that had reduced him to a long-necked, high-shouldered splinter of a boy who, out of exhaustion more than anything, had quit the world with a sigh of relief at the age of twelve. Then, last summer, Charlotte had all but eloped with Grant Peters and had left Nicola to fulfil Papa's hopes for the future of Craigiehall which, apparently, included marriage to his antique neighbour.

'Ah, yes,' Sir Charles said, nodding. 'I told your father it would be better to allow you time to ripen.'

'Ripen? I'm not an apple for the picking,' Nicola said. 'I'm quite old enough to know my own mind, sir. Whatever my father may have led you to believe, I am *not* going to marry you just to furnish Craigiehall with an heir.'

'An heir?' Sir Charles pressed a hand to his chest, his nails, close shorn, pink in the evening light. 'Nothing was said about an heir. The

7

provision of an heir might not—I mean—I am not a young man, Nicola, and nature . . .' He made to touch her sleeve but she drew away. 'I will not be—um—a demanding husband, I assure you.'

'Do you not love me?'

'No doubt I will learn to do so,' he said. 'The fact of the matter is that I have but few years left on this earth and I require a wife to protect me.'

'Protect you?'

'From my sons' interminable squabbling.'

'Is mediation to be my only role, sir?'

'You will be well provided for.'

'I am well enough provided for as it is,' Nicola said. 'What has my father promised you? And what will he receive in return?'

'That, my dear,' Sir Charles said, 'is none of your concern.'

'I see,' Nicola said. 'I am to become your wife to protect you from your sons but will receive nothing of value in return?'

'Coal working rights,' Sir Charles admitted, grudgingly.

'I don't doubt that my father will be delighted to work coal from your land but he also requires a suitable heir for Craigiehall,' Nicola said, 'and he will insist that you provide him with one.'

'That may not, in practice, be possible.'

'Stuff and nonsense!' Nicola had no experience of love or of courtship but she had been reared in farming country and was well enough versed in the facts of life. 'It *will* be possible, Sir Charles. I will make *sure* it's possible.'

'That is a very unseemly thing for a young woman to say, Miss Templeton. I am beginning to think that you are not the innocent flower your

8

father believes you to be and, indeed, may *not* be a suitable companion after all.'

'Companion, Sir Charles?'

'Wife: I mean, wife.'

'I regret that I must decline to be either your companion or your wife.'

'Are you rejecting my offer, Miss Templeton?'

'I am, sir. Indeed, I am,' said Nicola.

'Will you not give the matter more consideration? Talk it over with—'

'With my father?' Nicola said. 'No, Sir Charles, as far as I'm concerned my father may jump in the loch and, if he wishes, take you with him.'

Shocked, he staggered back, plucked a handkerchief from the pocket of his coat and held it to his lips. His eyes darkened and his cheeks took on a curious flush as if her forcefulness had finally stirred his ardour.

'Is that your last word on the matter, Miss Templeton?'

'It is, Sir Charles, it is.'

'Lassiter,' he called out, 'fetch the coach.'

*　　　*　　　*

It must have cost her father a mighty effort of will, Nicola thought, not to rush out of doors when Sir Charles's carriage clattered off towards the Ayr turnpike. He remained within the drawing-room, seated, rock-like, in a gilt-wood armchair, his long legs crossed, his lean, clean-shaven chin tipped up, his features carved with an expression of such severity that, not for the first time, she realised why he terrified not only felons but agents and advocates too.

9

'Well, girl,' he said, 'where has he gone to?'

'Home, I imagine,' Nicola said.

Hugh Littlejohn, her father's overseer, and Robertson, his manservant, lurked in the shadows of the hall and on the master's signal hastily closed the drawing-room doors.

Nicola's lips were dry, her throat sticky but, smothering her anger, she smoothed her skirts, seated herself on a black-and-gilt chaise and lay back against the cushion as if the events of the afternoon had merely bored her.

'What passed between you?' her father said.

'I think you know what passed between us. He asked me to become his wife and I turned him down.'

'You turned him down?' her father said. 'May I ask why?'

'I've no desire to become the wife of a man who has one foot in the grave,' Nicola answered. 'I'll not be traded away simply to advance your interests.'

'I trust you do not intend to follow your sister's example by marrying a penniless upstart.'

'Grant Peters is no upstart, nor is he penniless.'

'Peters is naught but a self-seeking lawyer with no rank or bottom. He will amount to nothing,' her father said. 'What's more, he'll have not one acre from me when I'm gone.' He leaned forward and thrust out his chin, as if pronouncing sentence. 'He's sharp enough when it comes to the practice of law, I confess, and I don't doubt that he has mastered all the prescriptions and obscure feudal acts that will enable him to lay claim to Craigiehall.'

'I want no part of your schemes to expand

Craigiehall,' Nicola said.

'If you choose to marry with my approval, Nicola, you'll have Craigiehall to pass on to your children; then, perhaps, you'll thank me for protecting you from the clamour that will hover over the inheritance.'

'I'm in no mood to be lectured on the laws of inheritance,' said Nicola.

'Perhaps not,' her father said. 'However, it's not given to mortal man to set a limit to his term on earth; that is a matter for God to decide upon. If I die without warning, believe me, Peters will have the skin off your back.'

Quite how Grant Peters had infiltrated Papa's stuffy clique was still something of a mystery. He had simply appeared one chill winter afternoon after service in St Giles, tagging along behind Mr Arbuthnot, the bookseller. He had been dressed in well-worn black gabardine, like an almsman, and had presented no obvious threat, save that he was young and more opinionated than he should have been given his rank and circumstances. He had courted Charlotte by letter and, later, at Craigiehall when Papa had been off on his Circuit journeys. He had proposed to her before Papa could return to prevent it.

'Why do you hate Grant Peters so much?'

'Because he's an upstart who took advantage of my hospitality to ingratiate himself into your sister's good graces. I had hoped that Charlotte would marry Arthur or possibly William de Morville but they were too impatient to wait for her to grow up. Tomorrow,' her father said, 'we'll ride over to de Morville's house and repair the damage. I'm sure that when you apologise for your

11

impetuosity Sir Charles will look more favourably upon you. He thinks very highly of you, you know.'

'He thinks of me hardly at all,' Nicola said. 'He thinks very highly of *you*, Papa. He is just as much in thrall to you as everyone else. Why don't you offer to lease the coal workings if you want them so badly? The bald fact of the matter is that you're so set against Grant Peters that you'll do anything to prevent him laying hands on Craigiehall.'

'Have I not just said as much?'

'Anything—including marrying me off to a decrepit old man. Well, Papa, I will not grovel to that horrid old fellow, not tomorrow nor any other day.'

'You will do as I say, Nicola.'

'No, I will not. I'm eighteen years old and quite able to take charge of my own life and my own destiny.'

'How will you support yourself?' her father said. 'Daughters of gentlemen are not equipped to provide for themselves. They are expected to make sensible marriages.'

'Surely you would not see me starve?'

'The letter of the law obligates me to attend to your welfare until you take a husband,' her father said. 'Starving is not an issue.'

He rose suddenly, looming up against the light. He had never struck her, or Charlotte, though once, many years ago, he had taken a cane to Jamie to teach him a lesson, the moral of which was long forgotten.

At sixty, he did not seem old. He was not stiff in movement and in spite of a thousand hours spent on the bench his spine remained straight. He closed his hands behind his back and tucked them beneath his coat tail.

'The truth is that I am not so well off as you might imagine,' he said. 'Balancing the running of my estate with a career in law has taken its toll. I may be a judge of the double robe and have an honorary title but my finances are not as sound as they ought to be.'

'Are we poor, father?' Nicola asked, with a hint of mockery.

'Poor? Nay, hardly that; not gruel poor, at least. However, now that Jamie's gone and Charlotte has put herself beyond reach it falls to you to secure Craigiehall's future by making a proper marriage.'

'Find me a husband then, a better, younger husband than de Morville.'

'Easier to say than to do. The world is full of selfish young rogues, Nicola, without a penny to their names or prospects worth the mention. I've gone to considerable lengths to encourage Sir Charles de Morville's interest. Whatever you may think to the contrary, he is, in most respects, an ideal husband for you.'

When he leaned towards her she saw the underside of his jaw, his thin lips and that formidable brow all foreshortened, just as she had done when she was small and he had slipped into the nursery to bid Charlotte and her goodnight. He had seemed quite fearsome then in the slanting light from the candle and she had often wished that he was more ordinary, like Mr Trench, the tenant of Kirkton farm, for instance, who was red-cheeked and jolly and who, risking Nanny Aird's wrath, would lift her up and twirl her about just for the fun of it; or like Mr Feldspar, the soutar from Kilmarnock who travelled about the shire with a cartful of boots and shoes and who always had a kind word and a square of brown candy for Charlotte and her, even though he took few orders at her Craigiehall's kitchen door.

'In most respects?' Nicola said. 'What respects, for instance?'

'By any calculation,' her father said, 'Charles de Morville will soon be called upon to pay his debt to nature.'

'His debt to nature?' Nicola said. 'What *do* you mean?'

'I mean,' her father said, 'that he will die within a year or two.'

'Is that what this is all about?' Nicola cried. 'You wish me to marry de Morville so that I may become his widow? Papa, that's a scurrilous suggestion.'

'It's not in the least scurrilous. If you marry Sir Charles you'll have your share of his lands to manage as you will. You'll be entitled to appoint your own factor, draw your own rents and be quite independent of de Morville's sons. In a word, what has been given you, you'll keep. Then you may marry anyone you choose, for a wealthy young widow never lacks suitors of quality.'

'And Craigiehall?'

'Craigiehall will be saved and increased.'

'Increased by my sacrifice, you mean?'

'Come now, whatever his faults, de Morville is hardly a Hottentot. He'll treat you with respect and obey your every whim.'

'But will he do the decent thing and *die*?' Nicola cried. 'Have you fixed a date in the nuptial agreement when he will politely give up the ghost?' She thrust her hands against her father's chest and

14

pushed him away. 'What if de Morville does not die? What if he falls into a dribbling sickness that does not prove fatal? Am I to nurse him? Am I to lie with him every night and keep him alive with the heat of my body as the Shunammite did to King David?'

'You have too much imagination, Nicola.'

'I have too much conscience, you mean,' Nicola snapped.

'He *is* seventy-two years old, you know.'

'And I'm eighteen. Great heavens, Papa, don't you care for me at all?' Nicola said and then, before she could burst into tears, added, 'I am going to my room now.'

'We'll sup at half past seven and talk of this matter at greater length.'

'I'm not hungry. I am going to bed.'

'Nicola!'

'Goodnight to you, sir.'

'Nicola!' he said once more.

But Nicola had already gone.

*   *   *

Waning sunlight was reflected in the bevel of the pier-glass, a sad little rainbow trapped in the darkened room. The four-poster that she had once shared with Charlotte seemed vast and with all Charlotte's boxes gone the room itself was depressingly empty. She loosened her ribbons, kicked off her shoes, threw herself on the bed and buried her face in the pillow.

Until now, her dreams of bridal nights had centred not on submission to a husband's physical demands but to a love that owed more to the

15

fairytale than the barnyard. She was afraid that Papa might somehow manipulate her into a position where she would have to marry Charles de Morville if only to save Craigiehall for children who had not been conceived and who, if Sir Charles was to be believed, might never be conceived at all.

Molly slipped into the room. She was six years older than Nicola and had served first in the scullery then as a housemaid and after Nanny Aird had passed away had been put to care for Charlotte and Nicola. She was a plump, red-haired woman whose bumpkin appearance disguised sharp wits.

She padded to the bed, seated herself on the counterpane and wiped away Nicola's tears with a none-too-clean handkerchief.

'What shall I do, Molly? What *can* I do?' Nicola sobbed. 'Tomorrow, or the next day, Papa will insist that we call upon Sir Charles, I will be forced to apologise and—and—it will begin all over again.'

'Aye,' Molly said, 'but this time you'll be ready for it.'

'Are the servants talking? Do they think me a fool?'

'It matters not a jot what the servants think,' Molly assured her. 'All that matters now is what you want to do.'

'What Papa wants me to do, you mean.'

'You refused the mannie once, you can refuse him again.'

'I cannot go on refusing him if Papa won't take *no* for an answer.'

'Sir Charles'll weary of it soon enough,' Molly

16

said. 'He was none too eager in the first place. He thinks you're o'er young for him an' he's frightened you'll wear him to a frazzle.'

Nicola sat up. 'Did Mr Lassiter say as much?'

'Mr Lassiter's far too grand to gossip wi' the likes o' me,' Molly said. 'If I know your father, though, he'll not let the matter rest. He'll want it settled before he goes up to Edinburgh for the summer term.'

'Perhaps he'll find another suitor, someone younger and more appealing than Charles de Morville. I'm not unattractive, Molly, am I?'

'You're far from that, Miss,' Molly said. 'It's my guess, though, his lordship'll leave you in Craigiehall. He's worried you'll have your head turned an' run off wi' an upstart like Mr Peters.'

'Mr Peters isn't an upstart; he's a well respected lawyer.'

'Maybe so,' Molly said, 'but he's not Sir Charles de Morville.'

'Why is my father so concerned with the de Morvilles? Sir Charles may be wealthy even by our standards but he's just a fusty old farmer with more land than he knows what to do with,' Nicola said. 'I've heard all the tales about the de Morville boys and their silly squabbles. Why Sir Charles imagines that having me for a wife will unite his family is quite beyond me. My father persuaded him, I suppose, bamboozled him with legal jargon. I'm sick of Papa's plots, sick of being shut away in Craigiehall like a prisoner in the Tolbooth.'

'Then go to Edinburgh,' Molly said. 'Now you've turned eighteen your father can't send the soldiers to fetch you back. Mr Peters'll take you in till this spot o' bother blows over. It would be a grand bit

17

of revenge for the way your father treated Mr Peters if he sheltered you for a week or two.'

'I cannot leave without Papa's permission.'

'If Charlotte had waited for his lordship's permission she'd still be sittin' here in Craigiehall or—worse—be wedded to old Sir Charles. When your Papa realises he has made a mistake he'll offer the olive branch, you'll see.'

Nicola thought about it for a moment. 'I'll write to Charlotte tomorrow.'

'If I was you, Miss Nicola, I wouldn't bother wi' a letter.'

'If you were me, Molly,' Nicola said, 'what *would* you do?'

'Pack an' leave for Edinburgh before his lordship can stop you.'

'But I've no money, not a penny to my name.'

'I've enough saved for two seats on the Flyer,' Molly said.

'I couldn't possibly take money from you, Molly.'

'Pay me back when we get there.'

'Where will I get the money to pay you?'

'Mr Peters'll take care o' it,' Molly said. 'Now what's it to be, Miss Nicola? Edinburgh—or another encounter wi' Sir Charles?'

'Edinburgh,' Nicola said. 'Even if it does turn out to be the lesser of two evils, yes, Edinburgh, first thing tomorrow morning.'

*   *   *

Charlotte was surprised and not entirely pleased, to find Nicola and Molly huddled on the landing at half past four o'clock on a rainy Thursday afternoon.

She had just entertained two ladies from the St Andrew's Charitable Foundation and had been reduced to a state of near torpor by their tedious harangue. In addition, the taking of tea at such an unfashionable hour had rubbed home the drabness of her life in the upper reaches of the massive tenement that towered over the Lawnmarket. Graddan's Court had originally been designed to provide the burgesses of Edinburgh with a little extra breathing space but having lost its wealthier citizens to the New Town across the North Loch, it had become a repository for those who had slipped from the upper rungs of society as well as those who, like young Grant Peters, were intent on moving up in the world.

Charlotte had a maid and a cook and her lot in life was not hard, though now and then she found it lonely, for Grant worked long hours to keep fees rolling in and he did not have a large circle of friends. Papa kept a spacious town house in Crowell's Close at the top of the Customhouse Steps, just a stone's throw away, but since the day of her marriage he had refused to communicate with Charlotte, let alone call upon her.

'My dearest girl,' Charlotte said, 'what a wonderful surprise. Look at you, though, you're quite soaked through. Did you travel on the post-chaise?'

'On the Flyer,' said Nicola. 'It took barely eight hours.'

Charlotte ushered them into the hall. 'Is Papa with you?'

'No,' said Nicola. 'Papa and I had a dreadful row and I ran off. May I lodge with you for a little

19

while—if it isn't inconvenient?'

'Of course it isn't inconvenient,' Charlotte said. 'I take it Papa knows where you are?'

'I left a letter with Mr Littlejohn.'

'Didn't Mr Littlejohn try to stop you?' Charlotte said.

'On the contrary. He had our boxes conveyed to the road-end.'

'Where are your boxes now?'

'At Mannering's Hotel in the New Town where the Flyer terminates,' Nicola said. 'We walked across the bridge from there.'

'Did you not think to hire a caddy?'

'I did not have money enough to hire a caddy,' Nicola said. 'I had to borrow the coach fare from Molly.'

'Oh!' said Charlotte. 'You really have run away, haven't you? Never fear. Grant will take care of everything. Now, why are we standing in the hall? Come into the parlour and take off your bonnet and cape. I'll have Jeannie make us fresh tea and some bread and butter. We sup, as a rule, at eight or half past, depending on when Grant elects to come home.'

'How is Grant?' Nicola said.

'He's well,' Charlotte said. 'Very well.' Then, throwing open the door, she ushered her sister into the parlour.

*   *   *

It was after seven o'clock before Grant Peters returned. He greeted Nicola warmly, listened to her story, nodded, and went off to find a reliable boy to retrieve her trunk from Mannering's yard

20

while Charlotte arranged with Cook to add more dumplings to the stew and Jeannie, the maid, lighted the lamps and set the table.

Nicola knew little about Grant Peters' pedigree. His family had elected not to add fuel to the flames by attending the Ayrshire wedding. Two brothers and a widowed mother were settled on one of four small farms that the Peters owned outside of Stirling. The oldest brother, Roderick, factored the holdings. The youngest brother, Gillon, had fought with the Highland Regiment in the American war but, having no cash with which to purchase himself a decent commission, had recently resigned from the King's service.

Grant had studied Latin, Greek and moral philosophy at the Universities of Edinburgh and Glasgow and had been mentored thereafter by Writer to the Signet Hercules Mackenzie, whose instruction had enabled him to pass his trials Civil Law and whose influence had gained him admission to the Faculty of Advocates, though Grant was still too young to have established the connections necessary to attract the most lucrative briefs.

The drawing-room, which also served as a dining-room, had precious few furnishings. There was no dresser or cabinet and only a small corner cupboard in which napery was stored. The rattle of pans leaked from the kitchen along with wreaths of steam and, now and then, an angry yelp from Mrs McCluskie, the cook; a far cry, Nicola thought, from Craigiehall's vast echoing dining-room.

Her brother-in-law uncorked two bottles of claret and filled the glasses. He was a large man, not tall but broad. His face, moistened by

21

perspiration, was all in proportion, with a strong jaw and high flat cheekbones. He had changed his coat and loosened the plain neckpiece that most advocates wore, though these days, so her father claimed, lawyers' stocks sometimes had more frills than a duchess's petticoats.

Grant chatted casually about crops and weather, as if her sudden appearance in his house was the most natural thing in the world, while Nicola studied her sister's husband with a degree of speculation, wondering, even then, if he had a friend, a fellow lawyer, say, as handsome and attentive as he was, to whom she might be introduced.

Mutton broth and brown bread, beef stew with onions and dumplings, pease pottage in a side dish, an orange pudding, strong cheese and oatcakes were washed down with several glasses of claret. When supper was over and the last crumbs swept from the table, Nicola assumed that they would move to the parlour, but Grant seemed content to stay where he was.

'Your maid—Molly, is it?—will be snug enough in the loft, though I fear she will have to share a bed with Jeannie,' he said. 'How long do you intend to stay with us?'

'Ah!' Nicola said. 'That depends.'

'On what?' Grant said. 'On your father?'

'On you,' Nicola said.

'The courts open in a matter of weeks,' Grant said. 'His lordship may come to retrieve you before then but somehow I doubt it. He'll retaliate in other ways.'

'Other ways?' said Charlotte. 'What other ways?'

22

Grant ignored his wife's question. He lifted a hand, brushed back the curl of dark hair that bobbed on his brow and looked squarely at Nicola. 'The boy will be here shortly, I fancy.'

'Boy?' said Charlotte. 'What boy?'

'With the baggage,' Nicola said. 'I think you read my father very well, Grant, particularly as you don't yet know the whole story.'

'What is the whole story?'

'Papa is pressing me to marry Charles de Morville.'

'And Sir Charles is not to your taste?'

'Heavens, no! He's well over seventy and in poor health. Besides, he has three sons squabbling to take possession of his estate.'

'Why does your father wish you to marry this man?'

'The de Morvilles have coal workings on their land,' said Nicola. 'Papa covets them. He has long had it in mind that either Charlotte or I would marry into the de Morville family to obtain possession of the mining rights.'

'It's true, Grant. Papa has been set on linking the Templetons with the de Morvilles ever since we were children,' Charlotte said, 'though I still find it odd that he did not encourage us to consort with the de Morville boys or invite them to visit us at Craigiehall.'

'We were too small for them,' said Nicola. 'Not, shall we say, quite ripe?'

Charlotte pursed her lips and fussed with her skirts. She had put on weight since marriage and her cheeks were fleshy. She had always been high-coloured and prone to blushing. Mr Watson, the music teacher, had been much amused and would

23

tease her just to watch the blood rise to her face. He had called her his little Redskin, his little Cherokee, which Charlotte hadn't considered much of a compliment and Nicola had thought in rather poor taste given the state of the war in America at the time.

'I heard nothing of this, Charlotte,' Grant said. 'Why didn't you tell me?'

'I had no reason to tell you,' Charlotte said. 'It was a silly thing, a storm in a teacup, all over before we met.'

'Nevertheless,' Grant frowned, 'you should have informed me.'

'I trust you don't think I married you just to escape de Morville,' Charlotte said, her cheeks burning. 'The whole affair was a mad scheme dreamed up by my father. Papa is not the sober man of sense and judgement that he appears to be in court, you know.'

'That does not answer the question, my dear,' Grant said. 'Did you or did you not marry me just to escape this Ayrshire fellow?'

'Stop it,' Nicola said. 'Do stop it.'

He glanced at her, one eyebrow raised. 'Stop what?'

'Teasing,' Nicola said. 'I know you are teasing, even if Charlotte does not. She has no more liking for Charles de Morville than I have, but that does not mean to say that she leapt into your arms unwillingly.'

'So, Charlotte, is your sister's defence true and accurate?'

'Charlotte is not on trial, sir,' Nicola said.

'Am I obliged to accept your word that my wife's integrity is unimpeachable without a shred of

24

evidence to support your claim?'

'You are,' Nicola said, firmly.

'And what of *your* integrity, Miss Templeton?'

'Mine? I have no reason to lie to you.'

'*Quid pro quo*: are you implying that Charlotte does?' Grant said then, noting his wife's distress, laughed and patted Nicola's arm. 'The question of your integrity, my dear sister-in-law, will have to be put into abeyance until it can be proved. What's not in doubt is your mettle. I wish that my brothers were as quick to defend me as you have been to defend your sister. I am, as you rightly suppose, just teasing.'

He pushed himself away from the table, bent and kissed his wife upon the brow then, stepping neatly around the chairs, cupped both hands on Nicola's shoulders. 'You are welcome to stay for as long as you wish, Nicola. I'm aware that your papa has considerable influence in the field of law but, be assured, I've no fear of him whatsoever. I've defied him once and it will give me great pleasure to add insult to injury by keeping you here for as long as you choose to remain.'

The touch of his hands sent a shiver of pleasure through her. To her surprise she found that she wanted him to kiss her too, on the brow, on the cheek, even on the mouth, but, as if he had guessed what was on her mind, he broke abruptly away and stepped to the door.

'What?' Charlotte said. 'What is it?'

'The boy,' Grant said. 'Do you not hear him on the landing?'

*   *   *

25

The boy was a great gangling lad not far short of six feet tall. His boots were muddy, his coat black with rain, his hair plastered to his scalp. He had hauled Nicola's trunk across the bridge and up five flights of slippery steps on his shoulder with Molly's little box tucked under one arm. He blew out his cheeks, gulped in air and eyed the gentleman with a degree of apprehension, as if he suspected that he might be ordered to take the luggage back again.

Digging into his pocket, Grant brought out a shilling and, to the boy's surprise, another. He took the boy's hand, cold as a cod-fish, and placed the coins upon the palm.

'Was only but sixpence was promised, sir,' the boy said.

'A good job, well done, is always worth a little extra,' Grant said. 'If you hurry, you'll have time to buy yourself a pie from Mrs M'Causlan's and perhaps a glass of punch at Mouser's.'

'Aye, sir, aye. I thank ye, sir. I do thank ye,' the boy said, slapping his hand to his brow in a grateful salute. 'Any more caddyin' you need done, sir, you know where I'm to be found.'

'I do,' Grant said. 'Now cut along before the pie-shop closes.'

He watched the boy lope off down the staircase, then, turning, called for Molly to come out to him which, quite promptly, she did.

'Your mistress's room is at the far end of the passage,' he said. 'Take her trunk there, unpack it and do whatever it is you do with her dresses. You will be billeted in the attic with Cook and Jeannie.'

'Aye, sir,' Molly said.

Grant dug into his pocket again and brought two

26

guinea pieces.

'Take them, Molly. God knows, you've earned them.' He watched the servant pluck the coins from his fingers and tuck them into her apron. 'You did well to bring her here.' Then stepping past her, he returned to the drawing-room to assure his wife and her pretty little sister that the baggage had arrived all safe and sound at last.

CHAPTER TWO

If Gillon Peters was famed for anything it was certainly not his modesty. At the drop of a hat or the offer of a glass, he would recount in grisly detail his exploits with the Highland Regiment and, if you were unwise enough to visit his lodgings, he would be sure to show you the bloodstained tomahawk with which he claimed to have scalped two renegades on a scouting expedition on the banks of the Brandywine. City ladies, young and old, drank in every word of this questionable tale but his brothers remained sceptical for, as Roderick pointed out, Gillon couldn't shear a sheep without three men and a dairy-maid to help him.

Several bloody battles and much hard travelling with the 42nd Royal Highland Regiment had left no visible marks on Gillon, none save a neat little scar the length of your fingernail that kinked the corner of his right eye and added a touch of insolence to features that were insolent enough already. He was two years younger than Grant and several inches taller. His hair was lighter in shade and his eyes piercing blue. For all that, the kinship between the brothers was obvious for their bantering familiarity had not yet been tainted by rivalry.

Grant looked up from the documents spread across the table.

'Ah!' he said. 'There you are. I wondered how long it would be before you deserted the lambing pens. You're back, I gather?'

'You gather correctly,' Gillon said. 'Our dear brother chased me away. Told me to make myself scarce. Took pity on my plight.'

'Which particular plight would that be?' said Grant.

'The plight of having no rapport with mutton unless it's glazed with red currant jelly,' Gillon said. 'Why does Roderick refuse to acknowledge that I'm not cut out to be a farmer?'

'He didn't think you were cut out to be a soldier,' Grant said. 'You proved him wrong on that score.'

'I did, did I not?' Gillon grinned. 'If, however, Roddy hopes that time and persuasion will transform me into an agriculturalist, he's sadly mistaken.' He kicked out a chair and seated himself at the table. 'What cause is this that has you chained to your ink-horn on such a sprightly May morning?'

'A dispute about heritable property,' Grant said. 'I've made the verbal pleadings and as soon as the session opens I will continue the process with representations and petitions.'

'Is a pretty girl involved,' Gillon enquired, 'or a wealthy widow?'

'I have no idea what the petitioners look like,'

28

said Grant. 'I haven't met them and probably never will. It's not an entertainment, Gillon. The case will drag on for weeks before the court provides a solution.'

'In a word, bread and butter.'

'In three words, yes.'

Grant conducted most of his business in Daniel Horne's wine cellar or, to be precise, in the large, well-lighted ground-floor room above it. Early that morning he had received written papers and printed indices from the hand of his clerk, Somerville, and would work over them until dinner time at half past one o'clock. He might, of course, have taken the material home—Horne's was not much more than a steep step from Graddan's Court—but he thought it best to allow the sisters time to gossip.

'I hear,' Gillon said, 'that you have a guest?'

Grant glanced up. 'Who told you that?'

Gillon shrugged. 'News travels faster than lightning in this town. Fact, I met Somerville, asked him where you might be found and he, for once, was remarkably forthcoming. I reckon he's as excited about the girl's appearance as you are.'

'I am not in the least excited,' Grant said.

Perhaps the wrath of the Lord of Session will add a little ginger to your water,' Gillon said. 'How long has she been with you?'

'Only a day,' Grant said. 'By the by, I'll be having a word with Somerville concerning his loose tongue.'

'Oh, you can hardly blame your man, Grant. It's too choice a piece of news to wrap in cheesecloth. You can't hope to hide her away for long.'

'I'm not hiding her. She's visiting Charlotte.'

29

'Alone and without a chaperone?'

'Her maid is with her,' Grant said.

'But Papa is not.'

'No, Papa is not.'

'Do you expect me to believe that Craigiehall granted her permission to come up to the city and lodge in your house? She's broken the halter, has she not, cantered off on her own?'

'She's not a child, Gillon, or a horse for that matter.'

'Indeed, she's not,' Gillon said. 'Tell me, is she as sweet and pliant as your good wife?'

'Have a care, Gillon.'

'I intend no insult. I have nothing but the highest regard for your missus, who is a woman of sterling virtue. What about the girl? Can the same be said of her?'

'She is, I believe, of good character—and intelligent.'

'With a figure to match?'

'Gillon!' Grant warned. 'That's enough! What are you doing here? I thought we agreed that you would spend time with Roderick and Mother at Heatherbank. You've been gone less than a fortnight.'

'What is there for me to do at Heatherbank?' Gillon said. 'Mother has everything and everyone under her thumb. I am nothing but an encumbrance there and, frankly, I got bored.'

'It's high time you found something to do, something that might spread a little bit of jam upon your bread.'

'I have my pension,' Gillon said, 'such as it is. I'll find myself "something to do", as you put it, all in good time. I am not yet fully recovered from my

30

military exertions, you know. Do I not deserve a little respite?'

'You have been in a state of respite for years, Gillon,' Grant told him. 'I would not want idleness to drag you down.'

'Down?' Gillon said. 'Down to what, I ask you? Besides, I'm not as idle as you seem to believe, Grant. I do have some irons in the fire.'

'Are you still paying court to Clavering's daughter?'

'Julia?' Gillon paused. 'No, alas, that came to naught.'

'Clavering put his hoof down, did he?'

'The girl was not passionate enough for me.'

'Hoh!' Grant said, sceptically. 'Is that your story?'

'It is,' Gillon said. 'And I am sticking to it. By the by, I notice that you have changed the subject. What of you and Craigiehall's daughters? You have both of them at your charge now, a situation that strikes me as nothing far short of greed.'

'Greed? How so?'

'Come now, two top cards from one pack. If that's not greed I don't know what else it can be. Unless . . .' He paused again. 'Unless, of course, you fetched the little one here for me.'

'If you mean Nicola, I did not fetch her to Edinburgh for you or anyone else. She came of her own free will,' Grant said.

Gillon nodded. 'To visit her sister?'

'Exactly so.'

'To stay in your house, under your roof, at your mercy?'

'See here,' said Grant, 'I have too much work to do to listen to your blathers. Nicola Templeton is

31

my wife's sister. I cannot refuse her hospitality, however odd the circumstances.'

'He'll come down on you like the wrath of God, you know.'

'I am prepared for that,' said Grant. 'There's little that Lord Craigiehall can do, though, given that Nicola is eighteen years of age and I'm not keeping her against her will. He may fume and threaten dire consequences but he cannot do me harm.'

'He can harm your clients in court.'

'Good God, Gillon! He is too honourable a judge to do any such thing.'

'I would not be so sure, if I were you. In any event, if the girl is presently part of your family so also is she part of mine,' Gillon said. 'I'm not averse to sharing the burden.'

'Burden? What burden? What the devil are you talking about?'

'She will require to be entertained, will she not?'

'Nicola Templeton is not for the likes of you, Gillon,' Grant said, sternly.

'Charlotte Templeton was not for the likes of *you*, dear brother, but that did not prevent you storming the temple—storming the Templeton, hah?—and making off with her.'

'Charlotte,' Grant said, 'is my wife.'

'If you were good enough for one Templeton girl why should I not be good enough for another?' Gillon said. 'She isn't ugly, is she?'

'No, neither ugly nor even plain.'

'So much the better.' Gillon rose from the bench, tugged down the wings of his waistcoat and flung back his greatcoat. 'I shall call upon you this evening for supper. You may alert Charlotte—and remind Cook that I do not care for onions. Shall we say eight o'clock, or would half past the hour be more suitable?'

Grant sighed. 'Eight will do,' he said, 'if you insist.'

'I do insist,' Gillon said. 'I would rather be an unwelcome guest than no guest at all. Shall I wear my surtout and my scarlet cloak?'

'Wear what you like,' Grant told him. 'Just don't bring along that damned tomahawk.' And with a curious sense of foreboding he watched his brother take his leave.

*　　　*　　　*

It had been a twelvemonth since Nicola had last been in town and 'Auld Reekie' had undergone several changes in that short time. Attended by Molly, Charlotte and she sauntered out into the spring sunshine not long after breakfast and, with bonnets firmly fastened against a fresh breeze from the Forth, tripped downhill to the bridge to survey the latest improvements.

The imposing span of the North Bridge had been open to traffic for several years but random bits of work continued on it still. That morning a gang of masons were setting the stones of a new baluster while caddies, carters and hordes of less than noble citizens trooped, grumbling, past, as if progress was nothing but a hurdle put up to annoy them.

To the east lay the estuary and the sea, the wave-whipped expanse of water that brought Edinburgh its fickle weather. Nicola held on to her bonnet with one hand and gripped Charlotte's arm

33

with the other. She had seen the vista many times before but it never failed to take her breath away and that May morning so lightened her mood that for a moment she forgot all about Papa, de Morville and Craigiehall.

Then Molly said, 'Is that who I think it is?'

Following the maid's pointing finger, Nicola saw Hugh Littlejohn striding towards them, chin tucked into his collar and his hat—a high-crowned, wide-brimmed thing—tugged down as if he were intent on hiding his face or, possibly, shutting out the city's many distractions.

'What's he doing in Edinburgh?' said Charlotte.

'We can make a fair guess, I'm thinkin',' Molly said. 'He'll have been sent here to offer you terms.'

Nicola had always been fond of Mr Littlejohn. His father and uncles had been gardeners at Craigiehall and his youngest daughter, Faye, was presently kitchen maid. Stepping away from her sister, she placed herself before him.

'Is it pleasure brings you to Edinburgh, Mr Littlejohn, or business?'

He glanced up and showing no surprise, said, 'If it was pleasure I was after, Miss Nicola, I would not be seekin' it in a wicked-busy place like this. Besides, I have too much to do at home to be gallivantin' at this time o' year.'

'Is Papa with you?' Charlotte asked.

'No, Mistress Peters, he is not. I'm his—uh, his emissary.'

'Why did he send you and not Robertson?' Charlotte asked.

'You must put that question to his lordship,' Hugh Littlejohn said. 'He was ill-pleased with me for helpin' Miss Nicola to the Flyer. I suspect sendin' me to Edinburgh is his way o' punishin' me.'

Mr Littlejohn carried no luggage save a small scuffed leather game-bag slung over one shoulder. He brought it round, dug into it and produced a letter packet, wrapped in brown paper and sealed with hard blue wax. He held it tightly in both hands as if afraid that the breeze might whip it away.

'For me?' Nicola said.

'For Mr Grant Peters. I'm to give it into his hands, an' his hands only.'

'Then you must find him,' said Charlotte, haughtily. 'If you can.'

'I'll wait at his house if necessary,' Hugh Littlejohn said.

Nicola touched his sleeve. 'Have you eaten breakfast yet?'

'I had a bite at the inn in Peebles afore I boarded the day coach.'

'Papa sent you by the overnight route, did he?' Nicola said. 'In other words, he would not pay for the Flyer? Are you going back to Ayrshire today?'

'If my business is concluded by four o'clock, aye.'

'I'll give the letter to my husband,' Charlotte offered.

'Nay, Mistress Peters, that will not do.'

'Do you not trust me?' Charlotte said.

'It's not a matter o' trust, Mistress Peters; it's a matter o' duty.'

'Very well,' said Charlotte. 'If that's the way of it, you must find Graddan's Court and sit upon the doorstep until my husband returns which, I might add, will be long after four o' clock. It may, indeed, be long after midnight if a reply is required, for my

35

husband will not put pen to paper without reflection.'

'Come now, Charlotte. Mr Littlejohn is only obeying Papa's instructions,' Nicola said. 'I, for one, have no intention of conducting a conversation in the middle of a public highway. If you breakfasted at six you must be hungry by now, Mr Littlejohn.' She turned to Charlotte. 'Where is he? Where's Grant? He will not be in Parliament House for the courts are not in session. Is he in a coffee house or tavern somewhere close at hand?'

'He may be,' said Charlotte, grudgingly.

'Which?' Nicola had heard enough table-chat at her father's house to know where advocates and writers convened. 'Horne's, Dow's, or the Slipper?'

'No,' said Charlotte, 'not the Slipper. He dislikes the Slipper.'

'Where then?' Nicola insisted.

'Horne's,' Charlotte conceded, 'unless he is elsewhere entirely.'

'Then we will go to Horne's and hope to find him there.'

'Thank you, Miss Nicola,' Hugh Littlejohn said. 'I admit I'm keen to be awa' back home as soon as possible. Where is this place, this Horne's?'

'Up there.' Nicola gestured towards the bristling tenements of the Old Town that fretted the ridge below the Castle. 'Do you have the breath for it, Mr Littlejohn?'

'It's not breath I'm lackin', Miss Nicola,' Hugh Littlejohn said.

'What is it then?' said Charlotte.

'Patience,' the overseer answered and, falling into step with Molly, followed Lord Craigiehall's recalcitrant daughters up into the wynds and smoky closes that protected the heart of the city.

*   *   *

Charlotte would not have had the nerve to enter Daniel Horne's wine cellar on her own. The sour smell of ale, tobacco smoke and the faint cloying sweetness of pickled herrings, for which popular delicacy Horne's was famous, would have put her off. In fact, the tavern was one of the most respectable in the vicinity of Parliament Square and a far cry from the vile drinking dens that crowded the vennels of the Cowgate and the Grassmarket.

Taking Charlotte firmly by the arm. Nicola dragged her through the doorway into the vast and gloomy tavern. Molly and Mr Littlejohn followed and, within a minute or two, all four, including the maid, were tucked into a corner booth and Charlotte's nerves were being soothed by a glass of sweet sherry and a cinnamon biscuit while Grant read the letter from Papa then threw it down upon the table and shook his head ruefully.

'What?' Nicola said. 'What is it, Grant? What does Papa say?'

Molly and Mr Littlejohn pretended to think of other things—family business was none of their concern—but it was difficult to remain detached when they were all seated together, elbow to elbow, at a corner table.

'He wants me to send you back to Craigiehall with Mr Littlejohn.'

'If I return to Ayrshire,' said Nicola, 'Papa will make sure I remain there until I'm so exasperated that I'll bend to his will and marry that horrible man.'

'You are under no obligation to marry anyone,' Grant said. 'We are sufficiently enlightened these days to acknowledge that women also have rights.'

'My father does not subscribe to that belief,' said Nicola. 'Look how he treated poor Charlotte when she married you.'

'True,' Grant said. 'On the other hand he was powerless to prevent it. He may grizzle to his heart's content but he cannot legally—or morally for that matter—force you to do anything you do not wish to do.'

'He will cut me off without a penny.'

'Does that matter?'

Charlotte sipped sherry, nibbled her biscuit and kept silent.

'He wants an heir for Craigiehall,' said Nicola.

'And he shall have one,' said Grant. 'In the fullness of time perhaps he'll have several.' He glanced up at Charlotte who, blushing furiously, looked away. 'In the meanwhile, he has issued an ultimatum. Either I see to it that you are bundled off to Ayrshire with Mr Littlejohn on the afternoon coach or . . .' He lifted the letter and read from it. ' " . . . or, Sir, you may keep her." '

'Keep her?' said Charlotte. 'What on earth does he mean?'

'He means that your sister will become my responsibility.'

'That's daft,' Molly blurted out. 'Plain daft.'

'Not so daft as all that, Molly,' Grant said. 'His lordship is well aware of my circumstances and unfortunately continues to harbour a conviction that I married Charlotte just to get my hands on Craigiehall.'

'Aye, he's said as much often enough.' Molly ignored the overseer's warning glare. 'It's breakin' no confidence, Mr Peters. We've all heard him rave about it. Is that not a fact, Mr Littlejohn?'

'What his lordship might think o' Mr Peters is not for the likes o' us to speculate,' Hugh Littlejohn said sternly. 'Now, hold your tongue, lass, an' remember your place.'

'My place,' said Molly, 'is here wi' Miss Nicola.'

'How will she manage your wages if his lordship cuts her off? Have you thought o' that, Molly Goodall?' Mr Littlejohn said.

'I'm not needin' wages,' said Molly. 'A bed an' a bite to eat will do me.'

'You're his lordship's servant,' Hugh Littlejohn said, 'not Miss Nicola's.'

'Oh, stop, stop,' Nicola cried, loudly enough to cause heads to turn. 'I cannot put this burden on your shoulders, Grant. I'll do as my father asks.'

'Marry de Morville, do you mean?' said Charlotte.

'No, not that, certainly not that,' said Nicola. 'I will return to Ayrshire with Mr Littlejohn, however, and try to make my peace.'

'If you do,' Grant said, 'you will never be free again. You've shown your mettle, Nicola, and you must not lose your nerve. If you return to Craigiehall at a snap of your father's fingers you'll either marry someone of his choosing, or die an old maid.'

'That's a frightful thing to say, Grant,' Charlotte admonished. 'Nicola has a mind of her own, I'm sure.'

'Then let her use it,' Grant said. 'Let her use it first of all by not making assumptions about what I will or will not do, what I can or cannot afford and what constitutes a burden and what does not. Nicola, do you wish to return to Ayrshire with Mr Littlejohn, or to stay in Edinburgh under my protection until such time as your father comes to his senses?'

'Devil a long while that'll be,' Molly murmured. 'I'm beginnin' to think I was wrong about him ever offerin' the olive branch.'

'Nicola,' Grant said, 'your answer, please.'

'Stay,' Nicola said. 'I'll stay, Grant, as long as you will have me.'

'Good,' her brother-in-law nodded. 'Now, if you ladies will excuse us, I'll order some dinner for Mr Littlejohn and compose my reply—in effect, your reply, Nicola—to Lord Craigiehall.'

'Tell him . . .' Nicola began.

'Tell him what?' Grant said.

'That I still care for him and regret that he no longer cares for me.'

Grant said, 'I think that you had better tell him that yourself,' and then, rather airily, dismissed them.

*   *   *

Small traders had crammed their stalls with the produce of the spring and the atmosphere at the top end of the High Street was nothing short of agricultural. Cattle had been driven across the pave and a trail of agitated brown splashes mingled with broken eggs, cabbage stalks and trampled potatoes. There were pigs, too, a pen of them, all snorting away, quite oblivious to the recent edict from city magistrates that had banned pork from

40

public highways.

'What is wrong with this city?' Charlotte complained, throwing the words over her shoulder at Nicola who was having difficulty in keeping up with her. 'Are there no laws and no constables to enforce them? Why are these traders not at the markets where they belong? Why are they here, fouling our pretty streets? It makes me feel quite sick.'

'It's commerce, dearest, just commerce,' Nicola answered.

Charlotte paid no heed. She was, Nicola realised, in full flow, though for a girl brought up in rough Ayrshire countryside her outrage seemed misplaced.

'I cannot imagine why I want to live here.' Charlotte plucked up her skirts and stepped over something indescribable. 'Small wonder that persons of genteel disposition wish to take up residence in the New Town. I would have Grant find us a house there too, but he pleads poverty. Poverty! He does not care a fig about my feelings. Even when he is off for weeks on end pleading causes before the Circuit Court, he is quite content to leave me cooped up like a pullet in that dismal apartment surrounded by this nauseating stink.'

'Charlotte,' Nicola said, 'where are we going?'

'Home,' said Charlotte. 'Home to have dinner. I'm hungry. After that, I am going to lie down. All this strife has made my head ache.'

'Strife?' Nicola tugged at her sister's sleeve. 'Is it me? Is it my fault you're so upset?'

Charlotte stopped so abruptly that Nicola almost ran into her and Molly, bringing up the rear, had to rein in sharply to avoid a collision.

'Why did he not consult me?' she blurted out. 'Am I not his wife? Is his house not my home too?'

'If you wish me to leave . . .' said Nicola. 'If you don't want me here . . .'

'Oh, stay, stay, by all means.' She wagged a finger angrily. 'I just wish he had thought to ask *me* before he issued his orders. It's obvious that Grant wants you here and that my opinion is of no consequence.'

'Charlotte, you're Grant's wife.'

'There are times of late when I wish to heaven I weren't.'

'Oh, Charlotte,' Nicola said, shocked. 'I thought you were happy.'

Suddenly aware that her hand was still poised, revealingly, in mid-air, Charlotte folded her arms across bosom and said, 'Yes, I am. Of course I am. Forgive me. I meant nothing by it. I just need my dinner, that's all.' Then, spinning on her heel, she set off once more in the direction of Graddan's Court, with Nicola and Molly trailing in her wake.

*   *   *

The roads that linked Edinburgh with Ayr had been sufficiently improved to accommodate fast four-horse coaches that halved the journey time for those willing to pay the ticket. Unfortunately, the same advances did not stretch to the ordinary service. Beds for the night in the filthy little inn at Peebles cost four pence and a supper of sorts could be had for sixpence: so, Grant calculated, even with the fare on top, John James Templeton was saving himself a mere three shillings by sending his overseer on the long route which, under the circumstances, did indeed appear less like thrift than spite.

Grant had not forgotten that Littlejohn was one of the few Craigiehall servants who had risked his lordship's wrath by turning up at Kirkton church to see Charlotte married. For this reason he had treated the overseer to a decent dinner and had accompanied him to the White Horse yard to catch the four o'clock standard back to Ayrshire.

The inn yard was busy at that hour of the afternoon. Pigeons whirred from the rooftops and waddled about on the cobbles, and gulls blown in from the estuary wheeled, shrieking, overhead. Footmen, carriers and post-boys lounged by the arch, smoking, laughing and exchanging gossip. The host of the White Horse, in buckled knee breeches and striped apron, occupied the doorway by the porter's lodge, affably, not to say unctuously, bidding a good afternoon to anyone who might be tempted to patronise his establishment.

The Border coach, a shallow, sagging, bone-rattling conveyance, was being harnessed with four sorry-looking horses. It would carry Mr Littlejohn as far as Peebles where he would spend the night. Tomorrow, in equal discomfort, he would trundle across the bleak moors of Lanarkshire and, with luck, arrive at the gates of Craigiehall by nightfall.

'Why did his lordship not provide you with a horse?' Grant asked.

'He's eager to have Miss Nicola back safe and sound,' Hugh Littlejohn answered, 'but not so eager that he'll pay to have it done quickly.'

'Does he not travel in style?'

'Aye, sir. He comes up to the capital by private

43

carriage but he usually breaks the journey at Salton House with Mistress Ballentine.'

'Mistress Ballentine, the widow of Lord Ballentine?' Grant said.

'Aye, she's my master's cousin, sir, an' just as severe as he is.'

'Severe—is that how you judge him, Mr Littlejohn?'

'It's not in my interests to judge his lordship.'

'Is he not a fair employer?'

'He is, sir, a very fair employer—if strict.'

'But not generous?' Grant said.

Hugh Littlejohn shouldered his bag and looked down at the cobbles.

'You're very loyal, Littlejohn,' Grant remarked.

'I hope it might be said that I am, sir.'

'Loyal to his lordship,' said Grant, 'and, equally, to his daughters.'

'It's not his daughters who employ me, though,' Hugh Littlejohn said.

'Nevertheless, you care enough for Charlotte and Nicola to serve their interests too, do you not?'

'As best I can, Mr Peters.'

'Did you not abet my courtship of Charlotte by turning a blind eye to our meetings when his lordship was not at home?' Grant said.

Mr Littlejohn chewed his lip and continued to stare at the cobbles.

'Did you not assist Nicola and her maid to fly from Craigiehall?'

'I did not assist them, sir. I just . . .'

'What? Turned a blind eye there, too?' said Grant. 'It occurs to me, Littlejohn, that for a fellow who professes loyalty to his lordship, you do not entirely approve of how he treats his children. It's also plain enough that his lordship is sufficiently dependent upon you to give you a certain amount of rope, otherwise he would have discharged you long since.'

'What is it you want of me, Mr Peters?'

'My letter to his lordship will not tell him all he needs to know. He's a man of the law and, as such, will seek out what lies behind it. In other words, he'll question you closely.'

'I expect he will, sir, aye.'

'May I ask what you will tell him?'

Mr Littlejohn raised his head and met the advocate's eye.

'The truth, sir,' he said. 'The truth as I see it.'

'And how,' Grant Peters said, 'do you see it?'

'I see that Miss Nicola doesn't wish to come back to Craigiehall.'

'That she is adamant on the score?'

'Nah, Mr Peters, she didn't strike me as adamant,' Hugh Littlejohn said. 'In fact, sir, she seemed uncertain what to do for the best.'

'There,' Grant said, 'you are mistaken. Take it from me, Littlejohn, Nicola Templeton is firm in her resolve not to return to Craigiehall.'

A wrinkle of understanding creased a corner of the overseer's eye.

'How else am I mistaken, Mr Peters? What else did I fail to notice?'

'That my wife is with child?' said Grant.

'I—I did not detect that, sir, no.'

'You may take it from me that it's the case,' Grant said. 'For that reason, if for no other, my wife wishes her sister to remain in Edinburgh to attend her in the early months of her term.'

'When is the child due?'

'In the neighbourhood of Christmas.'

'Is this the truth you're tellin' me, Mr Peters?'

'A truth not generally known, but a truth nonetheless.'

'Why does it fall upon me to convey this information to his lordship?'

'Because he'll believe you,' Grant said. 'He'll believe you because I signally failed to inform him of the impending event in my letter. If he enquires further, tell him that the news was leaked to you by Molly.'

'What reason do you have for keepin' it secret?' Hugh Littlejohn asked.

'That,' Grant answered, 'is for his lordship to worry about.'

'Aye, an' worry he will,' said Hugh Littlejohn. 'I'm not o'er keen to be the bearer o' this bit o' news, Mr Peters. What if he asks for proof?'

'He's not liable to ask for proof, knowing that you cannot be expected to provide it. It will be a case of *probatio probata*, evidence that cannot be immediately contradicted.'

'Is it your wish to bring his lordship to you, Mr Peters?' Hugh Littlejohn said. 'Are you hopin' he'll come rushin' up to Edinburgh to see for himself?'

'My concern is for my wife,' Grant said. 'I do not wish her to be distressed at this time.'

Hugh Littlejohn hesitated. 'If things are the way you claim them to be, Mr Peters, an' the child is a male, then the future o' Craigiehall will no longer be as unsteady as it is now.'

'It will not be in the least unsteady. I will see to it that it is secure.'

'Miss Nicola, sir, what'll become of Miss

Nicola?'

'She will be well taken care of, never fear.'

Hugh Littlejohn watched a fat cloth-merchant push his even fatter wife up into the coach and saw the vehicle list heavily to starboard. 'I'd better be boardin' now, sir,' he said. 'There's little enough room as it is.'

'Do you have the letter?'

'I do, sir, snug right here in my bag.'

'And the rest of it?' Grant enquired.

'Snug right here in my head,' the overseer answered with something that may, or may not, have been a wink.

CHAPTER THREE

Nicola was dozing in her room when whispers in the passageway roused her.

'What is he doing here, Grant?'

'He's come to eat supper.'

'Did you invite him?' Charlotte hissed.

'He more or less invited himself.'

'Why did you not give me warning?'

'It slipped my mind.'

'How could it possibly slip your mind?'

'I had other things to think about.'

'What, for an instance?' said Charlotte.

'Littlejohn, and the letter . . .'

'And my sister, I suppose?'

'Yes, of course, your sister—your sister's welfare, I mean.'

Nicola slid from the bed and tip-toed to the door. She was tempted to cough or clear her throat

47

to let Charlotte know that she was there but curiosity proved stronger than good manners.

'Have you told him?' Charlotte said.

'Told who?' said Grant.

'Gillon. You promised me . . .'

'I've told no one,' Grant said. 'But your condition cannot be kept secret for long. It's nothing to be ashamed of.'

'Promise me you won't tell Gillon.'

'Very well, I won't tell Gillon,' Grant said.

'Or Nicola.'

'Or Nicola,' Grant said. 'Where is she, by the by?'

Nicola pressed her hands to her breast to smother the sound of her breathing as someone rapped tentatively on her door.

'Nicola, are you there?' Charlotte asked.

She tugged off her cap, tousled her hair and manufactured a convincing yawn, before she called out, 'Who is it? What's wrong?' She opened the door a crack and peeped out. 'Oh, Charlotte, it's you. I'm sorry. I fell asleep upon the bed. I haven't kept you from supper, have I?'

'No,' Charlotte said, with a hint of suspicion. 'Were you really asleep?'

'It's Edinburgh air,' said Nicola, 'and all that walking about. What time is it? Has Grant arrived home?'

'Hmm, a half hour ago. Did you not hear him?'

'No, not a thing.'

'We have an unexpected guest.'

'Who?' said Nicola, then, inventively, 'Not Papa, surely?'

'No, not Papa,' said Charlotte. 'Grant's brother.'

'The soldier or the farmer?'

48

'Gillon, the soldier.'

'Then,' said Nicola, 'I had better make myself respectable.'

'I wouldn't bother, if I were you,' said Charlotte and stalked off, rather huffily, Nicola thought, along the passageway.

*   *   *

He rose at once from the horseman's chair and, swinging a leg over the worn leather crest, turned to face her. He was not what Nicola had expected. Charlotte's descriptions had been at best dismissive and at worst scathing; he was no ogre, no goblin. Nicola's first impression was of a man who was at one and the same time both dignified and raffish. She had hoped that he might be clad in regimental plaid but he was plainly dressed in clean, tight-fitting breeches with small buckles and a frock coat. Only his Hessian boots and fawn gloves tucked neatly into an epaulette showed soldierly.

'You have been left all alone, sir,' Nicola said. 'How very remiss of my sister and her husband.'

'Not at all,' Gillon Peters said. 'As family, it is assumed that I will not stoop to stealing the plate. It seems, however, that I must introduce myself without recommendation let alone fanfare.' He bowed. 'Lieutenant Gillon Peters, your humble servant.'

'Nicola Templeton, sir,' she offered her hand, 'is exceedingly pleased to make your acquaintance.'

'I am glad to hear it.' Gillon Peters took her hand and held it lightly. 'I have few allies in this household, or in this town, for that matter. I trust

49

that you will not be influenced by prevailing opinion as to my character.'

'I'm sure I don't know what you mean, Lieutenant Peters.'

'Of course you do,' he said. 'Your dear sister, for all her merits, does not hold me in high regard. Truth to tell, she considers me something of a plague.'

'I'm sure that is not the case.'

'Do you mean to say she has not libelled me in her letters?'

'She has said little about you, sir, except that you are a soldier.'

'A soldier without arms, alas, without cause or commission. I am, in a word, retired.' He looked around at the reading chair. 'I would offer you a glass to pique your appetite, Miss Templeton, but it seems that my brother has removed the bottles.'

'Where is Grant?'

'Gone down to his cellar to fish for a wine sour enough to suit his mood. Your sister, I believe, is in the kitchen negotiating with Cookie. In reference to "cellar" I speak generally, for there is no cellar in such a lofty apartment. Fact, he keeps his wine in a cheese locker in the depths of the pantry.'

'Where you, Lieutenant Peters, cannot readily get at it?'

He had blue eyes, piecing blue. For an instant they glittered hard, then he laughed. 'Libelled or not, Miss Templeton, it appears that you have me marked as a scrounger. Well, it's true that on occasions I do throw myself upon Grant's mercy, for I am a very hungry scrounger and would eat the poor fellow out of house and home if he would allow it. And you, are you ready for your supper?'

'Indeed, Lieutenant Peters, for I am a scrounger too, after a fashion.'

'Shall we go in then to scrounge our supper together?'

'I see no reason why not,' Nicola said.

'My name is Gillon, by the by.'

'And I am Nicola.'

'Nicola,' Gillon said, softly. 'What a pretty name that is.' And just as his brother came into the room, he offered her his arm.

*   *   *

The evening rolled along merrily enough at first and conversation swished forth and back with such gusto that it was all Nicola could do to keep up with it.

Claret was followed by madeira, madeira by port, and by the time the company repaired to the parlour she was glowing with good spirits and had failed to notice that Charlotte, who had touched hardly a drop, was less than entranced by Gillon's scandalous stories of his adventures in the American war and had confined herself to conducting the serving of the courses. At one point she had even vanished for several minutes, ostensibly to converse with Cook. She had returned flushed and perspiring and had seated herself without a word, and when Grant had touched her hand and enquired, tactfully, if she was feeling quite well, had answered, 'Quite well, thank you,' and with a little wave of the hand had sanctioned Gillon to continue his humorous tale of an encounter between a captured French bushman and a Highlander who spoke only Gaelic.

51

Nicola joined eagerly in the chit-chat. She was flattered that two handsome, well-bred young men obviously regarded her as something other than a brainless child. She was not so far gone in high spirits, though, that she neglected to smile with parted lips and, by instinct rather than calculation, flirt a little with both gentlemen, though rather less so with Grant, who was after all already married.

Fresh candles had been lighted in the parlour and the fire planted with new coals. A curtain had been drawn across the window to muffle the sounds of revelry from the street, revelry that now and then seemed to border on riot. No massive carved cabinets crowded the room, only a mahogany sideboard with a brass rail and a silk curtain behind which glasses and decanters were kept, a pedestal desk and a stout oval-topped table, and the settee and walnut armchair, like the horseman's chair, had seen better days.

Gillon was not one to stand on ceremony. Taking Nicola's arm, he danced her across the room to the settee and, throwing courtesy to the winds, plopped himself down beside her. Grant settled Charlotte into the armchair with a cushion at her back, then balanced himself on the horseman's chair, legs spread, and braced his forearms on the slope of the reading desk as if he were about to deliver a sermon. Nicola was aware of Gillon beside her, his thigh brushing her overskirt, aware too that Grant was staring at her or, possibly, at his arrogant young brother who had defiantly flouted the laws of etiquette to obtain the most desirable seat in the house.

'Is there no drink, old fellow?' Gillon said. 'Blinded by the beauty around you, have you forgotten your duties as a host?'

'Jeannie will bring in a bowl, shortly,' Grant said.

'A bowl?' said Gillon

'Punch,' said Grant.

'Punch!' Gillon said. 'Punch is not fit refreshment for a man of parts.'

'If you are so set against punch,' said Grant, 'I daresay I might find a little brandy to keep you quiet. May I remind you, however, that this is not the Reprobates Club. No one here is willing or, indeed, able to match you glass for glass, and there's no lackey to put you to bed when you fall down.'

'I never fall down,' said Gillon. 'Besides, there's no bed in this hovel in which a man might rest his head.' He paused. 'Is there?'

'No,' said Charlotte, 'there is not.' Gillon and Nicola lifted their heads as if her voice had emerged from thin air. 'No bed for you here and there will be no bed for you after our removal to a house in the New Town either, you cuckoo.'

'Oh!' said Gillon, stumped for a reply. 'Oh!'

'Unless,' Charlotte went on, 'my sister is willing to make room for you in her bed which thing, by all appearances, might suit you both.'

'Charlotte, please!' Grant said.

'Look at him,' said Charlotte. 'Look at you, for that matter, fussing over her as if you'd never seen a female before. By the by, I do not care for punch at this hour of the night. I will have tea, my dear, thank you.'

Grant cleared his throat. 'Very well, tea it shall be.'

For half a minute the silence was leaden, then Gillon said, 'Am I to take it, Charlotte, that you

53

have had enough of my company for one evening?'

'She's exhausted, that's all,' said Grant.

'I am not exhausted,' Charlotte corrected. 'I am weary, weary of listening to Gillon's bragging and weary of watching how you all fawn on him.'

'I think,' said Gillon, rising, 'I had better take my leave.'

'Why are you being so rude to Lieutenant Peters?' Nicola heard herself say. 'What's wrong with you, Charlotte? If you're not happy to have us here . . .'

'How long do you intend to stay?' Charlotte interrupted. 'Do you intend to remain throughout the summer to watch me grow fat and ugly?'

'Oh!' said Gillon, and sat down again. 'I see.'

Charlotte rounded on him. 'Do you, you devil? What do you see? An ugly woman growing uglier each day. Have a care, Gillon Peters, or that exquisite little sister of mine, of whom you are so enamoured, will soon become as hideous as I am.'

'What?' said Nicola, thoroughly alarmed. 'What is it?'

Gillon sighed and said, 'It's the legacy of Eve.'

'She's with child, Nicola, that's all,' Grant said.

'That's all!' Charlotte shrieked. *'That's all!* Is it not enough that you've taken me from my home, estranged me from my father and brought me to this miserable attic to satisfy your sordid appetites? Now you have to gloat over my condition and announce it to the world?'

'In fairness, Charlotte,' Gillon said, 'Grant did not announce . . .'

'Tea,' Charlotte said. 'I want my tea. Will someone please fetch my tea?'

Then, covering her face with her hands, she

54

burst into tears.

*　　　*　　　*

Molly removed the cloth from Charlotte's brow and lifting her head from the pillow, held the cordial glass to her lips.

'There, there,' Molly said. 'You'll feel better soon. It's perfectly natural an' nothin' to be afeared of.'

'How would you know?' said Charlotte. 'You've never carried a child.'

'That's true,' Molly said, 'but my mother carried plenty in her time an' every single one o' them afflicted her sore in the first months.'

'Months?' said Charlotte. 'Months, do you say?'

'Drink some more cordial.'

Charlotte sipped from the glass.

'What is it, Molly?' she asked in a small voice. 'The cordial, I mean.'

'Water of barley,' Molly said.

Charlotte sat up. 'Am I fevered?'

'A wee bit over-heated, that's all.'

'Am I—I mean, am I shedding it?'

'No, no,' said Molly. 'It's safe and snug.'

'How can you be sure?'

'I've seen too many sheddin's to be in any doubt.'

Propped on an elbow Charlotte plucked the cordial glass from Molly's fingers and drank the contents. She peered at her sister who sat, quiet as a mouse, in a corner of the bedroom.

'Well, Nicola,' she said, 'have you come to gloat?'

'I'm here in case you need me,' Nicola said. 'I'll

55

leave, if that's your wish.'

Charlotte shook her head. 'I'm sorry. I shouldn't have turned upon you. It's not your fault.'

Molly put the glass, the bowl and cloth on the table by the oil-lamp. The bedroom, like many in the old part of town, was furnished as a receiving room and chairs, foot stools, even a card table were ranged round the bed. Grant and Charlotte ate breakfast at the card table and in winter retired here in preference to the parlour, to play cards and other games.

'Where is he?' Charlotte said. 'Gillon—has he left yet?'

Nicola said, 'He's talking with Grant. He's very concerned about you.'

'Gillon Peters is not concerned about me.' Charlotte's voice strengthened. 'He is concerned only about himself.'

'I think you do him an injustice,' said Nicola.

'And I think you are dazzled by him.'

'I do find him amusing, I admit.'

'There is nothing amusing about any of the men in that family,' Charlotte said. 'Take heed of what I say, Nicola, or you'll regret it.'

Charlotte's gown, petticoats and stays were strewn upon the floor, her nightgown's frills twisted like a row of teeth nibbling at her neck. Nicola rose, came to the bed and took her sister's hand.

She said, 'Has your condition been confirmed by a midwife or a doctor?'

'No,' Charlotte answered.

'It would be as well to have a doctor's opinion, you know.'

'Oh, Grant will insist upon it, I suppose,'

56

Charlotte said, 'before he blares the sorry news from the rooftops.'

'Tells Papa, you mean.'

'Yes, tells Papa, I mean,' said Charlotte.

*   *   *

Grant sent Jeannie and Cook to bed before he fished out the brandy bottle, led Gillon from the parlour to the dining-room, lit two candles in the stick, and seated himself at the table with his brother, the bottle between them.

'Would you not rather be with your wife?' Gillon asked.

'Molly and Nicola will attend to her.'

'The better part of valour, eh?' said Gillon. 'I take it she is pregnant?'

'All the signs indicate that she is.'

'And the doctor's verdict?'

'She has so far refused to allow me to employ a doctor.'

'Is she embarrassed,' said Gillon, 'or ashamed?'

'I think she's afraid,' Grant said.

'If I were a woman I might be a mite jittery myself,' Gillon said. 'You're a sly dog, though, filling her up so quickly.'

'Nature cannot be denied.'

'Unless I miss my guess, Charlotte holds you, not Nature, responsible for what she seems to regard as a tragedy,' Gillon said. 'Does she not understand the simple mechanics of conception?'

'She is not by disposition passionate.'

'She seems passionate enough to me,' said Gilion, 'if tonight's outburst is anything to go by.'

'Charlotte is not a shrew, if that's what you're

57

implying.'

'Certainly not.' Gillon reached for the bottle. 'If I had been in your shoes, however, I think I might have plumped for the later edition.'

'The later edition?'

'Nicola.' He poured brandy into his glass and offered the bottle to his brother who, frowning, shook his head. 'Be that as it may, you've stolen a march on me this time, you dog. What hope have I of catching up now that you're about to present Craigiehall with a grandchild? Have you told him yet?'

'I sent a letter by Littlejohn's hand.'

'Without Charlotte's knowledge?' Gillon said.

'Yes.'

'Very prudent,' Gillon said. 'Bribed Littlejohn to say the servant girl let it slip and the condition has been confirmed? *Fait accompli*?'

'More or less,' Grant said.

'I am curious as to how his lordship will react,' Gillon said. 'Few men, even judges, can resist the lure of a grandchild. Perhaps now he will forgive you for stealing his daughter and will reward you with a share of Craigiehall.'

'A share?' said Grant.

'Oh, you want it all, do you?'

'At least I would know what to do with it,' Grant said.

Gillon laughed. 'Tell me, when do the courts resume?'

'On the eleventh day of June.'

'By which date his lordship must return to Edinburgh?'

'That is the case,' said Grant.

'I have but a month then, a short month at that.'

58

'A month—to do what?' Grant said.

'To woo the later version.'

'Nicola?' Grant said. 'What's the point in wooing her now when, by your own admission, I am several lengths ahead of you?'

'Been many a spill within sight of a winning post,' said Gillon. 'Am I not the one who knows that? After all, Charlotte may not come up to scratch. She may deliver herself of a daughter, then where will you be?'

'Precisely where I am now.'

'With one extra mouth to feed,' said Gillon, 'and Charlotte keening for a house in the New Town? Changed circumstances, my dear fellow, require a change of strategy.'

'On your part or mine?'

'Mine, of course, mine. You have already made your bed and picked a wife with whom to share it,' Gillon said. 'I am still footloose and free to pursue any girl of my choosing.'

'If you refer to Nicola,' Grant said, 'you may pursue her to your heart's content, Gillon, but you'll never catch her, not in a month, nor a year, nor ten years, for that matter. She is far too sensible to be taken in by your tricks.'

'Is she?' Gillon said. 'Well, my dear brother, let's see if your judgement is sound, shall we?'

'Yes,' Grant said, thinly. 'Let's see,' and reluctantly joined Gillon in clinking glasses above the candle flame.

CHAPTER FOUR

Small wonder, John James thought, not for the first time, that his cousin, Isabella Ballentine, received so few visitors. The road that meandered over the moors into the wilds of Clydesdale was, to say the least of it, execrable and even in the height of summer offered a sore challenge to man and beast. His liver had taken a pounding and his tripes felt as if they were being stretched like dyer's yarn as the chaise bounced and jounced, tilting first one way then the other, and the gaunt outline of Salton House hove gradually into view.

The rough ride was not his coachman's fault, nor could he chide Robertson, for his manservant, as usual, had turned the mottled colour of a toadstool and, after asking permission, travelled the final few miles with his head sticking out of the window.

If anyone was to blame it was Isabella. Thanks to his cousin's indifference and her tenants' laziness, nothing had been done to improve the sprawling estate that her husband, Clarence, had purchased thirty years ago, before he had taken a seat in the Westminster Parliament and had frittered away a deal of the family fortune by electing to live in London.

Sight of the ridge that backed the house made John James grimace; the irregular effect of ill-planted trees typified neglect and squandered opportunity. A quarter of Salton land was coarse and marshy but the larger part was made up of strong deep clay that might yield good crops if

60

properly drained. As it was, there was nothing to admire on the Salton acres but oceans of bent grass grazed by a few lean cattle. He had volunteered to send Littlejohn to organise improvements but his cousin had waved away his criticisms by pointing out that the sons of her ageing tenants had no fondness for splashing in bog and heather and, as soon as they were old enough, preferred to run off to sea.

Isabella might be stubborn but she was not entirely a fool.

Her elder daughter, Olivia, was married to a duke and lived in high style in Gloucestershire, while the other, Ariadne, was wife to an undersecretary in the Admiralty. The 'boy', Willy, now late into his thirties, had purchased his father's seat in Westminster together with an elegant mansion in the vicinity of St James's, and adamantly refused to return to Scotland to visit his sorry inheritance let alone his widowed mother. Why, therefore, Isabella declared, should she exhaust herself by building a portion for children who were not only well provided for but who regarded Scotland as so far north of Eden—by which they meant London—as to be almost off the map?

Salton House, though imposing from a distance, was mean and inconvenient, a spindle-shaped object, taller than it was broad. And the tower that leaned precariously over the courtyard was so far off vertical that it was less a monument to the days of Border raiders than a memorial to some forgotten architect with no eye for a plumb-line and a fondness for strong drink.

The only part of the house that John James

61

admired was not, strictly speaking, part of the house at all but a small sheltered rose garden that lay hard against the wall of the parlour. 'My sanctuary,' Isabella called it. 'My hermitage, my retreat,' and here on the ten or twenty fine days that made up a Scottish summer she spent most of her time.

The chaise rattled over broken cobbles into the courtyard and drew to a halt. Ignoring Robertson's trembling hand, John James got himself out of the vehicle unaided and, stretching his arms above his head to remove the creases from his spine, looked towards the arch of the main door. He was fond of his cousin and she of him but today there was no welcome awaiting him.

Shakily, Robertson began to unload luggage from beneath the boot while McNair, the coachman, did his best to prevent the exhausted horse from falling to its knees in gratitude.

'Hollah!' his lordship called out. 'Is no one here to attend us?'

The arrival of an unannounced conveyance at Craigiehall would have had servants running from all directions, with Robertson leading the charge. Here in Salton, however, both curiosity and good manners were unknown.

John James opened his mouth to call out again when the big weather-beaten door creaked and Dougie, her ladyship's one and only footman, peeped warily through the crack. 'Aye, so it's yoursel', sur, is it now?' he said as he drew open the door. His breeks were unbuttoned, his vest too, and he wore no wig. In his right hand he carried a pewter pot and in the left a slab of beef. 'Ah waur just havin' mah dinner.'

John James clamped his jaws and ground his teeth, a gesture that every advocate in Edinburgh would have recognised as presaging a sentence of death.

'Where,' John James asked, as evenly as possible, 'is her ladyship?'

'She's no' expectin' you, but.'

'Damn you, man, where is she?'

'In the gerd'n, ah think. Are you fur wantin' her fetchit?'

'Of course I want her fetchit—fetched.'

'Ah'll see if she's receivin' then, sur,' Dougie said and, without so much as a bow, slithered back into the hall.

At precisely that moment Isabella appeared from the little door that led through the mews to the garden. In a voice so warm that it might have melted butter, she cried out, 'Johnny! How lovely to see you,' and, trotting forward, kissed him. 'I did not expect you so soon. Is it June already?'

'No, my dear,' John James informed her. 'May, only May. This is not, as it were, an official visit. I came on the spur of the moment.'

'I have no rooms prepared and precious little in the larder.'

'That is of no consequence,' John James said. 'I'm here in search of advice, not hospitality.'

'Advice?' said Isabella. 'What advice could a poor old woman give to a great man like you, a man to whom the world bows down?'

'Oh, stop it, Isa,' he said. 'If I require to be flattered . . .'

'Which you often do,' Isabella put in.

'If I require flattery, which I do not, I would not be coming here to find it,' John James said. 'You

63

know me too well, far too well.'

'Aye, since you were in smallclothes,' Isabella Ballentine agreed, 'and I would wipe the saps from your mouth with grandmother's kerchief.' She put an arm about his waist and led him not towards the door but into the shelter of the mews. 'How long will you be with me, Johnny?'

'One night, that's all the time I can afford.'

'One night?' Isabella's voice echoed in the dank enclosure. 'It must be a very important matter to have drawn you out of Craigiehall for just one night?'

'It is,' said John James. 'Very important.'

'I see,' Isabella said. 'Is it Charlotte again—or Nicola?'

'Nicola. She's run off.'

'Run off, do you say? With a man?'

'With her maid. Run off to Edinburgh.'

'Oh, Johnny,' Isabella said, 'will you never learn?'

'Learn? Learn what?'

She slipped her arm from about his waist and took him by the hand as if he were still a child in smallclothes. She steered him forward into the rose garden, saying, 'Come, we'll have a bite of dinner out of doors while I remind you yet again that young women are a law unto themselves. Do you need to make pee-pee first?'

'No, Isa,' John James said, gruffly, 'I do not need to make pee-pee, thank you all the same,' and meekly followed his cousin into her sanctuary.

*   *   *

Any humble foot soldier of the Highland Regiment

64

might have told you that impetuosity was both Gillon Peters' virtue and his vice. He was first into the woods on the march to German Town and first out with the bayonet when the Americans attacked from the rear; yet he railed openly against General Howe whose dithering had permitted the indefatigable Washington to escape to rebuild his shattered army. If it had been left to Lieutenant Peters—so the story went—he would have plunged after the Americans and slaughtered every one of them there and then. And as if that was not enough, it was rumoured in the ranks that it was originally Gillon Peters' idea to cross the Acushnet river and destroy the ships of the privateers that lay at New Plymouth, though it was General Grey who took credit for that expedition and all mention of Gillon Peters was mysteriously left out of despatches.

Unfortunately Nicola Templeton knew no one who had fought with Lieutenant Peters in the American campaigns and she was obliged, at least initially, to take him at face value.

She had barely buttered a second breakfast muffin when he turned up at Graddan's Court carrying a basket of oranges and a small posy of spring flowers. Breezing into the bedroom without so much as a by-your-leave, he delivered a sweeping bow to Charlotte, who was still in bed, and dumped the oranges on to the counterpane.

'*Pour vous, Madame,*' he said, 'in the hope that these juicy orbs will stand as token of my contrition and sweeten your forgiveness.'

Charlotte tugged her morning gown over her breast and, leaning from the ramp of pillows, glowered at the fruit.

'Shrivelled,' she said.

'Only a little,' said Gillon, undaunted. 'Perhaps you would be shrivelled too if you had travelled from the coast of Spain in the hold of a cargo ship.'

'Spain!' said Charlotte. 'They've been nowhere near Spain. Where did you find them at this early season? The orangery at Castle Cuprigg?'

'What an infernal ingrate you are, Charlotte,' said Gillon. 'Even if they did originate no further south than the glass palace at Cuprigg they cost me a pretty penny. If you don't want them . . .' He shrugged.

'The juice will make a palatable addition to a cordial, I'm sure.'

Charlotte pulled her breakfast plate against her stomach, lifted a muffin dripping with honey and stuffed it into her mouth. Gillon grinned and, holding the posy safely behind his back, leaned over the bed and kissed his sister-in-law on the brow before she could protest.

'How's my little nephew this morning?' he enquired.

Charlotte's cheeks turned scarlet.

'Your little . . . wh-what?' she stammered.

'The heir apparent, the prince in waiting. The baby.'

'How would I know how he is?'

'Well,' said Gillon, 'if you do not, who does? I just hope he likes muffins.'

Then, laughing, he pushed himself away from the bed and, with a less theatrical bow than before, presented Nicola with the posy.

She took it, sniffed the soft yellow petals, placed it between the teapot and the marmalade dish on the card table and thanked him for his thoughtfulness.

'Gillon?' Charlotte said.

He turned. 'Madam?'

'Have you had your breakfast?'

'Indeed, I have. Hours ago.'

'Then why are you here?'

'To pay my respects,' said Gillon.

'If,' said Charlotte, 'you are in search of Grant, you're too late. He's gone out to meet Mackenzie.'

'Ah now,' said Gillon, 'what a great pity that is. I had hoped to petition him for permission to take Nicola out to show her the sights.'

'Sights? What sights?' said Charlotte. 'She's no stranger to Edinburgh, you know. She has seen all the sights before.'

'I would be delighted to accompany you, Mr Peters,' Nicola said, 'if, that is, the invitation extends in my direction.'

Gillon shook his head. 'I am a bold fellow, Miss Templeton, but I am not so bold as all that. Alas, you are now in the charge of my brother and it would be beyond the pale of decency for me to escort you into the streets without his sanction. Unless . . .' he glanced at the bed, 'unless Madam Peters, in the absence of her husband, would be prepared to act as surrogate.'

'Great God!' Charlotte snapped. 'Stop blathering. If you have nothing better to do with yourself, Gillon, and can contain yourself for an hour or so while I dress, you may escort Nicola and me to the Observatory.'

'The Observatory?' said Gillon. 'For what purpose?'

'To observe, of course,' said Charlotte.

'You're in no condition to climb a hill, dearest,'

said Nicola. 'Besides, the weather is unsettled and the wind will tire you. I am sure Mr Peters can be trusted to look after me.'

'I would not trust him to look after a pig,' Charlotte said. 'However, if you are determined to treat me as an invalid then by all means go—but take Molly with you.'

'Surely Molly has no interest in observing,' Gillon said.

'She will, on my instruction, observe *you*,' Charlotte said. 'She will report any flaw in your behaviour and the slightest impropriety towards my sister.'

'And you will do what?' said Gillon. 'Inform Grant?'

'Exactly so,' said Charlotte.

'And what will he do? Rap my knuckles and lock Nicola in her room?'

'Charlotte,' Nicola said, rising, 'I did not come to Edinburgh to exchange one harsh set of rules for another. I will, if you wish it, take Molly but I will not have you dictate what otherwise I may or may not do.'

'Oh, you were always stubborn,' said Charlotte. 'Always headstrong.'

'I'm not the one who was courted by a stranger behind Papa's back,' Nicola reminded her. 'I'm not the one who wed in secret.'

'It wasn't a secret.'

'Perhaps not,' said Gillon. 'If I had stolen the daughter of Lord Craigiehall from under the great man's nose, however, I would have been branded a blackguard. But it was Grant who led you into folly and Grant can do no wrong, can he?'

'Folly? Do you regard marriage as folly?'

68

Charlotte raised herself on the pillows and, picking up an orange, threw it at his head. 'Do you suppose that my present condition is folly, too?'

Gillon caught the orange and lobbed it underhand back on to the bed. 'No, my dear Charlotte, I do not suppose your present condition to be anything other than the natural outcome of a marriage made in heaven.'

'A marriage made in heaven! Is that how you see it, Gillon Peters? If so, then you are a bigger fool than I took you for.' She sucked in a breath and lay back. 'Besides, you would not have had the courage to pursue me, would you?' She tilted her head coyly against the pillow. 'Well, would you?'

'No, my dear,' Gillon said. 'I don't suppose I would.'

'You and your precious tomahawk,' said Charlotte, smugly. 'It took a man of passion to woo and win me; a better man than you will ever be, in spite of however many redskins you hacked to death in the colonies.'

It was on the tip of Nicola's tongue to point out the inconsistencies in her sister's argument but she was too eager to get out of the house. She brushed crumbs from her skirt and said, 'I will find my cloak and bonnet and alert Molly to our intention, though I still believe that Molly would be better left here with you, dearest, in case you have need of her.'

'I do not need Molly Goodall to help me rest,' said Charlotte. 'You may, however, instruct Jeannie to clear away the breakfast things and shake up the bedding while I attend to other necessary matters.'

'By all means,' said Nicola and, carrying her

posy carefully, stepped into the passageway, with young Lieutenant Peters hard on her heels.

* * *

Isabella's figure was as neat as it had been forty years ago when the French jacket had first come into fashion. The garment still fitted her snugly but the frogs and tassels were faded with age and, John James noted, the trimming of her small chip hat had not seen a needle in a decade or more. It hung down over one eye like a Cupid's curl so that every now and then she would crook her lip and puff out a little draught of air to blow it to one side.

Although her dress was slatternly she was still every inch a lady.

Grandfather Templeton had been a stickler for decorum and Isabella's mother, the late lamented Aunt Hankin, had been so refined that she would not visit the necessary place without putting on clean gloves and a spotless linen apron which she changed as soon as she had completed her business.

There were times when John James thought that the spirit of Aunt Hankin lived on in Charlotte. His elder daughter had always been uncommonly particular about trifles and in the month of her first bleeding had become so hysterical that a doctor had been summoned from Ayr to administer soothing elixirs. How, he wondered uncomfortably, had she coped with the sordid realities of marriage and how would she endure the strain of carrying a child, let alone the guddle of delivering it into the world?

'Is it true, Johnny?' Isabella tucked into a slice

70

of cold veal pie. 'Has the pregnancy been confirmed, or is it simply, shall we say, rumour?'

'Hysteria, you mean?' John James reached for the mustard pot. 'No, Isa, I doubt if Peters would be deceived by a phantom. It's real enough.'

'But neither he nor Charlotte communicated the news to you directly?'

'No,' John James said. 'I had it from Littlejohn, who had it in turn from the maid, Molly Goodall, who, if past experience is to be depended upon, knows everything that goes on with my girls.'

Isabella dabbed her lips with a napkin and looked up at the beeches that peered over the high wall of the garden. The trees were all in motion, new leaves flickering in the breeze that skimmed the bare acres of Salton moor. There was no trace of air in the garden, though, and so mild was the late spring sunshine that they might have been taking luncheon, as some folk called it now, on the shores of the Mediterranean.

She brought her attention back to the iron-legged table, poured a little more German wine into the old crystal glasses, and said, 'Peters made no mention of a child in his letter?'

'None.'

'Charlotte's condition would certainly explain why Nicola darted off to Edinburgh without seeking your permission.'

'Nicola received no missive from Charlotte.'

'That you know of?' said Isabella.

John James conceded the point: 'That I know of.' He shook his head. 'Whatever has transpired since, Nicola ran off to Edinburgh to spite me.'

'She took the servant with her, did she not?'

'She goes nowhere without Goodall. Indeed, it

was Goodall who scraped together the fares for the Flyer.'

'Did Littlejohn tell you that?'

'After a little cajoling, yes.'

'Tell me,' said Isabella, 'are the servants also conspiring against you?'

'They have no reason to conspire against me,' John James said. 'I have always treated them well. What are you implying, Isabella? Out with it.'

'We live in changed times, Johnny,' Isabella said. 'A father can no longer organise his children as if they were parcel of his estate. It occurs to me that since Jamie's passing the servants may seem more like family to the girls than you do, given that you are so often away from home.'

'I am not remote,' John James said, then added, 'Am I?'

'Why did you not warn Nicola that de Morville had an interest in her?'

'I was not at all sure that Sir Charles did have an interest in her.'

'It appears to me,' said Isabella, 'that Charles de Morville and Lord Craigiehall are two of a kind, by which I mean that you are, to a degree, indifferent to the wishes of others and interested only in heritage.'

'Which is more than can be said for you, Isabella.'

'Be that as it may,' his cousin went on, 'you have set your heart on acquiring a part of de Morville's estate . . .'

'Only the coal-workings,' John James butted in. 'De Morville will not part with one fertile acre, that much one can be sure of, but the coal that lies beneath his land is worth a king's ransom and is

72

presently wasted by mismanagement and a lack of capital investment.'

'How much would it cost you to acquire the workings?'

'More than I can afford.'

'More than the love of a daughter?' Isabella said.

John James paused. 'Nicola needs a husband.'

'Does Nicola think she needs a husband?'

'She does not know what she needs. She has reached an age in which skittishness overwhelms common sense. Take Charlotte, for example . . .'

'No,' said Isabella, sharply. 'Charlotte is not the problem.'

'That is easy for you to say,' John James told her. 'You have never had the misfortune to meet Grant Peters. Take my word on it, he is a grasping, ambitious upstart.'

'Like Grandpapa?'

'Not in the least like Grandpapa,' John James said.

'Come now, Johnny, however much we may have loved him, Grandfather Templeton was a greedy, grasping old rogue.'

'Who married for love.'

'How can you be sure that young Mr Peters did not also marry for love?' Isabella said. 'Is Charlotte so unattractive that a young man would only marry her to lay hands on Craigiehall?'

'I came to you,' said John James, 'in search of advice, not carping.'

'Carping, is it?' said Isabella. 'Tell me, my dearest Johnny, what do you truly want? Someone to replace Jamie? That can never be. If Charlotte is with child and the child is male, he will be your

73

heir and the future laird of Craigiehall. If you remain estranged from Charlotte, however, you will have no say in how the child is reared and will be handing Craigiehall to a stranger.'

'Grant Peters, aye.'

'Nevertheless, Charlotte's son—your grandson—will be born within wedlock. How stands the law in this matter?'

'Simply put,' John James said, 'in the absence of a son, daughters succeed, not the eldest to the exclusion of others, as it is with sons, but all equally as heirs-portioners. Charlotte and Nicola will divide the property between them—unless, that is, a male grandchild is declared.'

'Declared?' Isabella said.

'Daughters or no,' John James said, 'I may at my choosing transmit all heritable property into a male grandchild's name by means of declaration.'

'What if the child is not of an age to inherit?'

'A child may inherit at first full breath,' said John James. 'The property—Craigiehall—will then be managed by trustees until he reaches his majority.'

'Who nominates the trustees?'

'I do—assuming I am not taken suddenly.'

'Then you had better hasten to your writing desk, had you not?'

'It is not something to be rushed, Isa. I will choose very carefully whom I wish to care-take Craigiehall—a person or persons young enough to survive me by several years and with sufficient knowledge of management to ensure that the place does not run to rack and ruin or that its profits are not tapped off.'

'By which you mean Mr Peters?'

'Of course I do.'

The trees above the wall shivered in another gust of wind and, almost imperceptibly, the afternoon began to wane into evening. There were two thick slices of roast beef still on his plate but John James had lost his appetite. His cousin was no oracle, no Cassandra, but she had in her eye a far-away look that indicated inspiration. He watched her guardedly, saying nothing.

At length, she spoke: 'There is another way to shut Peters out.'

'Is there?' John James said. 'I cannot, offhand, think of one.'

'You might marry again.'

'Hah!' John James laughed. 'Who would have an old man like me?'

'You are naught but sixty, my dear,' Isabella told him, 'and, as far as I can tell, a model of rude health. Is that not so?'

'Well, yes, I am, I suppose, quite fit'

'Fit enough to find a wife to bear you a child?'

'Well, yes. Possibly. What, though, do I have to offer a woman who is still in the prime of her life, and still fertile?'

Isabella drew her chair closer to the table and motioned her cousin to do the same. She blew at the trailing trim, then took off her hat, rested her brow against her cousin's formidable dome and whispered, 'If I were forty years younger, Johnny, I would have you myself. That would solve all our problems, would it not? You would not have to borrow from me ever again. Most important of all, you would have an heir for Craigiehall, and not even clever Mr Peters would be able to wrest it away.'

'I'm flattered, Isa,' John James said, softly. 'However, you are not twenty again and cannot, alas, provide me with an heir.'

She sat back suddenly, not smiling.

'I know,' she said. 'I know. You must find another.'

'I will never find one like you.' John James surprised himself by his gallantry. 'Nonetheless, you've given me food for thought.'

'Find a wife, Johnny. Find a wife and fill her up with child,' Isabella said. 'If she happens to be rich, so much the better.'

'Play young Grant Peters at his own game, do you mean?'

'Precisely,' Isabella said. 'And you'd better be quick about it.'

*   *   *

They were both young and agile and made excellent time from the back of the Canongate to the new walk that spiralled up Carlton Hill. The hill, like many Edinburgh landmarks, was so pocked by works of building that it resembled a mason's yard. There were foundation stones here, mounds of earth there and, dotted about the slopes, strange men in black side-seamed coats and tall hats carrying lengths of cord and wooden stakes. Markers had already been erected and a large painted sign close to the western edge warned trespassers that this portion of the ground was no longer public and that approaching the digging, let alone the precipice, would constitute a hazard to life and limb.

'What we observe,' Gillon paused to catch his

breath, 'is not an Observatory at all but just another piece of private enterprise, a glorious vision of Athenian grandeur that, like so many schemes in this blighted country, will, in due course, go to pot.'

'I did not take you for a cynic, Mr Peters,' Nicola said.

'Oh, I am no cynic, Nicola. I am, if anything, a Stoic. I do not believe that the spectacle-maker from Leith who has promised to reveal to us all the wonder of the heavens with his optical apparatus— if, that is, the half acre of ground here apportioned to him by the town-council ever does get built upon—I do not believe that the said Mr Short, even though he be a Fellow of the Royal Society and an optician *extraordinaire*, will ever come to terms with the demands of the academic brotherhood, let alone the reluctance of the magistrates to release a farthing for the project, no matter how loudly they proclaim their approval. It will be another sad tale of reach out-stripping grasp, of promises made and broken, of money given and squandered, with nothing much to show for it in the end but a collection of uncompleted ruins which, I might add by way of conclusion, may stand only as a symbolic monument to our nation's destiny.'

'You are not a patriot, then, Lieutenant Peters?'

'Gillon, you really must learn to call me Gillon. No,' he sighed, 'I am not by any formal definition a patriot. That said, however, I will rise up and defend our hunchbacked little country against any person who slurs or slanders it for, like any true-born Scot, I am a muddle of contradictions.'

Nicola laughed. 'I do not believe you.'

'That is your entitlement, *Mademoiselle*, your privilege, and demonstrates wisdom far beyond your years.'

'If there is no Observatory, why have you brought me here?'

Gillon swung away from her and covered his face with his hand. For a moment she imagined that her question had opened some deep, mysterious wound in him, then she realised that he was laughing.

She touched his shoulder, laughter bubbling in her too.

'What do you find so amusing?' she asked.

He swung round and put his hand on her shoulder. For a moment they were balanced all of a piece in perfect harmony, like well-wrought statuary, before he blurted out, 'I brought you here, dear Nicola, to be alone with you.'

'Alone?' she said. 'On Carlton Hill, on this builders' site?'

'Which,' he said, 'proves evidence of just how deluded a fellow can be when he is drawn to favour a lady.'

'Oh,' Nicola said, 'am I in favour with you then, Mr Peters?'

'Gillon. Gillon,' he said. 'Yes, you are, though after this unfortunate "charade" I question if you will ever favour me again.'

'"Charade"? I have not heard that word before. What does it mean?'

'A French word, newly introduced. It's a game, a riddling sort of game in which meanings are expressed by gestures.'

'Have you seen it played, Mr Peters, or played it yourself?'

'Neither,' said Gillon.

'Is it to play this new French game, this "charade", that you have lured me to this lonely spot?' she asked, sarcastically.

'In a manner of speaking.'

'Can Molly play too?' She pointed downhill to the lower slope where Molly Goodall was seated upon the grass, staring out over the city.

'By all means, Molly may play the game,' said Gillon. 'But she cannot play with us. She must find her own partner.'

'I see,' Nicola said. 'It's a game for two people.'

'One male, one female.'

'I do not think this is a new game at all,' said Nicola. 'I think this game is as old as the hill upon which we stand. What is more, I think it is not a French invention but universal. I believe you are flirting with me, Mr Peters. Is that not a better way of describing it: flirting—a riddling game with hidden meanings expressed by gestures?'

Gillon Peters put his hands on his hips and, arching his back, let out a bellow of laughter so loud that several smock-clad diggers popped their heads out of their holes and one tall-hatted gentleman almost dropped his measuring pole. Molly, for all her discretion, glanced round in alarm.

'Oh-ah-hah!' Gillon said, at length. 'I see I have chosen to cross swords with a clever minx. I fear I must tread cautiously, Nicola, or you will parry every move I have in my repertoire.'

'So,' Nicola said, 'you *have* played this game before. You are practised in it and, I fancy, regard yourself as something of an expert. Well, Mr Peters, tell me this—what is the object of the game? What is its outcome? How do you know when you have won the round?'

'We are not discussing the French invention, I take it?'

'No,' said Nicola, 'the other thing, the metaphor.'

'How cold that sounds, how grammatical.'

'You have not answered my question,' Nicola said.

'I would regard it as a first small victory,' said Gillon, cautiously, 'if you were, for instance, to call me by my given name which is . . .'

'Gillon,' said Nicola. 'There, you see. You are on your way.'

'Am I? To what end?'

'Unless I am mistaken,' Nicola said, 'you will retreat; not far, a step to the side or backward. You will evince an interest in the scenery and point out to me the glories of Auld Reekie while, in the course of your instruction, you'll place a hand first upon my elbow and, if I make no protest or appear not to have noticed, you will then lay a hand upon my waist.'

'Stumped,' Gillon said. 'I am, I see, stumped.'

'If,' Nicola went on, 'I resist the first manoeuvre—which I would do without temper, of course—you will not be tempted to assume that I am a girl deficient in virtue and would not therefore immediately progress to cupping an arm about my waist.'

'Lest you cry out to your maidservant to rescue you?'

'Which, perhaps, I would do—like this,' said Nicola and, lowering her voice to a faint whisper, called out, *'Molly, Molly, save me, save me.'*

80

'Hah!' said Gillon. 'An excellent piece of play, Nicola, and thoroughly confusing to your opponent who, poor devil, would not know if you were advancing or retreating. I applaud your perspicacity. Did you learn these tricks in Ayr? If so, I have misjudged the amorous life of that shire.'

'I am, sir, my father's daughter,' Nicola said. 'I learned these "tricks", as you put it, by observing the behaviour of young men—and not so young men—in pursuit of the opposite sex. I noted, for example, how your brother's "charade" affected my sister and how she, less vigilant than I, was taken in by it; how she came hither and with astonishing rapidity went thither into marriage.'

'Is marriage then the objective?'

'For the female,' said Nicola, 'yes, I do believe it is.'

'And for the male?'

'There may be other aims, other distractions.'

'What if I were to tell you that it is not always so?'

'I would not necessarily believe you,' Nicola said. 'It is, after all, a riddle that cannot be solved without sacrifice.'

'Sacrifice?' said Gillon. 'What an odd word to use.'

'Would the word "love" be more fitting?'

'More alarming,' Gillon said, 'to some gentlemen, at least.'

'Not, however, to you?'

Gillon raised his chin and scanned her as he might have scanned a small, colourful reptile found in the grass, 'I have no answer to that question.'

'As I suspected,' Nicola said. 'When you have an

81

answer to give me, Gillon, we will "charade" again. In the meanwhile, you must be content with a gesture that may have no meaning at all.' Then, raising herself on the tips of her toes, she kissed him on the cheek and, laughing, caught up her skirts and headed down the slope to join Molly for the long walk home.

CHAPTER FIVE

They were hardly home from Salton ten minutes before John James set about arranging his departure from Craigiehall, a full fortnight in advance of the opening of court session.

Much to his chagrin Robertson was despatched to Edinburgh not only to prepare the apartments in Crowell's Close for his lordship's early arrival but to deliver letters to a handful of folk whom his master regarded as allies. Not least among this curious circle was the esteemed medical proctologist, William Gaythorn, M.D., who had nursed John James through several blistering encounters with haemorrhoids and a prolonged bout of the gleet, a discharge that in any other man might have signified at least one unfortunate instance of sexual laxness but that in John James's case stemmed from nothing more depraved than the eating of a polluted pheasant.

As the facilitator of such miracles of healing William Gaythorn had been bound into his lordship's employ at a retaining fee of twenty pounds per annum, though in the past couple of years he had done little enough to earn his oatmeal, a situation that according to all portents was now about to change.

'Who?' said Charlotte, sitting up in bed.

'He says he's a doctor, ma'am,' said Jeannie.

'A doctor? Mr Peters said nothing to me about employing a doctor. Where is Mr Peters?'

'Gone out, ma'am. He wented early.'

'And my sister?'

'Gone out too.'

'With Mr Grant?'

'With Mr Gillon, ma'am. They said I wisnae tae wake you.'

'What time is it?' said Charlotte.

'Wantin' a quarter tae eleven.'

Wide awake now, Charlotte experienced a sudden sense of desolation. Seated upright in the tousled bed with the curtains closed against the summer sunlight, she had never felt so utterly alone. She stared, round-eyed, at the scrawny little maid who crouched nervously in the doorway awaiting her mistress's instruction; then beneath the layer of quilt, blanket and sheets, her stomach went into a turbulent spasm that was not relieved by a discharge of noxious gas, and a pressing need to make water was abruptly replaced by an even more urgent need to vomit. She gasped, gulped, and held a hand to her throat to avoid the indignity of being sick in front of a servant.

'It's your breakfast you're needin', Mistress Peters,' Jeannie said. 'I'll carry it through in a minute. What'll I be doin' wi' the mannie, though?'

'Whuh—where is he right now?' Charlotte got out.

'I putted him in the parlour for tae cool his heels. He's no' verra pleased.'

83

Charlotte gulped again, closed her fingers over her windpipe and digging deeply into her scant store of Templeton grit, said, 'Fetch him in, Jeannie. And while you're about it bring me—bring me a—a bowl.'

'A bowl o' whut, ma'am?' said Jeannie.

'A bowl, a bowl, an empty bowl,' Charlotte cried and, lunging to the side of the big four-poster, threw up all over the carpet.

*   *   *

Precious few hackney carriages were to be found in hilly Edinburgh, though, as children, Charlotte and she had often ridden in sedan chairs lugged about the town by broad-shouldered highlanders. If hacks were few and far between, stubby little local coaches were not, and hardly a tavern or ale-house did not have stages at the ready to carry folk out to, as Gillon put it, near-flung places.

In the yard of Morgan O'Toole's Champion's Inn, amid high-sided carts, broken crates and decaying straw, four such coaches were horsed and harnessed.

'Where are you taking us today, Gillon?' Nicola asked.

'Hush!' Gillon raised a finger to his lips. 'It's a mystery and a surprise.'

'It'll be a surprise if it costs more'n sixpence,' muttered Molly, to whom the daily outings had become wearisome. 'It'll be Leith, like as not.'

'Can you be sure of that, Molly?' said Gillon. 'Are you possessed of the second sight?'

'There's a notice on yon chalk board,' Molly said. 'It says Leith.'

Smiling coldly, Gillon hopped around the back of the scruffy coach and spoke in private with the driver as if he hoped, still, to preserve the surprise for Nicola. He counted ten copper pence from his purse to pay for all four seats, for he had no wish to share a closed coach with a stranger. He would cheerfully have doled out three times that sum to be rid of Molly Goodall whose so-called 'discretion' was nothing but a mask for leech-like vigilance. He shoved the servant up into the coach then, with both hands about her waist, assisted Nicola into the cramped, damp-smelling interior.

'You'll not be gettin' much for your money, Mr Gillon.' Molly folded her arms across her bosom and sank, sulkily, into a corner. 'It's just as well we'll not be here for long or we'd all be smothered.'

'It's not, I confess, the Chariot of Meliadus,' Gillon addressed himself to Nicola, 'but it's snug enough for a short ride.'

'Perfectly snug,' said Nicola. 'Is it another abbey or a collection of ancient ruins you've selected to catch our interest today, Gillon?'

Molly snorted. The coach lurched. The driver urged the horse forward and coaxed the stage out of the inn yard.

Gillon flicked a glance at the servant who pretended to peer out of the tiny window, though the glass was so smeared with mud that it barely admitted daylight. He shifted his weight, pressed his knee into Nicola's pretty floral overskirt and laid a hand on her arm.

'Perhaps,' he said, 'I should blindfold you to preserve the mystery.'

'It'll take a better man than you, Mr Gillon,'

Molly said, 'to be tyin' a scarf round my eyes.'

'Molly,' said Nicola, 'please do be quiet.'

The horse trotted down hill. The coach dipped at a steep angle.

Gillon slid his hand through the folds of Nicola's overskirt. She did not draw away. He entwined his fingers with hers. 'Would that I might gag *and* blindfold your irksome maid,' he whispered. 'Will we never be alone?'

Nicola said, 'What would you do if we were alone?'

'Steal a kiss, of course.'

'Do you believe that stolen kisses are the sweetest?' Nicola said.

'Do you?' Gillon asked, still whispering.

'I have no experience upon which to base a judgement,' Nicola answered.

Gillon was silent for a moment, then said, 'Why *do* we have to be saddled with that woman everywhere we go?'

'Because your brother insists upon it,' said Nicola.

'My brother and, may I remind you, your sister too.'

Nicola pulled back an inch. 'Now you've spoiled it.'

'Have I?' said Gillon, frowning.

'I feel guilty at leaving poor Charlotte.'

'Leaving poor Charlotte fast asleep,' Gillon reminded her. 'What would you have us do, Nicola? Squat by her bed all day long listening to her snores?'

'Charlotte does not snore,' said Nicola. 'Does she?'

'How would I know a thing like that?' Gillon

said. 'Do you really feel guilty at shaking loose from her?'

'Indeed I do,' said Nicola. 'She isn't at all well.'

'My brother does not seem concerned?'

'I'm sure he is,' said Nicola. 'He merely chooses not to show it.'

'That may very well be true,' said Gillon. 'Grant and I are unalike in that respect. I cannot help but wear my heart upon my sleeve.'

'Did you not tell me that you were a Stoic?'

'Stoics too may fall in love,' Gillon said, and gave her hand a squeeze.

'Leith,' Molly cried out. 'Hah, I knew we was headed for Leith. What is there for to do in that dirty place?'

'We may walk out upon the stone pier, for one thing,' Nicola said, 'admire the great variety of ships moored in the harbour and watch mariners unloading cargo. Papa took us there once for an afternoon visit, to educate us in the way of trade. Everything is there, the product of every kind of manufacture from every country in the world. Oh, Molly—the delicious smells that come from the spice warehouses and the sugar-houses and the lofts where the coffee berries are stored. I have never forgotten it.' She sat upright and, undeterred by Molly's disapproval, gave Gillon a playful little pat upon the cheek. 'This is so much better than a meadow full of carved stones or the ruins of a nunnery or—or anything. Thank you, Gillon, for a wonderful surprise.'

And Molly, still scowling, snorted once more.

*   *   *

South of Grey Friars' church in the vicinity of George's Square, just beyond the reach of the City Council's jurisdiction, Hercules Mackenzie held court in a large mansion whose windows looked down upon the homes of the great and the good. Lords and ladies, dukes, duchesses, viscounts and countesses, even a few distinguished personages with no lineage to speak of, had recently migrated here to escape the flummery that surrounded the building of the New Town on the far side of the Castle ridge. Hercules Mackenzie was no aristocrat but he was, without doubt, wealthy and distinguished. From the apartments on the ground floor of his house in Rankin Street he conducted an astonishing amount of legal business on behalf of the pillars of society and an even more astonishing amount for those poor folk who dwelled below the salt.

Once, twenty odd years ago, he had been an advocate of considerable promise whose grasp of the intricacies of Scots law had brought many a panel of learned judges to its knees. What had brought Hercules to his knees, however, was not a fault of law but a confluence of bad breeding and riotous living for, at the age of thirty-one, the devil-may-care genius of Parliament House had been struck down by 'the wheeze', an affliction so severe and stubborn that the labours of young Hercules to draw breath, let alone argue causes, had suggested that his life, let alone his career, might well be in jeopardy.

Surgeons, physicians, street-corner leeches, experts in botanical remedies and healers by prayer and fasting had all applied themselves to ridding Hercules of his crippling illness, all to no avail. His intended bride had broken off their engagement. His mistress had abandoned him for an elderly woollen-draper. His surviving sister, Eunice, a harridan of the first water, had refused to have him in her house lest he contaminate her children, and his so-called brother advocates had scuttled off to Parliament House with hardly a backward glance in his direction. A man of less determination and character might simply have lain down and died at this turn of events but Hercules was made of sterner stuff. He had crept off to a trim little farm in the Stirlingshire countryside where clean air, fresh vegetables and the tender ministrations of Margo Peters, the farmer's widow, had restored not only his health but his ambition.

Six months later he had returned to Edinburgh, still wheezing, though only a little now, and had set about establishing himself not as a pleader but as a solicitor, a Writer to the Signet, a change of direction that over the years had rendered him rich and had brought him at length to the mansion house in Rankin Street where, on that morning late in the May month, he welcomed his young protégé, Grant Peters, with—metaphorically speaking—wide open arms.

The room was as broad as an assembly hall with flock wallpaper, a Turkish carpet and a fire screen the size of a portcullis. There were three sets of chairs, a striped sofa and, close to the fire, a huge well-padded armchair which contained, though only just, the huge, well-padded figure of Mr Mackenzie.

'Grant,' he said, slapping his thighs with both hands. 'As I live and breathe, there is no other man in Edinburgh that I would rather see at this hour of the morning.'

'Given that I was summoned, Hercules, it serves you ill to profess surprise at my appearance. If it is the Fifeshire dispute that bothers you . . .'

'No, no,' said Hercules. 'I take it that the petitions are all in order and you will lead with your usual efficiency and nary a rhetorical flourish to distract the Lords of Council from the pettiness of our client's claim.'

'Petty it is too in its essence, though the client does not think so.'

'Nothing petty about our fees, what?'

'As true a word as I've heard spoken since breakfast.' Grant seated himself on the striped sofa and, much at ease in the Writer's company, crossed his legs and leaned back against the cushion. 'Do you have another cause to put my way then, one more deserving of our attention, perhaps?'

'Deserving only of my attention,' Hercules said. 'I have been invited by a certain Mr Bunting, a writer in the parish of Galston in the shire of Ayr, to furnish the draft of a sale of a portion of land—a rather large portion of land that is presently attached to the estate of Sir Charles de Morville.'

Grant sat forward. 'Sale or lease?'

'Sale.'

'To Craigiehall?'

'No,' said Hercules Mackenzie. 'Not to Craigiehall.'

'To whom?'

'To a company masquerading under the name of the Westmore Coal and Mineral Trading Office.'

'Is there such a company?'

'Indeed there is,' said Hercules. 'In Glasgow.'

'I have never heard of it,' said Grant. 'How many barges do they have?'

'None,' said Hercules, with a hint of glee. 'No barges, no wagons, no operating crews, no traceable assets to speak of. The Westmore Coal and Mineral Trading Office currently appears to consist of four carts, eight horses and a hutch on a small piece of ground a little to the west of the Broomielaw, the hutch, I assume, being the office.'

'Then a masquerade it is, by all accounts,' said Grant. 'How did you come by your facts, Hercules—if the answer does not test your client's confidence?'

'I sent one of my clerks to Glasgow to investigate.'

'And he found?'

'Four carts, eight horses . . .'

'And a hutch,' said Grant, nodding. 'Is Craigiehall behind it?'

'I had hoped that you might be able to tell me that,' said Hercules.

'The lawyer in Galston, what light can he shed on the mystery?'

'Not a blink,' said Hercules. 'Or if he can, he will not.'

'Were the coal rights offered for sale by de Morville?'

'If so, it was done privately, not by public notice,' said Hercules. 'In view of the papers I have already received, the sum paid for the land and its mineral deposits is far in excess of what de Morville might have expected. It's my guess that some person or persons tendered an offer so outrageous that the old chap could not resist it.'

'But why would he sell at all?'

'Pique,' Hercules said. Grant had told him the story of de Morville's marriage proposal and Nicola's rejection. 'Pique at being turned down.'

'From what I've heard of him,' said Grant, 'de Morville is far too hard-headed to harbour resentment. We may, however, deduce that Lord Craigiehall will *not* be the new owner of de Morville's coal workings.'

'He will not be pleased about it,' said Hercules. 'By the by, Craigiehall could not afford to pay the sum offered to de Morville. Therefore, it's safe to assume that he is not the blind partner behind the Westmore Company.'

'He might borrow, I suppose.'

'Only a fool would lend Craigiehall money,' said Hercules Mackenzie. 'Between you and me, Grant, his finances are rumoured to be rather unsound.'

'The crops have yielded poorly in recent seasons,' Grant said, 'but surely his rent book remains healthy?'

'I take it the daughters know nothing of their father's affairs?'

'Ah,' said Grant, 'is that why you have summoned me this morning, to plumb me for information?' He shook his head. 'Be assured, Hercules, that the girls know nothing whatsoever about Templeton's finances. He would never confide in them. Never.'

'Because they are female.'

'Because,' said Grant, 'he is at war with them.'

'And with you?'

'That's no secret,' Grant said. 'What do you wish me to do?'

'Not a blessed thing.' Hercules slapped his thighs again. 'Bunting and I are more than capable of ensuring that the deeds are so tightly drafted that those quarrelsome sons of de Morville's will be unable to challenge them.'

'It may be,' said Grant, 'that you will discover the identity of the purchaser in the course of your application.'

'And it may be that I will not,' said Hercules. 'There's no tax levied on land used for coal working and no requirement under law for the names of participating partners to be registered in the purchase deed, not if the sum is paid in full on the striking of the bargain.'

'Will the sum be paid in full?'

'According to Bunting, yes.'

'Then we must wait,' said Grant, 'to see who extracts coal from the land and just how much capital is invested in the scheme. I wonder if Craigiehall has heard this piece of news.'

'He may have other more pressing matters on his mind, of course.'

'Charlotte, do you mean?'

'How is your dear lady wife?' said Hercules.

'As well as can be expected.'

'An heir for Craigiehall,' said Hercules, smiling wistfully. 'How I envy the unworthy old devil. There are times when I regret never having taken a wife; not for the pleasures of the marriage bed, which are, I believe, considerably overrated, but for the pleasure of having children and, now that I am in my decline, grandchildren to gather round my knee and be suitably awed.'

'Is it too late to take a wife, Hercules?'

'Oh, far too late,' said Hercules. 'Mrs Dalgleish would have a fit in purple if I brought another female to share her kingdom; no wife could possibly attend me as well as my housekeeper. Besides, there is only one woman to whom I ever gave my heart and she was but recently widowed. Is your mother well?'

Grant grinned. 'In the best of health, thank you.'

Hercules eased his buttocks forward in the armchair. 'Do you know why I invited you here this morning, Grant?'

'To warn me?'

'Aye, to warn you. If Craigiehall rumbled at his daughter's disobedience, when news of the loss of the coal workings reaches his ears he will become volcanic. And you, my dear boy, you will be held to blame.'

'I am always held to blame in Craigiehall's book,' Grant said. 'However, I thank you for your consideration, Hercules, and for the information. If anything comes to your ears regarding the mysterious purchaser . . .'

'You will be the first to know,' Hercules promised.

He hoisted himself an inch from the armchair and offered his hand.

'Good luck to you, Grant,' he said.

'Yes.' Grant shook his mentor's massive fist. 'I fear that I may need some luck when the Craigiehall returns to Edinburgh.'

'Oh, do you not know?' Hercules said.

'Know what?' Grant said.

'He arrived last night,' said Hercules.

*　　　*　　　*

The Nine-Headed Eel was the most popular of the many eating houses that had recently sprung up in

94

the neighbourhood of Leith harbour. It was owned and hosted by a mariner turned tapster by the name of Lucky Findlater and was not, as Molly had feared, a glorified knocking shop but rather a boisterous meeting place for the would-be dandies who trolled the esplanades of the sea port in search of diversion.

The stone-clad building was almost, if not quite, indistinguishable from the signal tower that propped up the root of the pier and the houses round it were still inhabited by rough-hewn, home-spun merchants who, Gillon said, were so shrewd that they could turn a profit on the sale of a hank of bladder-wrack or a cracked razor shell.

By the time Gillon informed the ladies that he was ready to eat neither Nicola nor Molly was willing to question his choice of tavern. Two hours of brisk walking along the banks of the river Leith had sharpened their appetites to the point where Molly, never one to hide her feelings, claimed that if Mr Gillon did not lead them to the trough quite soon she would be obliged to chew her mittens for sustenance.

Mr Gillon, still talking nineteen to the dozen, wended his way through the clutter of fishwives' closes and narrow causeways with a familiarity that was not lost on Nicola Templeton. She latched close to him, snaring his arm, and left Molly, as always, to chug along behind.

'Is it not odd to think,' Gillon waxed, 'that much of what we have seen this morning was once an uncultured wilderness that provided shelter to the galleys of the Roman legions as they came upon our shores; that once it was all just furze and golden broom, and elk and deer and white bull

95

calves came down to drink in the shallows in voiceless solitude?'

'Voiceless solitude,' Molly cried, from the rear. 'Would it not have been a mercy to be here in them days, sir?'

Gillon ignored the servant's jibe.

Inspired by the salty breeze that stippled the waters of the harbour and made the lighters and Fife ferryboats dip and bob alarmingly, he was in full glorious flow and truly believed that the girl at his side had been impressed by his witty accounts of local history, much of which he had made up on the spot. He had long cherished a desire to bring a woman here for there were few better places to woo an inexperienced girl and advance his cause, whatever that cause might be. If only, he thought, he could be shot of the impudent maid for a half hour or so, he might lavish charm on Craigiehall's daughter and, like his brother with Charlotte, sweep her off her feet.

He steered her around the corner of 'The Eel' into the slap of the breeze and watched, delighted, as little Nikki Templeton, laughing, clung to her bonnet and fought to keep her skirts and petticoats in place.

He pointed to the heavy wooden sign that swung above their heads.

'The Nine-Headed Eel,' he said. 'The lamphrey, in other words. The species was once profuse in the salmon pools of the river but, for some reason not known, it has greatly diminished in numbers in recent years. However,' he put an arm about Nicola's waist, 'there are still lobsters and crabs to enjoy, mussels too, and, need I add, salmon from the sea and every kind of fish you can imagine to

96

tickle our palates.'

'My palate tickles at the very thought,' said Nicola.

'Shall we step inside?' said Gillon.

'If you please,' said Nicola.

Gillon opened the door and ushered the girl and her maid into the tavern.

He knew 'The Eel' well, rather too well. On the uppermost floor, in an old rope loft, he had lost much of his hard-earned pension playing cards with other idlers from the city. Only a dazzling win at brag in April had enabled him to keep his head above water and Lucky Findlater's bully boys off his neck. He was currently in good standing with the landlord, however, and it would do his credit no harm to be seen in the company of a lovely young heiress whose connection to wealthy Lord Craigiehall would not go unnoticed by the scallywags who inhabited the parlour.

He raised a hand in greeting to Lucky Findlater and motioned that he intended to take his guests upstairs to the 'polite' dining-room where tables were clothed with linen and a long mullioned window provided an excellent view of the harbour. Best of all, behind a wooden screen, was a back room where valets and servants were stowed while their masters and mistresses enjoyed a little privacy.

The publican answered Gillon's signal with a sly grin and a gesture that wrung a grunt of disapproval from Molly. Shepherding the women before him, Gillon moved across the boards while, to his satisfaction, several gentlemen at several tables held their forks poised and left their glasses untouched to eye the silky young lady, Peters' latest conquest, as she tripped towards the stairs.

Gillon had barely set foot upon the stairs, however, when a familiar voice called out his name. He stopped in his tracks, turned and peered down at a man who was dining alone at a table beneath the staircase.

'Gillon, it's me.'

'God in heaven!' Gillon exclaimed. 'You. You of all people.'

A few steps above him Molly and Nicola turned too and looked down upon the man who, rising from the bench, brought himself into view.

He was exceptionally tall and as thin as a casting rod and wore no hat or wig. His hair was brown and curly, not cropped or even tied, a no-nonsense style, Nicola thought, that perfectly matched his demeanour.

Badly rattled, Gillon stretched out a hand for support and then, collecting his wits, brought Nicola down. 'Miss Nicola Templeton,' he said. 'My—ah—my brother, Grant's brother, our farmer brother—Roderick.'

*   *   *

The apartments in Crowell's Close were strewn with trunks and baskets and the long Jacobean table in the centre of the drawing-room was laden with documents, books and wig-boxes and draped with the lordly robes that Robertson had flung out to air. There was a hive-like buzz throughout the house, with Robertson barking orders to a swarm of servants who, it seemed, were irked at being summoned to attend his lordship when the opening of the summer session was still two weeks away.

In the midst of this activity, the great Lord Craigiehall sat motionless and calm, while a joiner with saw and mallet fitted new mouldings to the side of the chimney-piece and a curtain-maker, balanced precariously on a chair at the window, replaced a threadbare drawstring with a length of tasselled cord.

The din was tremendous and William Gaythorn, M.D., was rather upset that his lordship had not sent the tradesmen out of earshot of what was, after all, a private, not to say indelicate conversation.

'Is she, or is she not, pregnant?' his lordship asked.

William Gaythorn answered, 'The evidence suggests that the young lady is, indeed, with child.'

'Did you or did you not examine her?'

'I did, sir.' Gaythorn was not used to having his word challenged, not even by gentlemen of rank. 'I examined her thoroughly.'

'Yet still there is doubt?'

'A scintilla of doubt, yes,' Gaythorn admitted.

'Is she healthy?'

'Abundantly healthy.'

'But you cannot with certainty say about the child?'

'Not with absolute certainty.'

'I assume that my daughter did not take kindly to your ministrations.'

'No, Lord Craigiehall, she did not.'

'Did she complain?'

'She did.'

'Did her recalcitrance deter you from making a full examination?'

On his knees at the fireplace, the joiner held his mallet in abeyance and the curtain-maker craned so far back from the window that he was in danger of toppling to the floor.

Dr Gaythorn straightened his shoulders and, bridging his long white fingers before his chest like a parson in prayer, stared the learned judge directly in the eye. In his vast experience of the practice of midwifery he had rarely encountered a husband, or a father for that matter, who evinced much interest in the female reproductive system or what went on behind the elaborate screen of sheets and blankets during delivery.

Unfortunately the same could not be said for the lay members of the Odd Fellows club who were full of sly questions about the intimate parts of women and implied that the doctor's encounters with such hidden treasures brought him pleasure. Nothing, he assured his libidinous inquisitors, could be further from the truth and, if pressed, he would embark on a long harangue, filled with disgusting detail that rapidly removed the twinkle from their eyes and drained their saucy cheeks of blood.

'Do you wish me to continue?' the doctor asked.

'I do,' said Craigiehall, stubbornly.

'The examination is conducted by the introduction of the forefinger, lubricated with pomatum, into the—um—the vagina in order to feel the *os internum* and the neck of the uterus and, in this case, this morning, into the rectum to ascertain if the *fundus* was stretched.'

'Was it?'

'Not to any appreciable degree.'

'It's small wonder Charlotte complained,' said

100

his lordship. 'Go on.'

'In accordance with acknowledged practice,' Gaythorn said, 'I conducted my examination after the contents of the bladder and the rectum had been discharged and the stomach was empty. After persuasion, your dau— the patient submitted to the enquiry in a standing posture.'

'Standing? Why?'

'In that position, the uterus hangs lower in the vagina and the weight, however slight, is sensible to the touch. In some cases the vagina feels tense.'

'Thus it was with Charlotte?'

'No, not clearly. Hence, sir, my uncertainty.'

'When will you be able to tell with no shadow of doubt that my daughter has been impregnated?'

'By the fourth month.'

'Too late,' said Craigiehall.

'However,' Gaythorn went on, 'if my opinion has any value whatsoever, I think you may safely assume it that your lordship's daughter is entering the third month and will be delivered of a child shortly before Christmas.'

'Am I to conduct myself on your assumption, Gaythorn?'

'That, sir, is for you to decide. Medicine is not a precise science. Human anatomy, particularly that of the female, has many anomalies. But all the signs are that Mrs Peters will present her husband with an heir before the year ends.'

'How did Mr Peters greet the news?'

'Mr Peters was not present. He was not in the house.'

'Nicola, Mrs Peters' sister, was she . . . ?'

'She too was absent.'

'I see,' said Craigiehall.

He looked first at the curtain-maker who immediately plastered himself against the window glass and all but strangled himself with a loop of cord. He looked next at the joiner who began banging away with his mallet. Lord Craigiehall hardly seemed to notice the racket, let alone the workmen. He had about him, Gaythorn thought, the air of a man in a state of shock.

'If that is all, sir, I will take my leave,' the doctor said.

'Yes,' said his lordship, absently. 'By all means.'

Dr Gaythorn picked up the bag that contained the tools of his trade and, without so much as a fleeting glance at the artisans, headed thankfully for the door. He was almost there before Craigiehall called out to him.

He paused and turned. 'Your Lordship?'

'My daughter—Charlotte—did she weep?'

'Aye, sir,' the doctor informed him. 'She wept.'

'As well she might,' Craigiehall muttered, 'As well she might,' and with a little waggle of the wrist, dismissed the good doctor once more.

CHAPTER SIX

'Cattle?' Gillon said. 'The purchase of cattle brought you to Leith? Are we expected to believe that?'

'What other reason would I have for being here?' Roderick Peters said. 'There's quite enough risk in cattle dealing to satisfy my need for excitement without travelling thirty miles to join you at the gaming table.'

102

'Is it a bull you've purchased, Mr Peters?' Nicola asked.

'Aye, Miss Tempieton, a pure Banffshire longhorn to improve our stock.'

'To achieve a better yield of milk, or for fattening?' said Nicola.

'The milk will be less in volume but richer, which will help our output of butter,' Roderick informed her. 'The bull is a three-year-old and came at a bargain price. I'm transporting the animal by boat from Portsoy rather than have him travel with a rag-tag herd on a long drive. I know how lax some drovers can be and I prefer to have my lad arrive fresh.'

'I've heard that some Banffshire breeders now send their cattle all the way to London by boat,' Nicola said, 'but in this brisk weather your fellow may not have much stuffing left in him after his short sea voyage.'

'He'll be snugly penned and roped,' said Roderick. 'I have hired grass for him to rest in before we begin the drove back to Heatherbank.'

'We?' said Gillon. 'Who's with you?'

'McAllan and his boy.'

'Could you not have purchased a bull nearer to home?' said Gillon.

'Not one with a sound pedigree, not at that price,' said Roderick. 'It was Mama's wish that we strengthen the herd and you know how skilled she is at spotting a bargain.'

Gillon nodded dolefully, as if his mother's acumen had long been a thorn in his flesh. Nicola sensed that he was not well pleased at this chance meeting and even less pleased that she had taken it upon herself to invite his brother to join them for dinner.

Carrying his bowl of fish stew and his glass and bottle, Roderick had followed them upstairs. They were seated now at a table by the big mullioned window, eating and drinking like old friends. How odd, Nicola thought, that until a week ago she had known no interesting young men. Now she knew three, three personable brothers each as different from the other as chalk is from cheese. Roderick Peters was not daunting like Grant, nor garrulous and thrusting like Gillon; he struck her as a man who knew what he wanted and, when the time was right, how he would get it.

'How many beasts do you have in your fields?' she asked.

'Thirty cows in milk, twice that in fat cattle. We sell our sweet milk in Stirling and our buttermilk in Falkirk.'

'You have sheep too, do you not?'

'Aye, a small flock of Blackface. They thrive well enough on the heather on the hill but we bring them down to close pasture soon after Martinmas lest heavy weather cause the ewes to cast too soon.'

Gillon rattled his spoon in his bowl impatiently

'Come now, Roddy,' he said. 'Have we not had enough of agriculture that you must bring it to the dinner table with you, like dung on your boots? What have you done with McAllan and his boy?'

'I thought you were tired of agriculture,' said Roderick.

'Gillon may be, but I'm not,' said Nicola. 'My father . . .'

'Owns half of Ayrshire,' Gillon put in. 'Oh, by the by, talking of Martinmas, you are soon to become an uncle.'

'Surely not the Clavering lass?' said Roderick.

'What! Julia! Good God, no!' said Gillon. 'Grant—I mean Charlotte—is showing with child. Due, we believe, about Christmas.'

'Mama will be pleased,' said Roderick. 'She's long wanted a grandchild to pet and spoil. Is your sister well, Miss Templeton?'

'A little out of sorts in the morning, that's all,' said Nicola.

'Only to be expected, I suppose,' Roderick said.

'Do you have children, Mr Peters?' Nicola heard herself ask.

'Not him,' Gillon said. 'He's too busy to find himself a wife, too busy and far too ticklish.'

'Ticklish?' Nicola said.

'Fastidious,' Gillon said. 'Milkmaids are seldom ladies.'

'What do you mean?' said Nicola.

'My brother means that fine ladies do not wish to marry a humble farmer,' Roderick Peters said.

'What about the Gourlay girl?' said Gillon. 'She practically threw herself at your feet and you paid her not the slightest heed.'

'Lizzie Gourlay was not for me.' Roderick did not seem embarrassed by this turn in conversation. 'Besides, all that happened years ago, when I was not much more than a boy.'

'You were never a boy,' said Gillon. 'You were born into middle-age.'

Roderick shrugged. 'Someone had to look after mother and manage the holdings while you were off fighting redskins and Grant was transforming himself into a lawyer.' He took a mouthful of fish stew, extracted a bone from between his teeth and wiped it off on his napkin. 'Enough of your

105

slanders, Gillon. What of you? What brings you to Leith in broad daylight?'

'I am showing Miss Templeton the sights,' said Gillon.

'What sights are there to see in Leith?' said Roderick. 'It is not much more than a working port.'

'It makes a pleasant change from ruined churches, believe me,' Nicola said. 'Gillon has been very kind in keeping me entertained, but the sight I would much like to see is a bull being unloaded from a fishing boat. I cannot imagine how that feat is accomplished.'

'With difficulty.' Roderick tugged a watch from the pocket of his waistcoat and consulted it. 'If you are willing to tarry here for another hour or so the boat, and the beast, should arrive when the tide reaches full.'

'No,' said Gillon. 'We must be on our way back to Edinburgh.'

'Why?' said Nicola.

'In the event that your sister may need us.'

'Did you not say that Charlotte can take care of herself?' said Nicola. 'An hour or so will make no difference. We have light far into the evening. Besides, I have not nearly finished my dinner and by the time I do . . .'

'You're scuppered, Gillon, thoroughly scuppered,' Roderick Peters said and, to his brother's considerable annoyance, laughed.

*   *   *

If he had ever been asked to provide a maxim, or rule in life, that summed up his character, John

James Templeton would have declared, without a blush, that he was the sort of man who never began a thing without having an eye on its conclusion. Most of his friends and acquaintances would have crowed at such pompous nonsense and, without doubt, Lady Valerie Oliphant would have led the chorus. She was wife to Sir Archibald Oliphant whose fame as a man of letters was eclipsed only by the fact that he had more money than he knew what to do with and spent it lavishly on all sorts of eccentric pursuits, including funding theatrical companies to perform his execrable verse plays.

Lady Valerie's pursuits were somewhat less eccentric and a good deal less public. Her passions in life inclined not towards the arts but to playing cards, organising balls and, when Sir Archie was kind enough to leave town, to briskly swiving any handy young gentlemen imprudent enough to cross her path; and, this being Edinburgh, there was no scarcity of young gentlemen only too willing to accommodate the lady who, in spite of her advancing years—she was fast approaching fifty— was still slender and unblemished.

John James had never swived with Lady Valerie and when the rumour-mill ground out chaff about her ladyship's latest conquest, he covered his ears and pretended that, all evidence to the contrary, she was naught but the victim of drawing-room gossip. He had known her for many years and had been a friend of sorts since that night, long ago, when she had first fleeced him at whist in a private room above Fortune's tavern and being regularly skinned at cards by the lovely Lady Oliphant had become not just a habit but a substitute for other, less mercenary, desires.

It was not midnight in Fortune's now, though, but tea-time in the Oliphants' spanking new town house in Broughton Square.

John James entered the lady's presence, hat in hand. Her letter of reply to his request for a meeting was tucked into his spotless silk waistcoat, the French-style peruke that he hadn't worn in years sprinkling fresh powder in all directions as he fashioned a quaint leg and bowed. The little girl, Oliphant's latest prodigy, immediately stopped playing and as the tinkling of the piano died away, ten or a dozen heads turned and ten or a dozen pairs of eyes glowered at John James as if he had fallen from a branch of the silver candelabrum.

Behind John James's back a footman in full livery and snow-white wig, smirked at his lordship's discomfort and in a voice as plummy as a bishop warden's, announced a name and, without pausing for breath, recited all his lordship's sundry ranks and titles while poor old John James stood there, flushed and snorting like a horse in an auction ring.

'Lord Craigiehall,' Lady Valerie said at last and, rising from a silver-painted chair, advanced upon him with both hands outstretched. 'How honoured we are to have you join us for Mademoiselle Cadell's little recital. I did not expect you to come.'

He was tempted to catch her by the scruff of her slender neck and lead her from the room, for it was obvious that she had worked a mischief to make him look a fool. Instead, he took her hand and, stooping, kissed the stitching of her glove. Then, looking up into her pale blue eyes, he hissed, 'I was not informed that you were hosting a musical afternoon, Valerie, or I would have sought a more convenient time to call upon you.'

'Did I not say?' she asked, wide-eyed. 'Did I not mention in my letter . . .'

'No, you did not.'

Over her shoulder, through the nodding ostrich feather of her hair ornament, he saw how the folk whispered. He knew them all, or most of them, for hardly a one was on the sunny side of sixty and between them they represented the cream of Edinburgh's old society.

There was little Johnny Pritchard, Earl of Drumore, Lady Athelstane and her decrepit spinster sister, and that ancient crop-headed cutthroat, Admiral Staines, who was probably more interested in ogling the girl-child than listening to the music. There was no sign of Valerie's husband in the salon, though, for which small mercy John James was grateful.

'How remiss of me,' Valerie said. 'However, now that you are here, do come and be seated. The recital is almost over and we will have tea soon.'

'I did not come for tea,' John James said, 'nor for music. I will slip away, Valerie, and allow the child to continue. I will call another day.'

'Why *did* you call, sir? Was it to feast your eyes on my beauty or to pay me what is my due?'

The girl perched at the piano like a little pigeon and Staines, that ogre, had ambled over to flirt with her. Two maidservants by the window giggled furtively and one very old gentleman, Sanderson by name, had already fallen asleep, his head on Lady Athelstane's shoulder.

John James was well aware that he had breached good manners and could not delay the sedate progress of the afternoon's entertainment for long. He was also mindful that Valerie Oliphant held notes against his name amounting to almost one thousand pounds and that it would be advisable not to rile her.

'I am here,' he said, 'by invitation, if you recall.'

'I did not expect to see you in Edinburgh for another week or so.'

'I came early.'

'To settle your debts?' the lady said, winsomely. 'To ease your conscience, Lord Craigiehall, or to pile a few more coals upon the fire?' She did not require an answer and, twirling round, called out, 'With your pardon, I must excuse myself from your company for a few moments to attend to a sudden piece of business. Fleur, my dearest, do please continue.'

The girl, like an automaton, began to play again at precisely the point in the composition at which she had stopped. Lady Valerie took his lordship's arm and led him swiftly out of the room into the hallway and, with a nod to a footman to open the door ahead of them, straight into Sir Archie's library, where they might be alone.

*   *   *

The bull was a handsome brindled beast of forty or fifty stones, long-bodied, short-legged and, so Roderick Peters said, clean in the bone. He had, however, a fine springing pair of horns and a tongue so loud that his unhappy bellowing announced his arrival long before the smack reefed sail and poled into the harbour and drew a small crowd of spectators, Nicola among them, on to the quay to watch the fun.

110

Roderick's drovers, McAllan and his lad, appeared out of nowhere. The man was small and wiry and burned walnut-brown by sun and wind. The boy, much bigger than his daddy, carried a stout ash stick and a long pricking spear. They peeled off their coats and tied up their shirt sleeves and demonstrated a nervousness that, to Nicola's surprise, affected Roderick too.

The bull was penned in a narrow enclosure of unplaned timber, tethered to an iron hook by a muzzle-ring and chain. On the open deck were nine lean bullocks, curiously docile, who did no more than stamp and cough as the boat was brought broadside to the line of the quay and moored fast at bow and stern.

The skipper, it appeared, had dealt with live cargo before. He barked out orders to his crew who, dancing in tune to the dip of the vessel, ran out four heavy planks and secured them with ropes to piles on the quay.

'Are they yours, too, Roderick?' Nicola asked. 'The bullocks, I mean?'

'Aye,' he answered, curtly, then quitting her side, ran down the quay and, leaping like a deer, jumped on to the deck of the boat.

The McAllans, father and son, positioned themselves at the head of the ramp as Roderick drove the first of the bullocks on to the planking and chased it up on to the quay. The rest of the package followed, jostling and slithering, while Roddy Peters slapped and butted them into a single file. Once on the move, instinct drove them on. They trotted politely on to the quay where Daddy McAllan collected them and steered them away over the clattering cobbles into the streets of the town.

Nicola had seen cattle handled before but never so skilfully.

As she watched Roderick Peters at work, she detected in him a hint of kinship with his brothers; agility and directness of purpose and a certain buoyancy that linked him more to Gillon than to Grant. All three were clever in different ways and unaffected by the formal manners that genteel society imposed upon its sons. She could not imagine de Morville's boys being engaged in herding, or any of the young advocates that her father had allowed into the house now and then ever squaring off to a bull.

Behind her, Gillon shifted his stance and Molly, knuckles in her mouth, let out a little gasp as Roderick Peters, aided by two seamen, lifted down the timber barrier and waved the men away. He ducked under the bull's black-tipped horns and, squatting on his heels between its forelegs, unhooked the chain. He ravelled the chain in his fist and wrapped it around his forearm as if it were a strand of wool and, ducking again, brought himself out from under the bull's belly and held the big horned head fast on shortened tether.

For a moment, standing inside the sweep of the horns, he was eye to eye with the beast and close enough to mingle breath with it. The bull's head jerked and he let out a plaintive roar then, tripping daintily as a foal, he allowed the man to lead him forward towards the planking. He lashed out once, just once, and stamped his hoof with bone-breaking ferocity. Roderick, cinching the chain, drew himself even closer. His strength was no match for the bull's but, Nicola realised, he had put himself in command of the animal, both shielding and controlling it. Walking backwards, he guided the beast up the slope of the planking and on to the quay while the on-lookers whistled and cheered as if he had performed the feat solely for their benefit.

'My, my, my!' said Molly, at Nicola's shoulder. 'Now is that not somethin' to marvel at? I never saw the likes of that done at Craigiehall.'

'One day,' said Gillon, thinly, 'he will do it once too often and pay for his foolishness.'

'Do you consider it foolish, Gillon?' Nicola said. 'I consider it brave.'

'You are easily impressed, Nicola,' Gillon said. 'Compared with some of things I've seen and some of things I've done . . .'

Then, as the Banffshire bull lowered its head and Roderick, digging his heels into the cobbles, held it steady, he closed his mouth and moved sulkily away, and Roderick, with a glance and a nod in Nicola's direction, ran out the chain and led the bull off to the lairage on the outskirts of town.

*   *   *

Sir Archie Oliphant claimed that his creative forces could only be unleashed in total silence. For that reason the library door was quilted in plush velvet and trimmed with leather to keep out noise. It closed with a soft thud that stirred the languid air in the room like a fly alighting on treacle. Almost before it had settled, John James had blurted out the nature of the cause that had brought him here.

'A bride?' Lady Valerie cried. 'Are you asking me

113

to find you a bride?'

'A wife,' said John James, grimly. 'Not a bride, as such.'

'Do not split hairs with me, Craigiehall. First a bride and then a wife; is that not the natural order of things? Indeed, in our enlightened age does the progression not first begin with a lover?'

'I do not know how the progression begins.'

'But you, not even you, John James, can have forgotten how it ends,' Lady Valerie said. 'Is it a failure of memory that afflicts you or a sensibility that has grown frail with age?'

'Age?' said John James, scowling. 'I am not so old as all that.'

'Nor so poor as you pretend to be, in spite of the sum you owe me,' said Valerie. 'Why do you have need of my intervention, sir? Are you not well enough placed to pluck some plump young heiress from the shelf without assistance?'

'In fact, actually—no. My reputation . . .'

'Reputation! Hoh!' said Valerie. 'You are just as vain as any of the cockerels that strut the High Street, peeking from under their hat brims to see which tender young maid their tailoring has impressed.' She touched his shoulder. John James flinched. 'Go to St Giles—which, I believe, you do in any case—attend church, sir, and spy upon the beauties there. When you find one who takes your fancy, approach her Mama, hat in hand, and introduce yourself. You will, of course, have no need to introduce yourself for Mama will know only too well who you are and will tremble at the very notion that you have deigned to speak with her. Indeed, when you make it known that you have an interest in her daughter it would not

114

surprise me if she fainted dead away.'

'The matter,' said John James, 'is not suited to whimsy, Valerie. I need to find a wife who will bear me children—and with some urgency.'

'Is it the conceiving or the bearing thereof that is the urgent issue?'

'Beg pardon?'

'If a fire in the blood is all that troubles you, sir, I can, I believe, suggest several ladies of discretion who would be willing to . . .'

'I do not require a mistress, Valerie. I require a wife.'

'Is there no one in your set in Ayrshire who would do . . .'

'I have no "set",' John James interrupted her again, 'not in Ayrshire nor in Edinburgh. That is the crux of the problem. Why else do you suppose I would come to you? My cousin suggested it, for, it seems, you know everyone and everything that goes on in this town.'

'Is it a woman with a fortune that you seek?'

'No, damned be it!' John James said, then, closing his eyes for an instant, added more calmly, 'If she has property, of course, or the promise of a dowry, I would not be averse to that, but the necessary element, the essential thing, is that she is mild and well-bred and young enough to bear me a healthy child.'

'An heir?'

'Yes.'

'To replace poor young Jamie?'

'Yes.'

'To direct the inheritance away from your daughters?'

'In truth, yes.'

'Well,' said Lady Valerie, 'strange as it may seem I do not have a list of suitable candidates to hand.'

'Can you, however, help? I mean—will you?'

She walked away from him and toured the spacious room at no great rate, past the laden bookcases and the curtained window, and round again by Archie's huge sloping desk with its silver candlesticks, fresh-filled ink wells and sharpened quills. She stepped lightly, one hand raised, her forefinger pressed against her lips as if to check criticism or, perhaps, hold back laughter.

John James watched her, saying not a word.

He had always admired her and in his own stifled fashion had even desired her a little. Now, suddenly, it dawned upon him that even if Lady Valerie had been free—a widow, say—she was too old to suit his purpose and he realised with a start that he had just invited Valerie to guide him into marriage with a woman not much older than Charlotte, a woman who might turn out to be just as wilful, frivolous and immature as his daughter.

Valerie paused, one hand still raised, the muted light from the curtained window behind her, the ostrich feather bobbing.

'Yes, Lord Craigiehall,' she said. 'For the sake of our friendship—not forgetting that you are already in my debt—I will help you uncover a wife.'

'May I ask . . .' he began.

'How?' Lady Valerie said. 'That remains to be seen. However, you must promise me one thing, John James.'

'And what is that?' he asked.

'Your cooperation,' she answered. 'Your full, unswerving, unquestioning attention to the cause in hand. I will not have you make a fool of me, and

116

I will not be crossed or slighted once the game has begun.'

'I understand,' he said.

'Do you?' she said. 'I wonder, truly, if you do.' Then, touching him briefly on the cheek, she went forward to rap upon the quilted door to alert the footman to open it and let her return, belatedly, to her guests.

* * *

The coach had hardly left the vicinity of Leith harbour before Molly fell asleep.

She huddled in a corner, purring like a puss, her plump cheek resting against the glass. Nicola did not have the heart to waken her. Besides, she needed no chaperone now. All signs indicated that she was in no danger of being molested by Gillon Peters who seemed more interested in surveying the passing scene than in pursuing a conversation, let alone a seduction. Nicola was more relieved than disappointed. She had lost all inclination to flirt, especially with Gillon Peters whose churlish behaviour that afternoon had thoroughly annoyed her.

She lay back and closed her eyes as the conveyance came upon the first of the long hills that led up to the city and the coach tilted. She wondered where Roderick was, Roderick and his Banffshire bull. She wondered if he was thinking of her and, if so, what impression she had made upon him. There was so much that she did not know, not only about Roderick Peters but also about how a young woman should conduct herself in the company of a man so obviously self-contained.

117

She opened her eyes and said, 'You knew he would be there, did you not?'

'Pardon?' Gillon said, as distantly as if she were a stranger.

'You knew that Roderick would be in Leith today,' said Nicola. 'Do not lie to me, Gillon. It was a splendid surprise and a great pleasure to meet your brother and watch him at work.'

'Fact, I did not know he would be there,' said Gillon. 'It was mere chance. Given that Roderick rarely leaves the farm and that I am seldom in Leith, you may rest assured that it was no more than ill luck.'

Or destiny, Nicola thought, or destiny.

CHAPTER SEVEN

Papa, thank heaven, had never been a dedicated sermon-taster like so many of his peers. Not for him a dash from kirk to kirk from Sunday dawn until Sunday dusk to listen to the rantings of the latest controversial firebrand or the more considered preachings of famous Edinburgh divines. He attended church more out of a sense of duty than devotion and being not inclined to early rising took himself and his little flock to afternoon service in the New Church within the great decaying pile of St Giles.

Being a creature of pride as well as habit, he invariably occupied the cushioned chair within the box reserved for High Court judges. Many a time Charlotte and she had been propped beside him, too close to the prow of the pulpit to giggle, chatter or show off, and far too close for comfort to the tombs of long-dead Protestant barons whose disapproving effigies had haunted poor Charlotte's childhood dreams.

It came as no surprise to anyone in Graddan's Court when Charlotte, now recovered from her chastening experience with Dr Gaythorn, rose early enough that gloomy Sunday to eat a hearty breakfast, have Jeannie help her dress and, toddling into the parlour where Grant was working on papers and Nicola reading a dog-eared copy of the *Scots Magazine*, announced that, like it or not, they were all going to church.

Grant looked up from his papers, raised an eyebrow and said, 'Certainly we are, my dear. Do we not always go to church?'

'I am not fit to walk to the Tron, however.'

'Therefore,' Grant said, 'we will step over the road to St Giles.' He glanced at Nicola, who pulled a face, as if to say, 'I told you so,' then, pushing himself away from the table, he took his wife into his arms, administered a placatory kiss, and said, 'St Giles it will be, Charlotte. Come, we will confront God together, God and Mr Smellybelly and any other notables who happen to be worshipping there this afternoon.'

'I do not know what you mean,' said Charlotte.

'Of course you don't,' said Grant with a wink at Nicola. 'Of course you don't,' and, for the time being, let it go.

*   *   *

The Reformation had seen an end to the glory of St Giles, so her father claimed. Staunch

119

Presbyterian though he was, he bemoaned the fact that the four great brazen pillars that had propped up the high altar in ages past had been melted down to make cannon and that the church's once-tranquil precincts had become so secularised that lock-up shops—the famous luckenbooths—now bit into the fabric of the building itself. Lean-to wooden roofs nibbled at the buttresses and ate away the tracery of the windows, and the shanties of bookbinders, watchmakers and sellers of sweetmeats, toys and shoes so degraded the street that one practically had to rock back on one's heels and crane one's neck to see the majestic lantern tower at all.

Charlotte had no interest in the iniquities of the past and Grant, who did much business with the booksellers and printers who traded on his doorstep, valued convenience over history. But Nicola disliked the crude partitioning of the magnificent vaulted interior, though it had been completed at least a century before her birth, and following her sister and brother-in-law through the narrow transept and across what remained of the aisle, she felt a familiar Sabbath gloom descend upon her.

Molly, Jeannie and Cook dutifully joined the stream of servants that trickled into the fenced pews at the back of the New Church while Nicola trailed Grant and Charlotte to the strangers' box at the base of the pulpit.

She knew why Charlotte had insisted on bringing them to afternoon service and had chosen St Giles over the Tron. It was not to enjoy the enlightened preaching of the handsome, if ill-named, young divine, Mr Smellie, but to plant herself smack-a-dab in front of Papa who for the best part of four hours would thus have to endure the sight of his elder daughter side by side with her blackguard husband, and nurse his wrath in the knowledge that nature had been crass enough to dispatch a grandchild in the direction of Craigiehall.

It was, of course, Papa's own fault for sending Dr Gaythorn to Graddan's Court to confirm the pregnancy. Grant had been more amused than annoyed by his lordship's temerity. He had also been much amused to hear that Nicola had bumped into Roderick in Leith, and had displayed considerable interest in what his farmer brother had been up to and what she had made of his rustic kinsman.

There were no friendly faces in the New Church; Nicola recognised only a few of the deans, baillies and judges who occupied the steep-sided benches. In nearby rows advocates and Writers were twittering enthusiastically for their devotion to matters theological was secondary only to their love of exposition.

She did not meet her father's eye.

She folded her skirts under her and, clasping her hands, asked the Lord to forgive her transgressions and lead her into the path of enlightenment. She kept her head down, face hidden beneath the rim of her bonnet, until a stirring around her indicated the arrival of the preacher and his Bible-bearer.

And then she looked up.

Her father was propped in the fretwork chair and made no pretence of ignoring her. His implacable gaze was fixed upon her or, rather, upon Charlotte. He continued to stare at his girls

121

after the Bible-bearer had finished his chores and young Mr Smellie took his place before the altar and everyone rose for the intercessory prayer. He stared throughout the solemn intonement and refused to acknowledge the girls or react to their presence, even when Charlotte arched her back and, slipping loose the ribbon of her pelisse, placed both plump hands across her belly and, not without malice, grinned.

*   *   *

Nicola had assumed that he would slip away by one of the many doors that punctured the walls of the old cathedral, but he was more man than that. He came out at length by the aisle to the north transept where Robertson waited alone, the rest of Craigiehall's servants having been chased back to the house. Molly loitered there too and Jeannie, who knew no better, and a gaggle of other servants, together with wives and daughters, horses, carriages and sedan chairs.

Chatting to a fellow advocate, Grant leaned on the pillar by the steps while Charlotte and Nicola waited, nervously, a yard or two away. Little Johnny Pritchard paused to bid them a good afternoon, Lady Brancombe too, and the daughters of a Writer, whose name Nicola could not recall, lingered long enough to express admiration for Charlotte's hat and Nicola's shoes before, giggling, they scampered off to join their parents.

Papa was stiff-legged after the long service but looked very handsome and dignified, Nicola thought, though his old-fashioned French peruke seemed curiously out of character. He bowed this way and that way, unsmiling, then with Robertson falling in behind him came down the steps and placed himself squarely in front of his daughters.

'May I offer you tea, Papa?' said Charlotte.

'No, you may not.'

'We have brown bread and seed cake.'

'I am informed by Dr Gaythorn that you are expecting a child.'

'Not here and now, Papa,' Charlotte said, with astonishing boldness. It had been well over a year since Charlotte had addressed a word to Papa or he to her and in that time, for whatever reason, the balance between them had shifted. 'I will embrace motherhood late in the month of December.'

'Hmm,' her father said, through his nose. He looked down at Nicola. 'Am I to take it that you do not intend to return home, by which I mean to Craigiehall, that you will remain dependent on Peters' charity until such time as your sister is delivered?'

'I will not return to Craigiehall,' said Nicola, 'to be married off to Sir Charles de Morville in exchange for a few wagons of coal.'

'Did you know of your sister's condition when you ran off?'

'No, I did not,' said Nicola. 'But now I am here and have been made welcome, I intend to stay—at least until New Year, and possibly longer.'

'Do you not plan to return to Ayrshire at all this summer?'

'Not unless we are properly invited to do so,' Nicola said.

'We?' her father said.

'Charlotte and Grant are part of our family too.'

'It is a conspiracy then?'

'It's no conspiracy, sir,' Grant said from his lordship's shoulder. 'If, however, you have a mind to learn of a true conspiracy and are reluctant to take tea in my house, perhaps you would consent to walk a little way in my company so that we may talk privately.'

'Why would I walk with you, Peters?' her father said.

'Because, Lord Craigiehall, I have news to impart.'

'Concerning my daughters?'

'No, sir. Concerning your Ayrshire neighbour.'

'What does my Ayrshire neighbour have to do with you?'

'Not a blessed thing,' Grant said. 'I am but the bearer of information.'

'Information on what subject?'

'Coal-working rights,' said Grant.

She saw her father stiffen and his brows arch. He hesitated for a second, then said, 'I *will* walk a little way with you then, Mr Peters.'

Grant said, 'Take the ladies home, Molly, if you will.'

'Aye, Mr Peters.'

'Make sure the tea is brewed and ready, for I am thirsty.'

'Aye, Mr Peters. Will you be long behind us, sir?'

'No, not long,' said Grant.

*   *   *

Gillon opened his eyes and peered at the visage that emerged from the beam above his bed. It leered down at him with a wicked grin, as if it took

124

pleasure in his squeamishness. He blinked once and then again, his eyes as sticky as egg yolks. The face that fashioned itself out of knot and grain did not melt away but in the drab afternoon light from the unwashed window took on a fiendish clarity. Gillon closed his eyes and sank his head into the bolster which, to his disgust, was damp and sour where he had been sick upon it. Groaning, he swung his legs out of the bed and groped for the floor. He did not dare look up for he knew that the face in the roof beam would still be there, a remnant of nightmares that no amount of strong drink could dispel, dreams of dead men, Indians and French, butchered and buried long since but unwilling to lie quiet in their graves.

Arms hanging slackly between his knees, he stared at the floor and struggled to recall how he had managed to get home from the Reprobates' Club while filled to the brim with port and brandy.

Having no manservant to attend him, he had parted from his fellow reprobates in the region of the West Bow and—he remembered it now—had discovered a girl in the closes who was willing to be his friend. He had no recollection of her name or what she looked like, only that her thighs had been warm against his belly, her hair had smelled of vinegar and that despite his maudlin condition he had given her a good one or two.

Seated listlessly on the side of the mattress, he hitched up his shirt and studied his parts then, satisfied that no damage appeared to have been done, staggered to the cupboard where he kept the chamber pot and noisily relieved himself before he flopped on to a chair and peered about the tiny attic room.

Shoes, stockings, waistcoat and breeches were strewn across the floor where he had flung them last night. He grabbed his waistcoat, felt in the pockets and found them empty. He plucked up his breeches, dug his fingers into the hidden pocket in the waist, and found it empty too.

Lunging across the room he wrestled his greatcoat to the floor and hunted through the pockets, turning them out to the lining. Nothing, nothing but the plug from a pipe of tobacco and a single brown penny lodged in the stitching. He closed his fist on the penny and hurled the greatcoat against the wall.

Robbed! The bitch had robbed him. Robbed him of his handkerchief, his snuff box, his watch and fob, as well as all his cash.

One penny was all that remained of his savings after a week's futile wooing of the Templeton girl, after paying his split of the bill at the club which, now he thought of it, had come to a fifth part of six pounds. He had started out the week with almost nine pounds and had saved three pounds to stake him to a night at Fortune's; now he had lost it all.

Cursing, he sat back on his heels.

On Monday his rent was due. Mrs McCracken would come toiling up the staircase and with a simpering smile would deliver a harangue about the tribulations of widowhood and the necessity of keeping soul and body together and how she had so many debts to pay that she could not extend him even one week's credit, though it grieved her sore to say so and would grieve her burly son, Donald, even more if ever he got to hear about it which, Gillon knew from experience, meant a visit from Donald before the day was out.

Rent, or the lack of it, was a minor problem. He had banked on winning enough to resume his hectic courtship of Craigiehall's daughter. Unfortunately, Nicola Templeton was no harebrained wide-eyed child, like most of the promising young girls he had wooed. When she had responded warmly to meeting his farmer brother he had suffered a fearful loss of confidence in his ability to pull the wool over her eyes. Roddy had always intimidated him, Grant too, for he knew that he was no match for his brothers and had little to offer a woman but a faded reputation and a frisky substitute for love.

In the caddy was a single pinch of tea. In the bin were two stale oatcakes, in the kettle an inch of water and in the grate a few charred fragments that might be enough to brew him a breakfast of sorts. He considered taking himself to Graddan's Court to sponge off Grant, but he was not ready to face Nicola just yet. Besides, it was Sunday and to judge by the position of the sun not far short of mid-afternoon. If Grant had taken the family to service in the Tron they would not return until five at the earliest.

Kneeling at the fireplace in his soiled shirt, Gillon began to sort out useful coals and search for a wisp or two of kindling. In his day, he had lighted fires with less promising material and, cheered by that thought, had just turned his mind to how he would dig himself out of his present predicament when an imperious knocking sounded upon the door.

Fearful that he had slept the clock round and that Mrs McCracken had already summoned Donald to toss him out into the street, he croaked,

'Who is it? Who's there?'

'Am I addressin' myself to Lieutenant Gillon Peters, late o' the Royal Highland Regiment?'

Gillon hesitated. 'Who is it wants to know?'

'Am I or am I not . . .'

'Yes, yes, I'm Gillon Peters.'

'Got a letter for you, sir.'

'Letter?' said Gillon, suspiciously. 'Push it under the door.'

'Can't be doin' that, sir,' said the voice. 'Answer required.'

Tucking his shirt between his thighs, Gillon put his thumb to the latch and opened the door an inch.

'Tell me,' he said, 'who might this letter be from?'

'Lady Valerie Oliphant,' the cocky young footman replied.

*   *   *

'I don't imagine,' Grant said, through a mouthful of seed cake, 'that it will remain a secret for long. It would not surprise me if notice appeared in the *Courant* before the month is out. Meanwhile, I'd be grateful if you would say nothing of the matter outside of these four walls.'

'The owner, however, remains a mystery?' Nicola asked.

'That is the case,' Grant answered. 'To judge by his anger—which was, without doubt, unfeigned— your father knows nothing of the sale.'

'He was, I take it, furious?' said Charlotte.

'Quite beside himself,' said Grant.

'Is he hastening back to Craigiehall

128

immediately?'

'I doubt it,' Grant said. 'I believe I convinced him that the source of my information was unimpeachable and that the horse has already bolted.'

'He took *your* word on it, did he?' said Charlotte. 'I suppose that's something for which we should be grateful.'

'I wouldn't be inclined to read too much into it, my dear,' Grant told her. 'The best that can be said is that your Papa did not blame the messenger, no matter how upsetting he found the message.'

Charlotte hacked at the sugar loaf with a silver spike and spooned fragments into her tea cup. 'Mackenzie was your source, of course.'

'Your father did not ask and I did not tell, but I think he guessed that Hercules is the most likely person to have got wind of the sale.'

'Coal diggings,' said Charlotte, tutting. 'All this fuss about coal diggings. I do not know what the world is coming to.'

'There are,' Grant said, 'certain gentlemen in the community who firmly believe that in the not-too-distant future coal will be worth more than gold.'

'Why did de Morville sell the land and not simply lease out the rights?' said Nicola.

Grant shrugged. 'To spite his sons, maybe.'

'Perhaps,' said Charlotte, 'he was so upset at losing Nicola he decided to wash his hands of the whole thing, not to spite his sons but to spite Papa.'

'Or he has found himself another wife,' Nicola suggested.

Charlotte clinked down her teacup. 'Oh, I never thought of that.'

'A wife whose father has sufficient capital to exploit the potential of a coal-bearing field,' said Nicola.

'Now you *are* being fanciful,' Grant said.

'Why else would he sell?' said Charlotte.

'For capital,' Grant answered.

'Sir Charles is reputed to be among the wealthiest men in the shire of Ayr,' said Nicola. 'Why does he need capital?'

'To buy more land,' said Grant.

'More land? Another estate, do you mean?' said Nicola.

Grant nodded.

'Great God!' Charlotte exploded. 'Do you mean Craigiehall?'

Grant nodded again.

'Papa loves Craigiehall. He will never give it up,' Charlotte said. 'Oh, Grant, do you think he would sell Craigiehall just to prevent us inheriting it?'

'I doubt if he's as perverse as all that,' Grant said. 'There is, however, a whisper—no more than gossip, really—that your father has reached the limit of his borrowing.'

'Nonsense!' said Charlotte. 'Craigiehall is possessed of a rent book that's the envy of half the gentlemen in Scotland. Papa also has his court salaries and official emoluments. How can he possibly be bankrupt?'

'I did not say that he was,' said Grant, calmly.

'He hinted as much to me,' Nicola said.

'When?' said Charlotte.

'Just after I turned de Morville down.'

'Why did you not tell me?'

'I set no store by it,' said Nicola. 'I thought he was exaggerating.'

Charlotte shook her head. 'I cannot believe that Papa is poor.'

'The term, of course, is relative,' Grant said. 'Calm yourself, Charlotte. Your father would not be the first gentleman to discharge himself of a portion of his estate to set the remainder on a solid footing. Look at Lord Keppel, for instance, he . . .'

'I do not care about Keppel,' said Charlotte. 'Craigiehall is mine and I do not want it cut up like a round of cheese. You know better than I do, Grant, what happens when an estate is broken up. The best parts are sold and the rest rapidly falls to rack and ruin.'

'Not if it is well managed,' Grant said.

'Now if you were managing it, my dearest,' Charlotte said, 'I am sure you would make it yield ten-fold.'

'Littlejohn is a good overseer,' said Grant. 'It's not management but direction that Craigiehall lacks.'

Nicola had the uncomfortable feeling that Grant and her sister had discussed the future of Craigiehall many times before. Until now she had spared no thought as to what might become of her and what her future might hold. She had assumed that she would be well looked after. Charlotte was no longer the silly, submissive young woman who had deserted Craigiehall for a marriage made in heaven, however. She was not Grant Peters' pawn, but his partner in every sense of the word. Perhaps, Nicola thought, her father's judgement of Grant's intentions had been more accurate than she had supposed and that by flying here to Edinburgh she had played straight into Grant Peters' hands.

'The sale of de Morville's land to an unknown

131

buyer is not as inconsequential as you may imagine, Charlotte,' Grant Peters said. 'Indeed, it may favour us by prompting your father to reconsider his position. He did not turn away this afternoon, did not reject you. He's sufficiently interested in what you have in your belly to send a doctor to examine you and he cannot be entirely displeased with me for bringing such an urgent piece of news to his attention. Do you not see, dearest, that if your father acts rashly out of pique or panic he will isolate himself still further? He has no one to whom he can turn, has he?'

'His cousin, I suppose,' said Charlotte.

'That hermit,' Grant said. 'What can she offer?'

'True,' said Charlotte. 'She cannot even manage her own affairs.'

'It is only a matter of time,' Grant said, 'until your father is forced to face the fact that he has no one to whom he can safely turn—no one but us.'

'And Nicola, of course,' Charlotte said.

'Ah, yes, of course,' said Grant, sitting back. 'And Nicola.'

*　　　*　　　*

It was all very dramatic, Gillon thought, typical of the style in which the Oliphants conducted their affairs; Sir Archie might be dismissed as a brainless eccentric but Lady Valerie could be dangerously meddlesome. He approached the two-horse carriage by the locked gates of the old St Ninian's burial ground with caution. By the clock, it was still early evening but thick cloud had drifted in from the Forth and daylight was fading fast. The carriage stood out in the empty street like a silhouette. It was a fast rig with huge wheels and a high prow and, so he'd heard, a lining of copper sheeting to protect the occupants from highwaymen. There were no footmen on the step, though, and the driver did not raise his head when Gillon emerged from the Back o' the Yards and, glancing nervously this way and that, padded towards the vehicle.

Carriage lamps had not been lighted. Windows were draped with ruffled velvet. Nothing moved within or without, nothing save the coachman's arm as he tapped the butt of his whip upon the roof.

The door of the rig swung open.

A gloved hand beckoned.

Act Three, Scene Four of *The Elopement*, as performed by Didier's company in the Theatre Royal a season back, Gillon thought and, shaking his head ruefully, clambered up into the Oliphants' copper-lined chariot where Lady Valerie was waiting for him, *sans* maid and, naturally, *sans* husband.

She pressed herself into a quilted corner and drew up her fur-trimmed cloak to hide her face as if she feared that full exposure to her beauty might drive him to frenzy. He had locked with her before, of course, a single strenuous encounter in the garden of an oyster parlour near the Fleshmarket after a long evening of cards had left them both flushed and excited. They had met at the tables several times since but to his disappointment it seemed that once was enough for her ladyship, who preferred younger, less voluble gentlemen.

'Madam,' Gillon said, deepening his voice, 'you sent for me.'

'Did you come alone?'

'I did.'

'Not followed?'

'No, I evaded all pursuit.'

'Good,' she said. 'Excellent. We must not be seen together.'

'Really?' said Gillon. 'Why not?'

'I have need of you.'

'Do you?' Gillon said.

She lowered the cloak and dabbed a fleck of fur from her tongue with her fingertip. A small, flat candle floated in a dish on a shelf above her head. By its light he could just make out her eyes glittering in the half dark, her lips glistening. She looked younger by ten years, and almost desirable. He had eaten nothing all day but two stale oatcakes, however, and feared that a growling in the guts might break the mood and give the game away.

'What truth in the tale that your brother's wife is with child?'

Caught off guard, Gillon hesitated. 'Yes, Charlotte is—ah—with child.'

'Your brother is the father, is he?'

'What?' said Gillon. 'Yes, of course he is. Why do you ask?'

'I thought perhaps you had been scattering your seed immoderately.'

'Charlotte is a model of constancy,' said Gillon, 'and I am not so lacking in finer feelings that I would seduce my brother's brand new wife.'

'Tush! We are both worldly enough to know that such things happen even to high-minded ladies from honourable families. And you, my dear Lieutenant Peters, are not lacking in persuasive

134

charm.'

'Grant is the father, of that there's no doubt.'

'What of the other girl, the younger—Nicola, is it not?'

'What of her?'

'Has she succumbed to your wiles yet?'

'My wiles?' said Gillon. 'Miss Templeton—the younger sister—is a guest in my brother's house. I have been appointed to attend her welfare when my brother is busy with the courts.'

Lady Valerie chuckled, slyly. 'Do you believe that taking her to Lucky Findlater's on the waterfront at Leith is a proper way to attend her welfare?'

'Hah!' said Gillon. 'I was spotted, was I?'

'Given that you were parading her about the town and that gamesters are more prone to gossip than fishwives, are you surprised that word of your philanderings has reached my ears?'

'Possibly not,' said Gillon. 'Nevertheless, I am at a loss to understand why your ladyship is interested in me, or my family.'

'Not you,' said Lady Valerie, 'nor your family.'

'Why then have you brought me here?'

'To test your mettle, shall we say?'

Gillon was not at all sure that he was up to having his mettle tested. He recalled only too vividly how rapacious Lady Oliphant had been in the garden behind the oyster parlour and how he had ached for days afterwards. He wavered, torn between a desire to appease this influential vixen and fear that he would not be able to rise to the occasion.

She chuckled again, very softly. 'I have observed you at the tables often enough to reckon that you are not averse to taking risks.' She tossed aside the cloak and he saw that she was clad not in sober grey silk, as befitted the Sabbath, but in a fine-cloth riding habit in a colour that matched her eyes. 'Have you ever played whist with Lord Craigiehall?'

'His lordship and I travel in different circles,' Gillon said. 'He only plays in august company, so I've heard, and sometimes at formal winter assemblies.'

'You do not know him well then?'

'I do not know him at all,' said Gillon.

'Yet your brother is married to his elder daughter,' Lady Valerie said, 'and to judge by appearances you are wooing the younger.'

'I am not wooing . . .'

'Be that as it may,' Lady Valerie said, 'between you and your brother, are you not conniving to secure a hold on the Craigiehall estate through association with his lordship's daughters?'

'There's no sin in that,' said Gillon. 'Love is the great leveller, after all.'

'Love—*pshaw*!' said Lady Valerie. '*Marriage* is the great leveller.'

Gillon cleared his throat. 'Does one not marry for love, then?'

'Some women may, some foolish women,' said Lady Valerie. 'Some weak and foolish men, too, I suppose. But those of us who are ruled by more commanding passions are careful to avoid falling foul of Cupid's poisonous dart. Are you in love with Nicola Templeton, Lieutenant?'

'I—I admire her greatly.'

'Is she in love with you?'

'I am optimistic that she may be leaning in that

136

direction.'

'How far will she have to lean before she falls?' said Lady Valerie.

'I am nothing if not patient,' said Gillon, stoutly.

'You cannot afford to be patient, dear Gillon, not if your brother's wife is already pregnant. Are you banking on her producing a daughter?'

'I have given it very little thought.'

'Balderdash!' said Lady Valerie. 'Balderdash and piffle! I'll wager you have thought of very little else since your brother made the running.'

'Even if that were so,' said Gillon, 'I do not see what business it is of yours, Lady Valerie. I thought Lord Craigiehall was your friend.'

'He is,' the woman said, 'after a fashion.'

'Has he asked you to intervene on his behalf?'

'Intervene? Oh,' she said, 'to hinder your pursuit of the younger Templeton? No, no, my dear Lieutenant, that is not why I've arranged this meeting. In fact, I am here to help you.'

'To do what?' said Gillon.

'Attain your ends.'

And Gillon, sitting forward, said, 'How?'

PART TWO

The Bargain Bride

CHAPTER EIGHT

Out on the Circuits the appointed Lords of Session still paraded through the streets to demonstrate the might of the law and pay the price in pomp for the hospitality that was lavished upon them by their provincial hosts. In the capital, however, the pageantry that had once accompanied the opening of court term had been drastically pared down. The event was now marked only by a shifty assortment of peers and judges in drooping robes and full-bottomed wigs who shuffled into the stately hall where the Scottish parliament had met before the Union of Crowns had transferred power to London, and prayers and proclamations, tedious in the extreme, were quickly put over in favour of administering justice.

Those unfortunate advocates who had no causes on hand scampered off to pace the promenades and waiting rooms in the hope of catching a little casual business from a friendly agent, but Grant Peters had no need to scrounge for briefs. He had more than enough causes on his plate. None of the cases was of special importance and he did not anticipate that he would be ordered to present his arguments *viva voce*. Everything these days was committed to paper and most of his time was spent writing or dictating petitions while Somerville, his clerk, staggered under the weight of minutes, representations, memorials and replies that went forward for the judge's consideration.

As it happened, Craigiehall had been appointed Lord Ordinary for the first week of term. Peeping into the hall, Grant saw him, majestic in wig and robes, seated on what had once been the sovereign's throne.

Petitions were arrayed before him on long oak tables and the clerks of court danced about like monkeys while his lordship ground through the morning's proceedings with stamp and seal and signature.

Grant was just about to slip out of the hall when, to his surprise, Lord Craigiehall called his name and, slithering like a ferret through the maze of documents, Mr Leonard, his lordship's chief clerk, approached him.

'His lordship wishes a word.'

'What?' Grant said. 'Now?'

'Aye, Mr Peters. Now.'

Grant followed the little man through benches and tables while the clerks of court ceased their papery ministrations to observe this odd turn of events.

Curious but not intimidated, Grant came to the step that raised the judge a foot or so above the floor. He looked up at his father-in-law who, gathering his robe about him and controlling his massive wig with one hand, bent low and in not much more than a whisper, said, 'What news, Peters?'

'There is no fresh news, your lordship. Charlotte is well and Nicola . . .'

'From Ayrshire, I mean. News of de Morville's transaction.'

'None, sir, not a word.'

'Has Mackenzie heard nothing?'

'Nothing, your lordship.'

'Are you sure of this?'

'As sure as I can be, sir,' Grant said. 'What of your overseer, Mr Littlejohn, has he picked up no rumours on the ground?'

'It seems that this lawyer fellow in Galston is tighter than a clam,' his lordship said. 'He will give no hint of who his clients are.'

'He cannot be forced to do so, sir.'

'No, he cannot; nor, it appears, can he be bribed.'

'Bribed?' said Grant, more loudly than he had intended.

'Induced is perhaps a better way of putting it,' Lord Craigiehall said. 'In any event, Littlejohn has met with no success. Will you go there? Will you interview this Bunting fellow and find out what the devil is going on?'

'I am not free, your lordship. I have four petitions before . . .'

'Somerville can nurse them for a day or two, can he not?' Lord Craigiehall said. 'I'll pay you to act on my behalf, if you wish.'

'No, your lordship,' Grant said. 'Payment will not be necessary.'

'But will you do it? Will you go?'

'If your lordship insists,' Grant said, 'I will.'

'Soon?' said Craigiehall.

'I will leave this afternoon,' said Grant.

*   *   *

'Well, my dear,' said Charlotte, sitting up in bed, 'this is most certainly a step in the right direction. It would appear that my father is beginning to trust you.'

'It is not that he trusts me more,' said Grant,

143

'rather that he trusts everyone else less.'

'I'm not sure I understand,' said Charlotte.

Nicola had slept late that Tuesday morning. Now that Gillon had abandoned her—she had seen nothing of him for almost two weeks—she had no reason to bound out of bed at crack of dawn. Still clad in a dressing-robe, she had been dawdling over a late breakfast in Charlotte's room when Grant had burst in to impart the news that Papa had charged him to conduct an urgent piece of personal business.

'It means,' said Grant, 'that as Hugh Littlejohn has failed to elicit any information concerning the purchase of the coal field and, I believe, was unable to bribe the lawyer in Galston, I am being sent into the fray.'

'Why you?' said Charlotte. 'Why not Robertson, say, or . . .'

'Because Grant is an advocate,' Nicola put in, 'an Edinburgh advocate, as well as a relative, and may be able to intimidate the fellow in Galston in a way that a servant could not.'

'Now you have fuddled me completely,' said Charlotte. 'How long will you be gone, dearest?'

'Three or four days, Grant said.

'What of your clients?' said Charlotte.

'Your father will pass his interim decisions to Somerville and Somerville will impart the information to the clients via Mr Mackenzie. Your father will also ensure that I am not called to argue a cause in person.' Grant seated himself at the card table and helped himself to a muffin. 'I will leave this afternoon, head directly to Ayr, and thence to Galston. I'll make my appointment with Bunting for Thursday morning and return on the Flyer on

Friday.'

'Are you not going to Glasgow?' said Nicola.

'To Glasgow?' said Grant. 'Why would I wish to go to Glasgow?'

'Is that not where the company has its offices?' said Nicola.

Grant held the muffin an inch from his lips and blinked.

'There are no offices, only a hutch of some sort,' he said.

'Are you certain of that?' Nicola said.

'Well, Hercules told me . . .'

'How long ago?' Nicola interrupted. 'Almost a fortnight, is it not? It occurs to me that the purchaser may have marshalled his crew by now.'

'What do you know of crews?' said Charlotte, testily.

'I know that if Papa has entrusted this matter to Grant he will expect Grant to be thorough,' Nicola said. 'If the lawyer in Galston remains obdurate then Grant will have nothing to report. If it were up to me . . .'

'Fortunately, it is not up to you,' said Charlotte. 'Now, be quiet.'

'No,' said Grant. 'Let her continue. What would you do, Nicola?'

'I would go first to Glasgow and inspect this— this hutch to determine what, if anything, may be happening there. Then I would go to Kirkton, hire a horse from Mr Jackson's livery and ride along the wooded ridge that overlooks the north portion of de Morville's estate.'

'Trespass?' said Charlotte.

'The ridge begins its rise on Craigiehall and there is no boundary fence. Even without a

145

spyglass the coal field is plainly visible from the tail of the wood.'

'How do you know this?' said Grant.

'I have been there with Molly.'

'And a spyglass?' Grant said.

'No, to picnic.'

'And where, pray tell me, was I?' said Charlotte.

'Here, in Edinburgh.'

'When did this picnic take place?' said Grant.

'Last autumn, on a beautiful day in September.'

'So you know what the workings look like?' Grant said.

'I do,' said Nicola. 'There is precious little to see except some wagons and a very short measure of wooden way which has never been finished.'

'There may be more to see now, however,' said Grant.

'You might spend a night at Craigiehall,' said Nicola.

'Great heavens!' said Charlotte. 'If he does, Papa will have a fit.'

'Not if I'm there too,' said Nicola. 'If I accompany Grant, he will be made welcome at Craigiehall. Would you not like to visit Craigiehall again, Grant?'

'I would. Indeed, I would,' Grant said.

He put the muffin, untouched, back upon the plate and got to his feet.

Charlotte hoisted herself from the bolsters and wrung her hands. 'Am I to be left here alone while you gallivant about the country with my sister?'

'You've been left alone before. When I plead causes at Perth,' said Grant, 'you survive for days without me. Besides, you'll have Molly to look after you.'

146

'In my condition? What if there are robbers . . .'

'We do not live on the street,' said Grant curtly. 'Molly, let alone the town guard, will deal with any robbers who happen to climb our stairs. Robbers!' He shook his head. 'Look, Charlotte, this is too good an opportunity to ignore and Nicola has opened my eyes to the advantages of taking her with me.'

'Without a chaperone?' said Charlotte.

'She's my sister-in-law,' said Grant.

'Nevertheless, she is a young, unmarried girl, and . . .'

'Do you not trust me, Charlotte?' Grant said.

'Well, I—yes, I . . .'

'Then it's settled.' He tapped Nicola on the shoulder. 'Have Molly pack a valise. We will leave for Glasgow at noon.'

*   *   *

Lady Valerie had offered him a guinea and Gillon had accepted, thus, as it were, selling his soul for far more than his soul was worth. With a good supper inside him, he had slept well that night and had risen on Monday to greet Mrs McCracken at the head of the stairs and pay his rent, after which he had set off for The Nine-Headed Eel to turn his little windfall into decent working capital.

It was no easy task to accumulate cash at the gaming tables but for the best part of a fortnight he had reined in the bold side of his nature and exercised not only prudence but dexterity. In one evening of brag, as a guest of the officers of the 25th Foot in Mr Walker's Tavern on the Royal Mile, he had cleaned their clocks so thoroughly that they had threatened, only half in jest, to have him arrested and clapped in irons.

Meanwhile, he had steered clear of Graddan's Court, and had found to his surprise that he rather missed young Miss Templeton's pretty face. He was, therefore, more chastened than cocky when he turned up at the door of Grant's apartment to begin his courtship anew.

'Gone?' he said. 'Gone where?'

'To Ayrshire,' Charlotte told him.

Gillon groped for a chair. 'I should not have left her without word of my intentions. Why did she not wait for me? She's gone home to nurse a broken heart, I suppose.'

'You flatter yourself, Gillon,' Charlotte said. 'She's gone off with Grant to attend to some business my Papa put Grant's way.'

'With Grant?' said Gillon. 'To Craigiehall?'

'Yes,' said Charlotte. 'To Craigiehall, among other places. Where have you been hiding yourself these past weeks?'

'I had business of my own to attend to,' said Gillon. 'Has your father forgiven Grant for stealing you away?'

Charlotte shook her head. 'Only in part, a small part at that.'

'What nature of business requires my brother's attention?'

'That is not for me to say,' Charlotte answered. 'It is a family matter that does not concern you.'

'Does it concern Lord Craigiehall?'

'Did I not just say as much?'

'To do with the estate?'

'Perhaps.'

They were in the parlour. The sun shone

148

through the window and lit up the room. Motes of dust floated thickly in the air. Charlotte had taken tea early. The tea things were still upon the table. Crumbs still clung to the corners of Charlotte's lips. Gillon suffered an almost overwhelming impulse to pull out his handkerchief and wipe the crumbs away. He sat back in the chair and tucked his fists into his armpits. He had had his best shirt laundered. He had wiped the stains from his breeches with gin. He had even summoned a barber to shave him and dress his hair and was sure that he had never looked better.

'It must be very hard on you, my dear,' he said.

'Hard?' said Charlotte. 'What do you mean?'

'I mean, being left all alone in your condition while my brother trots about the countryside with your pretty little sister.'

'It is,' said Charlotte, 'hard, yes.'

'Pretty inconsiderate of Grant, if you ask me.'

'It is an opportunity that we cannot ignore.'

'Even so,' said Gillon, 'if you were my wife . . .' He paused.

'If I were your wife, which thank God I'm not, what would you do?'

'I would not leave you alone, not for one minute, not for any reason.'

Charlotte struggled to remain aloof but the trace of a smile indicated that flattery had paid dividends. He watched her shift her weight in the chair, wriggling her bottom, and pressed smoothly on. 'If I were your husband I would not be able to sleep of a night unless you were locked in my arms.'

'I think you have gone too far, Gillon,' Charlotte said in a tone that hinted that he had not gone far

149

enough. 'That is a most improper thing to say to a married person. Besides, do you not have a fancy for Nicola?'

'If I do,' said Gillon, 'it is only because the sister I truly desire has already been claimed by my brother.'

'Gillon Peters! Now really!'

She blushed and fluttered and before she could protest further, he rose from his chair, drew out his handkerchief—which, fortunately, was spotless—and leaning across the tea table, dabbed breadcrumbs from her lips.

She stared up at him, frightened and pleading.

He lowered his face to hers and kissed her. His fingers tickled the soft hairs at the nape of her neck. He felt her shiver, like a dog casting spray. Then he drew away and, puffing out his cheeks as if the kiss had set his blood on fire too, he stuffed the handkerchief into his pocket and, like an honourable gentleman, walked to the window to allow her time to savour the unexpected moment of intimacy, and to recover from it.

'Charlotte,' he addressed himself to the glass, 'the circumstances that keep us apart are gates of brass and cannot, alas, be breached. I wish you to understand, though, that I do not envy my brother the Craigiehall lands that your father is inclined to bestow upon him. What I envy him is—' he paused and turned, '—is you.'

'Oh, Gillon!'

'I may decide to give my life to Nicola, if she will have me, but I can never give her my heart, not all of it, anyway. A particular and special part will always be reserved for you.'

'Oh, Gillon, dearest!'

'There, it is said. I will never speak of it again.'

He returned from the window and positioned himself behind her so that she was obliged to twist a little to look up at him. Her cheeks were crimson, her eyes moist. He made as if to touch her then restrained himself.

'Oh, Gillon, I had no inkling that you felt for me,' Charlotte said. 'I—I am sorry, so sorry for your—your suffering.'

'I am reconciled to it,' he said, adding hastily, 'not that it makes it any easier to bear. Perhaps I had better leave before I forget myself.'

'No,' she said. 'Stay with me, please. I'll ring for a fresh serving of tea and we—we'll talk.'

'If that is your wish, Charlotte.' Gillon drew out a chair. 'What will we talk about? The weather? The state of the nation? Anything, I beg you, but the secret we share.'

She looked down at her lap. 'I—I don't know.'

'Well,' he said, as diffidently as possible, 'just to get us started, why don't you tell me where Nicola has gone, when she'll return, and what on earth she's doing at Craigiehall with Grant.'

'Yes,' said Charlotte, with a sigh, 'Yes, why not?' and within the space of an hour, had told him everything that he and Lady Valerie Oliphant needed to know about her father's passion for coal fields, and a great deal more besides.

*   *   *

The afternoon waned into evening. The coach, laden with passengers and luggage, clattered relentlessly on through a series of small towns and villages. Gentlemen of business and ladies of

151

dubious reputation rubbed shoulders with vulgar traders, one of whom made a point of announcing his financial worth in a dialect too guttural to understand. A little girl, not much more than ten, returning to Glasgow after a sojourn with an aunt in Edinburgh, prattled merrily to Nicola until her nurse—or was it her governess?—snapped at her to hold her tongue. Eventually the child fell asleep and soon after, her head resting on Grant's shoulder, Nicola dozed off too. When she wakened the light had gone from the sky, green fields and foaming hedgerows had been left behind and the coach was trundling through an abyss of blackened tenements.

Nicola peered through the window into the gloaming as a series of monastic-looking buildings trotted past and the coach dipped so violently that the passengers were shaken together like dice in a cup.

The little girl, startled out of slumber, shrieked loudly.

'It's the Bell o' the Brae, that's all,' the nurse told her. 'Sit up and tidy yourself. We will soon be home.' And a few minutes later a blast from the post-boy's horn cut through the hubbub and the coach lurched to a halt in the yard of the Tontine Hotel, a towering, three-tiered, four-storey construction of whitewashed stone and painted timber, pierced by jutting windows that reflected the light from the flares in the yard.

Nicola had never been in Glasgow before. Her first impressions were not favourable. The air reeked of tar and horse dung and a strange earthy odour that she suspected rose from the nearby river.

152

The hall was just as jostling and noisy as the yard, with waiters, pot-boys and porters milling about among a host of men, women and servants all demanding attention. Nicola looked round for the little girl and her nurse but they had vanished into the night. The door opening, closing and opening again brought in puffs of hot odoriferous air, and the strains of a fiddler playing a fiery highland reel somewhere in the darkness outside.

She sought Grant's arm and pressed herself against him as he glanced this way and that in search of service.

He turned at her touch and, smiling, said, 'Welcome to Glasgow, Nicola. Welcome to Glasgow, indeed.'

*   *   *

Gillon was not at his glorious best. Last night, after he had left Charlotte, he had gone walking in the West Bow in a vain attempt to track down the slut who had robbed him. He hadn't flopped into bed until well after two and was, therefore, somewhat put out to be roused at seven by a footman bearing a letter from Valerie Oliphant. Now, at just after nine, brushed, shaved and almost presentable, he loitered on the footpath that circled the flowerbeds in Broughton Gardens, awaiting the lady's arrival.

The lawns and footpaths were populated by nursemaids, small children, elderly ladies, gentlemen and valets and, entering through the iron gates, a colourful band of footmen and maids accompanied by a pack of six or eight small, very noisy dogs who raced in and out of the saplings without discipline or restraint. Heading the parade was Lady Valerie Oliphant, and a girl child dressed in imitation of a milkmaid, though no milkmaid Gillon had ever seen wore kidskin slippers and pantaloons trimmed with lace.

'Why, if it isn't Lieutenant Peters,' her ladyship called out, as the little dogs, still yapping, rushed upon him. 'Is this not well met, sir, since I have need of a word with you?'

Gillon resisted the temptation to kick the fluffy little brutes whose attentions threatened damage to his breeches.

'Down,' he said, smiling grimly. 'Down.'

'Ignore them, Lieutenant, and they will soon lose interest.'

Footmen and maids halted. The girl, who was not after all a child, dropped him a pretty curtsey.

'My ward,' Lady Valerie said. 'Mademoiselle Cadell.'

'Monsieur.'

'Mademoiselle.'

'Jackson,' her ladyship said, 'round up the dogs and take them and Miss Cadell off towards the fountain. I will join you there shortly.'

The footman, a haggard, elderly man who did not look comfortable in lilac, uttered a chirping noise to which the dogs and the girl responded. They moved off down the path with the rest of the entourage drifting behind them, leaving Gillon and Lady Valerie alone at last.

'Fleur Cadell is not, in fact, my ward,' Lady Valerie began. 'She is but the latest little waif that my husband has brought back from London. She does have a gift for music, however, and makes a pleasant addition to our household.'

'Is she not a trifle immature for our purpose?'

154

said Gillon. 'I question if Lord Craigiehall shares the Admiral's appetite for unfledged girls, no matter how drenched in musical talent.'

'I'm sure that he does not,' Lady Valerie said. 'In the light of what you have recently discovered concerning his lordship's obsessive pursuit of coal crops and your brother's advance upon Craigiehall, however, I believe we must move speedily. Fleur has an aunt . . .'

'Ah!' said Gillon. 'Ah-hah!'

'The woman is presently attached to Mr Didier's company . . .'

'An actress, do you mean?'

'Of some quality.' Her ladyship did not take kindly to being interrupted. 'And, so my husband informs me, of great beauty and charm. I am willing to take his word on it. Whatever his faults, Sir Archibald has always shown impeccable taste in regard to the female sex.'

'Where is this woman now?'

'In London.'

'Can she be summoned?'

'She can. My husband and Didier are close friends.'

'Is she French?' said Gillon.

'No,' said Lady Valerie. 'She comes, as I do, from good Saxon stock.'

'I see.' Gillon nodded. 'I suspect this "aunt" might stand in closer relationship to *la petite mademoiselle* than she is willing to admit. *N'est-ce pas?*'

'Even if that is so, the child will not be an impediment,' Lady Valerie said. 'Indeed, if Fleur is presented as my ward Craigiehall will be less cautious than might otherwise be the case.'

'Who is this actress?'

'Madelaine Young is the name she prefers.'

'How soon can she be brought to Edinburgh?'

'Within the month,' said Lady Valerie.

'Before the courts close for autumn recess?'

'Oh yes, certainly.'

'Has she performed at the Royal?'

'It seems not,' said Lady Valerie, 'nor anywhere in Edinburgh.'

'Craigiehall will not pitch himself at a jobbing actress, you know.'

'I am well aware of it,' said Lady Valerie. 'That is where you will step in. It will be your task, my dear Lieutenant, to make the introductions.'

'But I have never met Craigiehall face to face.'

'So much the better.'

'Where do you propose that these introductions take place?' said Gillon.

'Come, sir, use a little imagination, a little martial ingenuity. Think of it as a campaign to be planned and plotted. Where is Craigiehall liable to be found in the summer months when the formal assemblies are closed?'

'In court,' said Gillon. 'I could, I suppose, present her as a felon.'

Lady Valerie did not so much as smile.

'He attends afternoon service in the New Church faithfully every Sunday, I believe,' Gillon went on, hastily. 'He also frequents the bookshop, Atkinson's, on the Royal Mile. No, no, that is too random. Would he be drawn to a musical concert at your invitation, d' you think?'

'John James hasn't a musical bone in his body,' said Lady Valerie.

'Cards, then,' said Gillon. 'Our learned friend

156

will not be able to resist an invitation to a friendly evening of cards at the home of a noble lady.'

'And Mrs Young?'

'Oh, she's a widow, is she?'

'She is—or purports to be.'

'All to the good,' said Gillon. 'I will meet with her soon after she arrives and we will plot a strategy. If, that is, you approve?'

'I do approve,' said Lady Valerie. 'Will you bring the lady to the table?'

'I will,' said Gillon. 'It will be necessary for me to reveal my identity, however, and to admit that I am Grant Peters' brother.'

'His scapegrace brother.'

'Quite!' said Gillon. 'If the widow is all that you say she is, it may not matter who brings her. Indeed, it may heighten her appeal if Craigiehall thinks she's a *bel esprit* rather than a mere adventuress. Inform me when Mrs Young arrives and we will proceed along the lines we've discussed. If,' he added, tactfully, 'that is agreeable to you, Lady Valerie?'

'It is,' she said. 'Now, I must find my dogs before they create havoc.'

In spite of the fact that he had sucked upon her breasts and penetrated the aristocratic niche, Gillon did not dare touch her for, at least in broad daylight, she was a lady of rank. He took a half step forward. 'Wait.'

'What is it, Gillon?'

'Why are you doing this, Lady Valerie? Why are you so intent on bringing Lord Craigiehall to his knees?'

'I have my reasons.'

'Will you not share them with me? I am, after

all, your accomplice.'

'John James Templeton owes me a considerable sum of money.'

'My pardon,' Gillon said, 'but that is not reason enough.'

'Very well,' she said. 'I am acting on behalf of a friend, a better friend than Craigiehall deserves. Besides, I despise the man for the manner in which he treats his daughters simply because they have the misfortune to be female.'

'He is not unduly harsh with them,' said Gillon, 'certainly not so cruel as many fine gentlemen whom we might name. He may not approve of Charlotte's marriage to my brother but he did not have her dragged, wailing, from the church. And as for Nicola . . .'

'Lord Craigiehall does not need you to defend him, Gillon,' Lady Valerie said. 'I have given you my reasons. If that is not enough for you, you may put the rest down to the fact that I am notoriously meddlesome.'

'Is it then only a sport to you?' Gillon said, frowning.

'Everything is but sport to me, young man. Now, good morning to you.'

'Good morning, Lady Valerie,' Gillon said and watched the woman sweep off towards the fountain to collect her dogs and servants and the frilly little protégé whom Archie had brought back from London to keep them all amused.

CHAPTER NINE

The bed was clean and the room airy. Even so Nicola did not sleep well. Grant and she had supped on greasy chops in the barn-like salon and the meat lay like ballast in her stomach. It seemed unnatural to be alone in a strange room without Molly on hand to protect her.

Dawn was breaking over the spires of the city before she drifted into a restless sleep, then, not long after, she wakened to the sound of early travellers rising to greet the day. Surrendering to circumstance, she climbed out of bed, washed her face, brushed and arranged her hair, put on clean linen and a plain day dress and was ready and waiting when Grant knocked upon her door.

They ate breakfast in the cheerless salon, stored the luggage in a ground-floor closet and settled the bill. Then they set off for the Broomielaw.

Pale sunshine penetrated the haze and the river, such as it was, glinted like polished tin. Nicola found it hard to believe that this was the same river that fed the wide, wave-lashed estuary that lay on Craigiehall's doorstep for the Clyde here was as shallow as a saucer of milk. Cows stood placidly in midstream, women beat clothes, men fished, carts and horses splashed through the shoals and a clutter of lighters were grounded on the gravel mounds. Down river there were some signs of industry. Scaffolding poked up from the water's edge and two or three beetle-like barges were being unloaded.

Closer to hand, on a lozenge of ground raised

above the tide line, were four or five heaps of jet-black coal and a small wooden hut. An emaciated donkey cropped weeds in the lane between the coal piles and a dog, no less skinny, snuffled about the rear of the hut, cocking its leg and leaking water. Propped on a stool by the door of the hut was a very small, very old man wearing a battered three-cornered hat, an ancient frock coat and what appeared to be five woollen waistcoats. He was feeding bread scraps to a flock of sparrows and did not look up, even when the birds took wing and scattered into the air.

'Am I addressing the proprietor of the Westmore Coal and Mineral Company?' Grant said.

Very deliberately, the old man pursed his lips and dropped a globule of frothy white spit perilously close to Grant's shoes.

Grant stood his ground. 'Well, am I?'

At length, the old man answered, 'Nah!'

'Who are you then?'

'Watchman.'

'Where do you stay?'

'In yonder,' the old man said, jerking his thumb.

'So you sleep in the hut, do you?'

'Aye.'

'To guard the coal heaps, I suppose?'

'Aye, fur tae stop the beggars stealin'. Ah sees them aff,' the old man growled. 'Ah sets the dug on 'um.'

He raised his head and peered at Grant then, insolently, at Nicola. He was, she realised, the laird of this blackened patch, too old to care what anyone thought of him.

'I trust,' Grant said, 'that you are not going to

160

set the dog on us.'

'Ah might,' the old man growled. 'Depends.'

'On what does it depend?' said Grant.

The old man slid the plate to the ground and held out his hand.

Grant fished a shilling from his pocket and placed it gently in the grimy palm. 'Where might I find the owner of the property?'

'He's aff wi' the carts.'

'To collect coal from the pit?'

'Aye.'

'Where is the pit?'

'Knightswood.'

'How far off is that?'

The old man shrugged. 'Eight mile, or ten.'

'When will your master return?' Grant said.

'He's no' mah master. He's mah lad.'

'Oh, he works for you, does he?'

'Mah lad, mah lad, mah boy. Mah son.'

'I see,' said Grant. 'So you *are* the owner?'

'Never see him here no more.'

'Who?'

'Walter.'

'Walter?' said Grant. 'Who the devil is Walter?'

'Walter Buntin',' the old man said, and spat again.

'Bunting!' Grant glanced round at Nicola. 'Mr Bunting from Galston?'

'Never see him,' the old man said. 'Never comes bye the bit.'

Hunkering before the stool, Grant took another shilling from his pocket and held it between finger and thumb. 'How therefore does he pay for his coal?'

'Settles the bills tae the pits in the writin',' the

161

old man said.

'How do you pay him?' Grant said, patiently.

'We tak' what's due. The lad carries the rest o' the money tae the bank.'

'How much money, let's say, per week?'

'That no' fur me tae say.'

Grant eased the coin into the old man's fist. 'How much?'

'Thirty shillin'. Thirty-five in the dark o' the winter.'

'How many men are employed here?'

'Four wi' the horses, two wi' the spades.'

'How many horses do you stall?'

'Eight.'

'Do you really expect me to believe that Mr Bunting leaves the running of his business to you without any supervision?'

'Believe what ye like,' the old man said. 'Ticks.'

'Ticks?' said Grant, puzzled.

'Ticks like a clock that never needs no windin'.' The old man got to his feet and kicked away the stool. 'Ah'm sayin' nae mair till the lad get back.'

'When might that be?' Grant said.

'When the tide turns.'

'And when does the tide turn?'

'An hour past mah dinner time.'

'Thank you,' Grant said. 'You've been exceedingly helpful.'

'Ah have?' the old man said, scowling.

'Indeed you have,' Grant said and, turning, led Nicola away.

'Where are we going?' Nicola asked, as soon as they were out of earshot.

'Back to the Tontine to collect our baggage and hire a chaise to take us along the road to Ayr,'

Grant told her. 'No sense in wasting time.'

'Would it not be better to wait for the lad to return? He may be more forthcoming than his father.'

'Then again,' said Grant, 'he may not. It's all too clear that the old man knows nothing of de Morville or the purchase of a coal working in Ayrshire. I question if the lad will know more. It's a small family business that, as the old fellow puts it, "ticks like a clock". Whoever bought it from Bunting has not so far interfered with its management.'

'There is one question that you did not put to the old chap that might have yielded an interesting answer,' Nicola said.

'Oh!' Grant said. 'And what question is that?'

'How many sons he has,' said Nicola.

*　　　*　　　*

As the chaise clipped down the drive towards the house Nicola's apprehension increased. Although she had been gone for not much more than a month the place appeared to have changed. Trees were heavy with leaf and crops ripening in the fields. The setting sun sharpened the outline of the house but no lights showed in the windows and the door under the arch of the portico was closed.

The chaise drew to a halt on the gravel and Grant helped her alight. She stood uncertainly before the door while Grant saw to the baggage and paid the driver. She was waiting, she realised, for Robertson to hurry out to greet her, but Robertson too was in Edinburgh and without her father's presence the house seemed not so much dormant as deserted.

At this hour of a summer's evening, Mrs McGrouther, the housekeeper, would be tucked in her tiny parlour behind the kitchens or out walking with one of the maids, and Hugh Littlejohn would probably be sitting down to supper with his wife in the lodge cottage.

'Perhaps they have all gone tripping into Ayr to engage in riotous living,' Grant said, 'or, more likely, have fled into the hills at the first sign of my appearance, as if I were a Goth come to pillage.'

'If you were a Goth,' Nicola said, 'they would stand and fight.'

'Are they so loyal?'

'To my father, they are,' said Nicola.

The driver steered the chaise around in a circle and, with a wave and halloo, set off back up the drive.

'The fare,' Nicola said, 'was it costly?'

'Very,' Grant said.

'My father will see to it that you are reimbursed.'

'A good supper will be payment enough,' Grant said, then stepped into the portico and tugged on the iron bell-pull.

Nicola heard the echoes ring deep within the house. In her mind's eye she saw maids and footmen leap in alarm from the table below stairs or if they had been flirting in the library or the drawing-room—she knew perfectly well what servants got up to when Robertson was away—fumbling with buttons and strings in fear that the master had returned. Then the door opened and Gregory, the youngest footman, looked out, wide-eyed and red-faced.

'Why, Miss Nicola,' he said, 'is it yourself?'

'It is myself, Gregory.'

'An'—an' a man?'

'The man is Mr Peters, Miss Charlotte's husband. We have business to conduct in the neighbourhood and will be staying for a night or two. We require supper and our rooms prepared. Where is Mrs McGrouther?'

The maid who had followed Gregory into the hall rushed off downstairs, calling out, 'Mrs McGrouther, Mrs McGrouther,' at the pitch of her voice.

'Since you seem to be the only one capable of service, Gregory,' Nicola went on, 'you may fetch in the luggage and carry it upstairs. When that is done, find someone to bring hot water and fresh towels to the guest apartment and also to my room, my old room.'

'Aye, Miss Nicola,' Gregory said.

Though he wore neither cap nor wig, he knuckled his forehead and dived past Mr Peters to pick up the bags from the gravel just as Mrs McGrouther, puffing and not well pleased, emerged from the passage that led to the stairs.

'I had no word of this from his lordship,' she snapped. 'We are ill-prepared for unexpected guests in the term time.'

'I am not a guest, Mrs McGrouther,' Nicola said. 'Nor am I a stranger. Advocate Peters and I are here at my father's charge to conduct business on his behalf. If it is inconvenient to you, however, perhaps you would prefer us to put up at an inn or, for that matter, to sleep in the stables with the horses.'

'There is no need for the sarcasm, Miss Nicola,'

the woman said. 'Everythin' you require will be provided.'

'Supper, then,' said Nicola. 'In an hour.'

'Meat or fish?' the woman said.

'Is the fish fresh?'

'Fresh out the sea this mornin'.'

'Fish then,' Nicola said. 'We'll eat in the dining-room. First, though, find me a maid, for I have been travelling all day and wish to change my dress.'

'And Mr Peters,' the housekeeper said, 'will he be needin' a man?'

Grant shook his head, and Nicola said, 'Only for his boots and that will do quite well in the morning. Meanwhile, send a boy over to Mr Littlejohn's to tell him that we are here and that we will welcome his company at breakfast.'

'At what hour?' the housekeeper said.

'Seven,' said Nicola without hesitation and, ushering Grant before her, set off for the bedroom upstairs.

*   *   *

Intimate conversation in the vaulted dining-room was out of the question, particularly with servants ranked against the walls, ears pricked to catch any indiscretions that might be braided into gossip.

Grant chatted casually about the latest round of taxes that Westminster had imposed and how Scottish landowners, small and large, would be affected by them. He drank little but did justice to the lentil broth, fish stew, and apricot cake that Mrs McGrouther had stirred up from the kitchens. He seemed, Nicola thought, totally at ease in her father's chair at the head of the long table.

'Does the notion of a universal land tax amuse you, Nicola?'

'What?' she said. 'No, do pardon me. I was thinking of other things.'

'Of what we must do tomorrow?' Grant said.

'Yes, that,' Nicola said, vaguely.

Grant dabbed his lips with a napkin. 'I thought, perhaps, that you were thinking of my brother who, it seems, has abandoned you as a lost cause.'

'I'm not at all sure that I like being regarded as a lost cause.'

'On the other hand, knowing Gillon as I do,' Grant went on, 'it may be that he has exhausted his resources. It would not surprise me if he turned up again, ready to resume where he left off. Tell me, do you like him?'

Nicola glanced at the footman who stood at a respectful distance behind her chair; then, leaning forward, she said, 'I have no reason not to like him. He is amusing and attentive.'

'Is that all you require in a suitor?'

'Gillon is not a suitor. Is he?'

'He thinks of himself as a suitor.'

'Grant, this is not a suitable subject for supper time conversation.'

'No,' he said, 'perhaps not, at least not here in your father's house. What do you make of Roderick?'

'He is a very active sort of man, I think.'

'Shrewd, too,' said Grant. 'Mother and he make a formidable pair.'

'Formidable?' said Nicola, divided by a desire to learn more about Roderick and his 'formidable' mother and the knowledge that the servants were drinking in every word.

'Holding a small estate together in these harsh times demands a certain degree of ruthlessness,' Grant said. 'If the tenants do not match up to my mother's exacting standards then she calls upon them in person, and woe betide them if they do not change their ways. Roderick is a little more understanding. He allows them degrees of latitude in the matter of rent in seasons of scant harvests or when hard winters linger on into the spring. It's a fair policy, apparently, for we've had no changes in tenancy in many years.'

'No evictions?'

'Not a one that I recall.'

'Son to father, father to son?' said Nicola. 'In other words, it ticks?'

Grant laughed. 'Aye, that would sum it up, I suppose.'

'I would like to see your farm one day,' said Nicola.

'It's not my farm,' said Grant. 'I traded my interest in Heatherbank for a profession in law. It was no easy matter for Mam and Roderick to finance my tilt at learning. It was part of our agreement that I would forgo all claim on the holdings in exchange for an education. Heatherbank is entailed to Roderick and his descendents. I will have nothing from it.'

'What of Gillon?'

'He will inherit only if Roddy dies without an heir.'

'A situation that must surely test Gillon's patience to the limit.'

'Indeed, Roddy is careful never to show his back to our dear young brother lest the temptation to murder becomes too much for him,' Grant said. 'If Heatherbank ever does fall into Gillon's hands he will lose it within a year.'

'Lose it?' said Nicola.

'Fritter it away, furrow by furrow, at the gaming tables.'

'I see you have no high opinion of your dear young brother.'

'He is a rogue, Nicola, an out-and-out rogue.'

'Surely he would not stoop to murder?'

'No, no, of course not,' Grant said. 'He's far too frightened of being danced on the end of a rope to murder anyone, even Roderick. Besides, he has just as much affection for Roddy as I have, though to hear him speak sometimes you would not think so.'

'So my father's judgement was correct; you are without prospects?'

'I have my wits and my fees to serve my future,' Grant said.

'And Charlotte.'

'Oh yes, certainly—and Charlotte.'

'If Charlotte is delivered of a male child about the Christmas time you may have more future than you bargained for,' Nicola said, 'unless that is precisely what you bargained for when you persuaded my sister to marry you.'

'Did Gillon put that notion into your head?'

'Gillon did not have to,' Nicola answered. 'It's pikestaff plain that your marriage to Charlotte is only a means to an end.'

'There, my dear Nicola, you are wrong, very wrong.'

'I hope, for your sake, that I am,' said Nicola.

'Nicola,' he said, 'are you threatening me?'

169

'I am only looking out for my sister's best interests, as you are here in Craigiehall to look after mine.'

'Yours?'

'My father's, I mean, my father's best interests.'

'Ah, Nicola, Nicola,' Grant Peters said, shaking his head. 'I see that I've misjudged you. Perhaps I had better not show you *my* back too often.'

'At least I would look better treading air in the Grassmarket than your poor young brother,' Nicola said. 'I am no threat to you, Grant. Charlotte made her choice. I just hope it was the right one for all of us.'

'I was under the impression that you'd agreed to accompany me to Ayrshire to provide me with the pleasure of your company,' Grant said. 'I see now that your motives are more purposeful.'

'My father's interests are my interests too,' Nicola said. 'You would do well to bear that in mind when we meet Mr Bunting tomorrow.'

'Oh, I will, Nicola,' Grant said. 'Rest assured, I will.'

*   *   *

Hugh Littlejohn was chatting to Grant in the hall when Nicola came down for breakfast. A boy had already been dispatched to Galston to deliver a letter to Mr Bunting requesting that he make himself available for interview at the hour of noon. Craigiehall's chaise would convey Grant and her to the appointment, a journey that would take no more than a couple of hours on a dry summer morning. Mr Littlejohn too was bewildered by the de Morville affair. He had spied upon the coal

170

workings from the ridge and had discovered no change in practice there. If the new owner of the workings was intent on turning profit from his purchase he was certainly in no hurry to do so. Of the mysterious Walter Bunting, Mr Littlejon had gleaned little of interest beyond the fact that the lawyer had lived in Galston for many years. He was an active freemason in Lodge Kilmarnock, it seemed, and most of his cases came through that connection in the form of wills, deeds and the settlement of petty disputes among weavers and farmers in the parishes north of Craigiehall.

'Does he have a wife?' Nicola asked.

'To my knowledge, he has never married,' Mr Littlejohn answered. 'He lives in a stone house between the new school an' the old church with his mother, a woman of advanced years, an' a housekeeper. More than that, Miss Nicola, I can't be tellin' you for I have never met the man.'

'You've done well enough, Mr Littlejohn,' Grant said. 'How did you come by this stock of information?'

'At the Kilmarnock fair,' Hugh Littlejohn said. 'It's amazin' how a dram or two loosens even the tightest tongue.'

'I take it you have posted this news to my father?'

'I have, Miss Nicola, but it was not enough for him.'

'No,' Nicola agreed. 'The loss of the coal working has struck at him very hard, though I cannot imagine why.'

'He's too used to having his own way,' Grant said. 'It's a common failing in gentlemen of rank.'

'Do you wish to ride out to see the workin's, sir?'

Hugh Littlejohn asked.

'When were you there last?'

'On Tuesday afternoon.'

'Then, no,' Grant said. 'It will not be necessary. We'll take breakfast and avail ourselves of your offer of a chaise to deposit us on Mr Bunting's doorstep somewhat earlier than intended.'

'Will I have the chaise wait to bring you back?'

'I think not,' Grant said. 'Given that the great road passes through Galston and that our interview with Bunting may not take long, we'll try to secure a place on an afternoon stage and head for Edinburgh. Nicola?'

'By all means,' Nicola agreed. 'When our business is done, let us head at once for home.'

*   *   *

In spite of their early arrival Mr Walter Bunting was looking out for them from the gate of his solid stone villa. He was as round as a keg and sported a huge frizzy wig that gave his face the appearance of an amiable lion's. His coat was cut from thunder-and-lightning cloth, his breeches supported by embroidered gallowses in a style that had been out of fashion for twenty years. When Grant and Nicola alighted from the chaise by the gate he tugged out a kerchief the size of a tablecloth and waved it high in the air as if he feared that they might not notice him. He opened the gate and, still waving the kerchief, toddled out on to the road to greet them.

'Mr Peters, sir, an honour it is, indeed. And Miss Templeton. I have long been an admirer of your father's summations. Please, please step this way.'

172

He ushered them up a paved path through a garden bursting with shrubs and flowers. In the narrow doorway at the top of four steps stood a long, grey-clad droplet of a woman flanked by two short-haired cats.

'This is Tibby and that is Tabby,' Mr Bunting cooed, 'and the tall one is Mrs Phipps who looks after us all. Don't you, my love?'

'My love' refused to answer. Pivoting on her heel, she vanished into the depths of the house while the cats lingered just long enough to hiss at the intruders before they too went slinking off indoors.

'She'll have gone to attend to Mother,' Mr Bunting said. 'Mother is not too well today and will not be joining us for tea. You will take tea, Miss Templeton, will you not? And you, Mr Peters, a dram to revive you after your journey?'

'Tea will do me fine, thank you, Mr Bunting,' Grant said. 'It's a little early in the day for strong drink.'

'Hoh, then you are not an Ayrshire man, sir, I can tell, for it is never too early in the day for an Ayrshire man to tackle a dram. Come, come this way into my parlour.'

The house, unlike the garden, was drab. It smelled, Nicola thought, of boiled cabbage mingled with another odour that reminded her of cough drops. The parlour, Mr Bunting's place of business, lay to the right of the front door. It contained an upright desk and high stool, a small table and three unglazed bookcases crammed with calf-bound volumes. Four identical leather chairs, low backed and badly scuffed, consumed the rest of the space.

It was all Nicola could do to thread her way through the furniture and seat herself hard against a fireplace in which, fortunately, no fire had been lit. Mr Bunting inched out a chair for Grant and settled himself in another so that he and his guests were perched knee to knee.

The delivery of tea and oatcakes by the housekeeper involved a deal of shuffling and juggling before Mr Bunting, with an airy wave, dismissed the gloomy woman and through a mouthful of oatcake, said, 'Now that the niceties have been observed and our inner persons satisfied, shall we, my dear sir, proceed to what has brought you here?'

Legs wedged tightly against the fender, cup and saucer held to his chest, Grant said, 'First of all, Mr Bunting, may I enquire how you knew that my lady companion is, in fact, Lord Craigiehall's daughter?'

Mr Bunting blustered. 'Your letter . . .'

'My letter made no mention of Miss Templeton,' Grant said.

'The boy, your messenger . . .'

'Ah, he told you, did he?'

'Aye, yes, he told me.'

'What reason did he have for telling you?'

The beam had gone from Bunting's cheek and he looked less amiable now. 'Begging your pardon, Mr Peters,' he said, 'but I find it hard to credit that you came down from Edinburgh just to badger me about Miss Templeton.'

'Did your father tell you?' Grant said.

'My—my father?'

'Did your father take it upon himself to scribble a note and have it carried post haste from

174

Glasgow?'

'I have no idea what you're talking about, Mr Peters.'

'Perhaps it was your brother who wrote to you; the brother who acts as both carter and accountant and who sees to it that your profits are safely deposited in the Royal Bank? It is the Royal Bank, is it not?'

'Look here, sir, I resent being treated as if I were a common thief on trial for my life,' Mr Bunting said. 'My finances, let alone my family arrangements are no concern of yours.'

'Oh, but they are, Mr Bunting. Indeed, they are,' Grant said.

Grant had not been deceived by the Writer's quaint appearance or his affable manner. He reached behind him and placed the teacup and saucer upon a little table and, Nicola thought, might have got to his feet and paced about if there had been room enough to do so. She watched sweat form along the edges of the lion's mane wig on Mr Bunting's brow.

'Is it not fortunate for you that your father put aside his resentment long enough to warn you of our interest in your affairs?' Grant went on. 'Why, Mr Bunting, do you not give him the respect that is a father's due? Why do you use him so ill that he lives like a dog in a filthy hutch on the river side?'

Mr Bunting pursed his lips and expanded his cheeks to such a degree that Nicola thought he might explode. Then he blurted out, 'He deserves no better.'

'I see. You are punishing him, are you?'

'None o' your business, Peters. None o' your damned business.'

175

Nicola felt sorry for the provincial lawyer whose reputation in the north Ayrshire parish had been built upon secrecy and deception and whose fees were merely butter on the bread of a coal hauling business that ticked merrily away on the shores of the Clyde.

Grant went on, 'What crime did he commit, Mr Bunting, that condemned him to exile? Is he a drunkard? Did he beat you as a child ? Did he abuse your mother—or did you merely regard him as an embarrassment after you had risen to glorious heights in your profession?'

'How dare you, sir! How dare you!' Mr Bunting cried.

Grant reached forward and removed the teacup and saucer, now filled with slops, from Mr Bunting's hand. 'What portion of the sale fee will go into your father's pocket, I wonder? Did you have it written into the bill of sale that your father and brother will be employed by the new owner of the Westmore company?'

'New owner?' said Mr Bunting. 'What's this about a new . . .'

'Do not be obtuse, Mr Bunting,' Grant said. 'Do you expect me to believe that a company that yields profits of a mere thirty shillings in a week would tempt someone, anyone, to purchase it?'

'Mackenzie told you?'

'Of course Mackenzie told me,' Grant said.

'He has broken a confidence.'

'Given that you neglected to mention that you were not only acting as your client's agent but had a financial interest in the outcome of the sale, I think, sir, that you would be wise not to bleat about a breach in confidentiality. On paper, Mr Bunting, your company now owns a substantial piece of land that formerly belonged to the de Morville estate.'

'What I do with my company is not . . .'

'Someone,' Grant said, 'bought Westmore Coal to act as a veil for the purchase of de Morville's fields. I assume the transfer of the company to new ownership was concluded by private arrangement between you and persons not known, and that persons not known wished the contract for the purchase of de Morville's coal field to be drafted by a more experienced hand than yours, which is why Mr Mackenzie became involved. Am I right, sir?'

'I am saying nothing, Mr Peters. Nothing.'

'Who suggested employing Hercules Mackenzie, you or your client?'

'Not one more word will you get out of me,' Mr Bunting said.

Bunting's teacup and saucer were still in Grant's hand. He held them without a tremor at arms length until Nicola took them from him and placed them on the table. 'You, Bunting,' Grant said, 'or your client?'

The change was instant and unexpected; Mr Bunting was suddenly his old self again. He sat back in the armchair, crossed his ankles, laid both hands across the width of his belly and smiled benignly.

'Now, now, my dear Peters,' he said, 'you may fence all you wish but I won't be caught by a foul blow. If I confess that my client chose Mackenzie you might reasonably suppose that my client has done business with Mackenzie before and that his name will be recorded in Mackenzie's register. Well, sir, I may not be a clever Edinburgh lawyer

177

who struts about the Parliament House on sunny afternoons but I do recognise a pitfall when I see one. Hercules Mackenzie is my agent interim, and that is all about it.'

'What if I were to tell you that I have a client who wishes to top the present offer for the purchase of de Morville's coal fields?'

Mr Bunting chuckled and shook his head. 'Too late, Mr Peters. The sale is complete and there will be no going back on it. Besides, I doubt if Lord Craigiehall—to pluck a name out o' the air—would be in a position to match let alone top the sum paid to Sir Charles de Morville. Do you think de Morville would part with one acre of ground for less than a king's ransom?'

'A king's ransom, eh?' said Grant. 'Is that a clue, Mr Bunting, a hint that our illustrious majesty has purchased a stake in the shire of Ayr?'

Mr Bunting put a finger to his lips.

'Hush, sir,' he said, 'or you will see me hanged for treason.'

'I would see you hanged for a lot less than treason,' Grant said. 'Whoever elected you to represent them in this matter chose well. I am not going to wring a sensible answer from you, am I?'

'No you are not, sir, not you nor Mr Mackenzie, nor Lord Craigiehall.'

'Is it a brother, a fellow freemason?' said Grant, quickly,

'I wonder where Tibby's gone. She can, as a rule, smell fish.'

'Are you open to bribery?'

'Tabby on the other hand prefers meat.'

'How much meat?'

'She's very pernickety, Mr Peters. Besides, the

larder is full.'

'Yes,' Grant said, grimly, 'I rather feared it might be.'

*   *   *

The coach that picked them up at the crossroads had seen better days. The hinges that held the doors were strained and the doors chattered dementedly. The wind whistled through a rift on the underside of the roof and a torn strand of what had once been lining flapped and flapped until Grant, in none too good a humour, lost patience, knelt on the seat and ripped it off. None of the occupants of the coach complained and one wispy little woman with a linnet in a wicker cage on her lap let out a cheer as Grant tossed the remnant from the open window and sat down again.

For all its shabbiness, the coach was well-sprung and there was no crowding upon the outside so that good time was made along the road. Grant was hopeful that at the over stop he might be able to hire a chaise to carry them to Edinburgh that night. He seemed, Nicola thought, desperate to be home again, though whether it was because he had tired of her company or was simply anxious to be with Charlotte she did not enquire.

He sat beside her, sulky and unsettled, and appeared to have no appetite for conversation. They were ten or twelve miles along the road before he turned to her and said, 'Do you think I should have pressed him harder?'

'I think you played him as well as you were able.'

'Not well enough, however, to break down his resolve.'

She realised that he was smarting at his failure to carry out her father's wishes and regarded his encounter with the provincial lawyer as a defeat.

'You have gleaned certain facts to present to my father, facts that were not known before,' she said.

'But not enough, not enough.'

'It's all there is, all Bunting would give you,' Nicola said. 'He is the lynch-pin that will not break. There is no more to be done at present.'

'Gillon would have done better.'

'Gillon?'

'Aye, he'd have put a knife to Bunting's throat.'

'That is not your way, not—not advocacy.'

'Advocacy?' Grant said. 'Do you imagine that reason and logic are the only means of settling such matters? No, Nicola, there are times when a cudgel or a sharp knife can be more effective than rational debate.'

'It's my father who's being irrational,' Nicola said. 'Bunting has done nothing wrong. If he chose to banish his father and brother to Glasgow, what business is that of ours? If he wishes to sell his company then what law is there to stop him? If he is adamant in defence of his client and his client's need for secrecy then one cannot help but admire his loyalty.'

'Are you defending Bunting, taking his side over mine?'

'There is no side in this affair,' said Nicola. 'It is not a contest of wills, Grant. My father has lost whatever tenuous hold he believed he had on Charles de Morville's coal workings. The mystery, the real mystery, is not who bought the ground but why Papa was so obsessively eager to have the coal pit in the first place, so eager that he would trade a

180

daughter to get his hands on it.'

'He wants to increase his holdings,' Grant said. 'That's the force that drives the wheel of every landed gentleman who ever drew breath.'

'Well,' said Nicola, 'Papa has lost his chance. The coal workings have gone to someone else, someone with a greater driving force behind them and, perhaps, a bigger wheel to do the grinding.'

'But who?' said Grant. 'Damn it all, Nicola, who?'

'Do you know, Grant,' Nicola said, 'I find that I no longer care.'

'No longer care about Craigiehall?' said Grant, raising his brows. 'Craigiehall is your future, Nicola, your future and mine.'

'That,' Nicola said, 'is something I'm beginning to doubt.'

Grant stared at her for a bleak moment, opened his mouth as if to demand an explanation then, thinking better of it, inched away, folded his arms and lapsed once more into sullen silence. He was still sulking when, not far short of midnight, they arrived at Graddan's Court and Nicola, tired, dispirited and thoroughly sick of Grant's recalcitrance, refused the offer of a late supper and, leaving Charlotte to cope with her husband's mood, took herself straight to bed.

CHAPTER TEN

Nicola was bored, excruciatingly bored, so bored, in fact, that she would have welcomed Gillon with open arms had he deigned to call. There was no sign of Gillon at Graddan's Court, however, not so much as a note to excuse his absence. He had simply vanished into thin air. When she plucked up courage to beard Grant over the supper table and ask if he had heard from his brother she received short shrift for Grant, still brooding, could barely bring himself to be civil to his wife let alone his sister-in-law. Now that she had recovered from morning sickness, Charlotte, too, was bored and bad tempered. Elderly ladies from charitable foundations who called without invitation were sent away with fleas in their ears and persistent souls who broached her at church on Sundays were treated with sarcasm or disdain.

The weather did not help matters. June was marked by unrelenting rain and Jeannie and Molly were kept busy stoking fires to hold the dismal damp at bay. Gutters ran like rivers, eaves spouted torrents, huge puddles formed in cavities and hollows and the drains that had emptied the North Loch were so over-burdened that it seemed that water would once more cover the face of the earth, or at least that part of it that separated the Old Town from the New.

'Hearts,' Charlotte said, 'or cribbage, which shall it be?'

'I think,' Nicola said, 'that I prefer to read this afternoon.'

'If you're going to be stuffy what am I going to do?'

'You could sew, I suppose.'

'Sew? I'm sick of sewing,' Charlotte said. 'Come to think of it, I'm sick of playing cards too. Read to me, Nicola.'

'No.'

'What are you reading, anyway?'

'*The Pilgrim's Progress.*'

'Oh, I've read that one,' said Charlotte.

'No, you haven't,' Nicola said. 'You only think you have. Papa used to read it aloud to Jamie when he was poorly. We listened from the stairs until Nanny Aird dragged us off to bed.'

'Why did Papa never read to us?' said Charlotte.

'Perhaps he did not consider Bunyan suitable fare for girls.'

'He never read us anything.'

'Only the Scriptures,' Nicola said.

'And then not often,' said Charlotte.

They had eaten breakfast late, dinner early and were already looking forward to tea, each feeding ceremony spun out for an hour or more to peg the dreary day like markers on a cribbage board.

'A Polygon,' Charlotte said. 'It used to frighten me.'

'Appolyon, yes, and Giant Despair too,' said Nicola, closing the book. 'Everything used to frighten you, Charlotte.'

'It still does,' her sister said. 'I used to imagine that we lived in Doubting Castle and that Papa was Giant Despair. I wonder what Jamie made of it.'

'I expect he was comforted by the story of the Delectable Mountains and the promise of the Celestial City.'

'If Papa took him that far,' said Charlotte, then, abruptly, 'Where is he? Why does he not call on us?'

'Papa?' said Nicola. 'He is engaged on the business of the court and, in spite of Grant's efforts on his behalf, is still sour.'

'I do not mean Papa,' Charlotte said. 'I mean

Gillon.'

Nicola shifted uncomfortably. 'I think he has given up on me.'

'Is that sufficient reason to give up on *me*,' said Charlotte. 'He has been in love with me for years, you know.'

'Oh!' said Nicola. 'No, I did not know.'

'If he had met me before Grant . . . Oh, what's the point?' Charlotte said, waving her hands erratically. 'One cannot turn back the clock.'

'Are you in love with Gillon?' Nicola asked, cautiously.

'Having given up on you, no doubt he's pursuing some girl with a fortune attached and not a brain in her head.'

'You did not answer my question,' said Nicola.

'I have no answer to give, no proper answer,' said Charlotte. 'I have never encouraged him, if that is what you mean.' She paused. 'Still, it is flattering to know that someone cares for you.'

'I care for you,' Nicola said. 'Grant cares for you.'

'Does he?' said Charlotte. 'He has a queer way of showing it. Why will he not speak to me—or to you for that matter—except by means of surly grunts? What happened at Craigiehall, Nicola? Did he make advances on you?'

'Great heavens, no!' Nicola cried.

'I am not enough for him,' said Charlotte. 'He despises me.'

'He is in a black mood, I grant you,' Nicola said, 'but he does not despise you, Charlotte. He is disappointed, that's all.'

'In me, disappointed in me?'

'He had hoped, I think, to make headway with

Papa, to smooth things over before the baby is born. His pride was injured by his failure to come home from Galston with a name.'

'Do you know where he lives?' Charlotte said.

'Who?'

'Gillon: do you know where he lodges?'

'No.'

'Grant does not know either, or if he does he will not tell me,' said Charlotte. 'If we knew where Gillon lodges we might dispatch a letter inviting him to dine with us—or you might call upon him.'

'In this awful weather?' said Nicola, trying to make light of it.

'I want to see him again. I want a little merriment in my life, Nicola. Is that so wrong of me?'

'I thought you couldn't stand Gillon Peters,' Nicola said.

'I pretend not to like him,' Charlotte said. 'What's the point in pretence, however, when Grant has lost all interest in me and we are stuck here day after day with nothing to do but play cribbage and embroider mottoes that no one needs or wants?'

It was on the tip of Nicola's tongue to remind her sister that she was married and carrying a child and that Gillon Peters, however amusing, would be unlikely to provide a solution to her woes. She was well aware that any caddy worth his salt would soon track Gillon to one of the taverns where cards were played, but she kept that thought to herself.

'Perhaps he has gone to Heatherbank,' she suggested.

'If he had,' said Charlotte, 'then Grant would know of it. He receives frequent letters from

Roderick.'

'In that case,' Nicola said, 'might we not write to Roderick?'

'Hah!' said Charlotte, scathingly. 'Much good it would do us. They are as thick as thieves, those brothers. Besides, Gillon has no love for country life, particularly in wet weather. I'll wager he's found another heiress to pursue now that you have so cruelly cast him aside.'

'I did not cast him aside,' said Nicola.

'Where is he then?' Charlotte said. 'And who is he with?' And receiving no intelligent answer from her sister, rang the bell to summon Molly to heap more coals upon the fire.

*   *   *

Gillon had somehow imagined that she would be cast in the mould of stately Mrs Bellamy or full-bosomed Miss Lundy, actresses who had tickled the dreams of his youth, but at first glance Madelaine Young was not much more than a slip of a girl who, in shape if not feature, reminded him rather of Nicola Templeton.

As soon as she appeared at the door of the coach, three eager male passengers scrambled to assist her. So grateful was she for their attentions that she tossed back the hood of her cloak and blessed each gentleman with a smile so sweet and heartfelt that it was almost as good as a kiss. Greek, Gillon thought, or Italian? Only foreign blood could account for the liquid dark eyes that dominated her sallow, sharp-chinned face and almost, if not quite, overwhelmed a small puffy-lipped mouth that, to his astonishment, opened

186

wide as a water-lily the instant she caught sight of the girl who clung to his hand.

'Fleur, Fleur, my darling!' she cried. 'What have they done to you?'

'Auntie, Auntie.' Darting across the yard the girl threw herself into Mrs Young's arms. 'Oh, my Auntie Maddy, I am so happy to see you here at last.'

Floods in North Yorkshire had delayed the arrival of the London coach. Accompanied by the girl and by two footmen in Oliphant livery, Gillon had been hanging about Mannering's yard for what seemed like eternity.

'Fleur, Fleur, how you have grown.' Mrs Young studied her niece at arm's length. 'You are more beautiful than ever. Oh, how I have missed you.'

'I have missed you, also.' Fleur buried her head in her aunt's travel-stained cloak. 'I have been waiting and waiting with only Lieutenant Peters to amuse me. I thought you might have been swept away in flood waters and I could not sleep last night for weeping for you.'

'Well, dry your tears, my darling, for I am here now,' Madelaine Young said, 'none the worse for my adventures upon the road. We will both sleep soundly tonight, now that we are together again.'

'We will, we will,' the girl agreed.

Taking her aunt by the hand, she led her to Gillon who, sweeping off his hat, greeted the diminutive actress with a bow.

'Madam,' he said, 'a thousand welcomes to our fair city.'

'You're Peters, are you not?'

'I am, madam, for my sins, I am.'

'I thank you, sir, for looking out for my niece.'

187

'She is a delightful—ah—child and has given me nothing but pleasure,' Gillon said, then with military efficiency ordered the footmen to advance upon Mrs Young's luggage and transfer it to the waiting carriage. 'We will whisk you home in a trice, ma'am. It's but a step around the corner to Lady Valerie's house where friends and warm fires await you.'

'And a bath,' said Maddy. 'I must, simply must, have a bath.'

In spite of the rain and the activity around him, Gillon was smitten by a vision of the elfin actress arising nude from Lady Valerie's elegant copper-lined tub. He cleared his throat and dropping a hand to Fleur's shoulder, hastily steered the ladies through the crowd while the footmen, laden with luggage, trotted along behind.

*   *   *

As soon as the door of the carriage closed Madelaine Young leaned across the seat and said, 'So you're the sharper, are you, the expert in flim-flammery?'

'What?' Gillon was startled by her bluntness. 'Has this slander upon my reputation reached London now?'

'Word of your unusual skills has reached my ears,' said Madelaine Young, 'and that, Mr Peters, is all that matters.'

'I see,' Gillon said. 'Letters?'

The woman nodded. 'Letters.'

'From Lady Valerie?'

'And from Sir Archie.'

'I cannot claim much acquaintance with Sir

188

Archie,' Gillon said.

The carriage lurched as the footmen loaded on the baggage. Gillon put out a hand to steady himself and found it covered by the lady's dainty paw.

'Are you better acquainted with Lady Valerie?' she asked.

'To a degree.' Gillon cast a glance at Fleur who had snuggled into her aunt's lap. 'We are, shall we say, old friends, but these days our paths tend to cross only at the card table.'

'I gather that we are to be partners—at the card table, that is.'

'What, if I may make so bold, is your area of expertise?' Gillon asked.

'Crim Con,' the woman said. 'Do you know what that means?'

'Not,' said Gillon, 'precisely.'

'It's the lawyers' abbreviation for criminal conversation.'

'Criminal conversation?' said Gillon. 'Really?'

'In other words,' the woman said, 'a euphemism for adultery.'

'Oh!' said Gillon. 'How does one specialise in adultery?'

'Seduction might be a better way of putting it.'

'Ah yes,' Gillon said, 'that I do understand.'

The carriage lurched again and began to roll forward. Madelaine took her hand away and, sitting back, treated him to a dazzling smile.

'Will you be supping with us tonight?'

'No,' Gillon said. 'I am not suited to sup with the Oliphants.'

'Why not, indeed?'

'I am not a bluestocking.'

189

'No more am I,' the woman said.

'Nevertheless you obviously have the ability to create the illusion that you are one of them. Your talented niece has already prepared the way for your arrival and you will be taken at face value and accepted for whoever you say you are, particularly as you have Valerie Oliphant's backing. I will never be accepted in such circles,' Gillon said. 'I make no bones that I prefer cards to chitter-chatter. Besides, I have no bottom.'

'Bottom enough to do what Lady Valerie requires of you, however?'

'Bottom and nerve enough for that, oh yes,' said Gillon. 'When the cards are dealt face down all men are rendered equal.'

'And women, too?'

'And women, too.'

'We are two of a kind, I think,' Madelaine said. 'A matched pair. We will do well together, Lieutenant Peters, in bringing this noble lord to his knees.'

'Not my Admiral?' Fleur said, sitting up.

'No, my darling, not your Admiral, whoever he may be. Another gentleman altogether.'

'One with money?' the girl asked.

'Rich as Croesus, so I'm told,' Madelaine answered.

'As rich as our Mr Billington?'

Madelaine laughed. 'No, not quite as rich as all that.'

Fleur giggled and snuggled into her aunt's lap again, leaving Gillon to ponder just what sort of scheme he had stumbled into and who would finally benefit from playing this curious game.

*   *   *

It did not take long for news to circulate that Archie Oliphant had brought a beautiful English lady to town. Rumours soon abounded that she was a distant relative of the Queen or, possibly, a child of the late Marquess of Rockingham or even that she was descended from exiled Stuart kings and had been raised in secret in Paris and London, a princess of lost causes. How such ludicrous speculations took hold in the pragmatic world of Edinburgh society was inexplicable, but the Oliphants' friends and acquaintances were too artistic to permit truth to stand in the way of tittle-tattle.

It was known for a fact that Mrs Young had been at one time a player in M. Didier's London company, for the Admiral had seen her perform at Drury Lane. She had achieved a degree of fame with her impersonation of Shakespeare's Cleopatra and a degree of notoriety for her appearance in Thomas Zurich's *Salome*, after which she had vanished into the wings.

At what point in her career she had married Mr Young, who he was and how and when he had died were facts not known and Sir Archie and Lady Valerie remained provocatively vague on those issues. What matter! the Admiral declared. She was here now and if she hadn't been born a blue-blood he would eat his hat, braid and all, for the lovely Mrs Young was possessed of all the attributes that defined a lady, namely wit, charm and, of course, a matchless, if unconventional, beauty.

Toward the end of the month, when the rain

191

eased, Lady Valerie announced that she would host a musical evening to display the precocious talents of little Fleur Cadell and to introduce Mrs Young to cultured society by means of a reading from Sir Archibald's latest verse epic, 'Fingal's Return'. Invitations went out to those and such as those, which elite group did not include Gillon Peters but did incorporate the aloof, unmusical Lord Craigiehall who, unfortunately, was unable to attend due to pressing business in court.

Pressing business it was, too: a criminal charge brought by the Crown against two sisters who may or may not have wilfully murdered the wife of an inn-keeper in Glasgow's Saltmarket during an altercation over payment for a glass of spirits. The victim, it seemed, had been pushed or had tripped and had struck her hind head on the wall and had never stirred thereafter.

Acting for the defendants, Grant Peters petitioned that the sisters be tried separately so that the younger could speak in the elder's defence. Lord Craigiehall would have none of it, and the trial rumbled on until well after three o'clock in the morning when, in spite of Mr Peter's eloquent address to the jury, both girls were found guilty, sentenced to be hanged in the Grassmarket and their bodies given over for dissection to the Professor of Anatomy at the University. Small wonder that Lord Craigiehall was too tired to attend a musical soiree that evening, or that Mr Grant Peters remained sullen and uncommunicative at home.

Three days into the new month, Grant was summoned from the Advocates' library to the judges' robing room where Lord Craigiehall, still gaunt and weary, was being accoutred for another capital trial.

His lordship was nibbling thin slices of cold roast beef when Grant entered. He waved away his clerks and attendants and, when they had gone, rested on the edge of a table and after consulting his pocket watch, said, 'I have no wish to see a child of sixteen swing, Peters, but the jury, for some unfathomable reason, was adamant. If I were you, I would apply for leniency at the King's pleasure on behalf of the younger girl, Annie.'

'I have already discussed the matter with Mr Mackenzie,' Grant said. 'The evidence was not . . .'

'Yes, yes, Peters. I heard the evidence too, every blessed word of it. I am under no obligation to offer you advice on a decision which is already sealed but I suggest that you plead for the life of the younger girl alone.'

'And let the elder hang?'

'There is no help for it,' Lord Craigiehall said. 'She is twenty-two years old and must pay the price for her hot temper. The King's councillors will not reprieve both girls. If, however, you present your petition correctly I am sure decency will prevail and the younger of the two will walk free. Consult with Mr Mackenzie, by all means, but also with the Solicitor-General, whom you will not find unsympathetic.'

'Thank you for your advice, sir,' Grant said. 'I will follow it to the letter.'

'Better one than both,' Lord Craigiehall said, then, 'By the by, Peters, who is this woman, Madelaine Young, that Oliphant is so keen to foist upon us?'

'I really have no idea, your lordship.'

'Come now, there must be some chat on the promenade.'

'They say she is the granddaughter of Bonnie Prince Charlie and her sons, if she has any, will one day inherit the throne.' Grant snorted. 'That, sir, is the quality of opinion put out by my peers on the promenade.'

His lordship's long chin tilted and there may have been the hint of a smile on the corner of his lips. 'Do they not know that the Jacobite cause is dead and buried? I take they do not talk treason.'

'They talk garbage for the most part,' Grant said. 'I have heard little about the woman, only that she is an actress. I'm tempted to believe that Sir Archibald may have employed her to add polish to his latest drama.'

'She's an actress, then, not a lady of substance?' said Lord Craigiehall.

'She may be both of those things, I suppose,' Grant said. 'An absence of perspective on what constitutes a lady is the price we pay for living in enlightened times.'

'A fair point, Peters,' his lordship said. 'Is that all you can tell me?'

'It is,' Grant said.

'Then you may go and send in my clerk and my master of robes.'

'Yes, your lordship,' Grant said and, more than a little puzzled, left the great Lord Craigiehall making ready for another long day on the bench.

*   *   *

It was not until they reached the top of the Customhouse steps and Charlotte paused to catch

194

her breath that Nicola realised there was more to the outing than Charlotte had led her to believe.

Until that moment Nicola had been under the impression that her sister wanted no more than a breath of fresh air and a bit of exercise now that the rain had gone and the streets were drying out. She had not been at all averse to leaving the suffocating apartments in Graddan's Court and had dashed to put on a summery dress and a muslin bonnet and had trotted eagerly downstairs into the sunlight with Charlotte leading the way and Molly bringing up the rear.

They were not the only fashionable ladies out and about on that sparkling July afternoon. The Lawnmarket and Castle Hill Walk were as colourful as rose gardens with girls and women displaying their finery. They went up and they went down and then, with Charlotte still leading, came back at last to the rear of the Customhouse, climbed the steep steps and, at the top, stopped.

'Why,' said Charlotte, innocently, 'do you see where we are, dearest?'

'Aye,' said Molly, though the question had not been put to her. 'Home's but a hop in that direction an' it's gettin' fair near to dinner time.'

'I wonder if Papa is dining at home today,' Charlotte said.

'I think it exceedingly unlikely,' Nicola said. 'I have no intention of calling to find out.'

'Come now, Nicola,' Charlotte said, 'he is our Papa after all. He would hardly turn us away.'

'I wouldna be so sure o' that, Miss Charlotte,' Molly said, uneasily.

'Since we are in the vicinity . . .'

'We live in the vicinity,' Nicola reminded her.

'Since we are here, I think it would be only polite to drop in,' said Charlotte, with a prim pursing of the lips that Nicola recognised as obstinacy. 'My mind is made up. We'll step around the corner to Crowell's Close and pay our respects.'

'Did Grant put you up to this?' Nicola asked.

'Great heavens, no!' said Charlotte. 'Do you think I'm Grant's puppet? I do have a mind of my own, you know.' She paused, still breathing a little heavily. 'I've given the matter much thought of late and have reached the conclusion that it is unfair to blame Papa for the rift that exists between us. It is also unfair to expect Grant to put things right on our behalf.'

'Our behalf?' said Nicola.

'I am close to four months gone with child,' Charlotte said. 'My need is greater than yours.'

'If you mean reconciliation . . .' Nicola began.

'I do mean reconciliation,' said Charlotte. 'Whatever you have done to offend Papa it is time to make amends.'

'Whatever I have done?' Nicola said. 'I did not marry a scoundrel.'

'Is that what you think of my husband? After he has taken you in and succoured you without asking for a penny for your keep, you have the effrontery to call him a scoundrel?'

'Papa considers him a scoundrel, not me,' said Nicola.

'Then,' said Charlotte, picking up her skirts, 'it's high time Papa was made to change his mind. I am going to call upon him to tell him so. Come or not, Nicola, as you wish.'

'Best go, Miss,' Molly whispered. 'There'll only

be trouble otherwise.'

'Or trouble anyway,' Nicola said and hurried to catch up with her sister who had already vanished into the mouth of Crowell's Close.

*   *   *

Robertson neither smiled nor frowned but, lowering his eyelids, surveyed the women who fluttered on the doorstep as coldly as if they were strangers.

'Yes?' he said.

'Is my father at home?' said Charlotte.

'His lordship is at home.'

'Tell him that we have come to call,' said Charlotte.

Sunlight, streaming through a sloping skylight, illuminated the spacious hallway. That window had always bothered Nicola who, even now, could not understand how an architect had managed to place a glass skylight three floors below the roof. Staring up at the tinted glass, she felt like a child again. Bewildered and bashful, she half hoped that Robertson would turn them away.

'Is his lordship expecting you?' Robertson enquired.

'No,' Charlotte admitted. 'Please be good enough to inform him that we are here.'

'His lordship has company.'

'Company?' said Charlotte. 'Who?'

'Dr Gaythorn.'

Charlotte flinched.

'Is my father unwell?' Nicola asked.

'Nay, he's not sick, Miss Nicola, but he's been presiding at the court for half the night and he's exhausted,' Robertson said then, leaning from the waist, advised, 'Best come back another day.'

'Are they dining?' Charlotte insisted.

'No, they are takin' tea,' said Robertson.

'Then we will take tea,' said Charlotte and, giving Robertson a little shove with her elbow, stepped past him into the hall. 'Where is he?'

'In the breakfast room,' Robertson conceded. 'I'll announce you.'

'Do not trouble yourself,' said Charlotte. 'I know the way.'

With Nicola on her heels she charged across the hall and burst through the door into the breakfast room where her father, in dressing-gown and slippers, was nibbling on a piece of dry toast while Dr Gaythorn, with less than forensic interest, observed him over the rim of his teacup.

'Charlotte,' John James said, without a hint of surprise, 'what brings you crashing in on my breakfast? Do you have need of the doctor's attention?'

'No, Papa,' Charlotte retorted. 'I have need of your attention.'

'Indeed!' John James put down the finger of toast, said again, 'Indeed!'

'I shall leave now, sir,' Dr Gaythorn said, 'with your permission.'

'No, no, Gaythorn, stay by all means. You know my daughters, of course.'

'I do, sir, but—but the matter between you may be—ah—private.'

'Is it, Charlotte?' John James asked. 'Is it a private matter?'

It was typical of her father to remain unfazed, Nicola thought, a habit formed by many years sitting in judgement of criminals. He did look weary, though, and without a wig to hide his scant white hair, seemed closer to seventy than sixty. She felt a little stab of concern and, drawing out a chair, seated herself at the table and reached for his hand while the doctor escorted Charlotte to the little sofa.

John James allowed Nicola's hand to rest on his for a moment then put his question again. 'Is it a private matter, Charlotte?'

'No, Papa, it is not.'

'Does it relate to the child?'

'The child?' said Charlotte. 'Oh, the baby?'

'Yes,' said John James, with a sigh, 'the baby.'

'I am as well as a person in my condition can expect to be.'

'Does she look well to you, Gaythorn?' John James said.

'She does, your lordship, as far as I can tell without . . .'

'Quite!' John James said. 'If it is not the baby, is it, by chance, your husband who sent you here?'

'We were passing,' Nicola said, 'and decided to call to ask after your health, Papa, that's all.'

'I am in abounding good health, thank you, Nicola. Am I not, Gaythorn?'

'Well, I . . .'

'You see,' John James said. 'Now, Charlotte, about your husband: he has impressed me as an advocate who pleads well for his clients even if they do sometimes hang for it. I am less impressed by his complete lack of interest in our family's affairs.'

'It wasn't Grant's fault,' said Nicola. 'I was there, Papa. I saw with my own eyes how Mr

Bunting duped him.'

'Are you pleading Peters' cause too now, Nicola?'

'I'm only asking you to see reason.'

'There is no more reasonable man in Scotland than I am,' John James said. 'I am the very heart and soul of reason. Am I not, Gaythorn?'

'You do have that reputation, sir.'

'I reasoned long ago that Mr Peters cares not a fig for the future of Craigiehall, unless the future of Craigiehall will rest in his hands. Do you suppose, Charlotte, that your husband's failure to do that which I asked of him has altered my mind one whit?'

'I really think, your lordship, that I should take my leave,' the doctor said.

'Nonsense, man, nonsense!' John James said. 'We will have tea now and, as promised, dine about five with Mr Meegan and Mr Richards from the Royal Hospital so that we may extend our discussion on capital as an accumulation of anterior industry and its benefits to the health of society.'

'If that is your wish, Lord Craigiehall,' the doctor said.

'It is not just my wish but my intention,' John James said. 'I have nothing important to do today and after the exertions of the night—in court, that is—I'm looking forward to a lively debate on an interesting topic.' He paused, then said, 'Nicola, are you not inclined to come home yet? Have you not grown disillusioned with being a cuckoo in Grant Peters' nest?'

'No, Papa, I have not,' Nicola said. 'Besides, Charlotte needs me.'

'To protect her from Peters' indifference, I suppose.'

'My husband—my husband is not . . .' Charlotte blustered.

Nicola said, 'To protect her, if anything, from your indifference, Papa. Will you not acknowledge that we are grown up now and that you can no longer dictate how we lead our lives?'

'You, you at least, are still a child,' John James said.

'Old enough to marry, however,' Nicola said.

'Marry?' John James said. 'Is the purpose of your visit to inform me that you have fallen under the spell of some Edinburgh upstart?'

'The purpose of our visit,' said Nicola, 'is to effect a reconciliation.'

'Hah, I knew Peters was behind it.' John James wrapped the folds of his dressing-gown tightly over his breast, and laughed. 'Do you see how it is, Gaythorn, when a man has an estate at his disposal and naught but daughters to carry on the succession? You may think yourself fortunate, man, that you do not have children to plague your declining years.'

'My children died, both together, in infancy,' Gaythorn said. 'God, and my wife, decreed that there would be no more.'

'I was not aware of that, old fellow, or I would not have spoken of it.' John James had the decency to pause. 'However,' he turned again to Charlotte, 'I am, I assure you, quite the equal of your husband when it comes to processing statutes of succession and entail *ad longum*. Under the provisions of the law as it stands I can, and I will, prevent the esteemed Mr Peters from attaining his

201

ends. If the good Lord spares me for a few more years, I will ensure that Craigiehall remains in the Templeton family and does not become a toy for dirt-farmers. If you and your husband—and you too, Nicola—are willing to reconcile yourselves to that fact then I will be only too delighted to welcome you to my supper table, and, Charlotte, to be civil to your spouse.'

'What of my baby, your grandchild?' said Charlotte. 'Is he . . .'

'If it is a he,' John James put in, 'and not another blessed female.'

' . . .to be left penniless?'

'He will not be penniless, nor near it.'

'What you mean is that he will not be a Templeton,' Nicola said.

'Aye, Nicola, that's the nub of it. He will not be a Templeton. It will be up to Peters to look after the welfare of his children as I've looked after mine.'

'Looked after us?' Charlotte shot to her feet. 'You never loved us. You never cared for us. It was Jamie, Jamie, always Jamie,' she cried. 'It wasn't our fault that your precious Jamie died.'

'Now, now,' said Dr Gaythorn, catching Charlotte by the forearm, 'do not excite yourself, please, or the consequences . . .'

'Blast the consequences,' Charlotte raged, snatching her arm away. 'It would please you greatly, Papa, if I shed my baby here and now, would it not? If I spluttered him out on to your carpet and let you watch him expire, gasping like a poor wee fish? Well, damn you, I'm going to carry my term to spite you and deliver a fine, healthy baby whom you will never see, never hold in your arms. And when you're lying frail and dying in your

202

bed in Craigiehall you may look to your ghosts to comfort you for you will see neither my face nor Nicola's at your bedside, nor hear the voices of your grandchildren, whatever name they bear.'

Alarmed by the vehemence of his daughter's outburst, it seemed that John James was about to leap up and offer contrite apologies but then his crestfallen features hardened again and his chin tipped up defiantly, though whether he was defying Charlotte or his own sentimental weakness Nicola could not be sure.

'Nicola,' her father said, 'take your sister away.'

'I do not need to be taken away,' said Charlotte. 'I am perfectly capable of taking myself away, which is, indeed, what I intend to do.' She gathered her skirts and adjusted her bonnet. 'Come, Nicola. We have imposed upon Lord Craigiehall's hospitality long enough. Your arm, if you please.'

Nicola rose and gave Charlotte her arm.

She felt her sister's hand close on her elbow as they made their way to the door. Dr Gaythorn, quite put out, was on his feet but Papa remained seated, head turned haughtily away.

'Goodbye to you, Father,' Charlotte called over her shoulder. 'Next time we meet may it be in hell,' and then, before her Papa could answer, instructed Robertson to throw open the street door and let her out into the air.

CHAPTER ELEVEN

Whist was John James's only hobby. He did not regard himself as a serious gambler and had no particular fondness for other games of chance, but there was something so compelling about whist's strict rules and computations that, some years ago, he had attached himself to a group of reprobate lawyers who, when the court was in session, met for cards and supper in Fortune's every Friday night. There he had honed his skills and had rarely lost more than he could afford. Indeed, one of his fondest memories was of taking six guineas at a stroke from cocky young Boswell, Lord Auchinleck's son, before Boswell had achieved a measure of fame for his scribblings and before he, John James Templeton, had been elevated to the bench, after which he had been forced to be more circumspect where and with whom he played.

Card assemblies in the Baron's Hall were respectable enough even for a man of his rank and he'd spent many a happy hour partnering genteel ladies and gentlemen at a penny a point and sixpence the rubber. Then, out of the blue, he had been invited by Sir Archie to participate in one of Lady Valerie's private card parties in their vast drawing-room where supper consisted of truffles and *foie gras*, breakfast was served at four a.m. and the stakes rose to heights that almost took his breath away.

No novices were admitted into Valerie's inner circle. Little old ladies so frail they could barely stand upright and gentlemen so antique they might have sailed with Noah proved to be fearsome adversaries who were just as adroit in calculating odds at cock crow as they were at midnight. Of course, Lady Valerie was queen among them. John James had heard that not content with rooking her guests by her high play at home she spent her off nights in taverns and coffeehouses betting with riff-raff, a dangerous and demeaning pastime that Sir Archie apparently condoned.

To partner her ladyship was always a pleasure, though, to be matched against her a challenge. Thus, when the summons came, by way of a printed card, John James would put aside his papers, powder his wig, cancel all appointments and head out across the bridge to the big house in Broughton Square with nothing in his head but thoughts of quints, quarts and long trumps and how, God willing, he might finesse the lady into losing.

The warm wind that blew from the Forth that summer evening did not deter him. He held on to his hat and strode out as briskly as a young gallant. The recent trials over which he had presided had been prolonged and wearing, and his squabble with his daughters, Charlotte in particular, had so affected his nerves that he had lost the knack of sleeping soundly. He was anxious, distempered and filled with strange forebodings that, had he but known it, had more to do with loneliness than the uncertain future of Craigiehall.

When, however, Bradley, the Oliphants' butler, relieved him of his hat and gloves and he raced up the broad staircase and entered the gilded apartment and saw that the curtains were already closed, the candelabra lighted and four tables dressed for play, he experienced a lightening of the spirits so great that he almost danced for joy.

'Lord Craigiehall, how delightful,' Lady Valerie called from across the room. 'Is there no one for you to order to the gallows this evening?'

'Fortunately not tonight, your ladyship,' he

answered. 'And if there were I would see to it that they were hanged right quick for who could resist an invitation to play cards with you?'

'Not you, John James,' Admiral Staines bellowed. 'Come, split a bottle with me to clear your pipes.'

'I'll leave the bottle to you, sir. I prefer a clear head to clear pipes, particularly if I am to be matched against the navy.'

John James discreetly surveyed the room to weigh the strength of the opposition. Basil Stokes, the Earl of Inchinnan's nephew, was conversing with Miss Montgomerie, the only surviving daughter of a former British Ambassador, eighty if she was a day. The widow of Sir Lawrence Lawton, who had made a fortune importing cotton before the American War, was no spring lamb either but with a brain like a gin-trap deserved to be treated with respect. Evelyn Totterdale, another widow, clever but flighty, and Mr Raglan Pierce, a brewer who owned a string of thoroughbreds, were both risk-takers, and old Colm Leland, the Irish peer . . .

John James blinked and straightened his shoulders as if he were about to take wing, for there, chatting to old Colm, was a young woman he had never seen before; a perfect stranger, perfect in every respect, slight and shapely and pretty as a pixie, her head thrown back in polite laughter, her dark eyes ardent and sparkling as she caught and held his gaze.

'Who—who is that, pray?' he heard himself ask.

The Admiral answered, 'The musical child's aunt, lately arrived from London. Have you not heard the gossip that gathers about her, Craigiehall? Has the Parliament House gone dumb?'

'Ah!' John James got out. 'So that's the infamous Madelaine Young.'

'Oh, come now, sir,' the Admiral said, 'she is hardly infamous. Touched by a certain brand of notoriety, perhaps, a degree of intrigue, but she is a worthy enough woman, I assure you, and very lively.'

'I take it you know her personally?'

'We have conversed,' the Admiral admitted.

John James dared another peek at the actress. She was still absorbed in converse with the Irish peer, not so absorbed, however, that she was unaware of John James' interest and by fussy little motions of her fan seemed to beckon him and, at the same time, brush him away.

'I have also seen her perform,' the Admiral said. 'Three times, in fact.'

'Where?' John James turned reluctantly from contemplation of the celebrated stranger. 'In what play?'

'In the Lane, Drury Lane. In—um—Zurich's version of *Salome*.'

'*Salome*?' John James said. 'Good God! Was she . . . ?'

'Proficient,' said the Admiral. 'Very proficient.'

'The gentleman who attends her,' John James said, 'is he her husband?'

'No husband. She's widdered, I believe. The fellow at her heels is one of Valerie's strays. Soldier, or was, just home from the wars. Peters, by name.'

'Peters?' John James said. 'Gillon Peters?'

'Aye, aye, something of the sort,' the Admiral muttered, abruptly losing interest in John James as little Fleur Cadell was led into the room to kiss her aunt goodnight.

*   *   *

Cards were drawn for places and partners. To Gillon's relief, he was paired with 'Brewer' Pierce, not Craigiehall. After an interval for supper at ten-thirty cards would be drawn again and pairings changed and, by simple sleight-of-hand, he would ensure that Craigiehall and Maddy Young were brought together before the stakes were raised and play began in earnest.

Gillon did well enough in that first short session. He won seven pounds and eighteen shillings in nine deals, all without flim-flammery. He could see Craigiehall from the corner of his eye, tall and distinguished in a haggard sort of way, and Madelaine, at another table, laughing, always laughing. He had supposed that he would feel exhilarated in such rich company but as the sun waned behind the curtains, and the clocks of the New Town ticked away the minutes to supper time, the weight of responsibility began to bear down upon him.

Valerie, Maddy and he had played a few rubbers over tea yesterday afternoon, with Fleur, dementedly eager, standing in for Craigiehall. He had given them no hint when he was about to manipulate the pasteboards and throw suits in any direction that took his fancy—and he had been pleased when the ladies professed amazement and had praised his dexterity.

'Where did you learn such clever tricks?' Maddy had asked.

'On board the transport that took the Highlanders from Greenock to Staten Island,' he had answered, honestly. 'We junior officers had a long room to ourselves but it was a ruffian below decks who taught me how to sharp. He was a wild individual who had only just escaped the gallows by the skin of his teeth and wouldn't have been enlisted in the regiment if there had not been an urgent need of recruits.'

The women had been keen to hear more of his adventures at sea but he had politely changed the subject, not out of modesty but from fear that he would reveal too much of himself. How could he possibly tell them that it was only the greasy pasteboards that had saved his sanity during that hellish ten-week voyage to the shores of New York. That his guts had been ripped out by Atlantic gales, that he had wept into his bolster for fear of drowning and that the ruffian, Weaver, had pulled him out of it by showing him how to force cards and deal dicey and how he, then, had practised hour upon hour upon hour in the dank and dripping half dark of the subalterns' salon, squinting at aces, kings and knaves, dealing and cutting and dealing again, while his companions drank and vomited and squabbled.

'Lord Craigiehall,' he said. 'I am . . .'

'I know who you are,' Craigiehall said. 'What is it you want?'

'Lady Valerie has asked me to offer you the cards.'

Supper was almost over—it never took long— and the learned judge, dabbing gravy from his chin with a napkin, peered down at the reduced pack that Gillon held out to him, flat on one palm: four suits, spades to the fore, aces to fours in each suit, evens paired with evens, odds with odds.

'You bear no resemblance to your brother,' Craigiehall said.

'Indeed, no, sir,' Gillon said, 'which is probably just as well, given that we have no affinity other than kinship and are not, in character, at all alike.'

'You are a soldier, are you not?'

'I am no longer a soldier. I fought with the Highland Regiment in America but I confess that I had no stomach for spending my winters in idleness barracked in Nova Scotia. I resigned my commission.' Gillon said. 'Do you wish to cut the pack, Lord Craigiehall, or have me box for you?'

The learned judge was uncertain. He put out his hand, then withdrew it. He glanced up and around the room until his eye alighted on Madelaine Young who was eating strawberries with a silver fork and listening to some droning tale from Basil Stokes who, like every other man in the place, had been infected by Maddy's gaiety and was clearly out to impress her.

'Lord Craigiehall?' Gillon said, quietly.

'What? Yes, by all means.' His lordship picked a four of hearts from the top of the deck and held it up. 'My partner, who is my partner?'

'Mrs Young, I believe,' said Gillon.

And, to his satisfaction, heard his lordship sigh.

*   *   *

When, around four, a sleepy footman opened the curtains and sunlight seeped into the drawing-room, John James was richer by almost sixty pounds. The money, though welcome, was

210

less important than the astonishing affinity he had established with Mrs Young whose cards had mated so magically with his own and who had astutely followed his lead with trumps and tricks, deal after deal, much to the consternation of Grant Peters' brother and his unfortunate partner, Lady Valerie Oliphant.

By the time scores had been tallied and games analysed, and the players had risen and headed for the water closet or the coffee urns, John James was in a state of near euphoria. Not only had he bested Peters' brother and the indefatigable Lady Valerie, he had, without doubt, impressed the beautiful stranger and had earned the little kiss she gave him, behind her fan, before, pleading exhaustion, she took her leave to go to bed.

He was not tired, not in the least—and he was ravenous.

He ate three buttered muffins in quick succession and drank coffee, standing tall and strong and handsome, he thought, among the jaded elders at the breakfast table, for at that hour even the Admiral was inclined to sag a little. He noticed Valerie and Gillon Peters arguing in a corner, watched Peters turn on his heel and sulkily depart and, seizing his chance, hurried across the room to steal a moment alone with her ladyship.

'Luck,' she said. 'Oh, Craigiehall, you had the devil's luck tonight.'

'In respect of the cards that may be true,' John James said, 'but it wasn't luck that brought Mrs Young to my table, was it?'

Lady Valerie looked alarmed. 'Not luck? What was it then?'

'I had almost begun to believe that you had

forgotten your promise.'

'My promise?' Lady Valerie said. 'What promise would that be?'

'To find me a bride. How did Sir Archie discover such a jewel?'

'Madelaine—oh, you mean Madelaine,' Lady Valerie said. 'Archie did not bring her here for you, John James, if that is what you think!'

'What else am I to think? She is so—so ideal.'

'Madelaine Young is an actress and a widow, with precious few assets to her name. And she has a child—a niece—who would have to be included in any marriage arrangement.'

'Is the child hers?' John James said. 'I should not much mind that.'

'The child, I believe, was born out of wedlock to her sister when her sister was little more than a child herself.'

'Where is the sister now?'

'She died giving birth to Fleur. In Calais.'

'Calais?'

'The father was some licentious Frenchman whom the girl pursued to France after he had abandoned her.'

'And Madelaine's father?'

'John James, stop now, I beg you. Truly, she is not for you.'

'Is she with Peters, the soldier? Is she for him?'

'No, no.' Her ladyship shook her head emphatically. 'She has more sense than to throw herself on the mercy of a penniless soldier. Her husband—may he rest in peace—was a merchant in French wines. He died suddenly only months after the nuptials. There was no issue.'

'If he was a wine-merchant he must have left her

something?'

'Sons,' said Lady Valerie. 'He had sons from a former marriage. The usual sorry story; the sons claimed everything and tossed Maddy on to the street to fend for herself.'

'Poor woman,' John James said. 'She has met with much misfortune for one so—well—young. How old is she, by the by?'

'Enough, John James. I will answer no more of your questions.' Her ladyship pressed a wrist to her brow. 'It's four o'clock in the morning. I am weary to the bone and my head aches. A promise is a promise, however. If you will allow me a space to breathe, I will unearth a lady more suited to your requirements which, as I recall, were mild, well-bred and still of an age to produce an heir for Craigiehall.'

'In the meanwhile, Valerie,' John James said, 'would it do harm if I sent my card to your house guest?'

'Your card?'

'If, for instance, I invited her to supper?'

'It would do me no harm, Craigiehall,' Lady Valerie said, 'but I fear it will do *you* no good.'

John James opened his mouth to put another question then, thinking better of it, bowed, thanked her ladyship for her gracious hospitality and, after stealing another muffin to eat *en route*, collected his hat and gloves from the hall and set off to meander home through the warm summer air, humming to himself like a bee in a patch of clover.

CHAPTER TWELVE

It did not take long for word to leak out that stuffy Lord Craigiehall had been seen in the company of the mysterious Mrs Young, Sir Archie Oliphant's town-house guest. The pair were spotted playing whist at Fortune's and, a day or two later, were observed promenading quite openly in Broughton Gardens, escorted only by a servant. What Lady Oliphant, let alone her husband, made of the improbable friendship was open to speculation but it appeared, at least to the ill-informed, that her ladyship was not against it for as the month progressed the judge's chaise was often to be seen in the mews behind the Oliphants' house.

It was also said that the old boy had undergone a miraculous mellowing that showed all too clearly in his pronouncements from the bench. Fortunate, indeed, was the criminal whose cause was heard in those first court days of high summer when Craigiehall, sweating and smiling, would all but argue the case for the defence and during one late sitting almost came to blows with Dunbar, the Lord-Advocate, and accused him, without apology, of baying like a ghoul for the defendant's blood when the poor fellow, a cattle-thief, was patently the victim of a misunderstanding.

'If half of what we hear is true,' Nicola said, 'I fear Papa may have lost his reason. Do you think we have driven him to it?'

'To what? To making an ass of himself?' said Charlotte. 'He has always been an ass, don't you know? I for one am not sorry that it is now a matter for public acknowledgement.'

'Public acknowledgement?' said Nicola. 'Hardly that, Charlotte.'

'Mark my words,' said Charlotte, 'snippings will appear in the *Courant* before long and one of our satirists will compose a poem about him with the name barely concealed. Unless he mends his ways Papa will become a laughing stock—which, of course, is no more than he deserves.'

'You are very hard on him, Charlotte,' Nicola said. 'Why should he not enjoy a woman's company? It is, after all, eighteen years since mother died. Is Grant concerned in case this English person is setting her cap at Papa?'

'Setting her cap?' said Charlotte. 'God in heaven, Nicola, he's old enough to be her father. And she has a child—a child of dubious origin, I might add and not a penny to her name. Papa may be mad but he's not mad enough to be taken in by a woman of no background and no breeding who, so I hear, has not one crown nor one acre of ground with which to hansel her settlement.'

'She plays a decent game of whist, by all accounts,' Nicola said.

'Who told you that?'

'Grant.'

'That's more than he told me,' said Charlotte. 'He tells me hardly anything these days. How did you wheedle it out of him?'

'I did not have to wheedle,' said Nicola. 'One of Hercules Mackenzie's agents encountered Papa and this woman at the gaming tables in Fortune's. Half the young advocates in Edinburgh go there to gamble, so whatever the true state of affairs between Papa and Mrs Young I think we might

215

assume that it is not something he intends to keep secret.'

'Bad company,' Charlotte shook her head, scowling. 'He has fallen into bad company. Never did I think I would see the day when Papa became the subject of gossip. I'll wager Lady Oliphant's behind it. All that dabbling in art and literature can be very corrupting, you know.'

'The Oliphants have always been eccentric,' Nicola said.

'And trouble makers,' said Charlotte. 'Valerie Oliphant is famous for her mischief-making. In the light of what you've told me perhaps I will have a word with Grant to enquire what he intends to do about it.'

'What can Grant do?' Nicola said. 'Really, it's none of our affair.'

'If it's not our affair then whose affair is it, pray? I would not put it above Papa to marry again just to spite us. Grandfather did.'

'Grandfather married to acquire land,' said Nicola. 'I do wish you would be more consistent in your arguments. If, as you claim, this woman is indeed a penniless upstart Papa will see through her in an instant.'

'Unless he has fallen in love,' said Charlotte. 'He would not be the first old fool to be blinded by female charms.'

'Papa may be many things,' said Nicola, 'but he's no fool.'

'Now who's being inconsistent?' Charlotte said. 'Either he has lost his reason, or he has not.'

'It would not be unreasonable for a man in Papa's position to take a mistress,' Nicola said. 'I'm rather surprised he hasn't done so before now.'

'A mistress?' said Charlotte. 'How disgusting!'

'Papa is already a judge of the double robe and unlikely to rise higher. What is there to occupy him but Craigiehall?' Nicola said. 'We can hardly complain if he seeks a little female companionship to lighten his days.'

'Um,' said Charlotte. 'Yes, but a mistress is one thing and a wife quite another. I still think it's disgusting.'

'The court session ends soon,' Nicola said. 'Papa will either return to Craigiehall or take his turn on the Circuit. Perhaps that will be an end of it.'

'He wouldn't invite her to Craigiehall, would he? Can you imagine the look on Mrs McGrouther's face if Papa arrived with a mistress on his arm? There would be outrage and rebellion throughout the household. It will not come to that, will it?'

'No,' said Nicola. 'It will not come to that, I'm sure.'

'Then,' Charlotte said, 'we will put the matter to one side, for I am hot and thirsty and in need of refreshment.'

She stretched out her hand and rang the bell.

Two or three minutes later, she rang it again, impatiently this time. Molly, minus her cap, appeared in the doorway.

'Where have you been?' Charlotte said. 'Where's Jeannie?'

'Not well, miss,' Molly said. 'She's very poorly, to tell the honest truth. She's all sick an' drowsy an' sweatin' like a piggie. I sent her off to her bed.'

'Is it her time of the month?' said Charlotte.

'Nah, miss, she says it's not,' said Molly.

'Then she's malingering,' Charlotte said. 'What

217

does Cook say?'

'Cook says . . .'

'It's all right, Molly,' Nicola put in. 'Do not distress yourself. Tell us, please, what Cook said?'

'Cook says you'd better send for a doctor. Quick.'

*   *   *

Gillon said, 'What's wrong with the child, Maddy? I take it it isn't serious.'

'Of course it isn't serious,' Valerie Oliphant answered him. 'It's a summer cold, that's all. If it goes into her chest then we will seek medical advice but, believe me, it's nothing to be alarmed about.'

'Are you alarmed, Maddy?' Gillon said.

'I am, a little,' Madelaine Young admitted.

It was cool in the Oliphants' drawing-room. The windows had been unhooked since early morning and now that the sun had slipped to the west, the breeze that trickled in from the shaded gardens brought relief from the stifling heat, though there was still dust to contend with, the stench of dung from the mews and a cacophony from the streets that no amount of expense could muffle. Gillon hardly noticed the din and the dust; he was just pleased to be here, with Maddy, in the elegant house in Broughton Square.

Naked, without even a sheet to cover him, he had tossed and turned like a cod in batter night after night in the bed in his tiny tenement room; nor had he found respite in the shabby taverns along the Cowgate where he had gone, alone, to drink and gamble while awaiting a summons from high-and-mighty Lady Valerie whose 'scheme' had cut him off from his usual haunts and had ended his stuttering courtship of Nicola Templeton once and for all.

He had seen nothing of Nicola or Grant for weeks. He had taken to skulking in closes and vennels away from Parliament House, from Horne's and Mouser's, to avoid bumping into Grant. And when, last Monday afternoon, he had caught sight of Nicola, Charlotte and the maid heading towards the bridge he had scuttled off before they'd noticed him, for by accepting Valerie Oliphant's commission he had put Nicola Templeton out of reach.

On the other hand, mendacious Madelaine Young was a woman after his own heart and in her presence he had no need to pretend to be a gentleman. It galled him to think that she was spending her nights with Craigiehall and that he was no more to her than an accomplice.

'Are you playing cards, Gillon, or are you not?' Lady Valerie said.

'Give me the pack then,' Gillon said, reaching.

'Do you take me for a lunatic?' Lady Valerie said. 'I've seen what you can do with the pasteboards, young man. I've no intention of letting you cheat me at brag. I will deal.'

'Does Craigiehall play brag?' Gillon asked.

'Only whist,' said Madelaine. 'He's an excellent player too.'

'Is he, indeed?' said Gillon. 'Are you good at following his lead?'

'I am good at letting him think so,' Madelaine said.

Gillon stared at the fleur-de-lys pattern on the

backs of his cards. He wasn't used to playing with a clean pack. He tipped them, studied them for a moment then, rather casually, advanced a bet on the strength of a low pair.

Lady Valerie topped him immediately. Madelaine said, 'Blind.'

'Are you sure, my dear?' said Lady Valerie.

'Quite sure, thank you,' said Maddy.

'Where, by the way, is Sir Archie?' Gillon asked.

'Gone to London to search for a suitable Fingal,' Valerie answered.

'Is the play complete at last?' said Maddy.

'It will never be complete,' said Valerie. 'It is, I fear, a life's work—like Penelope's tapestry. He will have it privately performed in October or November. After which, knowing my husband, he will revise, alter and generally fiddle with the blessed thing before it is put before the public—if, indeed, it is ever put before the public'

'Will you still be here in October, Madelaine?' Gillon asked.

'Where else would I be?' said Maddy.

'Craigiehall, perhaps,' Gillon suggested. 'The chatelaine of Craigiehall.'

'Do not be impatient, Gillon,' Lady Valerie said. 'Lord Craigiehall must be roasted slow. Are you with me for four shillings?'

'I am,' said Gillon. 'Madelaine?'

'Blind, still blind.'

The hand progressed. Cards were dealt, bets increased. Maddy, for all her daring, had naught but scraps and Gillon lost twelve shillings to Lady Oliphant's treys. He watched her ladyship collect the cards and box them. He had no interest in the game and felt no compulsion to defeat either of the women or profit from their transparency. He could read the signs that announced deception as easily as he read text from a Bible, for women had too many frills to toy with and relied too heavily on flirtation to be very adept at the bluffing game. He said, 'How long has Fleur been poorly?'

'Three days,' Maddy answered.

'Is she fevered?'

'She has a cold,' Lady Valerie snapped. 'Will you please . . .'

'She is hot and cold by turns,' Maddy said, 'and complains of headache.'

'And drinks much but will not eat?' said Gillon.

'Yes, that's the case.'

'Where is she lodged?'

'Upstairs,' said Maddy.

'Can you not hear her snore?' said Valerie, making ready to deal again.

'A moment, your ladyship, please.' Gillon pushed back his chair. 'If it is agreeable to you, Madelaine, perhaps I might accompany you to look in on her?'

'Hah!' her ladyship snorted. 'Do you share the Admiral's taste for young girls, then? I would not have thought it of you, Gillon. There's no need for you to trouble yourself. My lady's maid is with the child.'

Madelaine was already on her feet.

'What is it, Gillon? What do you fear?'

'He fears nothing,' Valerie said. 'He is merely trying to impress you.'

Gillon put a hand on Madelaine's sleeve. 'Take me to her.'

And ignoring her ladyship's protests, Maddy led him upstairs.

221

'Smallpox?' Charlotte cried, her face chalk white. 'No, it cannot be smallpox!'

'I'm in no doubt whatsoever,' Dr Gaythorn said, 'that your maid has been struck down by the contagion. Has it escaped your notice that folk are flocking to the public ward of the Royal Infirmary to have their infants inoculated? The disease is rampant in certain quarters of town.'

'What will become of us? Will we die?' said Charlotte.

'Calm yourself, please, Mrs Peters,' said Dr Gaythorn. 'The servant—Jeannie, is it?—is unlikely to succumb. Unless the strain is inordinately virulent or the person weak, the condition is seldom fatal in an adult. Did you not suffer the disease in infancy?'

'I did, sir,' Molly put in. 'It was mild an' left no scars.'

'Miss Templeton?'

'No, not that I recall.'

'Neither of you were inoculated?'

'My father did not believe in inoculation,' Nicola said. 'He claimed it was flouting God's will to pierce the skin with infected material.'

'An old-fashioned attitude, if I may say so,' Dr Gaythorn said. 'Rendered correctly, inoculation is a sound defence against the worse forms of the disease. If you wish I will inoculate you both now. I have samples of dried tissue in my bag. It takes no time at all. Given that you have been breathing the same air as your little servant, however, it may be . . .'

222

'Too late, it's too late,' Charlotte said. 'Oh God! We are doomed.'

'Charlotte, for pity's sake, be still,' said Nicola. 'We must put Jeannie's welfare first. What is to be done for her, Dr Gaythorn?'

'The eruptions have not yet appeared,' the doctor said. 'When they do the fever will abate and I will be able to tell from the hue of the pustules just how deeply seated the disease may be. It's fortunate that you summoned me in preference to some quack who would bleed and blister the poor wee creature and thus suppress the proper workings of nature. Balm-tea and barley water will be nostrums enough, and the girl should be encouraged to rise as soon as she is able, to sit up and have her legs and feet bathed.'

'I'll see to that, sir,' Molly said.

'And who will see to me?' said Charlotte. 'We must send Jeannie back to her family in Pennicuik. Let them take care of her.'

Gaythorn shook his head. 'It would not advantage her health to undertake a trip, however short. In fact, I insist that she be not moved until the disease has run its course.'

'How long will that take?' Nicola asked.

'If there are no complications, three to four weeks.'

'Be not moved?' said Charlotte. 'I've witnessed women by the roadside clutching children dripping with pus. Being moved does *them* no harm.'

'Would you have me put your maid out on the roadside?' said Gaythorn. 'Smallpox is a condition that yields best to careful nursing.'

'The Royal, then, the infirmary?' said Charlotte, desperately.

223

'There are no beds to be had in the infirmary,' the doctor said. 'The disease is not yet epidemic but it may soon become so, in which case there will be panic and an exodus from town will begin in earnest.'

'Leave town?' said Charlotte. 'Yes, we must leave town at once.'

'And go where?' said Nicola. 'To Craigiehall?'

'No,' Charlotte said. 'No, I will not return to Craigiehall, no matter how circumstances may urge me in that direction.'

'Where then?' said Nicola.

But Charlotte, breaking down in tears, had no ready answer.

*   *   *

She was gone before nightfall. She took with her half the servants, all the dogs, and a great quantity of baggage, and rode out of the mews in the four-horse carriage without a backward glance or a word of farewell.

'I take it,' Gillon said, 'that her ladyship is heading for her country seat at Kingsley where Archie will join her on his return from London?'

'She did not say as much,' Maddy said, 'but if Kingsley is in the shire of Perth then I believe I did overhear her mention it.'

They were alone in the gilded drawing-room, looking down from a half-open window at the cloud of dust that the departing carriage had left behind. Cards and coins were splashed across the table and the chair that Lady Valerie had knocked over in her haste lay upturned on the polished floor. Gillon righted it and set it in place. He gathered the cards and put them in the ornamental box from which her ladyship had removed them, then he divided the crowns and shillings into two heaps and, nodding, said, 'An even split, I believe.'

Madelaine scooped the coins into the purse at her waist.

'Smallpox,' she said. 'How could I have ignored the signs?'

'I assume you've seen cases in London?'

'Far too many,' Maddy said. 'My sister died of it when she was four years old. I had the contagion too but my father cured me.'

'How did he cure you?'

'By dint of prayer.'

'Prayer?' said Gillon, surprised.

'He was a preacher in Nottingham.' Madelaine hesitated. 'A Methodist. He may still be there for all I know.'

'Did he cast you out?'

'I cast myself out,' Maddy said. 'I followed a man to London in the belief that he loved me which, perhaps fortunately, he did not—at least not enough to forsake his wife and family.'

'Was he also a Wesleyan?' said Gillon.

'No, he was a travelling man who sold religious tracts from a wagon and preached salvation when ever an opportunity presented itself. Preached and prayed and dandled every young girl who was foolish enough to be deceived by his promises of marriage.'

'Were you carrying his child when you left for London?' Gillon asked.

She shook her head. 'No, no child.'

'Fleur . . .' Gillon began then, thinking better of it, changed tack. 'Fleur will need more attention

225

than we can give her. I've seen the pox rage through an army encampment. I've attended men on the march so encrusted with pustules that they looked like fir cones but, to be honest, not all of them survived my rough and ready treatment.'

'Are you immune, Gillon?'

'I've had a brush with the villain, aye,' Gillon said.

'Then you must stay with me.'

'What? Here? Oh no,' Gillon said.

'Are you afraid that the servants will tattle to Lady Valerie?'

'Partly that,' Gillon admitted. 'The butler . . .'

'Bradley.'

'Aye, I prefer not to tangle with Bradley. He'll have been given instructions even if we have not. He'll tell you what Valerie intends you to do which, I imagine, will be to remain here until the crisis is well and truly over and her ladyship is able to return to Edinburgh without fear of having her features scarred by a disease that has neither aesthetic nor moral inhibition and admits no difference between a harlot and a peer.'

'Eloquent,' said Madelaine, 'if not tactful.'

'I'm not concerned with Valerie Oliphant or her wayward husband,' Gillon said. 'I'm only concerned with you—and with Fleur, of course. Fleur must be visited by a doctor, a reliable doctor, and it must be done without delay.'

'Reliable doctors cost money.'

'I have a little money,' Gillon said, 'but, unlike you, I do not have powerful friends.'

'Craigiehall, you mean?'

'Yes,' Gillon said, thinly. 'Who else but Craigiehall?'

226

*   *   *

It had been a long, hot, dreary day in the Court of
Session and Grant was in no mood to sup at home
and put up with his wife's scolding. He had
received an invitation to call upon Hercules
Mackenzie at an hour that suggested supper and as
soon as he had delivered his last amendment,
asked Somerville to find him a chair to carry him
to George's Square.

He sank back into the canvas-covered cushion
and, with the door closed but the window open,
watched the boy—for he was hardly more than
that—grip the shafts of the sedan and in harmony
with the burly highlander at the rear cry out, 'Hup,
Daddy,' and felt himself being lifted into the air.

Being carried aloft at walking pace was an odd
but not unpleasant sensation, one that Grant had
never quite grown used to. The heat had made him
just a little light-headed and he closed his eyes and
let his body relax as the carriers tramped out of the
heart of the city.

At first he had tried to ignore the malicious
rumours that were circulating in the Parliament
House and the taverns and coffee-shops in its
vicinity. He had never had much, if anything, to do
with the Oliphants and the arrival of an actress,
even a pretty one, from London had impinged
upon his consciousness hardly at all. Not until his
father-in-law's name had cropped up in a less than
casual conversation with Somerville had he
realised that there might be fire beneath the
smoke. And when Lord Craigiehall, who had
always been known for his rectitude, had blistered

227

Dunbar, the Lord-Advocate, and publicly accused him of blood lust Grant had pricked up his ears.

Scandal, he knew, was like an intricate piece of clockwork that once wound would tick away as mercilessly as time itself. It was too soon, however, to predict how this turn of events might affect his relationship with his father-in-law. He had sent a note to Gillon requesting a meeting, for Gillon had been at one time an intimate of the Oliphants. But his brother had failed to reply and Grant had had no option but to raise the matter with Charlotte and Nicola, if for no other reason than to share the burden of his concern.

The sun, slipping towards the west, struck blinding reflections from the mansion's box windows. Grant tugged down the brim of his hat as he climbed from the chair. He paid the carriers and, carrying his court bag across his shoulder, strode down the path that led to Hercules' front door.

He was admitted at once, relieved of his bag and hat and shown directly into the dining-room on the ground floor.

The four gentlemen at the table had already made inroads into pitchers of ice-cold beer that stood in ceramic pots on the side-board. How Hercules had acquired such a quantity of ice in the midst of a hot spell was more than Grant could imagine. He accepted a tankard from the butler and to relieve his anxiety as well as his thirst sank the contents in a single swallow. He rifted politely into his closed fist, seated himself on the last vacant chair and, with a deferential nod that was almost a bow, bade a good evening not only to Hercules but to the lords Buller, Marsh and

Dunbar, three of the most powerful men in Scottish legal circles.

'Gentlemen,' Hercules said, wheezing a little, 'now that Mr Peters has joined us, perhaps we may sup. I've taken the liberty of ordering cold this evening and of serving only German wines. If anyone prefers hot meat and full-blooded Burgundy, though, just say the word. My cook is standing by with the oven blasting and the pan spitting, and my cellar door is always open.'

The decision was delivered as portentously as a jury ballot.

'Cold,' said Buller.

'Cold,' said Marsh.

'Cold will do fine,' said Dunbar.

'Grant?' Hercules asked 'You?'

All eyes turned to the callow young advocate.

'Cold, by all means, Hercules.'

'Unanimous,' said Buller.

'Unanimous,' said Marsh.

And Dunbar, with a nod, agreed.

*   *   *

Aunt and niece shared a big bed in a small room on the third floor. The maid that Lady Valerie had appointed to attend the girl had fled or had been removed by Bradley, the butler, whose authority was absolute. On his instructions a fire had been lighted and the window draped with a heavy velvet curtain to keep out not only light but air.

By the time the doctor and Lord Craigiehall arrived poor little Fleur was not the only occupant of the sick-room who was gasping and sweating. Gillon had removed his coat, waistcoat and necktie and had unfastened the ribbons of his shirt, and Madelaine had reduced herself to a stuff jacket and petticoat, a state of dishabille that his lordship found shocking.

'What's going on here?' he cried. 'You, Peters, what are you doing?'

'Lieutenant Peters is the person who sent for you,' Maddy said. 'It was his suggestion that Dr Gaythorn be summoned and that you be informed of our unfortunate . . .'

'Yes, yes, quite!' Lord Craigiehall said. 'Where is her ladyship?'

'Gone,' said Maddy. 'She so feared for her health that she left for the country as soon as Lieutenant Peters breathed the word "smallpox".'

Gaythorn moved to the bed and after a brief inspection of the little patient, who lay like a corpse beneath the sheets, swung round and angrily demanded to be told who had ordered the window closed and a fire to be lighted.

'You, sir?' he snapped. 'Is this your notion of a restorative regimen?'

'Not my notion,' said Gillon. 'It was done without my knowledge.'

'Well, man,' said Gaythorn, 'undo it at once before you suffocate the child and the rest of us with her.'

Gillon hauled the curtain from the rail and flung open the window. He tossed the curtain into a corner then, kneeling at the grate, raked the coals and poured water from the wash jug over them, releasing a hissing cloud of coarse white dust. Lord Craigiehall coughed and covered his nose with a handkerchief, while Gaythorn peeled back the bedclothes, stripped off his coat and began to fan

230

Fleur with it, flapping the garment as if he were ridding a blanket of fleas.

'Is it the smallpox?' Maddy asked.

'Of course it is,' said Gaythorn, still flapping. 'What imbecile thought to break a pustular fever by applying heat and denying oxygen? Good God! I'm surprised you haven't murdered her.'

Lord Craigiehall said, 'If you are done showering us with ash, Peters, perhaps you would be good enough to relieve Dr Gaythorn who, I do not doubt, has had a tiring day at the infirmary.'

Gillon took up his jacket and easing Gaythorn aside, commenced fanning while the doctor examined the patient. Madelaine and Lord Craigiehall looked on with more concern than embarrassment, though Fleur had leaked from bladder and bowel and her gown was soiled.

Gaythorn unfastened the neck of the gown, furled it over the girl's shoulders, down the length of her body and neatly over her feet. He held the gown out behind him. Madelaine took it from him. Gillon glanced at the judge to see what effect the sight of a naked young female might have upon him, but Craigiehall's expression showed no hint of excitement.

Fleur was small-boned, like her aunt, but she was not, Gillon thought, quite so young as she pretended to be. Her breasts were prominent, her belly and hips already shaped like a woman's and a dense growth of dark-blonde hair, matted with urine, protected her intimate parts. He felt no twinge of lust, only surprise that Gaythorn had thrown professional courtesy to the winds by exposing her to the gaze of two unmarried men.

'Look,' said Gaythorn, 'we have caught the

eruption just as it's breaking. The secondary stage is upon us. Full pulse and a dry skin indicate that she is not sufficiently plethoric to benefit from a bleeding. She will become, I believe, less turbid and more restless as the eruption progresses. I'll leave with you a glass of poppy syrup in case she becomes agitated. Rest and quiet are prime requirements. Is there a servant to sit with her?'

'I will sit with her,' Madelaine said.

'You must not risk contagion, Madelaine,' Lord Craigiehall said. 'It would not do for you to fall sick.'

'I have no fear of falling sick,' said Madelaine.

'Nor I,' said Gillon. 'If, I mean, nursing assistance is required.'

Lord Craigiehall lifted his head and stared at Gillon, his eyes flinty with suspicion. 'You?' he said. 'What are you to this girl?'

'A friend, sir, that is all,' said Gillon. 'A friend in time of need.'

'As you have proved yourself to be, John James,' said Maddy. 'I did not expect you to come in person. When we are all well again, I must find a way to repay your kindness.'

'Hmm,' said John James, under his breath, then started when Fleur, naked as a nymph, suddenly opened her eyes, tilted her flushed face towards him and cried out, 'Papa? Papa? Is that you?'

*　　　*　　　*

Moorcock, smoked hams, poached salmon and hard-boiled eggs were served on massive silver platters and washed down with chilled wine and ice-cold beer. When Buller requested gin he was presented with a bottle of best Dutch Blue and a jug of water to mix his own refreshment, which he did with relish. It was not the manners of the men or their capacity for drink that troubled Grant but, rather, their delight in picking over the bones of old scandals while approaching, more or less obliquely, the matter that really concerned them.

He was delicately paring the shell from a hard-boiled egg with the edge of his knife when Dunbar finally got around to it.

'It will be a winter in the theatre for you, young man, will it not?' Dunbar said, in a measured tone. 'I have not seen the early playbills but the bent will be towards comedy, I imagine.'

'The theatre?' said Grant. 'I rarely attend the theatre, sir, unless my wife insists upon it.'

'Or your father-in-law?' said Marsh.

Marsh was thin to the point of emaciation. He wore a bleached wig so tight-fitting that it resembled a schoolboy's cap, spoke in a quick sparrow twitter and had the habit of concluding every statement with a little snigger.

'I am unclear as to your meaning, your lordship,' Grant said. 'To the best of my knowledge my father-in-law is not an habitual playgoer.'

'Times change and men change with them,' said Dunbar.

'Do you play whist, Mr Peters?' said Buller, dabbing gin from his chin with a napkin. 'Do you frequent the Baron Hall assemblies, say?'

Grant put down the egg, half-peeled. 'No, sir, I do not play whist.'

'You appear to have little in common with Lord Craigiehall,' said Dunbar, 'family being the exception.'

'It's no secret, gentlemen, that my relations with his lordship are somewhat less than cordial.' Grant paused. 'If you are concerned about his lordship's behaviour in recent weeks and are in hope that I may be able to shed light upon it then I'm afraid you will be disappointed. I am just as much in the dark as you are.'

The judges, a little disconcerted, glanced one to the other.

Hercules said, 'Did I not warn you that Peters' directness is a mark of character and not merely an advocate's ploy? Come now, Grant, you know why you are here and what his lordships want from you.'

'I do not have Lord Craigiehall's confidence,' said Grant.

'But you do have his daughters,' said Buller.

'That's true, sir,' Grant conceded.

'And women talk—heh, heh,' said Marsh.

'My wife and her sister are just as mystified as I am by what Lord Craigiehall is up to. I mean . . .' Grant cut himself off abruptly.

'What *do* you mean?' said Hercules.

Grant picked at the egg shell on his plate for a moment before he plunged into deep waters. 'Is my father-in-law's competency under scrutiny?'

'Insofar as such charges lie within our power,' Dunbar answered, 'we are a far cry from summoning his lordship to answer them. As yet there's no substance to justify it. To besmirch the reputation of one of our great jurists on the back of mere rumours would damage the integrity of the justiciary.'

'He insulted you in open court, man,' said Buller.

'And contrary to witness evidence and over my strenuous protests,' Marsh twittered, 'he permitted that damned cattle-stealer to evade the gallows. Is that the action of a man in full command of his senses—heh?'

'That,' said Hercules, 'is a matter of law and interpretation, Charlie. I've reviewed the printed record of the trial and I believe that Craigiehall's remarks to the jury were not entirely devoid of humanity.'

'The defendant did not ask for nor deserve clemency,' Dunbar said.

'Enough, gentleman, quite enough,' Hercules put in. 'If a slip in judgement in a single trial was Craigiehall's only error then there would be no need for us to meet here tonight.'

'It's the woman, is it not?' Grant said.

'Yes,' Buller said, 'it's the woman.'

'And the gambling,' Marsh added.

'It's all very well for young reprobates fresh to the bar to seek amusement in Fortune's of a night—we have all done that in our day—but for a man in Craigiehall's position to put his integrity on the block is quite another matter,' Lord Buller said.

'Clinging on to a harlot, too—heh?'

'Mrs Young is hardly that,' Grant said. 'She's a house-guest of Sir Archibald Oliphant.'

'A harlot consorting with a harlot, if you ask me,' Marsh said. 'We all know what sort of a reputation Oliphant's wife has. If it weren't for Archie's title she'd be stalking the streets of the Cowgate with her skirts over her waist.'

'Now, now, Charlie,' said Hercules. 'You profess to be a God-fearing Christian yet here you are casting stones in all directions. Are you sure you have no sins of your own tucked away?'

'None that I care to discuss with you, Hercules,' Marsh said. 'None, certainly, that would bring dishonour to my rank.'

'So far, Lord Craigiehall has not behaved dishonourably,' said Grant.

'Oh, you're standing up for him now, are you?' Buller said.

'I am expressing an opinion, sir, an opinion based on evidence that has a firm foundation on fact,' Grant said. 'There is, to my knowledge, no regulation to prohibit a member of the justiciary playing whist or, indeed, from enjoying the companionship of a young woman. There are, as I'm sure we're all aware, much worse things going on behind closed doors. Why are you bent on destroying my father-in-law's reputation?'

'No, lad, no,' said Buller. 'You have grasped the wrong end of the stick. We are keen to defend, not destroy, Craigiehall's reputation. While we may not always see eye to eye with him in and out of the Parliament House, it is our duty to protect him from disgracing himself.'

'What,' said Grant, 'do you want me to do about it?'

'Warn him,' Dunbar said.

'Warn him?' said Grant. 'I'm the last person that Lord Craigiehall will listen to. He regards me as a blackguard who stole away his daughter. He will hardly give me the time of the day, let alone heed anything that I might say to him, especially on such a delicate subject as this. Why do you, one of you, not broach him? You are, after all, his peers and counsellors. He is more likely to listen to you than to me.'

'If not a warning, *per se*,' said Buller, 'a quiet word in his ear, perhaps?'

'I tell you,' said Grant, 'we are not on intimate terms.'

'Yet he trusts you,' said Hercules. 'If he did not trust you, he would not have sent you to attend to that private matter in Ayrshire.'

'In that matter,' said Grant, 'I failed him, as you well know.'

'So you won't wish to fail him again—heh?' said Marsh.

Grant could not hide his irritation. 'What are you afraid of, gentlemen? Why do you wish to keep this silly business within the walls of the family?'

'For the very reason that it is, at this point, a family matter,' said Hercules. 'His lordships are anxious that it remains so.'

'Aye,' said Dunbar. 'One more outburst in court, one more wild slander on another lord's competency and we will have no choice but to challenge Craigiehall in review and once that challenge is made and reported there will be no turning back for any of us, least of all for Craigiehall.'

'He's on a slippery slope,' said Marsh. 'He must be coaxed back from the brink before it's too late.'

'John James Templeton has done nothing,' said Grant, 'nothing to deserve your censure. Great God in heaven, he has lived a blameless life since the death of his wife. He does not even have a mistress.'

'He insulted the Lord Advocate,' said Buller.

'If it happens again,' said Dunbar, 'be assured I'll challenge him.'

'Challenge him?' said Grant. 'What—to a duel?'

'Possibly,' Dunbar said.

'But he's an old man,' Grant protested.

'His hand is steady enough to hold a fan of cards,' said Buller.

'And can, therefore, cock a pistol,' said Marsh.

Grant fashioned a whistling sound to signal incredulity. 'The Lord Advocate shooting at a judge on the Meadows in the cold light of dawn? Now that, sir, would be a scandal to shake the nation.'

'It will not come to that,' Hercules said, 'Not if you do what's asked of you. Think of it as a test of your powers of persuasion, your skill as an advocate.'

'Which will not be forgotten,' said Dunbar.

'And will not go unrewarded,' said Buller.

Grant sat silent for a long moment. He was well aware that these gentlemen, the great panjandrums of Scots law, could smother his career or, conversely, could raise it to illustrious heights. What he did not understand was quite how they expected him to influence his father-in-law or, even more puzzling, why they had chosen such an underhand method of drawing the noble lord back into line.

He looked up and said, 'I'll do it, gentlemen. At least I'll do what I can.'

'Good man,' said Hecules, relieved. 'Good man,' and raised a glass to toast his protégé's sagacity.

CHAPTER THIRTEEN

They clattered out of Mannering's yard through an early morning haze that, according to Charlotte, stank not of horses and wood smoke but of disease. She fastened a large cambric handkerchief over her nose and mouth and refused to remove it even to take breakfast in the inn at Kirkliston, though she nibbled bread and sipped tea beneath the lace edge and, Nicola thought, managed to sustain herself well enough in spite of the impediment.

They ate at a trestle table outside and as the haze dispersed watched the unveiling of the coast of Fife across the Forth and the high hills of Perth and Stirling, blue and distant, far to the west.

They were travelling without a maid. Molly had been left behind to look after Jeannie and ensure that Mr Peters did not suffer inconvenience in the absence of his wife.

'Heatherbank,' Grant had said, and Nicola's heart had leapt a little. 'I'll send you to Heatherbank. The air there is clean and if either of you do succumb to the fever my mother will be on hand to nurse you. Unless you would prefer to seek refuge at Craigiehall.'

'No,' Nicola had cried and Charlotte, holding up her hands, had snapped, 'Over my dead body,' which had settled the matter on the spot.

It took all morning and most of the afternoon to cover the cranky road that linked Edinburgh to Stirling. It was early evening before they arrived at the inn at King's Park and, after some argument, engaged a boy to ride the six miles to Heatherbank to deliver the letter that Grant had written to Roderick.

Nicola was thrilled by the sight of the rock, topped by an ancient castle, that soared sheer out of the plain. Here, or nearby, King David had held court and Wallace and Bruce had fought their famous battles against the English. She was less impressed by the number of low ale-houses that lined the winding streets of the town and least of all by the King's Park inn itself where the crew that manned the taps was made up of coarse, foul-mouthed soldiers who, she gathered, had been invalided out of service, lived in asylum in the castle and spent their miserable pensions on drink.

Charlotte and she sat out in what passed for a garden. There was no tea, no seed cake or fresh-baked scones, none of the comforts that the new inns of Edinburgh offered. They drank lukewarm ale and ate oatcakes and stale cheese to sustain them while they waited for Roderick to collect them. An hour passed, then another and the mountains to the north, where the Highlands began, had turned cool and sombre before the post boy returned.

Charlotte leapt to her feet. 'Did you deliver the letter to Mr Peters?'

'Aye,' said the boy, cockily. 'No reply.'

He had already been paid and having sized up the women and reckoned that no extra would be coming his way, felt no obligation to be polite.

'Wait,' said Charlotte, in a tone that not even a Stirlingshire post boy dared ignore. 'Did you put the letter into Mr Peters' hand?'

'Gave it tae the wumman at the ferm gate.'

'Was Mr Peters not at home?' said Nicola.

'Nah, just the wumman.'

'Where was Mr Peters?' said Nicola.

The boy tutted and shook his head at her ignorance. 'Takin' in the hay, o' course,' he said and, tipping his cap, led his weary horse off to the stable.

'Does Roderick intend to leave us stranded here until his precious hay is raked and stored?' Charlotte said.

'He'll come soon,' said Nicola.

But another half hour passed before a cart appeared on the dusty road that snaked across the plain and as Nicola and Charlotte watched trundled up the slope to the apron of the inn.

'Is it him?' said Nicola. 'Is it Roderick?'

'No,' said Charlotte. 'It's her?'

'Her?' Nicola said.

'My mother-in-law,' said Charlotte. 'The blessed saint Margo.'

*   *   *

The meeting of the Lords of Session in the Council House at the Parliament building had been convened to debate a ticklish point of law that occupied the councillors until well past tea time.

It was uncommonly warm in the high-ceilinged room and at one stage in the proceedings John James felt as if he might faint away. Every pore in his body was leaking sweat and only constant swabbing with his big red handkerchief kept sweat from blinding him. He barely listened to Buller's pronouncements, Marsh's gibbering, and Lord Sandiman, now in his seventieth year, spewing out Latin epigrams like a broken spigot.

241

'Craigiehall?'

'Uh?'

'Are you ailing, man? Are you sick?'

'No.'

'Then be so good as to answer Lord Sandiman's question.'

'Improbior multo quam de quo diximus ante; quando blandior haec, tanto vehementius morde.' John James could have sworn he heard Sandiman quote from Lucilius' Law of the Twelve Tables— 'She is much wickeder than he about whom we spoke before; the more she fawns the harder does she bite'—but for the life of him he was unable to fathom what relevance it had to the business in hand. He paused for a moment, then said, 'It is not so much an answer that the noble lord requires as agreement. I, for one, remain unconvinced that we have reached the point where agreement is possible, at least in the particulars.'

'What?' Buller said. 'Are you suggesting a more extensive review of sources and precedents before we proceed?'

John James had meant no such thing; he had only been playing for time.

Nonetheless, he said. 'I am, sir, I am—which is not to say that the Lord Advocate has been negligent in his preparation of the paper, only that in my opinion it requires a modicum of adjustment before we can, in conscience, approve the amendment with our signatures.'

'The point is well made,' Dunbar said, much to John James's surprise. 'I will instruct my clerks to delve deeper into original sources and, if you agree, we will return to the matter on the first Monday of the month.'

'Agreed?' Buller asked.

'Agreed. Agreed,' came the answer.

An hour later John James stood erect in a wooden tub in his bedroom clad only in his bathing shirt. He sighed luxuriously as Robertson trickled cool water from a huge earthenware jug down his back.

'Better, sir?'

'Much better,' John James said. 'For a little while this afternoon I thought I was about to expire.'

'Aye, hot it is today, sir.' Robertson tilted the jug again. 'Will I leave the soap an' the brush an' let you steep for a bit?'

'In a moment,' John James said. 'Have you laid out the frock with the round cuffs, and the short-cut waistcoat?'

'I have, sir, an' the braced breeks.' Robertson splashed water on his master's thighs. 'Are you for goin' out to sup tonight, your lordship?'

'I am. At Lady Oliphant's—though her ladyship is in the country.'

Robertson rested the jar gracefully against his hip, like a statue of Aquarius. 'An' the other lady, sir, the one with the sick bairn?'

'Ah, Robertson!' John James said, without rancour. 'Is it my health or my morals that concern you? In neither case do you have need to worry. I will stay only long enough to put that autocratic butler in his place and sample some of Sir Archie's wine. I am in Session tomorrow and need to bed early.'

'Will I have the chaise run out, your lordship?'

'No, now the air is cooling, I will be better for the walk.' He glanced round at his manservant.

243

'Tell me, Robertson, are you afraid of the contagion?'

'I'll confess, sir, I'd feel safer at Craigiehall.'

'The summer session will soon be over and we will be free to go home.'

'Aye, sir,' Robertson said. 'Will we be . . . ?'

Without warning the door fanned open and Isabella Ballentine stepped into the bedroom, a maid fluttering anxiously at her heels.

Pretty heels they were too, John James thought, incongruously, as he clapped an arm across his breast, cupped a hand between his legs, and cried, 'Isa, what the devil are *you* doing here?'

*   *   *

Mother Peters was a very large woman with a deep bosom, broad shoulders and upper arms so muscular that they strained the stitching of her dress. She had a flat nose with a curious twist to it, wide slanted cheekbones, and wore her hair cropped like a girl's. She eased the cart close to the bench and reined the horse to a halt. Several men appeared in the doorway of the inn and two stable boys cantered out of the yard for a sight of the matron of Heatherbank who jumped from the board and wrapped her arms around Charlotte as if she intended to lift her daughter-in-law and toss her into the cart like a sheaf of oats.

In a lilting voice, quite at odds with her appearance, she said, 'There now, my love, we'll soon have you an' your precious cargo safe home.'

The men—soldiers—chirped and mooed. 'Get awa' wi' ye, Margo,' one of the men shouted. 'If they pretty lassies had telt us they was your kin we'd ha'e gi'en them plenty o' cuddles.'

'Keep your dirty tongue to yoursel', MacLean,' Margo Peters called out, 'or you'll have had your last keg from me.'

'Last leg, Margo?' another man shouted. 'Nae mair leg frae you? Now there's a threat if ever was,' and everyone, including Margo, laughed.

'You, Stoner, you shiftless beggar,' Margo said, 'hoist the girls' baggage on to my cart since I'm tired out with the day at the hay.'

'In the hay, was it, Margo? In the hay wi' auld Tam again?'

'I'll "auld Tam" ye,' Margo said. 'I've worn out better men than him, in the hay and out o' it. Now, jump to it if you're wantin' this sixpence.'

Charlotte continued to cling to her mother-in-law while Stoner and MacLean shambled to the bench and lifted the bags into the cart before approaching Nicola in a manner that, while not threatening, was certainly not courteous. They were a rough pair, ill-kempt and unshaven, clad in bits and pieces of regimental uniform, including, Nicola noticed, swords and scabbards. They smelled strongly of ale and sweat and when they flanked her, grinning, she saw that neither man had a sound tooth in his head.

'You're next, Miss,' Stoner said and crouching on all fours at the gate of the cart, allowed Nicola to step on to his back then on to the bed of the cart.

There was no bench or box to sit upon, only a cushion of new-mown hay piled into a corner. More amused than embarrassed, she spread her skirts and sank down into it while Margo helped Charlotte on to the board.

Stoner bobbed to his feet, tugged his weathered cap and winked.

'Aye, Miss, you're as light as a cock's feather,' he said. 'Ye can use me as a steppin'-stane any time ye fancy.'

'Thank you, Mr Stoner,' Nicola said. 'I will bear that in mind.'

A coin changed hands, then with a 'hup' and a shake of the rein Mother Peters brought the cart round and headed down the road that would take them through the gloaming to the farm far out on the Carse.

*   *   *

'For heaven's sake, Johnny, do complete your ablutions,' Isabella said. 'If I were more suitably accoutred and did not have a palsy in the wrists I'd scrub your back as I used to do in times past.'

'When,' said John James, through his teeth, 'I was three years old.'

'Robertson, I imagine, has gone to fetch a screen,' Isabella said. 'Perhaps it's as well for you do not present a very attractive picture in wet cambric.'

'Isabella,' John James sighed, 'what are you doing in Edinbugh?'

'I came to visit you.'

'In the middle of summer with smallpox rife in the city?'

'I was concerned about you,' Isabella said.

She showed no inclination to turn away. John James was tempted to sink into the tub for modesty's sake but he recalled how his long shanks persisted in sticking up and how ungainly, not to say undignified, he looked in that position.

'Robertson,' he roared, 'haven't you found that screen yet?'

'Aye, sir. It's here.' The man servant edged through the door with a tapestry screen from the drawing-room in his arms. He dragged it to the middle of the bedroom and, with an apology to Mrs Ballentine, propped it in front of the tub. 'Your clothes, Lord Craigiehall?'

'Yes, my clothes. Of course, my clothes,' John James snapped. 'Isa, do you wish tea—or something?'

'Neither, thank you.' Isabella seated herself on a chair. 'Perhaps someone would be good enough to collect my boxes from the hall, however, and convey them to my room.'

'Your room?' John James said. 'Are you staying?'

'I did not come all the way from Salton just to watch you bathe, Johnny. Yes, I'm staying, but I promise you won't have to put up with me for long,' Isabella assured him. 'I have a deal of business to attend to in town but as soon as it is completed I will return home.'

'I thought you came to see me?'

'I did,' said Isabella. 'I'm here, am I not?'

'Why did you not give me warning?'

'In case you had another guest. Do you have another guest?'

'Hmm?' said John James. 'What is that supposed to mean?'

'I hear you have a new friend, a female friend.'

'Where, in God's name, did you pick up that piece of gossip?'

'Gossip? Is it gossip? I thought perhaps you had

247

followed my advice and had found yourself a bride.'

'Phah!' John James exclaimed. 'Women! Can one not indulge in an innocent game of whist with a female person without it leading to the altar?'

'Is it leading to the altar?'

'Of course it's not leading to the altar.'

'To the bed chamber, then?'

'Isabella,' John James said, 'there are times when I doubt that we are even vaguely related. How can you be so—so crass? Do you suppose that I would take advantage of a lady whom I have only just met?' He popped his head over the top edge of the screen. 'Where is that fellow with my clothes?'

'Are you properly dried?'

'Damn it, Isa, *yes*.'

Robertson brought in a bundle of clothing and, with another apology to Mrs Ballentine, vanished behind the screen.

Crooning a little to herself, Isabella waited for her cousin to appear, splendid if somewhat damp, from behind the tapestry.

When John James finally came into view, with Robertson still fussing with the ribbons of his shirt, she said, 'Are you calling upon her tonight?'

'What if I am?' his lordship said. 'What business . . .'

'I will accompany you,' said Isabella.

'Aren't you tired after your journey?'

'I am never too tired to look out for you, Johnny.'

'Look out for me? What do you mean?'

'Where does this woman reside?'

John James pushed Robertson away. Peering sternly down his long Templeton nose, he said, 'I

248

have a feeling that you already know not only where she resides but who she is and what colour of stockings she wears. What are you up to, Isa? I do not need your approval.'

'To do what, Johnny?' Isabella said. 'To fall in love?'

'You cannot come with me. There is sickness in the house.'

'Valerie Oliphant's house?'

'See. I was right. You *are* up to the mark.'

'Yes, my dear, but the question is—are you?'

'Am I what?'

'Up to the mark,' said Isabella.

Robertson cleared his throat and asked, tactfully, 'Will I have the chaise run out now, your lordship?'

'Perhaps you had better,' John James answered. 'And while you are about it, please show this interfering woman to her room.'

Isabella Ballentine gazed up at her cousin, undaunted.

'Are we going to sup in the house of sickness after all?' she asked.

'Aye, we are,' John James told her. 'If you are up for it.'

'Will I meet your lady love?'

'Yes, damn it, Isa, you will meet my lady love.'

'Then I am up for it,' Isabella said and, rising quickly, kissed him, like a little Judas, on the cheek.

*   *   *

'Sorry,' Gillon said. 'Can't stop. Must trot. Late for a supper engagement.' Grant's grip on his arm bit

249

like a carpenter's vice. 'Something wrong, old chap? Charlotte all right?'

'Where the deuce have you been, Gillon?' Grant said. 'We've seen nothing of you for weeks.'

'Busy,' Gillon said. 'Irons in the fire. Is Nicola well?'

He had rushed out of the tenement without due care and Grant, lurking by the wall, had snared him before he could slide away. Lucky for Grant that he hadn't been wearing his sword or his brother would be dead by now.

He wrenched at his arm again. Grant held firm.

'You've been avoiding us, have you not?' Grant said.

'Certainly not,' said Gillon. 'Fell out of favour with Nicola. Went my own way to—ah—lick my wounds.'

'Balderdash!' Grant said. 'You've been gambling.'

'True, yes, that's true. Guilty on that charge. Now, if you please, I really must be on my way.'

'Where are you going?' Grant said. 'To the New Town?'

'Well, fact is . . .'

'I'll walk with you.'

'Aren't you expected at home? Will Charlotte not . . .'

'I've sent Charlotte and Nicola away.'

'Oh!' said Gillon then, in a higher pitch, 'Oh! To Craigiehall?'

'Heatherbank.'

'Good God! That's risky!'

'Risky?' Grant said. 'What's risky about it?'

'Mother,' said Gillon.

'Mother will look after them perfectly well.'

'Is Charlotte ailing?' Gillon said.

'No, but there's smallpox in my house—the kitchen maid—and I thought it best to send the ladies to the country out of harm's way.' He released his grip on Gillon's arm. 'This urgent business, this supper that you cannot afford to miss, will it take you to Sir Archie Oliphant's house, by any chance?'

'In that direction, yes,' Gillon said.

'Then,' said Grant, 'I will walk with you.'

'If you insist,' said Gillon.

'And as we walk you will talk to me.'

'Really?' said Gillon. 'Talk about what?'

'Learned judges and pretty actresses.'

'Oh, is that all?' said Gillon, brazenly. 'What is it you wish to know?'

*   *   *

The Carse, or plain, of Stirling had once been marshland, Mother Peters explained, and the fields that covered the slopes of the Lennox hills were composed of till and peat earth and were reputed to provide the finest grazing in Scotland. It crossed Nicola's mind that Mrs Peters might be attempting to justify her son's rank by boasting about the quality of the land but she could not have cared less about till and peat earth, or the size of the Peters' holdings.

She lay peacefully on the bed of warm hay and watched the hills change from blue to inky-black, while Mother Peters, an arm about Charlotte's waist, went on and on in that country lilt of hers, mingling husbandry with history until her words became as bland and soothing as a lullaby, and

251

Nicola fell asleep.

She wakened with someone licking her face, soft little kisses from a soft wet tongue. She heard someone laugh and a man's voice, say, 'Come away now, Pup, before I take the stick to you,' and the tongue went away and she opened her eyes and saw his face there, upside-down, the dog beside him with its head cocked and tongue lolling as if she were a biscuit or a tasty bit of marrow bone.

She brushed hay from her breast and sat up.

'Are we here?' she asked, sleepily.

'Aye, Nicola,' Roderick said. 'You're here, with me, at last.'

*   *   *

Bradley, the butler, was furious, though he took some pains to hide it. With his master and mistress both out of town he had obviously expected to have the rest of the summer to bully the young footmen and bruise the tender feelings of the maids to his heart's content; in other words to abuse his position, exercise his power and generally behave like a tyrant.

Once, many years ago, Isabella had employed a house-keeper of that ilk, a tight-lipped, scowling martinet who had ruled the staff of Salton House with a rod of iron and might have ruled the mistress too if Isabella had not put her foot down. When Clarence had left for London she had insisted that the housekeeper accompany him, which was no more punishment than her husband deserved.

It did not take Isabella long to realise that the pretty little creature who had entranced her cousin

252

was in awe of the butler. However artfully Mistress Young might flutter her eye-lashes and flap her fine-boned hands she made no impression on the servant who, Isabella thought, probably regarded the house guest not only as a thundering nuisance but as seriously deficient in class.

Lord Craigiehall, of course, was another matter. However much the butler might fume in private he did not dare disobey his lordship's orders which, Isabella noted, were issued not as requests but as commands.

She might treat John James as if he were still a boy but it stirred her soul, and other less mystical regions, to watch her cousin take charge of Archie Oliphant's household as if it were his own and, within minutes of arrival, organise not only supper but also a sick-room roster and the appointment of a maid to attend to Mistress Young's needs.

After introductions had been made and the woman had gone so far as to curtsey, Isabella said, 'How is your daughter today, Mrs Young?'

'My niece: she is not at all comfortable. Now the smallpox is rising she is greatly distressed about her appearance, and very cross and restless.'

'Did Gaythorn call this morning?' John James asked.

'He did. He seemed pleased by the violence of the outbreak which he regards as a laudable sign.'

'His approach is rather modern, Madelaine, but he has much experience,' John James said. 'What treatment did he recommend?'

'He administered an emollient clyster and insisted that poor Fleur walk about the room—supported, of course—to help her release her water.'

253

'Effectively?' said John James.

'Yes,' the woman said. 'Quite effectively.'

'And you, Maddy, how are you bearing up?' John James said.

'As well as one can expect,' the woman said. 'I am pleased to see you, however, for it is lonely here and I am always glad of your company.'

She angled her head, Isabella noticed, and delivered a limpid glance out of the side of her dark eyes, a look that had her cousin wriggling like a maggot on a fish-hook. He was both proud of and flustered by the young woman's gratitude, though it had within it, Isabella thought, just the merest hint of calculation, of which, naturally, John James was quite insensible.

She could hardly blame her cousin for being taken in.

The woman was uncommonly pretty and had so thoroughly refined the art of flirtation that it did not seem like flirtation at all. If the English widow had indeed set her sights on becoming the second Lady Craigiehall she would make a formidable opponent, for she would not seem like a bargain bride, at least not to a sixty-year-old anchorite whose only diversion these past dozen years had been losing heavily at cards.

'If your niece is presently settled,' John James said, 'shall we repair to Lady Valerie's withdrawing-room and seek a little refreshment while supper is being prepared?'

'Oh, I would like that,' said Mrs Young. 'If it is agreeable to Lady . . .'

'Ballentine.' Isabella added, 'But I have no title now, Mrs Young. I am, as you are, just a plain and ordinary widow.'

254

'Oh no,' said Madelaine Young, 'you are anything but plain.'

'And, as you will soon discover, anything but ordinary,' John James said and offering an arm to each of the ladies, nodded to the footman to open the door to the drawing-room.

*   *   *

It soon became clear to Madelaine that she had the dowdy widow, as well as Archie Oliphant, to thank for bringing her to Edinburgh and raising her prospects to new and giddy heights.

Fleur had paved the way, of course. Without Fleur's musical talent and her ability to lure well-to-do gentlemen into believing that she was not much more than a child, they would surely have wound up being cared for by some music-hall clown, for sooner or later she would be forced to acknowledge that her productive years were behind her and let Fleur go, which, Madelaine knew, would not only break her heart but would put an end to her dreams of finding a man who would make her both happy and rich.

On the surface there was nothing laboured in the drawing-room conversation that filled the hour before supper. However untidy her appearance, Isabella Ballentine's wits were neat enough to balance a harmless exchange of pleasantries with a series of questions so sly and penetrating that it was all Maddy could do to deflect them. In another setting, she might have found the thrust and parry stimulating but she was limp with concern for Fleur and how Fleur's illness would affect her future.

She was relieved when Bradley announced that supper was served in the dining-room, even more relieved when, a moment later, the butler reappeared to inform Lord Craigiehall that Lieutenant Gillon Peters of the Highland Regiment was waiting below.

'Hmm!' John James was already on his feet. 'What do you wish me to do, Madelaine? Shall I send him away?'

'No,' Maddy heard herself say. 'Please have him admitted.'

'Your son-in-law's soldier brother?' Isabella put in. 'Oh, I've been longing to meet him.'

'Have you?' John James said. 'May I ask why?'

'To hear at first hand how we managed to lose the war in the Colonies.'

'Well, I doubt if Gillon Peters even knows that the war is lost,' John James said, 'or if he does, will not admit it. However . . .'

'Invite him to sup with us,' said Isabella, 'if he has not already eaten.'

'I'm quite sure he won't have eaten,' John James said. 'If you wish him to sing for his supper, Isa, so be it,' and signalled the glowering butler to escort Gillon up from the hall.

PART THREE

The Fields of Fortune

CHAPTER FOURTEEN

All the things that Nicola loved about Heatherbank, Charlotte hated. She hated having to share a cramped loft with her sister, hated the ripe smells of byre and barnyard; hated crowing cocks, bellowing cows and the all-too-cheerful shouts of milkmaids at crack of dawn; hated, too, the rough-and-tumble of the big earth-floored kitchen perpetually wreathed in steam; hated the old grey-bearded dogs that slumped on doorsteps and the cats that crouched, scowling, on the windowsills. Most of all, Charlotte hated her mother-in-law who was, in Charlotte's eyes, a paradox personified; a soft-spoken, foul-mouthed harridan whom everyone, including Roderick, adored.

Charlotte had never met anyone like Margo Peters before, nor, indeed, had Nicola. For all that they had been reared in an agricultural community they had been wrapped in the comforts of the big house of Craigiehall and only now did Nicola realise how hard life must be for her father's tenants and why Charlotte and she had never been allowed to accompany Papa and Mr Littlejohn on their rounds of inspection.

From the first hour—an early hour at that—of her first day at Heatherbank, she experienced an exhilarating sense of freedom. She was already awake when a fat-faced little butter-maid kneed open the door of the loft and with a cheery greeting, dumped a jug of water on the stand by the window. She tugged open the ragged cotton curtain that singularly failed to keep out daylight and, hands on hips, leaned over Charlotte and said, 'You'll be gettin' up for your breakfast now, Miss.'

'Breakfast?' said Charlotte blearily. 'What hour of the clock is it?'

'Past five, Miss,' the girl said.

Charlotte glowered over the edge of the sheet. 'Are you to be my maid?'

'Nah, nah, Miss. I'm awa' tae skim the cream.'

'What?' said Charlotte, nudging Nicola. 'What is she saying?'

'It's summer,' said Nicola. 'Milking is done early in summer.'

'Aye, Miss,' the girl agreed. 'An' we're late. An' Mistress Peters is no' pleased. She says you've to get up if you're wantin' your breakfast.'

'God in heaven!' Charlotte said. 'Breakfast—at five in the morning?'

*　　　*　　　*

There were no muffins, no toast, no dainty little cups of boiled milk, no jam, let alone marmalade. There was no sign of Margo or Roderick in the kitchen, only an old man in a grubby smock who knelt by the fire, frying bacon on a griddle. He had a wire fork in his hand and a plate on his knee and, spearing a rasher, slid it on to a plate and, rising, put the plate on the table in front of Charlotte and, moments later, delivered a second plate of bacon to Nicola.

'Tea, ladies?' he said.

'If you please,' said Nicola.

The tea was poured straight from the kettle into cups without saucers; tea so strong that it made

260

Nicola's tongue curl. She watched Charlotte sip—and spit.

'What is *that*?' said Charlotte.

'Gunpowder,' the old man said, and winked at Nicola.

'It tastes like gunpowder,' Charlotte said. 'Is there no tea?'

'It is tea, Missus, green tea.'

'Oh, pellets!' said Charlotte, in disgust.

'Aye, expensive pellets,' the old man said. 'Grand it is for the bowels.'

Bracing herself, Nicola drank again. She felt her eyes open wide, as if the liquid had flooded her brain with light. She lifted the bacon rasher with her fingers and nibbled fat from the rind while Charlotte observed her sister's breach of good manners with undisguised horror. A huge oaten loaf, like a cartwheel, was placed before them, and a pat of butter in a lidded dish.

'Bread, ladies?'

'Thank you, yes,' said Nicola.

She watched the old man carve the loaf.

Charlotte said, 'Where is Mrs Peters?'

'Out yonder in the byre.'

'Fetch her for me.'

'Nay, lady, she'll be far ow'er busy to be fetchit right now.'

'Do you know who I am?'

'Aye, you're Grant's wife.'

'And who, may I ask, are you?' said Charlotte.

'Grant's grandfather.'

'Oh!' Charlotte hesitated. 'Are you, indeed?'

He winked again at Nicola who, having finished the bacon, was munching bread and butter as if she had not seen food in a week.

'Aye,' he said. 'Indeed, I am.'

'What's your name, sir?' said Nicola.

'Ralston,' he said. 'Duncan Ralston.'

'You're Mrs Peters' father, are you?' said Charlotte.

'Well, so her mother telt me, anyway.'

'How old are you, Mr Ralston?' said Nicola for she had judged, rightly, that he would be proud of his years.

He put a hand behind his head and primped the fringe of white hair that hung over his collar. 'Eighty-three,' he said. 'An' still pretty as a pictur', eh?'

Nicola laughed. 'Still turning the lassies' heads at the market.'

'Aye, turnin' them awa' in disgust,' he said. 'Eat up, ladies, for I'm to guide you round the farm an' show you the best o' the walks.'

'Walks?' said Charlotte.

'Margo says you're to walk, to take the fat off.'

'Fat! What fat!' said Charlotte.

'Margo says walkin's beneficial for ladies in your condition.'

'Oh, she does, does she?' said Charlotte.

'Exercise an' quantities o' good fresh air,' said Mr Ralston, 'those are Margo's recipes for healthy babies.'

'Well, I am not here to exercise,' said Charlotte. 'I am here to rest.'

'No rest in this household,' Duncan Ralston said. 'If you're done wi' your breakfast, come an' I'll show you where to empty your pots.'

'Empty our pots?' said Charlotte. 'The maid does that, does she not?'

'Maid? What maid?' said Duncan Ralston. 'I

262

might tak' a turn at the cookin' when Margo's busy elsewhere but I'm all there is, an' I'm no maid, so you'll have to empty your own pots, or leave them for the flies to find—an' Margo won't like that.'

Charlotte pursed her lips. 'I see. We're to be treated like prisoners in the Tolbooth, are we? Well, be assured that my husband will hear of this and he will not be pleased.'

'Grant'll be pleased enough to have you safe out o' Edinburgh,' Duncan Ralston said. 'He trusts his mother to do right for you an' his child. Better a wee bit discomfort, lady, than a bout o' the pox, eh? Come along, fetch down your night-pots an' I'll show you the ash-pit.'

'The ash-pit?' said Charlotte. 'Oh, I can hardly wait!'

*   *   *

Butter and cheese, wool crop, mutton and fat cattle were the mainstays of Heatherbank's economy, the tenants tithed in hours of labour as well as kind. The contrast with Craigiehall's traditional methods—which only her father considered 'modern'—impressed Nicola and she questioned Mr Ralston closely as he toured them through the outbuildings.

Charlotte, of course, had no interest in rural affairs. She was too offended by the stink and slather of the byre to venture inside, though the blessed St Margo was seated there, on the far side of a cow, tugging away at the teats and swearing cheerily.

Mr Ralston guided them out to admire the vegetable garden.

The Carse stretched flat as far the eye could see with only the castle crag poking out of the plain in the distance. Behind the farmhouse, to the north, the river's winding loops were packed with willow and hawthorn, the air so clear that Nicola could make out individual sheep, white as daisies, high on the heathery hillside to the south, and, in splendid isolation, the steeple of the old parish church which, for a reason that not even Mr Ralston could explain, had been built not in the village but on the lip of the moor.

'Aye, it'll be fair again today,' Duncan Ralston said, with a sigh of satisfaction. 'They'll have the last o' the hay strewn and dried e'er the day's out.'

'A good hay harvest, then?' said Nicola.

Charlotte picked a few sticky white petals from her skirt. She had spoken hardly a word since they had left the kitchen and gave the distinct impression that she found everything, including Mr Ralston, decidedly offensive.

'Aye, a better crop than last year,' Mr Ralston said.

'Is that where Roderick is?' said Nicola. 'At the hay?'

'Like as not,' said Mr Ralston, and gave her a queer, quick wee glance.

After a tactful pause, Nicola said, 'Where *is* the hay field?'

'Follow the footpath past the ash-pit, lass, an' when you come in sight o' the river, you'll see it awa' on your left.'

'Is it far?'

'Nay, not much more than a quarter mile,' Duncan Ralston said. 'I'd take you there mysel' but the old shanks might not bring me back.'

'The new bull,' said Nicola, 'I'm not likely to encounter him, am I?'

'Nah, nah,' said Mr Ralston. 'He's barracked safe in his own pen. If any wee bullocks trot forward to greet you, just wave your bonnet an' they'll be more feared than nosey.'

'Charlotte,' said Nicola, 'shall we walk to the river?'

'Walk!' said Charlotte. 'Bullocks! Hah!'

'What do you wish to do?'

'I am going to my room to write to my husband,' Charlotte said and, turning on her heel, headed back to the farmhouse without a thank-you or a word of farewell.

*   *   *

The hay field was hedged but not fenced. The gate at the near corner, propped open with stones, was guarded by a lively black-and-white collie who barked in warning before she came up, sniffing and slavering, and poked her snout into Nicola's hand. The cattle that had trailed Nicola out of the willow groves broke away and galloped madly off across the field, kicking their legs and tossing their heads, before huddling at a safe distance to peer at the strange creature in the lemon yellow dress whose appearance had so intrigued them.

There were two women in the hay field, and two men. The men were armed with long-handled wooden rakes, the women with switches. The men tossed the hay and the women, following on, flicked and fluffed the swathes into long, loose ridges that, Nicola guessed, would dry quickly in the sunshine. More than half the field had been

265

shorn and gathered. It basked naked in the heat, gulls, crows and pigeons picking over it, and a mist of insects hovering above.

She breathed in the cloying scent of mown hay and, leaning on the gate with the collie panting beside her, watched Roderick stroke the scythed grasses with a motion that looked effortless, though Nicola was sure that it was not. It did not occur to her that there was anything unusual in a landowner pulling in his hay. Roderick Peters seemed no different from the man who flanked him and might, she thought, have been husband to the woman, bare-legged and weather-brown, who followed him across the field.

Swinging on the gate, she watched the haymakers reach the end of the cut and, after a pause so brief that a blink of the eye would have covered it, turn and come back towards her.

She took off her bonnet, and waved.

Roddy lifted the rake and saluted her and, losing hardly a beat, called out, 'Dinner time, Nicola. We'll talk at dinner time.'

Pleased with that promise, she waved again, then set off across the pasture towards the river and left Roddy to get on with his work.

*   *   *

John James stifled a groan when, on entering the breakfast-room, he found his cousin already there, delving into a dish of chopped eggs and chives and chatting to one of the little serving-maids who, when the master made his appearance, blushed and cowered and scuttled off back to the kitchens.

Isabella looked up and treated him to one of her

dimpled smiles.

'For a man teetering on the verge of ruin, Johnny,' she said, 'you do yourself very well. Coffee?' She poured from the long-spouted pot and pushed the cup across the table towards him.

He was already dressed for a stint in the Court of Session. Marsh, a notorious hypochondriac, had declared himself unfit and he, Craigiehall, had drawn the short straw for extra duty. There would be an amended calendar today, of that he was sure, for a number of advocates had already claimed extensions and taken their wives and children off to the country out of the sluggish heat and away from the breath of contagion.

'I am not teetering on the verge of ruin, Isa,' he said. 'I am tight but not strapped, in spite of the sums I owe you which, by the by, will be paid in full by the year's end.'

'I would have that promise in writing, signed and witnessed, if I thought it would do the least bit of good,' Isabella said. 'How much do you owe to Lady Oliphant, apart, that is, from a note of apology for appropriating her town house in which to entertain your paramour?'

'I have already written to Lady Valerie,' John James said. 'Under the circumstances, I question if she will consider my actions a breach of protocol.'

He reached for a muffin and buttered it. 'She, after all, abandoned her house guests without a qualm.'

'I liked the young man.' Isabella added pepper to her eggs and wielded her spoon vigorously. 'Is he your rival?'

'My rival! Do not be ridiculous.'

'He is certainly very personable,' said Isabella.

'If I were thirty years younger than I am, I might have a fancy for him myself.'

'He is an even bigger wastrel than his brother,' John James said. 'He does nothing, nothing for a living, except gamble. And his pension—pish, that's hardly enough to keep a cat let alone a wife.'

'I would not necessarily have a fancy for him as a husband,' said Isabella. 'I have more than enough of the wherewithal to employ him as a pet.'

'I do wish you wouldn't talk like that, Isa,' John James said. 'I don't know what's come over you of late. Besides, thirty years ago you did not have two halfpence to call your own. If grandfather hadn't dowered you . . .'

'I would not have married Clarence. Forty years, Johnny, forty years.'

'God, so it is.'

'Is Gillon Peters your rival?'

John James put down his coffee cup and paused to consider his answer.

At length, he said, 'Better my rival than my son-in-law.'

'Oh, Gillon is courting Nicola, is he?'

'He was, I have reason to believe, inclined in that direction,' John James said, 'until the redoubtable Mrs Young put in an appearance.'

'Did you persuade Valerie Oliphant to send for her?'

'No, no, no,' John James said, quickly. 'That sort of manoeuvre is beyond my powers of invention, Isa, but then, as a mere male, I'm not as devious as the members of your sex.'

'Do you consider me devious, Johnny?'

'No worse than the rest of them.'

'Valerie Oliphant is devious,' Isabella said, 'the

lovely Mrs Young even more so, I imagine. I am but an amateur in such company. Mark my words, Johnny, that pretty little widow is yours for the asking, but if I were you, I would keep a close eye on the lieutenant who, if I read the signs correctly, is fast falling in love with your actress. You may have to fight for her, you know.'

'It would not become a man in my position to fight over a woman.'

'Then you will lose her.'

'Gillon Peters is no threat to me,' John James said. 'Is he?'

Isabella scraped the last of the egg from the corners of the dish and sucked it from her little silver spoon. 'What a tangle you have fashioned for yourself, Johnny,' she said. 'In debt to at least two women, lost to your daughters, and without the spunk to fight for the woman you love.'

'I am not in love with anyone,' John James said, haughtily.

'No, and that, I think, is your trouble,' his cousin said. 'What time do you make your grand entry into the Parliament House?'

'Soon,' John James said, and shouted, 'Robertson, Robertson,' to summon his trusty man-servant to come and rescue him.

*   *   *

It was not yet eleven o'clock when dinner was served. A satirist might have applied the French word 'buffet' to the spread but to Charlotte it was nothing but an unholy mess. There were pans of lukewarm stew, heads of lettuce in watery dishes, a pot of soup, two loaves of oat bread and a massive round of cheese whose odour added a final base note to the medley of smells that greeted her when she came downstairs.

The problem was that she was hungry and could not deny that however disgusting the aroma that had drifted up to her hide-out in the loft, it had made her stomach rumble and her mouth water.

She had found paper, yellowing and rather greasy, in a drawer in the dresser in the small room that passed for a parlour and a blunt black-lead pencil in a jar. She had carried her treasures up the crooked little staircase to the loft where the bed was unmade, the floor had not been swept and her belongings, and Nicola's, were still strewn where they had thrown them last night.

She had pulled out the loft's only decent piece of furniture, a rush-bottomed chair, had perched herself upon it and, using the window ledge as a desk, had scribbled a long demented letter to Grant demanding that he come and fetch her and transport her by some means or other to a more salubrious place where she might ride at anchor until the tide of contagion receded. She knew that she would have to find a means of sealing the letter before she handed it over to be delivered to the coach office in Stirling but she was too hungry to apply herself properly to the problem.

Mr Ralston had charge of the ale—there was, it seemed, no tea—and rationed out one beaker to everyone and resolutely refused all pleas for more.

She approached the old man with a show of meekness.

'May I have some, please?'

'Aye, lass, you may.'

She watched him fill a beaker with the pale

brown liquid and, remembering her manners, thanked him before she took the beaker and drank.

The ale was weak, bitter and very refreshing.

She went to the table and surveyed the mess that, oddly, seemed just a little less unholy than it had done at first glance. She watched a young man saw off a piece of bread and lather it with gravy. He bit into it, said, 'By Gad, that's good.' He offered the titbit to Charlotte. 'Care for tae try some, Mrs Peters?'

Charlotte recoiled. 'No—ah—thank you. How do you know my name?'

'A body knows your name, Mrs Peters. It's you who'll be makin' Margo a grandmother e'er the year's out. There'll be an eighth part o' auld Mr Ralston in the bairn in your belly tae.'

Oh God, Charlotte thought, with a shudder, *he's right!*

Cutting herself a slice of bread and a slab of cheese, she took herself outside where four female farm-hands were picnicking on the grass. The moment she appeared their chatter ceased. Four pairs of eyes followed her as she looked around for a place to put herself, four pairs of eyes that seemed to look through her skirts and petticoats directly into her womb.

The soft little 'Awww' that rose from the girls was, she knew, a response to the thing inside her, Margo's grandchild, who was as yet too unformed to make his presence known save as a faint swelling beneath her clothes.

'Sit here, Mrs Peters, sit here.'

'Nah, nah, sit by me, Mrs Peters, sit by me.'

'Leave the poor woman alone,' Margo said.

'She'll sit where she likes.'

The grass was worn and weedy in the shadow of the byre. There were no benches or trestles, only two or three milking stools that looked to Charlotte's eye dangerously unsteady. She juggled the beaker, the bread and cheese and, after a moment, lowered herself gingerly to the ground by Margo Peters' side.

'Pay no attention to those daft bitches,' her mother-in-law told her. 'You'd think they never seen a cow in calf before.'

'A cow?' said Charlotte.

'Manner o' speaking, love,' Margo said. 'You'll have to get used to my rough tongue. I'm o'er long in the tooth to practise refinement. Are you happy there?' Charlotte nodded, though in fact she felt like a straw doll with her legs stuck out and nothing behind her. 'Here,' Margo Peters said. 'Lean on me,' and offered her broad back for support.

Charlotte could smell the woman, a strange odour, not sour or unwholesome. She could feel the heat from the woman's body and in spite of herself, snuggled into Margo's back and, comfortably positioned at last, fell to eating her bread and cheese.

'Are you well enough?' the woman asked. 'No sign o' fever?'

'No,' Charlotte answered. 'I'm hot, but I have no fever.'

'Why did you not go walkin' with you sister?' Margo said.

'I had a letter to write.'

'To Grant?'

'Yes.'

'You'll want it took to the post, I suppose,' Margo said.

'It isn't packeted,' Charlotte said.

'Roderick has a letter for Grant too, so they can be sealed in the same packet. Give your letter to Roddy.'

'I—well—yes, I will,' Charlotte said. 'Where is—ah—Roddy?'

'At the hay.'

'Does he not come in to dinner?'

'Not when the weather's fine,' Margo said.

Charlotte stopped chewing and glanced round.

'Is that where my sister is?' she asked. 'With Roderick?'

'Aye,' Margo answered. 'Out in the field with Roddy.'

*   *   *

The smallpox outbreak had interrupted the drift of summer term and the court as well as the town was possessed by a spirit of urgency that stopped just short of panic. Jeannie, the Peters' maid, was in the throes of secondary fever but Dr Gaythorn, who had called late last evening, was of the opinion that the pox would not blacken and turn in on the face and that the patient would soon be over the worst of it. As a precaution, he had shown Molly how to pierce the soft yellow pustules with a heated needle and draw off the foul matter with dry lint, a procedure that neither Cook nor Grant could bring themselves to watch.

Grant had dined with Hercules and later had supped in Horne's with Somerville and, in a quiet corner, had dictated a week's worth of depositions to present to session. He had been nagged all the while not by concern for Charlotte or Nicola but by the burden that Hercules had put upon him, a burden that his encounter with Gillon had lightened not one whit.

The hot weather had eased and a welcome breeze swirled through the columns as he paced the promenade in Parliament House and rehearsed a variety of introductions to the subject of his father-in-law's behaviour. He was making his tour for a second time when, to his dismay, he all but bumped into the great Lord Craigiehall who, it appeared, had slipped out of the hall to catch a breath of air and eat an apple while his clerks attempted to rearrange the quota of causes and muster the relevant documents.

Of all the breaches of custom that Craigiehall had committed—precious few, in fact—leaving the hall in robe and wig seemed to Grant the most heinous. He stopped short, blinking, and might have slunk off through the pillars if his father-in-law had not spotted him and, tossing away the apple core and wiping his hands on his robe, hailed him like a long-lost brother.

'Grant, my good fellow,' he called out. 'What news do you bring me from the nether regions?'

'Nether regions, your lordship?'

'That nether world where advocates dwell when not in court.'

The old man, Grant realised, had made a joke. He blinked again and after looking round to see who might be watching, approached.

Lord Craigiehall leaned against the stonework by the small door that led into the judges' chamber. He had the attitude of a lounger, much at ease, legs braced, hands stuffed into his pockets beneath the ornamental robe.

'You have packed your ladies out of town, so Gaythorn tells me,' he said. 'One cannot be too careful, can one? Sent them to your farm, I believe. Do both my girls a world of good. I supped with your brother last evening.'

'Gillon?'

'Aye, the soldier.'

Gathering his wits, Grant said, 'Whist?'

'In point of fact, no,' Craigiehall said. 'Not a card was cut, though I have had the pleasure of trumping young Gillon on several occassions recently. We came together on a mission of mercy at Lady Oliphant's house.'

'With her—I mean, with Mrs Young present?'

'Oh, yes.' His lordship smiled at mention of the name. 'With Mrs Young. Poor woman, her niece is languishing on a bed of sickness and she is not at all her usual self—Mrs Young, that is, not the niece. I would have them both conveyed to Craigiehall to recuperate if the girl was in a fit condition to travel which, alas, she is not—not yet, at any rate.'

'Ah!' said Grant. 'Ah!'

'Why do you frown?' his lordship said. 'Do you not approve?'

'It is not up to me to approve or disapprove,' said Grant.

'Gillon told me.'

'Told you what, sir?'

'That you do not favour my friendship with Mrs Young.' His lordship threw back his head and, clutching his wig, laughed. 'It seems that no one likes poor Maddy.'

'It's not Maddy,' Grant blurted out. 'It's you that concerns us.'

'Me? Why? I am a widower, am I not, and a free spirit?'

'Lord Dunbar does not think so.'

'Dunbar, that pompous fool!'

'Your lordship, really! Dunbar is, after all, the Lord Advocate.'

'One must respect his position, if not his opinions, I suppose?'

Several young advocates, accompanied by clerks, trotted past and bowed in the direction of his lordship who, holding on to his towering wig, responded in kind. Grant stepped closer, so close that his father-in-law drew in his legs and stood upright, like a thief braced by a member of the guard.

'It's a question of appearances, sir,' Grant said, before his nerve failed. 'Dunbar, and others, are against you; I know not why. They disapprove of your recent behaviour.'

'My behaviour?'

'They wish to protect you from gossip—or so they say.'

'To whom did they impart this information? To you?'

'Aye, your lordship, to me. They are anxious to avoid a scandal.'

'What, in God's name, leads them to believe that playing a few hands of cards with a lady will cause a scandal?'

'May I ask, sir,' Grant heard himself say, 'who introduced you to Mrs Young? Was it, by any chance, my brother?'

'I do not see the relevance of that question.'

276

'Was it, Lord Craigiehall, was it Gillon?'

'He was, I believe, at the tables that evening,' his lordship answered. 'Are you implying that your brother and Mrs Young were previously acquainted? If so, what does that have to do with me?'

'With the greatest respect, Lord Craigiehall, I am merely passing on the concerns of certain members of the fraternity.'

'The fraternity? Hah, some brotherhood!' his lordship said. 'Out with it, Peters, what are they saying about me?' Then, without awaiting an answer, he rattled on, 'Buller, I suppose, Buller, Marsh and Dunbar are behind the slanders. Are they using you as an emissary because they are afraid to face me?'

'I think, sir, that they prefer the matter to go unrecorded.'

'So they pulled you from the rack to do their dirty work, hmm?' His lordship's good humour had evaporated. 'Why? Because you are my son-in-law? Because their lordships wish to pretend that my private life is a family matter? Which, damn it all, it most certainly is.'

'I agree with you wholeheartedly, sir,' Grant said, as obsequiously as his nature would allow. 'I did not invite this queer commission. It was foisted upon me against my will.'

'At Mackenzie's suggestion, no doubt?'

'Mr Mackenzie felt that tact . . .'

'Tact!' His lordship spat out the word. 'Tact! Well, by God, Mr Peters, I'll give them tact. I'll give them something to talk about, believe me. If Dunbar thinks he can oust me from office by stirring up slanders behind my back, then

Dunbar has another think coming.' To Grant's astonishment, his father-in-law snared him by the folds of his collar and pulled him so close that he collected a little spray of infuriated spit from his lordship's lips. 'When I am in court I am Craigiehall, and I do my duty fairly and serve my King's pleasure as I have always done. But when I take off this infernal wig and these arse-scratching robes I answer to no one, not to you or my daughters, not even to my cousin, and not, most of all, not to that conniving piece of horse manure, Dunbar.'

'Your lordship?' said a trembling clerk from the doorway.

'What?' Lord Craigiehall cried. *'What is it now?'*

'We are—ah—we are assembled, sir, and—ah— are ready to begin.'

His lordship released his grip on Grant's collar and with a gesture that was not in the least apologetic, smoothed the ruffled fabric with his knuckles. His nostrils flared as he sucked in breath and in a voice that quivered like a fiddle string, said, 'And so am I, Peters. So am I,' then gathering his robes about him, he swept past the clerk of court and out of sight.

*   *   *

The canvas sack that Margo had given her was heavy. It contained not only bread and cheese but a large green-glass flagon filled with ale. By the time she reached the hayfield, Nicola, sweating and out of breath, had begun to suspect that she was too soft and well-bred ever to make a farmer's wife. She put the sack down on the grass in the

278

shade of the hedge at the far end of the field and unpacked it while the women watched her, warily.

The man, Calum, went off to make water out of sight and Roderick, kneeling, did not offer to help her as she extracted a couple of tin cups and the parcels of cheese and bread that Margo had packed with her own none-too-clean hands. Also in the sack were several thick strips of cold mutton which Nicola laid out on the striped kerchief in which they had been wrapped as if she were offering them for sale. The women, kneeling too, eyed the food but did not reach for it and even the collie, who had accompanied Nicola from the gate, lay low on the grass by Roderick's heels, panting quietly.

'Eat,' Roderick said. 'For God's sake, Marie, you are not usually one to stand on ceremony when dinner is brought out.'

'Will we not be sayin' a prayer then?' Marie asked.

'Do you wish me to say a prayer?' said Roderick.

'Nah, but I thought the lady might need a grace.'

'The lady does not need a grace, I'm sure,' said Roderick, not sternly. 'You are not going to shock Miss Templeton if you just snatch and guzzle as you usually do.' He lifted the thickest strip of mutton and tossed it to the collie who caught it deftly in midair and had it half devoured before her paws touched ground. 'Here, Cathy,' he said and, pulling the cork from the flagon, handed it to the elder of the women. 'I can see you're gasping for a suck, so go to it.'

Cathy had thick greying hair, a square jaw and large blunt-fingered hands. She grasped the flagon, tipped it up and gulped down several mouthfuls before she passed the flagon to Marie who handled it no less skilfully.

Both women were loose-dressed in Scotch-cloth skirts and cotton smocks. Their bodices were untied and they wore no stays. The clefts of their breasts were glossy with perspiration and sun-browned, but neither they nor Roderick seemed to care, and Calum, when he returned from behind the hedge, was more interested in food than women.

He picked up a strip of mutton and a slice of bread, seated himself, cross-legged, a yard or two away and began, rather fastidiously, to feed himself. He was a man about fifty, Nicola guessed, wrinkled by weather and lean as a rake-handle. She wondered if Cathy might be his wife, but he said nothing to her, or to anyone, though his silence was not sulky or forbidding.

'Will you be done by this evening?' Nicola asked.

'Yes, and glad of it,' Roderick answered. 'It's a rare season, indeed, when the rain does not come driving in just as we're sharpening our scythes, is that not so, Calum?'

'Aye.'

'We'll have the lofts full to busting this year. If the barley and the corn stand up, we need have no fear of beasts starving in the field or cows drying up this coming winter for there will be feed and bedding enough and to spare.'

'If the harvests come in good,' Marie said. 'It'll no' be a real summer wi'out a drenchin' rain tae spoil it, though.'

'What a pessimist you are,' Roderick said.

'Winters are hard, whatever the crop,' Cathy

said.

Nicola, nibbling cheese, said, 'Do your fields flood?'

The women looked up, surprised that she had addressed them directly. They glanced at Roderick before answering.

Marie said, 'The hill drains well enough, an' the Carse too.'

'But the river comes o'er an' covers the meadow,' said Cathy.

Marie said, 'Times are, all ye can see are the tops o' the willows.'

'Three late calves we lost the year afore last,' said Cathy.

'Drowned,' Marie said. 'Swept awa' afore Mr Roddy could get to them. Poor wee creatures.'

'Did you recover the carcases?' Nicola asked.

'All swole up,' Cathy answered.

'Too swole for even the dogs to eat,' Marie added.

She was a handsome young woman, Nicola realised, flaxen-haired and shapely. Her eyes were sea-green and sharp. The little exchange had given her enough confidence to ask, 'What is it we're to ca' you, since we're told you'll be here for a while?'

'Nicola will do,' Nicola said.

'Miss Nicola, it had better be,' said Roderick. 'Miss Nicola.'

'Well, Miss Nicola,' Marie said, 'would you like a taste o' our ale?' and, with a flourish, offered her the flagon.

*   *   *

John James was so involved with his own affairs

that it did not occur to him to ask what sort of business had brought his cousin to town. He strode into the drawing-room roaring for Robertson to fetch him brandy and to lay out clean linen. His cousin, who had returned to Crowell's Close only a half hour before, was already sipping tea.

Tea! John James thought, was there no escape from the constant drinking of tea, from the clicking of spoons and the measured refinements of serving, consuming and clearing the stuff away?

He tore off his coat and neck-cloth and tossed them over the back of one of the little gilt chairs that had come with the lease of the apartments. He despised the pretty little chairs which did not seem suited to accommodate one manly buttock let alone two and might, indeed, have been manufactured exclusively to support the dainty bottoms of women and girls.

'Good evening to you, Johnny,' Isabella said. 'Am I to take it from your demeanour that it was not a good day in sessions?'

'It was a perfectly fine day in sessions,' John James snarled.

'The passing of sound judgements does seem to have taxed your patience, however, to say nothing of your manners.'

'I am in no mood for one of your lectures, Isa.'

'A dish of tea will calm you, I'm sure.'

John James glowered at the tea things then, planting his hands on his hips, roared again for Robertson to bring him brandy.

The manservant appeared as if by magic and presented a tray with a glass upon it. John James plucked up the glass, downed the fiery liquid and then, not much mollified, ordered Robertson to pour him another.

'If,' Isabella said, primly, 'you intend to go courting this evening, Johnny, might I suggest that strong drink and a foul temper make ill bedfellows. Your English widow, in spite of her cosmopolitanism, may not care to be wooed by a suitor too bleached to stand up.'

The brandy lay on John James' tongue, stinging a little. He let it trickle slowly down his throat before he advanced upon his imperturbable cousin. 'Are you implying that I am not man enough to hold my liquor?'

'Oh please, please, Johnny,' Isabella said, 'do not try to prove me wrong. I have never been one to equate masculinity with an ability to consume vast quantities of strong drink. You are, by nature and habit, temperate—and I, for one, prefer you that way.'

'Strange as it may seem, it is not my purpose in life to please you, Isa,' John James said, 'nor, for that matter, to please anyone. I am sick, sick unto death, of being told that I must do this and do that, that I must behave in a certain manner and never be myself.'

'Yourself?' said Isabella. 'Which particular self would that be?'

'Beg pardon?'

'Are you Templeton of Craigiehall, an Ayrshire landowner, or the noble Lord Craigiehall, pillar of the courts of the Parliament House?'

'Well, I suppose I am both.'

'Are you a demon at the card table, a solitary widower, a distant father, or still, at heart, a boy pretending to be a man? Are you all things to all men or nothing, John James, nothing in the eyes of those who love and respect you? Tell me the truth. Do you regard yourself as a failure, or as a sham?'

He hesitated. 'What do you think I am?'

'Oh, no!' Isabella wagged her finger. '*I* know what you are, Johnny. My question is—what do *you* think you are?'

He was aware of Robertson hovering by the door, the silver tray held down by his leg, the brandy bottle in his hand. For a split second he was tempted to put the question to his man-servant who, when all was said and done, had studied him for many years in all, or most, of his sundry roles. He was still Robertson's master, though, and Robertson would tell him only that which a loyal servant thought his master wanted to hear. He could no more trust Robertson to tell him the truth than he could trust Grant Peters, or Charlotte, or Isabella, for that matter, though she had known him longer than anyone.

He grinned, crookedly, and said, 'I must take your question and reflect upon it, my dear Isabella, for it represents a problem in condescendence, in separating facts from opinions.'

'Now you are being a judge again?'

'Aye,' John James agreed. 'I am. I've seen many a man condemned by juries who could not separate one portion of truth from another. Meanwhile, as you rightly surmise, I'm going to call upon Mrs Young, though whether it is to enquire after the health of her niece or to lead the lady into the ways of wickedness, I leave you to decide.' He gave his cousin a formal bow. 'I am calmer now, and still sober, and for keeping me so, I thank you.'

'May I not accompany you to Lady Oliphant's?' Isabella said.

'Not tonight, Isa,' Lord Craigiehall told her. 'Tonight I wish to have Maddy all to myself— whichever "self" that may be.'

'Johnny,' Isabella said, 'be careful.'

'Am I ever anything else, my dear?' his lordship said, and hurried off to the bedroom to change.

CHAPTER FIFTEEN

Although Nicola had been led to believe that the course of true love did not run smooth her early days at Heatherbank seemed to give the lie to the adage. Roderick was considerate almost to a fault, a near perfect amalgam of Gillon and Grant, displaying all Gillon's charm without his garrulousness, all Grant's caution without his moods. He remained the same from day to day, even-tempered, equitable, always in control and tolerated Charlotte's constant complaints with remarkable equanimity.

It was left to Margo and her bluff old father to lick Charlotte into shape.

Charlotte, of course, did not take kindly to being licked into shape.

The maids in the buttery or raking curds in the cheese trough were often treated to sounds of discourse between the elder Mrs Peters and the younger, a weird duet of shouts and responses, spiced by an occasional oath and an ensuing cry of outrage, 'Oh! Oh! Oh! How dare you speak to me like that!' Then Charlotte would prance off to her room to scribble a furious letter to her husband, whose reluctance to respond had become another thorn in her flesh.

'Is that the post?' she said. 'Is there no letter for me? What is the man thinking of? If he does not reply within the week, I will take myself home. And damn him. And damn the risk of smallpox.'

'Nah, nah,' Mr Ralston told her. 'It's o'er soon, lass.'

'How do *you* know whether or not it's too soon? Do you have a correspondent in Edinburgh who relays you the latest news? Tell me, Mr Ralston, have you ever set foot in Edinburgh?'

'Once or twice,' Duncan Ralston said. 'As for news, I can read the paper as well as anyone an' by all reports the contagion's still rampant. If you're not willin' to take my word on it you can always plead wi' your daddy to come an' take you away?'

'That I will not do. I have cast my father from my life for good and all.'

'For all, perhaps, but not for good,' Margo told her. 'It takes more than one hand to mend a fence.'

'You may know how to mend a fence, Margo, but I doubt if you know much about the agitation that exists between Lord Craigiehall and myself.'

'I know more than you might imagine, dear,' Margo said. 'I know, for instance, that he's never forgiven you for marryin' my son. By-the-by, have you sorted out the eggs?'

'No, I have not sorted out the eggs.'

'Then you'd better get on wi' it before the cart leaves.'

'Eggs!' said Charlotte. 'What am I expected to do with eggs?'

'Clean the shells an' set them in the basket,' Duncan Ralston said, 'just like you did yesterday.'

'Is this what I have become?' Charlotte whined.

286

'A farm servant, good for nothing but wiping filth from egg-shells?'

In view of her husband's silence, however, and the absence of anything better to do, she reached for a cloth and the straw-filled collection box and began, quite carefully, to clean the eggs and bed them in a wicker basket, while old Duncan, hiding a smile, watched over her, and Margo, with a rueful snort, went off to attend the business of the farm elsewhere.

*   *   *

Nicola was too sensible to assume that farm labour required no special skills. She applied herself diligently when Roderick showed her how to skim cream, operate the butter churn—which she found very tiring—and rake the rubbery curds in the cheese trough. He even led her into the byre one evening and, much to the amusement of the other girls, persuaded his mother to let her try her hand at milking, which was much more difficult than Nicola had assumed it would be, though she had no fear of the cattle and did not, like Charlotte, recoil from the smell and the mess.

She found the menial tasks of lugging water from the pump, draping sheets on the hedge and scouring cooking pots easier to cope with and was quite proud of the watery red blisters that blossomed on her small hands. She uttered no more than a little gasp, half pain, half pleasure, when Roderick bathed them with weak vinegar and a compress of camomile flowers. She was somewhat less sanguine about the freckles that appeared on her cheeks and the flakes that peeled from the bridge of her nose and, alone in the loft by candlelight, rubbed in a greasy sweet-smelling unguent that the woman, Cathy, had slipped to her to offset the effects of too much sun upon the skin.

In spite of her nickname Margo Peters was no godless heathen. Every evening, after supper, she insisted that everyone link hands in prayer and had one of the men read a passage from the Bible. She was also much concerned with the welfare not only of her tenants but of the sick and aged of Heatherbank parish. Once every week her father would be sent out on the pony-cart to deliver butter, milk and eggs to the manse by the church high on the hill. No beggar or pedlar was ever turned away from the farmhouse door and Margo would always spare time to chat with them while they devoured a bowl of soup or a dish of stew so that the sixpence or shilling she pressed into their hand would seem more like hospitality than charity.

The cows did not respect the ordinances of a Scottish Sabbath and went on converting grass into milk willy-nilly. Margo had devised a rota that permitted one third of her workers to don their best clothes on Sunday morning and attend service in the parish church while the rest stayed home to see to the necessary chores.

As the third Sunday in the month approached a feeling of anticipation crept over the Peters household.

'What'll you wear, Nicola?' Margo asked. 'Have you a fine gown, not too heavy, an' a dandy bonnet? It'll be dry, Daddy says, so we'll walk to the kirk without fear o' gettin' our feet wet. Are your shoes well-shod, though, for the path up the hill is steep an' stony.'

'I have half-heels,' said Nicola, 'that will do, I think.'

'I will wear black,' said Charlotte. 'I always wear black on Sundays.'

'It's a bit warm for black,' said Margo. 'God knows, though, I'm stuck with an old brown thing in Padua serge that makes me sweat like a piggie.'

'Och, I'll just be wearin' my cloak o' purple velvet an' all my medals, as usual,' Duncan Ralston said, puffing on his clay pipe. 'What about you, Roddy; the scarlet cape an' the blue satin breeks?'

'Medals?' said Charlotte, sitting up a little. 'Do you have medals?'

'One medal for ploughin' the straightest furrow at the Thornhill fair,' Margo said. 'An' that was given him back in the year o' the short corn. Don't pay any heed to his blathers, Charlotte. He's playin' the fool again.'

'Satin breeks would suit you, Roderick,' Nicola said. 'Sky blue, perhaps?'

'Prussian,' Roddy said. 'I wouldn't want to be dubbed a showman.'

'In satin breeks,' said Mr Ralston, 'you'd be showman enough, m'lad.'

And everyone, except Charlotte, laughed.

*   *   *

The pony-cart was rolled out early. With Duncan Ralston at the reins and Charlotte beside him, it set off a good half hour before the others. It was still dry, but the crippling heat had diminished, a gusty wind bowled streaky cloud across the tops of the mountains and, Mr Ralston said, the weather was on the change.

Weather hardly seemed to matter to Margo. She gathered her little flock about her in the yard and made sure that every child had a hand to hold on to and a lump of peppermint candy to sustain them on the journey.

Cathy and Marie were both in the party, each with a child by her side.

'Where are their husbands?' Nicola whispered.

'Cathy's husband is a Hebrew,' Roderick told her. 'He worships with others of his faith in Stirling and otherwise he keeps himself to himself.'

'And Marie?'

'She has no husband.'

'What of the children? Are they Cathy's?'

'The girl is,' Roderick said. 'A latecomer, the youngest of six.'

'And the boy, the little boy?'

'He belongs to Marie.'

'Where is the boy's father?'

Roderick answered with a shrug that was not quite nonchalant, then scooping a watch from his pocket, consulted it. 'Make haste, Mother,' he said, 'or we'll be late and Mr Devlin will chastise you from the pulpit.'

'He wouldn't dare,' Margo Peters said.

The stay-at-home servants waved as the big woman led her little troop out of the yard and on to the track that ran straight between hedges and ancient dry-stone walls, walls, Roderick informed Nicola, that may once have marked the route of the Roman legions as they marched north to fight the Pictish tribes. She waited for him to go on at length, as Gillon would have done, but Roderick was content to let that fragment of history stand.

He wore stout top-boots, polished to a high shine, a plain double-breasted coat and, to Nicola's disappointment, long breeches of cloth, not satin.

She felt conspicuous in her Edinburgh finery. The women around her were dressed in clean, patched garments decorated with ribbons and cheap bits of lace and even Margo, though her bonnet was as large as a corn-sheaf, had settled for a cloak that was more like a shawl than anything, a worked muslin jacket and a washed-out dark green sash.

There was no order in the ranks once the plain had been left behind and one of the smaller children, already leg-weary, had to be carried up the last steep mile. When Nicola, glancing round, offered to drop back to help, Roderick said, sharply, 'No, that would not be wise,' and she saw Marie, the little dark-haired boy draped against her shoulder, signal that all was well and felt, rather than saw, Roderick nod.

Close to the crest of the hill she glimpsed through the trees the whitewashed cottages of the village and found Charlotte and Mr Ralston seated on a bench outside the mill-house that backed on to the stream. They were drinking small beer and chatting to Mr Thomson, the miller, and his wife. To Nicola's surprise, Charlotte was laughing in an animated fashion and, when she caught sight of her sister, waved, then, accompanied by Mr Ralston, rose and followed the little procession up the last few hundred yards to the church.

It stood hard and solid against all the winds that blew, its stout, blunt-edged steeple rearing against the sky with nothing but heather behind it. There were sheep-droppings on the path, rabbits in the graveyard, and a kestrel hovering high overhead, as if the church had sprung out of the bracken and heather, like one of the stones that the ancients had worshipped. Nicola felt the power of the old religions close about her, the root of the love of an invisible God, for the little rural church had an enduring quality that the decaying pile of St Giles had sacrificed to grandeur and her home church in Ayrshire had lost to pettiness, bickering and division.

She filed through the doorway and followed Margo to the pews on the left of the aisle. The Peters had no box, unlike the heritor of the parish whose special place was raised eight or ten feet and faced across the line of the altar to the pulpit. Sir Ranald McIver was not in residence, apparently, and the box was empty, save for three women, his wife and her sisters, who floated like ghosts in the strong light from the window behind them. There was no gallery. Servants and children were penned in raked tiers split by a broad passage in which the smallest children could stretch their legs or crawl about when the solemn weight of words became too much for them.

Mr Devlin was, as his name suggested, an Irishman, a fugitive from Ulster, a tall, plump, fresh-faced man in his fifties with a manner neither arrogant nor assertive. He addressed the congregation in the same familiar tone as he addressed his prayers to the Lord, as if God had somehow come among them, slipping in, modest and unnoticed, before the elders closed the doors.

During prayers Margo sighed from time to time and murmured under her breath, 'Aye, sir, aye. Amen. Amen.' Roderick, shoulder to shoulder with his mother, knee to knee with Nicola, bowed his head and prayed with eyes tight shut. Nicola wondered what he prayed for so fervently, for it seemed that Roderick Peters had already been blessed with everything that he might need to make him happy. She too squeezed her eyes tight shut, though, and sent her small, selfish message upward in the hope that God, in His infinite mercy, might grant her wish and bring her not peace but love.

*   *   *

The facility provided for the minister and elders was quite inadequate to deal with the needs of the multitude. As soon as the service was over and the doors opened there was a general scatter in the direction of the dry-stone walls that enclosed the graveyard, the gentlemen heading in one direction, the ladies and small children in the other to relieve themselves in the tall fronds of bracken that fringed the moor. When modesty had been restored, folk congregated outside the church to exchange greetings and gossip or, with dinner on their minds, to look about for carts and traps or brace themselves for the long walk home.

Margo was in no hurry to set off. She conversed at length with the minister, the elders and sundry villagers and even to the heritor's three wispy women who paused to acknowledge her before they climbed into their carriage.

There was no sign of Mr Ralston, Charlotte or the children, but Marie remained, loitering on the fringe of the crowd, and watching Roderick who, it appeared, was almost as popular as his mother.

293

Half a dozen lassies of various ages ringed him, chattering away, while he, not at all displeased at being the centre of attention, smiled and nodded and answered each of the questions put to him, questions, Nicola suspected, that may well concern her.

She considered going forward to introduce herself, then thought better of it. Stepping back, she almost bumped into Marie. 'Come on, Miss Nicola,' the woman said. 'I'll take you down to the mill where the others are. Roddy'll find you there when he's had enough o' bein' worshipped.'

'Is it always like this?' Nicola said.

'Always—an' sometimes worse.'

'They are all spinsters, I take it?' Nicola said.

'Aye, desperate for to find a man,' Marie said, 'though some o' them are past it an' others o'er young to know what they would be doin' with a man even if they found one. Mr Peters is not for them, an' never will be.'

'Is Mr Peters not interested in finding a wife?'

'None o' us—none o' them are good enough.'

'I would not have thought that Mr Peters was a snob,' said Nicola.

'It's not him who'll choose his wife,' Marie said. 'His mammy has first an' final say—an' Margo is not easy pleased.'

'Has Roderick no say at all in the matter?'

'Precious little,' Marie said.

They left the scattered crowd and walked down the steep track that followed the line of the stream. The mill tower was visible above the pines and the plash of the wheel, low after the dry spell, rose pleasantly into the air. The pony, not yet hitched to the cart, grazed on the lush weeds on the verge of

294

the mill-race. Children gathered about the mill-house steps eating barley cakes and drinking milk. Duncan Ralston, Charlotte and Cathy were enjoying a glass of ale and a crack with Mr Thomson who was, to judge by appearances, a jolly sort of fellow and fond of company.

The little dark-haired boy was seated on Duncan Ralston's lap, a barley cake clutched in his fist.

'What is your son's name?' Nicola said.

'Iain,' Marie told her.

'Is he called after his father?'

'He is called after no one but himself,' Marie said.

Nicola had sense enough not to ask the question that would surely cause offence and that might bring an answer that she did not wish to hear.

She said, 'He is a fine, sturdy wee boy.'

'He is, he is,' Marie agreed and, rather abruptly, abandoned Nicola to go in search of drink.

* * *

Feathery clouds had thickened on the mountains. A rumble of thunder drifted over the Carse on a tide of wind that shook the trees and hedgerows and made stragglers quicken their pace to reach shelter before rain came sweeping in. The pony-cart, laden with children and women, Margo among them, had trundled past some twenty minutes ago but Nicola could still see it, isolated on the broad expanse of the plain, and beyond it, livid in the gathering gloom of late afternoon, the farmhouse and its outbuildings and the tiny bald patch of the hay-field, shorn, it seemed, not a day too soon.

Alone on the long stretch, she walked arm-in-arm with Roderick at no great rate. Avoiding the subject of Marie's son and the father she would not name, they talked of sermons, dreary Sundays and the promise of life hereafter.

'I have always loved the way this world wags,' Roderick said, 'with hills and valleys, lochs and streams, rivers, trees and grass—and the sky, that ever-changing sky. Only a generous God could have made such things and given us such gifts to live under and among.'

'In your view this then is Eden?' said Nicola.

'Aye, I suppose it is.'

'An Eden without an asp?'

'No, there are vipers everywhere, even here,' Roderick said. 'You just have to be careful not to tread on them.'

'How does one do that?' said Nicola. 'By prayer and fasting?'

'By vigilance,' said Roderick. 'Vigilance, and guilt.'

'Guilt?'

'By allowing yourself to experience shame.'

'Shame!' said Nicola. 'How odd! Do you mean guilt as in "once bitten, twice shy", or do you mean the shame that eats away the soul?'

'Deep waters, Nicola, deep waters,' Roderick said.

'I'm not afraid of deep waters. Have you no answer to give me?'

'None that would satisfy you, I fear.'

'Your brother has no shame.'

'Grant, do you mean?' said Roderick.

'Gillon: I doubt if he has ever experienced a

moment's shame, or the least twinge of guilt, in his whole life.'

'I would not be so sure of that, nor so hasty to condemn poor Gillon.'

'I do not condemn him,' Nicola said. 'In fact, I rather envy him.'

'Now you do surprise me.'

'He leads such a blameless life—inside his head.'

'Possibly, but what of his heart?' said Roderick.

'I am not at all sure that he has a heart.'

'There,' said Roderick, 'you are quite wrong. What of Grant, however? Do you not envy Grant? He plots his courses with such care that he rarely ever puts a foot wrong. There's small chance of Grant ever treading on a viper, except to crush it before it bites.'

'You think highly of your brothers, do you not?'

'I do, though I am not blind to their faults.'

'What,' said Nicola, 'do they think of you?'

'Grant thinks me—well, noble. And Gillon thinks I'm a fool.'

'It is Gillon who's the fool then,' said Nicola.

'I thank you for the compliment,' Roderick said. 'I'm not at all noble, though, not in thought or deed. I've done many things I'm ashamed of.'

Nicola paused. 'What, for instance?'

He laughed. 'No, no, Nicola. I am not being caught out by your trickery. The time is not ripe for confessions. If you wish to unravel my secrets you must be patient, very patient indeed.'

'Are your secrets worth unravelling, Mr Peters?'

'Are yours, Miss Templeton?'

A few spots of rain tumbled out of the sky and, closer now, thunder growled. Roderick took her hand and broke into a run. She skipped beside him, holding up her skirts.

Rain splashed upon her brow and pocked the dusty surface of the track. The cart was no longer visible. Farmhouse and outbuildings were veiled, the air restless now and cold. She clung to Roddy's hand and ran until she was out of breath, then, in the corner of the track where it turned towards the farmhouse, she could run no further and stopped. Roderick stopped too. He pulled her to him and before she could catch her breath, he threw off his hat and kissed her, his mouth wet against her lips, his hair wet against her cheek. He kissed her without haste, with a strange detached sort of passion that she found unnerving.

'There,' he said, releasing her. 'Now we both have a secret.'

'A secret to share,' said Nicola. 'Yes,' and, taking his arm, accompanied him sedately into the yard where, in the doorway of the byre, Margo Peters waited anxiously for her son to return to her, unscathed.

*   *   *

'If I had married Gillon,' Charlotte said, 'I would not be in this predicament.'

'Married Gillon?' Nicola said. 'You can't stand the sight of Gillon.'

'Gillon would not have abandoned me. He is a gentleman.'

'Grant is a gentleman,' Nicola said. 'Grant is also your husband.'

'By default,' said Charlotte. 'Only by default.'

'What nonsense!' Nicola said, raising her head

298

from the pillow. 'How much ale did you consume this afternoon? It seems to have addled your brain.'

'If I had been fortunate enough to meet Gillon first . . .'

'Oh, stop,' Nicola interrupted. 'If you had met Gillon Peters first you would have sent him off with a flea in his ear. When did this passion for our soldier laddie come over you, Charlotte?'

'Gillon wouldn't have sent me to suffer in this place.'

'Come now, you can hardly blame Grant for sending us out of town. As I recall, you insisted upon it.'

'I want to go home.'

'If you are so unhappy here, Papa will take you to . . .'

'Home to Edinburgh. Why does Grant not write?'

'Because he's engaged in court business, earning fees while he can.'

'Gillon, I mean,' said Charlotte.

'What, do you tell me you wrote to Gillon too?'

'No, but he must know where I am and how I am suffering.'

'You are not suffering, Charlotte. We are perfectly comfortable here.'

'You are, perhaps,' Charlotte retorted. 'You and your farmer lover.'

'Lover!' Nicola sat up, shedding bedclothes in all directions. 'If you're implying that Roderick Peters and I have—have engaged in impropriety . . .'

'It's only a matter of time,' Charlotte said. 'Any fool can see that he desires you and that you are so enraptured by him that you will do anything he asks of you. It's but a short step from scouring pots and skimming milk to lifting your skirts and throwing yourself down in the muck.'

'How dare you say such a thing?'

'I dare say it because it's the truth. I have heard the girls talk.'

'The girls?' said Nicola. 'The farm hands, do you mean? And what do the farm hands say, tell me that if you will? What do the girls say about me?'

'It's what they say about Roderick,' said Charlotte. 'They say he has a passionate nature, and will take his pleasure wherever he can. They say that the only reason he has not married is because his mother turns a blind eye to his indiscretions and will not let him wed a woman who does not have a dowry.'

'So,' Nicola paused, 'because I have no dowry, he cannot marry me?'

'Has he talked of marriage?'

'Of course he hasn't talked of marriage.'

'He is not wooing you, Nicola,' Charlotte said. 'He is seducing you.'

'Did Grant seduce you?'

'What? No, of course not. That was—that was love.'

'A love that has already flown from the window, it seems,' said Nicola.

'How cruel of you, Nicola! I fell in love with Grant.'

'Do you love him still?'

Charlotte did not answer at once, then, snuffling and tearful, she said, 'I want to go home. I hate it here. I want him to fetch me and take me home. I want my husband. That's all I want—my husband.'

Nicola sighed. Reaching out, she fished the sheet and blankets from the floor and draped them over her sister. 'There, there,' she said. 'Summer will soon be over. Grant will come for you, for both of us. He will be just as anxious as you are to have you home again.'

'Do you think so?' Charlotte said. 'Do you think he still loves me?'

'Yes,' said Nicola, soothingly. 'I'm sure of it,' though she was less sure now of Roderick and why he had kissed her that afternoon in the rain.

CHAPTER SIXTEEN

It did not occur to John James that he might miss his cousin after she had gone back to Salton House. Before her departure she had extracted a promise that he would write regularly and when the courts closed for summer recess he would call in on his way back to Craigiehall to deliver a report in person on the progress of his 'romance' with the lovely Madelaine Young. He was by no means averse to enlisting his cousin's aid in pursuit of his objective and wished that she had tarried longer so that she, like a good general, might direct the focus of his advance on the citadel of marriage day by day, if not, indeed, hour by hour.

Fight, Isabella had told him—though not in so many words—fight for the woman you love. And he had set off determined to do just that. The truth was, though, that he did not know how to fight, how to court a widow thirty years his junior who was a cuckoo in the nest of another man, Oliphant,

301

and had for a friend and confidante a sly young lieutenant with a reputation for being a heartbreaker and a mountebank.

Night after night, there he was, Gillon Peters, seated by Fleur Cadell's bed, mopping her brow or feeding her sips of Peruvian tea. Once, to John James's horror, he had even caught the fellow washing the girl's feet, a chore that by any standard of decency should have been left to a chamber maid. And when the girl's condition had improved enough for her to sit up and take notice of the world it was Gillon Peters who reassured her that her tender skin had not been pitted and that, within a week or two, she would be as right as rain.

It was all too apparent that Madelaine was impressed by the lieutenant's devotion to her niece and that he had made progress where he, John James Templeton, for all his courtesy, had failed. Try as he might, he could not tempt Maddy to leave Broughton Square to sup with him in a candlelit corner in Horne's or partner him at whist in Fortune's. She was, said Maddy, afraid of the contagion. To appease her apprehension and demonstrate concern for her niece, therefore, he contrived a plan. He set down his intentions in a letter to Isabella but, thanks to muddy roads, failed to receive her reply before, dressed in lordly style and steeled in his resolve, he clattered through the drizzle to invite Madelaine and her niece to accompany him to Craigiehall as soon as the court recessed.

Bradley admitted him to the hall. Relieved of his greatcoat, hat and gloves, John James headed directly for the staircase and would have been half way to the second landing if the butler had not called out, 'Sir, sir, your lordship, this way, if you please. Mrs Young awaits you in the library.'

'The library? Is Lieutenant Peters with her?'

'Lieutenant Peters is with Miss Fleur, your lordship,' Bradley told him. 'I have been instructed to show you to the library.'

'By all means,' John James said, 'show me to the library.'

The first thing he saw when Bradley pushed open the door was Madelaine outlined against the light from the window which, grey drizzle notwithstanding, seemed to add lustre to her appearance. She wore a long apron over an open robe, a large hat tilted back from her brow and shoes—new shoes?—with full Italian heels that added inches to her height. She looked, John James thought, not so much regal as rapacious. For an instant he was almost overwhelmed by fear, a fear so subtly mingled with admiration that he could do no more than stammer out her name.

'Ma—Madelaine!'

'Ah, there you are, Craigiehall,' said a voice from the shadows. 'Maddy assured me that you would turn up in time for supper.'

'He comes every evening without fail,' Madelaine said. 'He has been very kind and attentive, Archie, and unswervingly loyal to my poor niece.'

'Good for him,' Sir Archie Oliphant said. 'If you can't trust a judge of the double robe to stand in for you, who can you trust?'

Sir Archie had been hidden behind the door and, it appeared, had been reading to Madelaine from a sheaf of manuscript. It took John James no more than a half second to realise that a fourth

303

party had entered his relationship with Mrs Young and that from now on he would have to contend with yet another rival in his claim for her attentions.

'Fingal?' he said.

'Aye,' Sir Archie cried. 'Fingal has returned.'

'Complete at last?' John James asked.

'Almost so,' Sir Archie told him. 'A touch here, a dab there, a readjustment of inflexion to suit the vocal range of my fair stranger.'

'I take it, then, that you are back from London?' John James said.

'From London? No, from Ireland, from the emerald island itself, sir, where I have tramped the rocks where bold Cuchullin roved and splashed through all the bogs where Fingal and his lover roamed.'

'In the footsteps of Ossian, in other words?' John James suggested.

'Ossian, that myth, that charlatan. No, no, Craigiehall, I've eschewed the bye-ways that James MacPherson followed to cobble up his mock epic in Ossian's name. I have delved into sources unknown to Ossian or, rather, to the unscrupulous MacPherson. I have uncovered the real poetry, the *vox populi* of that heroic age and, dare I say it, have rendered it in verse the like of which has not been heard since the Bard of Avon tossed away his quill.'

Oh, John James thought, he's full of this latest damned verse-play and more obsessive and self-aggrandising than ever. Of all the dilettantes in a city crammed with dilettantes Sir Archie Oliphant was by far the worst.

He glanced at Maddy whose raised eyebrow

spoke volumes.

She, he guessed, was already bored with the pretentious gentleman and his hackneyed verse, with the price she would have to pay for the Italian heels and all the other benefits that her patron had bestowed upon her. She looked so beautiful, so stoical, that John James was tempted to throw his career to the winds and sweep her into his arms and carry her off to the nearest anvil.

'Would you care to hear a few stanzas?' Sir Archie said, eagerly.

'What?' John James was startled out of his fantasy. 'No—I mean, yes. I'd be flattered to receive such a treat, old fellow, but I confess I'll be more receptive after supper. I've eaten nothing since breakfast and an empty stomach is often linked to an empty head, do you not think?'

'Supper?' Sir Archie said. 'Why, yes, of course. Forgive my lapse. I have been gone so long a while that I had quite forgotten that you had become dependent upon my hospitality. Come, we will summon the young man from his vigil in the sick-room and break bread together, then you shall hear what I have made of the dolorous tale of Fingal and his beautiful lover, Nu-ala.'

Still clutching the manuscript Sir Archie hauled open the door of the library and called to Bradley to rouse the cook and kitchen-maids, while Maddy laid a hand on John James's sleeve and whispered in his ear, 'I know, my love, I know,' which, John James supposed, was some small consolation for the long and dreary night that lay ahead.

*　　　*　　　*

305

'So,' Hercules said, 'the bold Sir Archie has returned at last, has he?'

'Full of wind and literature,' Grant said. 'According to my brother, the woman and the girl are being whisked off to Kingsley for the rest of the summer to assist Archie in rehearsing his latest masterpiece.'

'Is the girl recovered?'

'She is, or soon will be, fit to travel,' said Grant.

'And your patient at home?'

'Jeannie is not so far advanced along the road to recovery.'

'Will she be marked?' said Hercules.

'Gaythorn says not.'

'What else does Gaythorn have to say—about Lord Craigiehall, for instance?' Hercules said.

'He tells me little,' Grant said. 'He's a medical man and you know how jealously they protect their confidences.'

Hercules chuckled and slipped another oyster down his throat.

They were taking a casual supper in Mouser's tavern. Now that the hot weather had given way to cool rain Hercules had been coaxed out of his mansion to observe the progress of his cases at first hand. He had, it seemed, no fear of catching smallpox and scoffed at the idea that a virus would choose to inhabit a body as unhealthy as his.

'This play of Oliphant's,' he said, 'has it but a cast of one?'

'No, no, players from London will be hastening north in the autumn to enhance the performance.'

'A private performance?'

'By invitation only.'

'Oh, my! What would I not give for a ticket to

that debacle?' Hercules said, wheezing with laughter at the prospect. 'I assume there will be no public showing?'

'There never is,' said Grant. 'I am no ardent play-goer, Hercules, but I gather from reports that all of Archie's masterworks have been butchered by the critical *cognoscenti* after which he retires to lick his wounds for a year or thereabouts before beginning another assault upon immortality.'

'These little shows of his must cost a pretty penny.'

'I am sure they do,' Grant said, 'but Oliphant does not lack for cash. His banking interests probably earn more in a month than most of us see in a year. At the least of it Oliphant's reappearance has saved my father-in-law from making too much of a fool of himself.'

'I have heard that he goes about the courts wearing the glazed look of a cock pheasant in the May month,' Hercules said. 'Is he in love with this actress or merely stunned by her physical charms?'

'The distinction is too fine to measure,' Grant said.

'Has he bedded her yet?'

'No.'

'Are you sure?'

'As sure as I can be. My brother has been in and out of Oliphant's house for most of the month but even he cannot be sure. Lady Valerie has some sort of mischief afoot and might have trumped Craigiehall by now if the pox had not sent her chasing off to Kingsley.'

'Does the mischief concern the sale of de Morville's coalfield?'

'There's no indication that the Oliphants are

even aware of de Morville's existence. Have you heard anything to the contrary?'

'Nary a word,' said Hercules. 'The deeds have been completed and approved and I have received my fee. But the identity of the purchaser remains a mystery.'

'There is no sign of change at the Ayrshire pit,' said Grant.

'Who told you that?'

'Hugh Littlejohn, Craigiehall's overseer. He and I have struck up a friendship of sorts and correspond quite regularly.'

'You sly dog,' Hercules said. 'You're still after the estate, aren't you?'

'It's my entitlement, Hercules, or, rather, my wife's entitlement.'

'Is that why you married her, because of her "entitlement"?'

'I'd have married Charlotte if she had come without a ha'penny to her name,' Grant said.

'You hypocrite!' said Hercules, jovially. 'Your Mama—for whom, as you know, I have nothing but respect—your Mama would not have allowed it. Is Craigiehall's estate to be her reward?'

'Unlike Buller, or Marsh or any of the other great lords of Session, I have not one acre of ground to call my own.'

'True,' said Hercules. 'You did not trade your birthright for mere pottage, however. You traded it for entry into a noble profession. By all the signs, you will go far in the law.'

'Not without land,' Grant said.

A waiter brought to the table two plates of beefsteak glazed with egg yolk, and a side dish of boiled onions. Hercules tucked his napkin into his collar and reached eagerly for his supper. He speared an onion and sprinkled it with salt and, filling his glass as he spoke, said, 'Come, Grant, out with it. There are no secrets between us.'

'I do not wish to see Craigiehall brought down.'

'The man, do you mean, or the estate?'

'Both,' Grant said. 'I do not wish to see my father-in-law end his career in ignominy, nor do I wish to see his lands thrown away on some scheming harlot from London.'

'On that,' said Hercules, 'we are agreed. May I eat my beef now, please?'

'By all means,' said Grant, magnanimously. 'Eat away.'

'When,' said Hercules, 'will you fetch Charlotte back to the fold?'

'As soon as it is safe to do so.'

'Do you miss her?'

'I do.' With a forkful of meat half way to his mouth, Grant paused, then said again, more forcefully, 'By God, Hercules, I really do.'

*   *   *

Summer rains were misery for Charlotte. Her shoes were ruined, her skirts soiled and her intimate garments long overdue for laundering. And still the rain came down, mizzling and mild, day after day. She worked in a state of sullen boredom at the small jobs that Margo gave her to do and only ventured out of doors when necessity demanded it.

The old man did his best to entertain her with tales of the Jacobite rebellions and the battles he had witnessed, though he had not borne arms and had not favoured the Bonnie Prince. He spoke too of Margo's husband who had died young, dropping behind the plough in the last furrow of the last field with his wrist still snared in the traces and how the horse had plodded home, dragging the plough and the body behind it. Margo had shed not a tear for half a year until one Sunday in November on the way to church she had crumpled in a heap and had wept and wailed and ripped her breast and had had to be carried back to the house and a doctor summoned. She had lain for weeks mute and sick in the bed she had shared with her husband until Roderick, a half grown boy, had spoken to her calmly and without sentiment, and soon after Margo had got out of bed, put on her dress and had gone out to tend the cattle wintered in the byre.

The following spring the young lawyer, Hercules Mackenzie, had arrived from Edinburgh crippled with an inflammation of the lungs. Margo had nursed him as she would have nursed a sickly calf and had brought him back to life and had thus gained a patron for her middle son.

Margo had left early that morning in the pony-trap to deliver cheese to the inn at Kings Park and, Charlotte thought, to drink and argue with the rough-tongued, ill-mannered old soldiers whose company she found so congenial. Charlotte was toasting her shins by the fire and shelling peas into a bowl, while Duncan, an expert with thread and needle, was replacing broken buttons on a favourite old coat, when the trap came into the yard and, a moment or two later, Margo entered the kitchen.

'By God, dear, you're early home,' Duncan said.

'I'm wet through,' Margo said, shivering. 'Soaked to the bone.'

Her skirts were black with rain and her boots squelched when she stooped to unloose them. Her hair was lank and straggling and she smelled, Charlotte thought, uncharitably, like an old sheep. Duncan brought a towel and, kneeling before his daughter, helped her off with her stockings.

'You shouldn't have gone out in this weather, darlin',' he said. 'They could've waited another day or two for their cheese. Are you chilled?'

'I'll be fine when I warm up,' said Margo. 'God, what's happenin' to me, Daddy, when I can't stand up to a sprinkle o' summer rain?'

'Aye, lass,' Duncan said. 'It's age, an' it happens to all o' us.'

'Age!' said Margo. 'Pish! I'm not old, not as old as you, anyway.'

'What's that?' Charlotte said. 'On the table; the packet?'

'Oh, aye,' said Margo. 'It's post.'

'For me?' said Charlotte, shrilly. 'A letter for me?'

Dumping the bowl on the hearth, she leapt up and snatched the brown-paper packet from the table. 'Grant, it's from Grant. For me, from Grant!'

She found a knife, hacked open the packet and revealed not one but two covering envelopes, both sealed and stamped. She tossed Grant's letter to Roderick on to the table with the spoiled wrapping, tore open her letter and scanned the pages quickly.

Shaking the paper triumphantly over her head, she cried, 'He's coming. He's coming to take us

311

home as soon as the courts close next week!' and ran out into the yard to share the news with her sister.

*   *   *

It would, Nicola thought, have been demeaning to be found tumbling in the hay like the couple in one of the naughty prints that Charlotte and she had happened to catch sight of in the window of Mr Higgins' bookshop on the corner of the Fleshmarket. Charlotte had squeaked and feigned horror but had not, Nicola recalled, hurried on, not before she had studied the print in detail and, flushed and puffing, had declared it an affront to decency and had insisted on entering the shadowy little shop to tell the proprietor what she thought of him, while poking about to see what other filthy prints he might have on display.

The gossip that Charlotte had blown her way had made her wary of Roderick's intentions, though not quite wary enough to deny herself the pleasure of allowing him to kiss her now and then when no one was watching.

She loved the touch of his lips, the pressure of his hand on the small of her back, the gentle growling sigh he emitted when she drew back to breathe. He asked no more of her than that, though once, in the buttery, he had turned her round and held her against him, her back to his front, and had kissed not her mouth but her neck, and even through her skirts she had felt the satisfying solidity of his thighs while he supported her.

Roderick and she were not locked in an

embrace that afternoon. They were merely toying with the kissing game behind the timber posts that supported the hay loft. Hens clucked on the earthen floor, pecking at damp straw, and the larger of the two roosters, Auld Cockie, strutted arrogantly about, his bright beady eye on the scout for something to eat, or mount. When Charlotte burst into the barn the hens scattered in all directions and Cockie, shedding his dignity, flew up and down again, squawking loudly, and then, rain or no rain, shot off into the yard.

Smoothing her skirts and combing hay from her hair, Nicola stepped from behind the timber post and, forcing a taut little smile, said, 'Charlotte! How nice to see you.'

'Who's that hiding there? Oh, need I ask?' Charlotte said as Roderick, not at all shame faced, showed himself. 'What are you doing with my sister.'

'Ratting,' said Roderick.

'Ratting?'

'Plugging the holes in the floor where the rats nest.'

'Feeeh!' said Charlotte. 'Well, I have news, good news, and it comes, I think, not a moment too soon.' She held out the letter. 'Grant is coming to fetch us as soon as the courts close.'

'Is Jeannie well again?' Nicola said.

'Well enough, it seems, to be returned to her family in Pennicuik to recover her strength.'

'Has the contagion in the city burned itself out?' Roderick asked.

'If Grant considers it safe for us to return to Edinburgh,' Charlotte said, 'I do not intend to argue the point. I've had more than enough of

313

country matters. Edinburgh.' Charlotte raised her eyes to heaven. 'Think of it, Nicola: our own beds to sleep in. Molly to bring us breakfast. Oh, how I long to have cobbles under my feet and dear old St Giles peering over my shoulder.'

'Edinburgh in August is dead,' said Nicola.

'How do you know?' said Charlotte. 'You've never been in Edinburgh in August. Papa always took us home to Craigiehall.'

'For good reason.' Nicola adopted a belligerent stance, feet spread and hands on hips, like a Newhaven fishwife. 'I'm not going.'

'What, then, will you do?' said Charlotte.

'Stay here,' Nicola said. 'I've been invited to spend the rest of the summer here at Heatherbank.'

Charlotte rounded on Roderick. 'You scoundrel. Stealing away my sister when I need her to look after me in the last weeks of my condition.'

'Last weeks?' said Nicola. 'You're not due to drop until Christmas.'

'Drop!' said Charlotte. 'Drop! Is that the language of a lady? Besides, you will have no chaperone.'

'Mrs Peters will be my chaperone,' Nicola interrupted.

Charlotte flapped her hands distractedly. 'I'm at a loss to understand you, Nicola. Are you intent on becoming a gypsy, sleeping wherever your head comes to rest and scraping your food from a pot?'

'Do not be ridiculous, Charlotte. I'll return to Edinburgh to assist you in the final weeks of your term. Until then I prefer to remain in the country.'

'Has this farmer fellow here so turned your head that you will discard your obligations to your family?'

'This "farmer fellow", as you call him, is your brother-in-law.'

'And what of Gillon?' said Charlotte. 'I thought you cared for Gillon?'

'Gillon, it seems, no longer cares for me,' said Nicola, 'We have seen nothing of him for weeks. Besides, I do not care for Gillon as much as you do.'

'May I remind you,' Charlotte said, her cheeks scarlet, 'that I'm a happily married woman, not a silly little girl without prospects scrambling to find a husband.'

'Do think I'm so desperate for a husband that I'd throw myself away on a penniless soldier?' Nicola said.

'Better a penniless soldier than a penniless farmer,' said Charlotte.

'To the best of my knowledge, Nicola has no intention of throwing herself away on anyone,' Roderick put in. 'She has been invited to spend the autumn here and if there's no other call on her time I see no reason why she should not do as she wishes.'

'Oh, yes,' said Charlotte. 'Let her do as she wishes, but after you have ruined her reputation do not depend on me taking her back.'

'Ruined my reputation?' said Nicola. 'What reputation? I may be Lord Craigiehall's daughter but no one really gives a fig about me.'

'There,' Roderick said, 'you are wrong. You may be a perfectly fine wife to my brother, Charlotte, but here you are nothing but an impediment or, to put it another way, an infernal nuisance. It's high time you went back to Edinburgh where your virtues are more appreciated. Now, tell me, was there a letter for me in the mail packet?'

Charlotte opened her mouth, gaped for a moment, then nodded.

'Where is it?' Roderick said.

'In the house. On the table.'

'Thank you,' Roderick said and with a curt nod and a brusque little bow strode hastily out of the barn.

CHAPTER SEVENTEEN

Lord Craigiehall was not the first judge to be granted a night's lodging in the city guardhouse, nor Madelaine Young the first fair lady. Many years ago the illustrious Lord Buller had awakened in the Burghers' room, one of the guardhouse's four apartments, with no memory as to how he had got from the Union Club to the building by the Tolbooth; and it was not uncommon for Lord Conway's daughter, Barbara, and her maid to finish off an evening of wild carousal as guests of the town guard; a youthful advocate and a wilful girl were one thing, however, a sixty-year-old judge of the double robe quite another.

The guards, amused, had tossed coins to decide whether or not his lordship, whom they recognised, and the lady, whom they did not, should be caged together like turtle-doves, or if it would provide more entertainment to throw the pair into the common hall and let them sleep it off among the night's catch of thieves, whores and habitual drunkards.

Common sense, not decency, won out in the end, however, and when John James opened his eyes at around half past six o'clock in the a.m., the first thing he saw was Madelaine, specifically Madelaine's head, cradled in the crook of his arm. The arm itself had lost all feeling, a loss more than compensated for by the feeling in his temples which throbbed and pounded monstrously with the slightest movement of his eyeballs, and the sensation in his bladder which was like to that of a broth pot simmering close to the boil.

His first coherent thought, if one could call it that, was that he had been smitten by a paroxym of the brain, akin to that which had carried off his father, and that he was now in the infirmary— which did not, of course, explain why Maddy was clasped in his arms or why the bed that held them was nothing but an old straw mattress that reeked of vomit.

He struggled to apply logic to the situation but the effort proved too much for him. Instead he contented himself for a moment by admiring the woman's features, beautiful and serene, as she slept her angel sleep.

Then, suddenly, he sat upright.

Maddy slipped from him and all but rolled from the mattress to the floor which was no more than inches away; a stone-flagged floor, stained here and there with nasty substances, in an oblong room without windows and no furniture save a rusty bucket placed close to an iron-studded door. There were, thank God, no other occupants of the cell, for cell it surely was, and crawling carefully over his lady-love, John James just managed to reach the bucket before his bladder exploded.

He relieved himself in a kneeling position for his head was not steady enough to allow him to stand. He let out a sigh and then a groan and, glancing round, saw to his dismay that Madelaine's eyes were open and that she was watching his every move.

'Good morning, my darling,' she said, rather hoarsely. 'May I ask where we are and why you have brought me here?'

Crouching, John James fumbled with his flies. His stockings were looped round his ankles. The knees of his breeches and the elbows of his coat were caked with mud. He groped a hand to his head and found that his both his hat and his wig had disappeared, exposing his thin grey hair.

'I take it,' Madelaine raised herself, gingerly, 'that we are not in your apartments?'

'We are, I believe, in the city guardhouse,' John James said.

'In prison?' said Madelaine, without alarm. 'Will we be hanged for being sweet together? Is love-making a capital offence in Edinburgh?'

'Love-making?'

'Do you not remember?'

'No, I—no, not much.'

Madelaine rose cautiously from the mattress. She was, he judged, in no better a state than he was, though her head, it seemed, was clearer and her memory unimpaired. She put out a slender arm and he, hobbling over the flagstones on his knees, took it and steadied her.

She was fearfully dishevelled, her petticoats torn, her skirts stained, her stockings, too, wrinkled around her ankles. She had also lost her hat and hairpiece and her dark hair hung in frantic little curls across her brow. She fashioned a smile, though, placed an arm about his shoulder and kissed the top of his head.

'What a man, you are, Lord Craigiehall,' she murmured. 'More man than I have ever had before,' then, detaching herself, lifted up her skirts and headed for the bucket while John James, like a true-blue gentleman, buried his face in the mattress and covered his ears with his hands.

*   *   *

It was but a step from Graddan's Court to the long, low ugly building planted in the middle of the High Street. Grant had been on the point of leaving for Stirling when a grinning captain of the guard, complete with braided coat, cocked hat and sabre, appeared at the door to inform him that his father-in-law and a lady unknown were presently in custody in the guardhouse and that Lord Craigiehall would be most grateful if Mr Peters would pop down without delay to assist in his release.

'Captain Struthers, is it not?' said Grant, calmly.

'It is, sir, it is.'

'What is Lord Craigiehall's crime, Captain Struthers?'

'No crime, Mr Peters, sir, no felony to speak of. Stumbled on by the second watch, drunk and incapable in the company of a woman on the slope of the Castle Hill. Recognised by the lantern-bearer who deemed it wise to bring his lordship in for his own protection, and to preserve public order.'

'Was he obstreperous?'

'Quiet as a lamb, sir, just a-layin' there asleep on top o' the lady.'

Grant cleared his throat. 'Is the—ah—the lady known to you?'

'No, Mr Peters, sir, not one o' our naughty girls, too well turned out for one thing. She was just sensible enough to stagger along to the guardhouse supported by my arm. His lordship, I'm sorry to say, was too far gone in his cups to be roused and had to be carried in on a board.'

'Will my father-in-law be mounted on the wooden horse and dragged through the Old Town as an example to others?' said Grant, not seriously.

The captain, a cheerful soul, laughed. 'Nay, Mr Peters, that punishment has gone clean out o' favour in our enlightened age—more's the pity.'

'More's the pity, indeed,' Grant said.

'Will you come down now, Mr Peters, sir?'

'I suppose I had better,' said Grant.

*   *   *

The door of the slate-roofed building opened directly on to the street. It was not uncommon for idlers to gather in the vicinity to jeer at the poor loons who reeled, blinking, into the daylight after a night on the guardhouse floor.

Sometimes a distraught father or mother would be lying in wait to grab an errant son and cuff him about the head before leading him off home for more punishment, or a tear-stained wife would be hanging about the doorway to redeem a husband whose surly scowl marked him as incorrigible. And, more often than not, a paid-by-the-piece correspondent for the *Courant* or the *Mercury*

320

would be lurking in a nearby close, ready to pounce on any little tit-bit of gossip that might earn him a shilling or two.

Unfortunately, the correspondent that shiny August morning was a fellow by the name of Jack Cattenach, who published under the pen-name of 'Cyclops'.

His knowledge of the higher reaches of society enabled him to identify not only Lord Craigiehall but also his somewhat bedraggled companion, the actress Madelaine Young, as, escorted by the advocate, Grant Peters, they stepped into the morning light. In the doorway, waving farewell, was a certain grizzled Highlander who was fond of a tipple and, being seldom in funds, was usually willing to trade information for a pint of whisky which, Mr Cattenach reckoned, was a reasonable price to pay for a scandal in the making.

It did not take Mr Cattenach long to learn that Lord Craigiehall been celebrating the close of another court session by supping *à deux* at Fortune's with the pretty little actress. Egged on by his partner, it seemed, his lordship had thrown caution to the winds and a great deal of brandy over his throat while losing several large-stake rubbers in rapid succession. Quite how the couple had found their way from the card table to the grass on the side of Castle Hill, though, not even the inquisitive 'Cyclops' had been able to discover, but what had taken place there he could very well imagine.

The Old Town was bustling. The courts had closed the previous forenoon and those judges, advocates, writers and clerks who had not slipped away early were heading out to their country

321

residences or, the lesser among them, casting about for clients on the autumn Circuits. Not a hackney was to be had and even at that early hour all the sedans were occupied.

'Did you not bring my carriage?' his lordship croaked.

'I had no time,' said Grant. 'I came without delay. It isn't far to walk.'

'Far enough, far enough,' his lordship said. 'I have no particular desire to be seen in public in this sorry condition.'

Grant was tempted to tell the old fool that he should have thought of that last night but he felt a degree of sympathy for his father-in-law who was clearly suffering not only the ravages of drink but also of conscience. His lordship was gracious enough to allow the woman to take his arm, however, and after a few tottering steps managed to straighten his shoulders, lift his head and glower at the little crowd as if they, not he, were the spectacle.

'You, sir,' the woman said, 'are Mr Grant Peters, are you not?'

'I am,' said Grant, curtly.

'I am Madelaine Young.'

'I had assumed as much,' Grant said.

In spite of the fact that she looked as if she had been dragged through the Cowgate by the heels, she was, he realised, just as petite and pretty as Gillon had claimed. For a fleeting second he found himself staring into her dark, slightly bloodshot eyes with something other than disgust. In his bachelor days, he had admired many pretty women, and one or two famous beauties, but none, not one, could hold a candle to the English actress

322

when it came to character, by which he meant, he supposed, allure.

'We drank too much,' the woman said, with a lift of the shoulders. 'I am to blame for that, I fear. I have been confined indoors without amusement for so long that my excitement at being released quite robbed me of prudence.'

'How is your niece?' said Grant.

'Ah, Gillon told you of our misfortune, did he?'

'Yes. By-the-by, where is Gillon?'

'He sat with my niece last evening. He will have gone home by now.'

Grant nodded and turned his attention to his father-in-law. 'You have caught me at an inconvenient time, your lordship. I was just about to leave for Stirling to collect your daughters from my brother's farm.'

'Really!' his lordship said.

'However, my house is but a step away. If you wish you may rest and refresh yourself there and I will send Molly to Crowell's Close to alert your manservant and have him bring down your carriage.'

'No,' his lordship said. 'If you are up for it, my dear Madelaine, we will put on our bravest faces and walk the rest of the way to my building.'

'By all means, John James,' Madelaine said. 'I am quite ready for my breakfast. The air has revived me.'

'Oliphant will be anxious to have you back,' his lordship said. 'I will send you home in my carriage.'

'After breakfast?'

'Aye, after breakfast.'

She cuddled close to him, petite and exquisite even in her raddled state, and, craning her neck, whispered into his lordly ear, whispered something that made the old boy wince and brought a faint rush of blood to his ashen cheeks.

He closed his eyes and shook his head, 'No, Madelaine, no. My cousin is expecting me this evening. I must set out no later than ten.'

'Then there is time, ample time, to fashion our fond *adieus*.' She cast a glance at Grant to make sure that he was listening. 'I meant every word of what I said this morning, John James. It was no lie, no idle flattery.'

'Be that as it may,' his lordship said, gruffly, 'I cannot.'

'Cannot?' said Madelaine.

'Tarry,' his lordship said.

'Are you not free to tarry,' Madelaine said, 'even for a little while? It will be an age until we are together again, an age interminable, for, as you know, Archie will have me reciting verse in the great hall at Kingsley until the leaves turn brown and the sun grows cold. Can you not come to Kingsley?'

'I have much to do—too much to do—at Craigiehall.'

'Then we must part,' said Madelaine, 'with no more than a kiss and a good breakfast to warm me through the autumn months?'

'So it would seem,' his lordship said, just a little too brusquely.

Then, after shaking Grant's hand and thanking him for his assistance, he went on up the slope of the Lawn Market with the amorous English beauty glued to his arm, while Grant, at the door of Graddan's Court, watched them, wondering.

324

*   *   *

Gillon was seated on the top step of the house in the New Town with Fleur, well wrapped up in a velvet cloak, by his side. He was feeding her little pieces of biscuit as if she were a parrot brought out from her cage.

It was a bright mild morning with a breeze from the west that, Gillon thought, would surely bring more rain before evening. He would not have been seated on the step below the front door if Bradley had been at home. But Bradley had gone off with Sir Archie, leaving a footman in charge of the household, a footman who was far too timid to order Lieutenant Peters to stop behaving like a vagrant and come indoors.

The unearthing of Fingal, that sad god-like warrior who had united Scotland to Ireland far back in the murk of pre-history, apparently meant more to Sir Archie Oliphant than wife, family, friends or plain good manners. Last evening he had received a letter from an antiquarian in Morven that had so excited him that he had packed his travelling bag, dragged Bradley from his cubby and, with airy instructions to Gillon to look after the ladies, had been on the road north before dawn broke over Arthur's Seat.

Gillon did not object to being given the run of a spacious town house, of course. He accepted it as no more than a just reward for the hours he had spent tending the invalid, Fleur. Indeed he had grown quite fond of the odd little creature and had learned a great deal from her about Madelaine and their life in London, information that the girl would not have revealed if she had not been so

325

light in the head, and so trusting of him.

He broke off another piece of sweet biscuit.

'Open wide.' Obediently Fleur opened her mouth. He placed the biscuit on her tongue and said, 'Chew before you swallow.'

'Yes, Gillon.'

She chewed and swallowed.

She was, he thought, almost well enough to travel. Yesterday afternoon, when Gaythorn had dropped by, she had played a short piece on the piano to entertain the doctor who had applauded both her performance and her recovery. But although she was Sir Archie's protégée, his 'discovery', the master had not emerged from the library to hear her play and, later, at tea, had expressed irritation at being distracted from his poetic labours by 'that tinkling noise'. He had punished Maddy for her thoughtlessness by taking her off to the library to read aloud the latest adornments to his epic and had left her precious little time to dress and arrange her hair before Craigiehall had arrived to carry her off to supper at Fortune's.

'Are we waiting for Auntie to come home?'

'No,' Gillon said. 'We are just enjoying the sunshine.'

'She did not come to bed last night,' Fleur said. 'Was she with you?'

'What?' said Gillon. 'No, she was not with me.'

'She was with Lord Craigiehall, was she not?'

'Indeed, she was—playing cards.'

'Were you not playing cards, also?'

'I was not invited,' Gillon said. 'Besides, I sat with you until quite late, if you recall, and then—then I went home.'

'Did you come so early this morning because I am sick again?'

'I came early this morning because Sir Archibald asked me to.'

'Has Sir Archibald gone to be with Lady Valerie?' Fleur said.

'He has gone on a jaunt—a trip to visit an acquaintance in the Highlands.'

'Is that far away?'

'Far enough, and very remote,' said Gillon. 'The roads are bad in most parts and he will be gone for at least a week.'

'Then I will be well and he will take us to visit with Lady Valerie.'

'To his country house at Kingsley, yes.'

'Is there a piano in his house in Kingsley?'

'I imagine there will be,' Gillon said.

'Have you not been there?'

'No.'

'Will you not come with us to this house in Kingsley?'

'No,' Gillon said. 'I have things I must do in Edinburgh?'

'What things?' said Fleur. 'What do you do, Gillon?'

The truth was that he had no occupation other than gambling. If he read the signs correctly the task for which Lady Valerie had employed him would soon be completed and he would no longer be made welcome in the Oliphants' house. He had been well enough paid for the shady labour of bringing Craigiehall and Maddy together and, paradoxically, for keeping them apart. Nursing Fleur had been an unforeseen burden. He did not resent the extra duty, though, for it had kept him close to Maddy. With Sir Archie gone and Lady Valerie unlikely to return soon he might yet extend that tormenting pleasure until Sir Archie whisked Maddy away to Kingsley or his lordship plucked up sufficient courage to defy convention and carry her off to Craigiehall.

'You have not answered me, Gillon?' Fleur said. 'What is it that you do?'

'What do you think I do, Fleur?'

'I think that you do nothing, like Mr Billington.'

'Your Mama's friend?'

'My friend, also.'

'Well,' said Gillon, 'I do not have as much money as Mr Billington.'

'If you did, Auntie would not have gone to play cards with his lordship,' Fleur said. 'She would have stayed to play cards with you.'

'I see,' said Gillon. 'Aunt Madelaine only plays cards with wealthy gentlemen, does she?'

'It is not cards, not just cards.'

Gillon was well aware of the games that Madelaine played with wealthy gentlemen but to hear it confirmed by this pathetic girl galled him. However he might pretend otherwise, he was more than half in love with Maddy and knew that he would lose her soon.

He stared bleakly along the street towards the Broughton Park.

It was now in the region of ten o'clock. Madelaine had been gone all night which indicated that she had probably achieved her, and Lady Valerie's, objective by coupling with or at least compromising the learned judge and that it would only be a matter of time before Craigiehall was brought to book for his indiscretion and, by some means or another, made to pay for it.

'Look,' said Fleur, 'I see a carriage.'

Turning his head, Gillon watched the vehicle clatter into the Square and draw up at the carriage-step before them. There was no boy to open the door, only a driver who, it seemed, did not consider his passenger worthy of attention and remained where he was on the board.

Gillon rose, stepped to the pavement, pulled open the door of the carriage, and caught Madelaine as she fell, almost, into his arms.

She was mussed and roughened, hatless too, but jolly enough.

'Madelaine,' Gillon said, still holding her, 'where have you been?'

'I have been—oh, a prisoner of the guard,' she said. 'If you must know, I spent the night in a cell with our John James.'

'In a cell?'

'In the guardhouse, yes.'

'So,' said Gillon, softly, 'nothing happened?'

'Ah, but it did,' said Maddy. 'Indeed, it did.'

'What?' said Gillon. 'Tell me.'

She reached up and ruffled his hair. 'I will tell you all, my dearest, but first I must bathe. Fleur! There you are, out and about at last!' And detaching herself from the soldier, she took her niece by the hand and, prattling nineteen to the dozen, led her up into the Oliphants' house, leaving Gillon to trail disconsolately after them.

*   *   *

Nicola was in the niche at the rear of the dairy working the crank of the butter churn when

Charlotte tracked her down. The milk had become thick and sloppy and quite soon she would extract the bung at the bottom of the churn and run off a little of the thin buttermilk, as Roddy had taught her to do. She was sweating in a most unladylike manner and switched the crank handle from hand to hand to protect her palms and ease the strain on her forearms.

'Look at you,' Charlotte said. 'You have become his slave.'

'Nonsense!' said Nicola. 'Look at *you*, though, caped and shod as if the coach were on the doorstep. Has Roderick not told you a dozen times that Grant will not arrive in Stirling much before nightfall?'

'He may come early.'

'He will not come early,' said Nicola. 'No amount of wishing will bring him here before dark and you cannot possibly leave for Edinburgh before tomorrow forenoon. Of course, Grant may decide to stay on for a day or two to spend time with his family.'

'I am his family.'

'You are his wife,' said Nicola. 'His family is another matter.'

Charlotte caught her sister's arm. 'What is this man to you?'

'Roderick?' Nicola stopped cranking. 'He is more attentive to me than any other man I've ever met.'

'Just how many men have you met?' said Charlotte.

'Is it my fault that Papa would not allow us to meet young men unless he thought they could be of use to him?' Nicola said. 'Has it not occurred to

330

you, Charlotte, that Roderick has no interest in Craigiehall, that he simply likes me?'

'Oh, you are worse than Papa, sometimes,' said Charlotte. 'I wish you to come back to Edinburgh to look after me.'

'You'll have Grant to look after you, and Molly too. I'll return to Graddan's Court in ample time to comfort you through the last weeks. Are you ailing again?'

'What? No,' said Charlotte. 'I'm as well as can be expected.'

'If you become unwell, I promise I'll return to Edinburgh immediately. Meanwhile, I'm enjoying myself pretending to be a country girl. And if I am being groomed to be the wife of a farmer, what harm is there in that?'

'What harm! What harm!' Charlotte rolled her eyes in despair. 'You are Lord Craigiehall's daughter. Washing clothes, fetching water and emptying slops is not what you were bred for, Nicola. Whatever transpires with Papa and Craigiehall, Grant will see to it that you are looked after.'

'I do not want to be looked after. I want to look after myself.'

'That is not how it is done.'

'How is it done; tell me?'

'You must find a husband.'

'Without a dowry, an income, or prospects?' said Nicola.

'Better a ragged farmer than no man at all, is that it?' said Charlotte.

'Roderick is your brother-in-law; how can you slander him so?'

'You do not want to look after yourself at all.

You want Roderick Peters to look after you. Well, hell mend you, Nicola, hell mend you,' Charlotte snapped and, angered at not having things her own way, stalked off into the yard and left Nicola alone with the butter churn.

CHAPTER EIGHTEEN

They spent the afternoon in Broughton park, strolling a little then resting on the grass on a blanket that Gillon had fished from a chest in one of the attic rooms. They did not return to the house for tea but Gillon walked to Prince's Street, near the theatre, to fetch from a stall there three baked apples and a pocketful of sugared almonds. They ate the honey-coated apples with much hilarity, licking away the stickiness, wiping their faces with Gillon's big handkerchief, engaged in the kind of horse play that Fleur found amusing, though snooty ladies passing with their maids sniffed in disapproval at the unseemly display.

Maddy told him all about her adventure with John James, how the mighty Lord of Sessions had lost his senses as well as his cash by staring deep into her eyes while she plied him with fine brandy, glass after glass, and how it had taken all her wiles to lure him from the gaming table and out into the night air before he collapsed; how he had fallen on her, pinning her to ground, behind the wall that topped the slope on the side of the Castle Hill, and how relieved she'd been when the watch turned up to rescue her not from his lordship's wickedness but from imminent suffocation.

Liberated from Craigiehall and Oliphant, she was no longer obliged to act out a role and could be, for once, her natural self. She had no need to court Gillon's good opinion for they were kindred spirits. He might laugh and mock the stuffy jurist but he of all people knew that a long trick demanded concentration and more than a little suffering and that she had sold her dignity dearly. Besides, he was just as cynical as she was and would not be deceived by mere flirtation or gulled into believing that she loved him.

Later that evening, as soon as supper was over, Madelaine dismissed the servants. Fleur was already nodding at the table for a glass of watered wine on top of all the fresh air she had enjoyed that day had almost sent her to sleep.

The girl did not protest when Gillon scooped her up and carried her upstairs in his arms. He laid her down upon the bed and took off her shoes. She sang to herself, a French rhyme, and when he kissed her on the brow she draped a sleepy arm about his neck and brought him down and kissed him on the lips then, purring like a kitten, obligingly closed her eyes.

He left them alone, Maddy and Fleur, and went out on to the landing at the top of the stairs. He felt strangely at ease in the vast rambling mansion, not at all like an intruder. He took a candle-holder from the window shelf and lit the candle with his flint before he padded down to the half-landing above the long corridor that led to the drawing-room.

The shadows that the candlelight cast upon the walls led him on. He opened a door and found himself in a dressing-room and went through it

333

into a bed chamber. The bed had been stripped to the mattress, the curtains pulled down for washing. He did not know whose bedroom it was; not Archie's and not Valerie's. There were no tables, no chairs, no clothes or trinkets and when he brushed his hand across the top of the mattress a little trail of dust followed his fingers. He returned to the half-landing, put the candle-holder down upon the stair and settled himself, his back to the newel post that supported the handrail.

One leg stretched out, the other drawn up in a minstrel pose, he waited for Madelaine to come to him. He knew that she would come as surely as he had known that the Indian scout would come out of the grove of pines that hid the river and that he would not hesitate to kill the Indian, ripping his throat with a knife or driving a sword up into his belly, sudden and swift, before conscience could take hold.

At length he heard the door above him open and close.

He looked up.

She wore no cap or stockings, only a muslin night dress, without bodice or petticoat, a flimsy thing that wisped and wafted in the up-draught from the hall until she gathered it into her lap and, drawn by the candlelight, came down the steep stairs to join him.

He remained where he was, seated on the floor.

'Is she asleep?' he asked.

'Fast asleep,' Madelaine answered.

She stood above him, bare-foot and bare-legged, legs spread. She placed one foot, arched and graceful like that of a dancer, against his thigh, her toes small with pale, trimmed nails. The heel, browned a little where her shoe had rubbed, pressed into him. After a moment, he caught her ankle and took her foot away. He could see the shape of her now, curves and hollows lit by candlelight, her feet planted on either side of him, her slender thighs aligned with his face.

She uttered no sound, save a little 'shish' of breath, when he ran his hands under the garment and spreading her with his thumbs, kissed her through the muslin, his mouth slithering against the flesh beneath the cloth; then one hand was behind her cupping her thigh, the other busy between her legs, until, with a yielding sigh, she sank against him and he rose and lifted her, her legs locked about his hips, and carried her clumsily into the darkened room, and closed the door behind him.

*   *   *

The pole stuck out over the pony's ears and jiggled a little on the rutted track. The circle of light from the dangling lantern wobbled and waned but the beast was used to travelling in the dark and, finding its own pace, ignored the slap of the rein and the nip of the switch on its rump and drew the cart on at not much more than a walking pace.

Seated by his brother's side on the board, Grant laughed and said, 'I see this is one mare that you haven't managed to train.'

'No, nor never will,' said Roddy. 'She'd rather have a flayed backside than a broken fetlock, which shows sense, I suppose. At least she won't trot us into the ditch like old Harriet used to do. Do you remember old Harriet?'

'Only too well,' Grant said. 'I still have the bruises.'

'Well, she did it just once too often,' Roddy said. 'She almost killed Grandpa during one dash for the feed-bag and Mama sold her off for dog meat.'

'She was old, though.'

'Aye,' Roddy agreed. 'She was old.'

'When did this happen?'

'Oh, three or four winters ago.'

'You didn't tell me,' Grant said.

'I don't tell you everything, you know,' said Roddy.

'You always were a secretive beggar,' Grant said. 'If anything, I do believe you've got worse with the advance of years.'

'I take it you're referring to my relationship with Nicola?'

'Obliquely, yes,' said Grant. 'How are you coping with my lovely sister-in-law or, more to the point, perhaps, how is she coping with you?'

'She copes well enough.'

'Which means, I imagine, that she adores you?' Grant said.

'She's a willing worker, that I will say, not spoiled.'

'Unlike Charlotte, do you mean?'

'Well, yes, but it comes as no surprise to either of us that Charlotte did not take kindly to farm manners. She will throw herself into your arms, Grant, and appreciate you all the more for her month among the primitives.'

'Will she appreciate what I have to tell her about her father's behaviour and that he spent a night in the cells of the city guardhouse?'

'This actress obviously led him from the path of

336

righteousness. What is her motive?'

'Marriage would seem to be the answer but I'm not entirely sure that is the case. The involvement of Valerie Oliphant in all this is rather puzzling.'

'I do not know these people,' said Roddy.

'Of course not. Why would you? They are as far removed from your reality, or mine, as the earth is from the moon. I have a suspicion that my father-in-law may owe the woman, Valerie Oliphant, money.'

'Has he borrowed from her, do you think?'

'Possibly, but an outstanding gambling debt is more like the thing.'

'Do you know,' Roddy said, 'I find that knowing the old boy has a vice or two tucked up his velvet sleeve makes him seem more human.'

'Oh, he's human enough,' said Grant. 'He's proud, greedy and concerned about dying and, beneath it all, he cares for his daughters.'

'One wouldn't think so by the way he's treated them,' Roddy said.

'They are not the uncomplaining little creatures among whom he was reared. They have minds of their own.'

'Are you winning the old boy round, Grant? Will you have Craigiehall for your own?'

'I am optimistic,' Grant said.

'But what will you do with it?' said Roddy. 'How will you manage it?'

'There's an overseer in place, a youngish man; he will keep me right.'

'I take it,' Roddy said, 'that his lordship has gone home.'

'Aye, he left at once for Ayrshire. He won't show his face in Edinburgh until the courts reopen in

October.' For several minutes the brothers watched the dance of the lantern on the track as intently as if it were a fairy-light, then Grant said, 'Why is Nicola determined to stay on at Heatherbank?'

'She likes the simple life,' said Roddy, casually.

'Is she in love with you?'

'Perhaps a little.'

'Damn it all,' Grant said. 'I do have to worry about you.'

'First Gillon, now me,' said Roddy. 'What a worrier you are, Grant.'

'Have you kissed her?'

'Yes.'

'Have you . . .'

'No, of course not.'

'Have you told her about Marie?'

'Mother would never forgive me if I did,' said Roderick.

'Mother, do you blame Mother now?'

'I blame no one,' Roderick said. 'Nor should you.'

'We are none of us blameless, are we?' Grant said.

'No, that's true,' said Roderick and, whether she liked it or not, cracked the rein against the pony's crupper and urged her into a trot.

*   *   *

The sun had slipped behind the rim of the moor before John James reached Salton House. The topmost chimneys and the balusters of the teetering tower trapped the very last of the sunlight and, being still wet with rain, shone golden for a few brief seconds before dusk snuffed them out and left no sign of welcome save a lamp flickering in the window of the first-floor drawing-room.

He had slept through the first leg of the journey and, though not much refreshed, had eaten and held down a modest dinner in the inn at Peebles while Robertson saw to the change of horses. He, like his servant, had driven the last few rugged miles with his head sticking out of the carriage window, not because he felt unwell but, rather, because the heathery breeze helped blow away his daft romantic notions in respect of the pretty young actress who had led him astray. He thanked his stars that the session had closed, that he would be stowed safe in Craigiehall for the autumn months and that any lingering wisps of scandal would evaporate before the courts convened again.

'Are you sure, Johnny?' Isabella waved away the maid and sliced up the gigot of mutton with her own fair hands. 'It seems to me that your indiscretion may not be forgotten so quickly.'

'Oh, Buller and Dunbar will grouse a bit,' John James said, pouring wine from a chipped crystal decanter, 'but the winter term is crowded with too much business and the town with too many diversions for the stain to stick.'

'Stain?' Isabella pushed a plate towards him. 'What a curious word to use, John James.'

'It is merely a figure of speech.'

The mutton had been trimmed of fat, cooked in milk and served with a caper sauce. He lifted his fork and spoon and with his cloth tucked into his waistcoat in traditional style, attacked his supper with appetite.

339

'Nine-day wonder,' he said, chewing.

'And Madelaine Young,' his cousin said, 'is she too a nine-day wonder?'

'A mistake,' said John James, 'a misjudgement.'

'So,' said Isabella, 'there will be no wedding after all?'

'A fine woman,' John James said. 'Do not mistake me, Isa, a very fine woman, but not "fine" enough by our lights, if you take my meaning.'

'I'm not sure that I do,' said Isabella.

She ate a dainty mouthful, sipped wine, and cast an eye on the maid who was hunched on a stool in a far corner of the room, apparently asleep. Robertson was below in the kitchens, presumably having the whole story teased out of him by Dougie and Cook, all the sordid details that would be revealed to her after her cousin left.

'Do not misconstrue what I am about to say,' John James said, 'but Madelaine Young is more suited to being a mistress than a wife.'

'You are not in the market for a mistress, are you, Johnny?'

'Certainly not.'

'And are you no longer in the market for a wife?'

He sighed and dabbled gravy with his spoon. 'It was, shall we say, an adventure—oh, very well, an infatuation—but it is over now. Young women with old men,' he shook his head, 'no, not a combination that is liable to bring lasting happiness to either party, I fear.'

'Have you apologised to Nicola?' his cousin said. 'If you had had your way you would have married *her* off to an old man. I trust that you have learned a lesson from this escapade, John James.'

'Damned be it, woman, it was your suggestion.

340

Are you telling me you merely set out to teach me a lesson? In any case, there's no parallel between Nicola and me. I wanted a wife to bear me a son.'

'And you wanted Nicola to do what—bear you a coal mine?'

He sat back, the chair creaking, and wiped his lips with his cloth. He had the decency, Isabella noted, to grimace. 'Aye,' he said. 'Your point is made, Isa. By God, though, the older you get the more scheming you become. I may have lost the coal workings but I have not lost my daughters, have I?'

'No, not yet,' said Isabella. 'Tell me, did your witty little actress disappoint you? I have never known a gentleman's infatuation with a pretty young woman cool until he has had his way with her. Did you bed her?'

'No,' John James stated; then, 'Yes.'

'Which is it?'

'It seems that, circumstantially, I may have done.'

'Does Madelaine have no recollection of the momentous event?'

'She did indicate that—ah—something had taken place.'

'Oh, I see,' said Isabella. 'You are in retreat, Johnny, not because you were disappointed in Mrs Young but because she was disappointed in you.'

'I have no wish to discuss it.'

'Very well,' said Isabella, and continued eating.

'However . . .'

'Yes?'

'Maddy did not indicate that she was disappointed,' John James said, smugly. 'Quite the contrary, in fact.'

'I thought you did not wish to discuss it.'

'I simply wish to make certain facts plain.'

'Well, you have done so,' said Isabella. 'Now let us put the subject aside.'

They ate in silence for several minutes.

Then Isabella said, 'How is that nice young man, Gillon Peters?'

'I have no idea. Why do you ask?'

'He impressed me,' said Isabella.

'So impressed you that you thought he might be my rival,' John James said. 'Indeed, you told me to go and fight him for Maddy's affections.'

'Hardly that,' said Isabella. 'I liked Madelaine Young. I found her charming and witty—but I did not think that she was for you.'

'Is that why you warned me to be careful?'

'Did I?' his cousin said, innocently. 'Yes, perhaps I did.'

'You did, most certainly,' John James said. 'You once asked me what sort of man I was, how I saw myself. Well, now I can give you an answer: I am first and foremost Lord Craigiehall of Craigiehall. I cannot blind myself to that fact, however much I may wish to do so. To seek a wife out of spite was not becoming to a man in my position. If I had persevered in my pursuit of Madelaine Young my reputation would surely have suffered and my peers on the bench would have used my folly as a means of bringing me down.'

'Do they wish to bring you down?'

'Oh, the noble lords may appear to be gentleman of great gravity, Isa, but, believe me, they are as petty as children in a schoolroom. They believe that because they have made me, they can also break me and that it will enhance their

342

authority and prove their integrity if they do.'

'Do you owe them money, Johnny?'

'No, I do not owe them money. You will be paid, you will be paid.'

'I'm not asking to be paid,' said Isabella. 'Where is Madelaine now?'

'Gone off with Oliphant to Kingsley.'

'Does Mrs Young know that you have broken with her?'

'If she does not, she will soon enough,' John James said. 'I will write to her and make it clear that our relationship is at an end.'

'Will it then be over?'

'Of course it will,' his lordship said. 'Over for good and all.'

PART FOUR

Breach of Promise

CHAPTER NINETEEN

Heavy rain in the harvest month was the curse that every farmer feared. More than once in recent years it had fallen to Mr Devlin to dismiss his congregation to wrestle with their consciences and, if they saw fit, put up the crop on a dry Sabbath, while he, later, faced the censure of the Synod and pled the case for 'mercy and necessity', which argument was, of course, supported by Mother Peters who had her own way of dealing not only with the Lord but with the institutions of the church.

On the ninth day of September, a Tuesday, word went out that the oats were ready for cutting. Every man, woman and child who did not have cattle duties gathered by the barn and rode or walked to Tom Hadley's field to draw the first crop of the season. The day was dry and warm, not sunny. Nicola rode in the cart beside Mr Ralston who surveyed the sky as if his vigilance might keep the rain at bay. The Hadleys were waiting by the field gate, Marie too. The bright, dark-haired boy darted about like a leveret, while scythes, sickles and rakes were allocated, but Nicola noticed that he avoided Roderick and when Roderick came to speak to Marie, hid behind his mother's skirts or vanished into the waist-high oats.

'He does not seem to take to Roderick,' Nicola said, casually.

'If it's Iain you're meanin', lass,' Duncan Ralston said, 'he'd come to Roddy soon enough, or to me for that matter, if he was not discouraged.'

'Discouraged?' Nicola said. 'Who discourages him?'

'She does—Marie—an' you can hardly blame her for it.'

'Because she thinks of Roderick as her master?'

'She admits no master,' Duncan said. 'She's a wild spirit, only half tamed. Her parents an' her brother have never known what to do with her.' He shrugged. 'Listen to me gossipin', when there's work to be done.' Then he clambered down from the cart and hitched the pony to the gatepost while Nicola, more puzzled than ever, hurried off to join the women for another long day in the field.

*   *   *

'Are you not throwing your weight behind the Circuit courts at all this autumn?' said Isabella. 'Do you fear ridicule even on the road?'

'I do not fear ridicule, Isa,' John James said. 'I have too much to do here at Craigiehall to ensure that the harvest tops its yield. I admit that I prefer not to sit with Maynard who would be my Circuit companion and would without doubt subject me to an inquisition that I'd rather avoid. I've agreed to sit at Dunbarton, Inverary and Glasgow in the latter part of the month. Maynard will have gone home by then and Jackson will be my running mate. He's a congenial enough fellow and will not tease me more than a little.'

'Have you seen the letters in the latest issue of the *Courant?*'

'Yes,' John James said, curtly.

'Much is being made of it, still.'

'Damn it, woman, I know.'

'Do *you* regard the Parliament House as an Augean stable in sore need of cleansing?' Isabella said. 'Mr Peck of Carluke seems to think so.'

'What do I care what Mr Peck of Carluke thinks?' John James said. 'Look here, Isabella, if you persist in this nagging, I will send you home again.'

'Why did you send for me in the first place, Johnny?'

He did not answer her at once but did not, she noticed, remove her arm from his. They were strolling across the lawn that fronted the house. The evening air was cool and free of insects and there were no fractious sounds in the air, only the cooing of wood pigeons and the pulse of the sea from the shore. It was, she thought, peaceful here in Craigiehall, peaceful in a gentle way, unlike the wind-swept isolation of Salton House.

'I—ah—I am concerned,' John James said, at length.

'Money again?'

'No,' he said. 'A matter of the heart.'

'Have you not had enough of matters of the heart?'

'It seems not,' John James said. 'I have received a letter from Madelaine Young; a letter in response to my letter to her.' He cleared his throat. 'It appears that she is not willing to be dismissed quite so lightly.'

'Where is she?'

'Still at Kingsley with the Oliphants.'

'When will she return to Edinburgh?'

'I have no idea,' John James said. 'At a guess— late this month.'

He fished in his pocket and brought out a letter

349

written in a small crabbed script that leaned distinctly to the right of the page and by the page's end had become almost vertical.

'Here,' he said, giving her the letter. 'What do you think?'

She read the letter carefully, then, looking up, said, 'Are you sure that Madelaine Young wrote this?'

'It's her signature.'

'Are you sure?'

'What is your point, Isa. It's literate enough, is it not?'

'Too literate, perhaps,' Isabella said. 'In spite of the script, it has the feel to it of an older hand, written not in haste but carefully composed.'

'I had not detected that,' John James admitted. 'Is it a love-letter, Isa?'

'Or is it,' his cousin said, 'a threat?'

'What do you think?' he said again.

'I think, dearest Johnny, that I should be irked with you for inviting me to Craigiehall not for my company but for my opinion of a letter that is overflowing with innuendo that you are too blind to see for yourself.'

'It is a threat, then?'

'Of course it's a threat.'

'She won't let me go?' John James said.

'Apparently not.'

'She wants me to marry her?'

'Now, now,' said Isabella. 'Do not get carried away. There is no mention of marriage on the surface.'

'But beneath the surface . . .'

Isabella held the letter down by her hip for her eyesight had been fading a little in recent months and she had left her spectacles in her luggage. She scanned the page, looking down her nose in a manner that seemed to indicate distaste.

'Is she in love with me?' John James said.

'If she is,' said Isabella, 'I can't think why,' then, relenting, added, 'Her letter, if it is her letter, is a masterpiece of ambiguity. To reply to it point by point, John James, will only lead you into deep waters.'

'Is she not in love with me?'

'There is no more mention of love than there is of marriage.'

'What *does* it mean, then, Isa? And how should I reply?'

'Do you want this woman for your wife?'

'No,' said John James, emphatically. 'No, no.'

'Or for your mistress?'

'Does she say . . .'

'Or for your mistress?'

'No.'

'Then do not, under any circumstances, reply.' She folded the letter into a small, neat square and handed it back to him. 'You have made your intentions clear. To enter into further correspondence will only lead to trouble. Come now, Johnny, how many times have you seen a man hanged on the strength of a few words rashly committed to paper?'

'Hmm,' John James said, 'if not hanged, certainly condemned.'

'If you do not reply then she will know that you have written her off.'

'And I have, haven't I? Written her off, I mean?'

'I must take your word on that, Johnny. One can only hope that Mrs Madelaine Young is sensible enough to write you off too,' said Isabella then, taking his arm again, steered her troubled cousin past the matrimonial oak and safely back to the house.

*   *   *

Dust made her itch, stubble had drawn blood from her ankles and the muscles across her shoulders burned like fire but the stooks that she had helped bind stood out like sentinels against the evening sky, and tomorrow, if the weather held, they would do it all again, gathering from McAllan's ground.

The bottle shook in her hands but ale had never tasted better.

'Enough!' Marie said. 'I wouldn't have you fallin' down on me.'

Nicola laughed and gave the bottle to Marie who took it in both hands, lifted it to her lips and drank in odd little sips that seemed too fastidious for a woman reputed to be wild. The harvesters were heading homewards. There was no sign of Roderick or Duncan Ralston, though the old man had promised to come back for her. She waited by the gate with only Marie for company.

'Where is your boy?' Nicola asked.

'Gone in with his Gran,' Marie said. 'He'll have had his supper an' be tucked up in bed by now.'

'Bed,' said Nicola. 'What a wonderful thought.'

'Aye, you'll sleep sound this night, Miss Nicola,' Marie told her. 'It'll be a different tale in the mornin', though. You'll be lucky if you can crawl.'

'Do you not grow used to it?'

'To what?' Marie said. 'To the labour? Nay, you never get used to it. But this is the lot God's given me an' there's no help for it.' She drank again and handed the bottle back to Nicola. 'I've never known another way o' life. I was born there at the end o' the oat field an' I've never strayed from Heatherbank.'

'There are worse places,' Nicola said.

'Where you come from?' Marie said, with a little edge.

Nicola hesitated. 'Do you know where I come from?'

'Aye, from Ayrshire, daughter to some laird— like her.'

'Like who?' said Nicola.

'The woman Grant married, the one who was here. Your sister,' Marie said. 'She'd never make a farmer's wife.'

'Charlotte might have been brought up in the country but she much prefers the town.'

'Spoiled bitch!'

Nicola felt a little stab of anger at the woman's presumption and was tempted to remind Marie that it did not become a lowly farm hand to pass judgement on the daughter of a lord. Aware that Marie was watching her, she drank another mouthful of ale and wiped her mouth before she responded.

'You must have known the Peters boys well when they, and you, were children,' she said.

'We learned our tables together when Mr Jamieson came.'

'Does Mr Jamieson still come?'

'Nay, he's gone. A woman takes the lessons now.'

'In the village, a school in the village?'

'Not so far as the village. Over by Gleddon.'

353

'Will Iain go there to learn his ABCs?'

'In a year, when he's old enough.' Marie said. 'If she wants to send him away for more learnin', I'll not let her.'

'If *who* wants to send him away?' said Nicola.

'Margo Peters.'

'Send him where?'

'To Stirling, to the academy.'

'Is that what they do with boys, furnish them with an education?' said Nicola. 'Education is no bad thing, you know.'

'Not our boys,' said Marie. 'Only her boys, her precious bloody boys.'

'Then why would she want to send your son . . .'

'Bitch!' Marie said, viciously, then realising that she had already said too much, flung open the field gate and tramped off across the stubble without another word.

*　　　*　　　*

If Charlotte had been opposed to taking exercise in the sweet fresh air of Heatherbank she was a deal less reluctant to do so in the hazy atmosphere of Auld Reekie, particularly when she had Grant's arm to support her and his promise that he would show her the New Town, or what there was of it. So, on that dry, dull Tuesday afternoon the advocate and his portly wife had sallied forth across the bridge and along what existed of Prince's Street while Grant discoursed on contract law and feu dispositions and explained the merits of biding time until the town council and the heritors settled their disputes and agreed what could and could not be built, and where.

It was a boring subject, though Grant made it as interesting as possible, and Charlotte remained optimistic that he would lead her to a plot and point and say, 'There, my dear, there we will have our mansion.'

Grant, of course, could give no such guarantees. The gulf between plan and execution was wider than the North Loch and bits of fencing and rows of painted posts were not enough to ignite Charlotte's imagination. She was happy enough, therefore, when Grant bought her a pear and urged her to sit for a while in Broughton Gardens, near to the house where Papa's mistress had lodged before she went north with the Oliphants for the summer.

Papa's indiscretion and the subsequent notices in the press had been done to death in conversations between the advocate and his wife, for Grant was well informed and Charlotte more intrigued than seemed quite wholesome for a woman in her condition.

Her 'condition', however, had brought benefits that neither Charlotte nor Grant could have foreseen. A strange, avid hunger for intercourse had taken possession of Lord Craigiehall's elder daughter, and Margo Peter's middle son, not unwillingly, was stretched to the limit to keep up with demands that began before breakfast and ended long after dark, when pride was no longer enough to stave off exhaustion and his candle was thoroughly extinguished.

It was as well for Grant that his ledger was light that September for as Charlotte's shape became ever more voluptuous, her character changed accordingly. She might, in fact, have had him dandle her in the park that dull Tuesday afternoon for her kisses, damp with pear juice, left him in no doubt that her blood was on fire again and that for the sake of his health as well as his reputation, he had better get her out of there.

He ran off to find a hack to whisk them to Denholm's tea shop at the bottom of the Canongate where he stuffed Charlotte full of brown bread, fresh apple pies and about a quart of best Indian before he led her on foot up the long hill home in the hope that exercise might tap off a little of her energy and leave him time to write a letter or two and, possibly, sup before Molly, smirking, was sent to fetch him to her lady's boudoir.

He'd had lovers before marriage, of course, country lassies whose ardour was usually tempered by fear of making babies. He had spent one glorious winter's afternoon on an ottoman wooing the daughter of a titled client whose reluctance to surrender even a little of her virtue had added mustard to his conquest. Since marriage, however, he had been true to dull Charlotte, for reasons that were not entirely honourable. But now, almost on the eve of fatherhood, he found that he had wedded a strumpet, who without fear of consequence and protected by her wedding band felt entitled to do anything she liked with him.

As they passed the Luckenbooths, she drew him close and, lips against his ear, whispered, 'What of *that* girl, dearest, what would you do with a buxom young jade like her?'

'Stop it, Charlotte, for heaven's sake stop it.'

'Would you not like to take her "walking" on the Castle Hill?'

'Charlotte, what's come over you?'

'I know what men are like—and *what* men like.'

'That,' said Grant, grimly, 'is no excuse.'

'Dr Gaythorn says it is not uncommon.'

'You've spoken of this matter to Gaythorn?'

'Of course. I was concerned that your antics would harm the baby. Dr Gaythorn says not. Dr Gaythorn is very enlightened. He says that our child is well protected, that the female body . . .' She paused, brought her mouth to his ear again, and murmured, 'Oh look, Grant, look at her, the fair-haired girl in the green dress. Would she not give you pleasure?'

'This is not only unseemly,' Grant cast a glance at the fair-haired girl popping out of her green dress, 'it is obscene. Is it your intention, Charlotte, to drive me into the arms of other women?'

'You will look at them differently when I am fat and suckling.'

'No, I will not.'

'You will, I know you will.'

'What have you heard? What's been said about me?'

'If my papa, at his age, cannot control his instincts . . .'

'Oh, Papa, is it?' said Grant, relieved. 'It's your father's behaviour that's brought on this fit, is it? Are you testing me, Charlotte? Well, be assured that I am not like your papa. Besides . . .'

'Besides?'

'I love you.'

'Do you?' Charlotte said.

'How can you possibly doubt it?'

'It is not enough to say it. You must prove it.'

'Have you not had proof enough these past

weeks,' Grant said.

'Do you not feel it?' said Charlotte, gripping his arm tightly.

'Feel what?'

'Time, time slipping past us. In a month I will be too fat to fit into bed with you and in two months thereafter I will bear you a child.'

'Bearing a child is not the end of the world, Charlotte.'

'I will become a mother—and you will love me no longer.'

'For the love of God, Charlotte! I will love you all the more.'

'What if I die?'

'You will not die. You are strong, as strong and as healthy as a horse.'

'A horse, is it? Is that how you see me, as a brood mare?'

'I meant . . .'

'My mother died soon after Jamie was born,' Charlotte told him.

'You are not your mother any more than I'm your father.'

'Will you marry again?' she asked.

He could not be entirely sure that she was not teasing, though she had never, like Nicola, been witty enough to do so effectively. He was caught, cleft-stick, by her question. If he admitted that he would in all likelihood remarry then she would hold it against him; if he declared that, no, he would mourn her for the rest of his days she would accuse of him lying.

It crossed his mind, not for the first time, that she had heard tales about his fecklessness, that someone at Heatherbank had spoken out of turn or, worse, had practised malice against him in a spirit of revenge. Why, he thought, could he artfully plead causes for other men yet be so tongue-tied in his own defence?

'If you were to die, Charlotte,' he said, 'what would *you* have me do?'

'You are too much of a man not to marry again.'

'I will take that as a compliment, but not a proper answer.'

'You could not marry Nicola?'

'No, I could not—nor would I wish to,' Grant said.

'Who would look after you? Who would look after our child?'

'If it came to it, which it will not,' Grant said, 'I would employ a nurserymaid to look after our child.'

'And you?'

They were within sight of Graddan's Court now, thank God. He was tempted to be brusque with her, to tell her to put all this nonsense about dying out of her mind and consider instead what they would have for supper and what they would do after supper but he sensed that her fears were deep-seated and that to dismiss them out of hand would be cruel.

'Charlotte,' he said, 'what are you afraid of?'

'If I were to die,' said Charlotte, 'then would you do as Papa did and put our child into the charge of a hired servant and give him no affection?'

'I would raise him close under my care, Charlotte, I promise.'

'And if it's a girl, a daughter?'

'I would love her all the more,' Grant said, 'because she would remind me, always, of you.'

'Oh!' Charlotte said. 'Oh! I had not thought of that.'

'Well, think of it now, dearest,' Grant said. 'And when we are tottering down the Lawnmarket to St Giles in forty years time with a skein of grandchildren trailing behind us, I will remind you of my promise and we will laugh at your foolishness.'

'And there will be no one else?'

'No one,' said Grant.

'Oh, Grant,' she said. 'I'm so frightened.'

'Of what, my darling girl?'

'Everything,' said Charlotte and, less than an hour later, sent Molly, smirking, to fetch him from his writing-desk.

CHAPTER TWENTY

Sir Ranald might assemble a dainty orchestra of spinet, harp and viol in the great hall at Gleddon, his ladies done up in gowns of silk and gentlemen ruffled like heads of lettuce in a ballroom lit by a thousand candles, but in the laird's mansion the spirit of the harvest was honoured by little more than a basket of fruit and two or three corn-dollies pinned above the doors.

Margo Peters' harvests, however, were celebrated by traditions that reached far back in time. She might lead her flock to church on the last Sabbath in September to give thanks to God for His bounty, but she would not forgo for anyone the revel that preceded it, the Saturday dance at Heatherbank, where ale flowed like water, the reels were fast and furious and more than one maid would find her destiny among the stooks that ringed the stackyard.

The appearance of Habbie Gow and his brother Birnie at any gathering was enough to make the toe tap before a note was played or a posture struck. The evening was sharp and clear. The moon shed light on the fields and silvered the white-washed cottages as lads and lassies, scrubbed and sparkling, wended in from the steadings. Four or five old soldiers had tramped in from Stirling to keep Habbie and his brother company and soak up as much free liquor as they could stomach. They would blearily emerge from the hay-loft tomorrow afternoon in search of a hair of the dog and a gentle ride back to the fortress.

Well fed and watered, Habbie was at it early. He was seated on a barrel and was as round as a barrel himself, fat legs bulging in his old regimental trews, matching stockings tight over his stumpy calves, his foot, a tiny foot in a black leather slipper, tap-tapping away while his bow danced over the strings and the strains of 'Glendevon's Farewell' rose into the crisp night air. His brother, Birnie, the piper-mannie, warmed the bag and wetted the pipe while strutting up and down between byre and barn until Habbie finished his set, then out Birnie came, hoisting the pipes against his shoulder, filling his cheeks and letting rip so strong with the jig 'Jenny's Lost Amang the Clover' that heads were raised from the meal dish near as far away as Doune.

Milking had been got through with an alacrity that if done any faster would have singed the poor cows' teats. Kegs of ale and barley brew, tankards, cups and glasses were spread on the tables along with potatoes roasted in mutton fat, pies and pastries, cheese and bread, and a great cauldron of soup, made to Mr Ralston's recipe. Roderick and the boys had dragged out the tightest stooks and lined them against the walls and, since the night was fine and windless, planted big tarry torches on poles close to the house and hung capstan lanterns on hooks below the eaves and, just as darkness fell, lit them, one by one.

When the first of the tenants began to arrive Nicola hurried upstairs and put on the dress that she had dug from her luggage, a gay striped garment with light petticoats, and pinned on the impertinent little straw hat that Margo had found for her which was more suitable than a bonnet for a country dance.

The loft was bright with light from the lanterns and her shadow danced on the wall to the fiddler's tune. Although Papa had forbidden attendance at balls and assemblies, Nana Aird had taught Charlotte and Nicola many familiar steps and one afternoon, when Papa was away, Nicola had danced a Strathspey with Mr Littlejohn when an itinerant fiddler had come by and had played so enthusiastically that neither she nor the overseer could resist, though they had both been embarrassed about it afterwards.

Now she danced with her shadow on the wall, trying hard to recall all that her old nurse had taught her about pivot steps and points in the hope that she would not make a fool of herself and disappoint Roderick.

She heard a knock upon the door, opened the latch and found him there, stooped under the low

362

beam, his coat thrown open and his shirt white as milk in the gloom of the stairs. 'Ma'm'selle,' he said. 'Are you ready?'

'I am, M'sieur, I am,' Nicola answered and taking his hand, let him lead her down through the kitchen and out to join the jollity in the yard.

*   *   *

It was late evening when John James returned to Craigiehall after his Circuit journey. He had survived the trip into the Highlands well enough for he loved the rugged landscapes of Argyll and had received hospitality from Sir Andrew Aitchieson who was far too much of a gentleman to raise the subject of the *Courant* pieces. Glasgow, though, had been another matter. The court parade was as splendid as ever but there had been a cat-call or two from the crowd on the High Street and some booing and whistling within the courtroom until Sergeant Traynor and his guard had rooted out the offenders and evicted them.

The public dinner had been even more of an ordeal for all sorts of questions, sly and sleek and quite impertinent, had been put to him. Seventy-eight cases, mainly involving theft, had taken up the best part of the week and if Jackson and he had not dispensed with the absurd practice of sermonising on Christian virtue to men and women to whom theft was next door to a way of life, would have taken a great deal longer. It was late on Friday evening before the court had closed and, after supper with Sheriff McMenemy at Possil House, John James had had Robertson pack his bag and order the carriage for seven in the a.m, at which hour, with the Sheriff's best wishes ringing in his ears, he had set out for Salton House to call upon Isabella.

To his astonishment, Isabella had not been at home. The incorruptible Dougie had claimed that he had no idea why the lady had left or when she would return, and no amount of persuasion could wring from the dour old beggar so much as a hint as to where she had gone. John James had not been too dismayed for he had managed to convince himself that Isabella had gone on to Craigiehall and would be waiting there to surprise him. 'Mrs McGrouther, Mrs McGrouther,' he called, striding into the hall. 'Where is Mrs Ballentine? Has she had her supper yet?'

The housekeeper appeared at the top of the stairs, sour-faced as ever.

'Well?' John James said, jauntily. 'Where is she? Where's she hiding?'

'Mrs Ballentine isna' here, your lordship.'

'Not here?' John James looked hither and thither as if he suspected that his housekeeper was in on the prank. 'Then where is she?'

'I'm not the one to be askin' that, sir,' said Mrs McGrouther.

'No, I don't suppose you are,' John James said, trying to hide his disappointment. 'Where are my letters?'

'On the table in the drawing-room, your lordship,' the housekeeper told him. 'Are you wantin' fed?'

'What? Yes, of course I want fed.'

The housekeeper bowed and went off downstairs to rouse the cook from her slumbers, while John James headed for the drawing-room to sift through the mail that had accumulated in his absence. A young footman, buttoning up his tunic, slipped into the room before him and lit from a taper four of the eight candles in the holder on the table. It was very quiet in the big room, very still.

The curtains had not been closed and pale shafts of moonlight streaked the polished floor. John James seated himself at the table and rested his chin on his hand. He still wore his greatcoat and smelled of the road. Robertson would be upstairs unpacking his bags, fetching hot water for the jug, laying out his nightshirt and cap, and that, John James thought, was all very well, but Robertson was not true company, not family.

How many times had he returned from long days on the road to find Marion waiting up for him, her smile soft, her pleasure at seeing him quite genuine? She would take his dusty coat and hand it on to a servant, his hat too, then she would put her arms around him and hug him and, for a moment, rest her head on his chest, and he would feel superior to any man alive, for he knew that in spite of all his foibles, all his faults, he was loved. He had not thought of Marion much in recent years, had not missed her as he missed her now. Jamie had been there, little motherless creature, all patient and sleepy in his gown as he waited up for Papa's return, for Papa to pick him up and carry him to bed. Later, the girls: never quite the same with the girls, for they were never so uncompromisingly eager to greet him when he had been away too long.

'Will that be all, your lordship?' the young footman asked.

'Aye, that will be all, lad,' John James answered.

365

Rousing himself, he reached for the basket of letters and sorted through them in search of a note from Isabella that might explain her absence.

There was no missive from Isabella, only, as expected, packets of mail from his peers on the bench dripping with monogrammed seals and, no doubt, recriminations. Hidden in the professional debris, were two—no, three—letters addressed in Madelaine Young's small, slanting hand. He slit them with a knife and spread them in order of receipt upon the table. He cupped his hands over his ears and read and as he read the blood drained from his cheeks and a violent shivering took hold of him. He read each letter once and then again, then, rising, crushed the pages against his chest and charged out into the hall.

'Robertson,' he bellowed. 'Robertson!' And when his man-servant appeared at the head of the stairs, he cried, 'Send a boy to the stables to have fresh horses put to the chaise and the chaise brought round.'

'Tonight, your lordship?' Robertson said, astonished.

'Aye,' John James shouted. 'We are leaving for Edinburgh at once.'

*　　　*　　　*

When midnight came Habbie would case his fiddle and Birnie drain his pipes and the dance would dwindle into memory. What went on after twelve in the fields and hedgerows or off behind the byre was not Margo's concern. She was a country woman born and bred, and sufficiently realistic to acknowledge that the line that divided Saturday frolic from Sunday reverence was thin at best and on the night of the harvest-home might waver a bit on the side of the secular.

Nicola was too caught up in the lather of the reels to spare any thought for tomorrow. As the evening progressed the lads became less considerate of the Edinburgh lassie's gentility and swept her, as they swept all the girls, clean off her feet and caught her again as cleanly as they might catch a leaping lamb or a calf on a rampage: Jamie McAllan, young Gibbie Crowe, the Macpherson lads—and Roderick, always Roderick, his hands in hers, his face gleaming with sweat, and that eye on him, arrogant and amused, when they were paired together in circle or rank, making sure that he was her partner when Habbie tapped his bow and the music stopped and the kissing began. After the youngest children had been taken home and whisky in shiny jugs had appeared, the laughter, clapping and kissing became less ordered. It was all Habbie could do to pull the sets together, three here, four there, and trim the ranks for the 'Pearie-Whup' or, with the clock ticking towards midnight, spread the circle wide for 'Babbity Bowster', a game imported from the bridal feast.

Nicola had seen little of Marie Hadley. She had been playing with her little boy in a corner in the early part of the evening and drinking ale with an arm about Duncan Ralston's waist later on, but no man, young or old, courted her and when the kissing started in earnest Marie had stepped back into the shadows for, it seemed, she preferred ale to osculation.

Nicola had watched the dance performed at a rowdy hiring fair in Kilmarnock and was just as

367

exuberant and flirtatious as any girl there. Habbie struck a long chord and the clapping and singing began.

'Wha' learnt you tae dance,
Babbity Bowster, Babbity Bowster,
Wha' learnt you tae dance,
Babbity Bowster Brawly.'

Tom Hadley pranced into the circle and plucked up the sack that substituted for a bridal bolster. He slung it over his shoulder and skipped energetically around the ring, grinning and winking at every lass he passed, then whipped the sack down and threw it at the feet of a pretty wee girl, not more than fifteen years old, who pressed her hands to her bosom, such as it was, and shrieked as her friends pushed her to her knees.

'My Meggie learnt me tae dance,
Babbity Bowster, Babbity Bowster,
My Meggie learnt me tae dance,
Babbity Bowster Brawly'.

Habbie scraped the bow on the strings above the bridge and brought forth a squeak as young Meg, kneeling on the sack, offered her mouth to Tom's kiss which, when their lips met, raised a huge cheer.

Rising, gallant Tom offered his arm to blushing Meg and they circled the ring together, save that it was the girl now who had the 'bolster' and gave the eye to every boy she passed. Impatient to be kissed again, she tossed the sack down before a startled ploughboy and threw herself to her knees, lips pursed in expectation. While the onlookers cheered, clapped, and chanted, little Meggie got her kiss, albeit a clumsy one, and the dance went on.

No one invited Marie Hadley to join the circle, no one knelt at her feet. She appeared without warning, pushing into the ring, arms raised, her hair tossing wildly about her shoulders. She thrust aside the girl whose turn it was, stripped the sack from the girl's shoulder and linked arms with an astonished young man who, not knowing what else to do, let her drag him round and round while the clapping became sporadic and the chanting ceased.

When Marie dropped the sack at Roderick's feet, Habbie lowered his fiddle. She knelt there, chin lifted, eyes open, arms spread like a martyr, defying Roddy to kneel down and kiss her.

Nicola heard him sigh then watched him lower himself before the dark-haired woman. He took her hands in his and said quietly, 'Marie. Oh, Marie.' He kissed her briefly on the mouth, then jumped to his feet and signed to Habbie to draw the bow in one long trembling sweep to signal that the dance was over and the harvest celebrations at an end.

*   *   *

The loft was dark, with no more light than the moon provided, and not much of that. Roderick opened the door and peeped in.

Nicola raised herself on an elbow. 'What is it you want with me?'

'Have you been crying?'

'No,' Nicola said. 'I'm worn out.'

She had thrown off her dress, kicked off her shoes and peeled her stockings but had forgotten to remove the little straw hat. She pushed at her petticoats to preserve her modesty when he came to her and seated himself on the side of the bed. When he brushed her cheek with his fingertip she flinched and drew back.

'You have been crying,' he said. 'Why, Nicola, why?'

'Do you not have brain enough to know why?'

'It's Marie, is it not?'

'Why did you have to kiss her?'

'I would not see her humiliated.'

'She humiliated herself,' said Nicola. 'She had no right.'

He brushed her cheek again and endeavoured to put an arm around her. 'Aye,' said Roderick. 'She had every right.'

'What is she to you?'

'She's a farm servant, Nicola, and I am no ill master.'

'Is she waiting for you in the hay-loft? Will you go to her after you've done with me?'

'Her brother took her home.'

'You act as if it were nothing,' Nicola said.

'It is nothing,' Roderick told her. 'She's made a fool of herself too many times for it to matter.'

'It matters to me.'

'Does it?' Roderick said. 'Why does it matter to you?'

'Because I—I thought . . .'

He reached for her again. This time she yielded, resting her shoulder against his arm. She waited for him to tell her that he loved her, that the woman meant nothing to him. He slipped the pin

370

from her hat and put it in the hat and placed the hat upon the floor. He cocked his knee and stretched out beside her.

He kissed her ear, then her neck and then her bare shoulder. In a moment he would slip his hand to her breast and though she had expected it and had prepared herself, now she resisted. It was not enough to want him. He was too glib, too tender and solicitous, too good, in fact, to be true.

She rolled away and found the floor with her feet.

She said, 'I think it's time I went home.'

'I thought you liked the country life?'

'I promised Charlotte I would look after her and I believe in keeping my promises. I'll travel to Edinburgh tomorrow.'

'Tomorrow is Sunday.'

'Monday then, Monday first thing,' Nicola said. 'I would be obliged if you would arrange for someone to take me to Stirling.'

Keeping the width of the bed between them, he got to his feet.

'All this,' he said, 'because of a silly prank.'

'Was it a prank for Marie Hadley when you fathered her child?'

'That's what you think, is it?' Roderick said. 'Very well, Nicola, if you insist on leaving, I'll arrange for a cart for Monday morning.'

'Is that all you have to say?' said Nicola.

'It's all I am prepared to say,' Roderick told her and, without so much as a bow let alone an apology, flung open the door and clattered downstairs.

CHAPTER TWENTY-ONE

It was a little after four o'clock when Hercules Mackenzie returned from attending service at the New Grey Friars' Church. He had worshipped there since he had first arrived in Edinburgh, though it had been less convenient to his lodgings in those days. He had tarried outside the church to chat with Mr Austin, a fellow Writer, and his charming wife, and with the Duchess of Gordon, a client, and her companion, Miss Wade, who, though pretty, was just a tad too frisky for Hercules' liking. Accompanied by his manservant, he had then walked home—his weekly constitutional—for a light dinner and a snooze before he took himself into the old town to sup with Lady Colquhoun who had just returned from the country and would no doubt be all agog to hear the latest tittle-tattle.

The moment his housekeeper opened the front door, however, Hercules knew that dinner was going to have to wait.

He had not encountered Craigiehall's manservant before and did not recognise the man who, listing like a sand-hopper, occupied the chair that guarded the entrance to the drawing-room.

'Is that him?' came a voice from the drawing-room. 'Is he here at last?'

The drawing-room door opened with enough force to shake the paintings on the walls. The man on the chair wakened with such a start that he fell to his knees and, scrambling to find his feet and his senses, bleated, 'Sir, sir, your lordship, sir . . .' in a voice weakened not by drink but by exhaustion.

Paying no heed to his servant's distress, Craigiehall raised an arm above his head and waved it about. 'Thanks be to God, you're here at last, Mackenzie,' he cried. 'I have urgent need of your services.'

'My services?' Hercules was not unused to squaring up to desperate men and despairing women, though rarely on a Sunday afternoon. 'Is it the Ayrshire coal-workings again?'

'What? No! God, no!' Craigiehall roared, caring not a fig who heard him. 'I'm being sued, man, *sued.*'

Hercules slipped off his coat and handed it to his house-keeper.

'On what grounds?' he asked.

'Breach of promise,' Craigiehall answered. 'Breach of bloody promise.'

And Hercules, pursing his lips, said, 'Oops!'

*   *   *

Brandy calmed the learned judge a little. He looked, Hercules thought, like a wounded heron, all grey and bedraggled. He limped nervously about the room while Hercules, comfortably seated in his armchair by the fire, read through the letters that had given Lord Craigiehall such fits.

'How long have you been on the road?' he asked.

'Days,' said Craigiehall. 'Or so it seems.'

'You travelled overnight from Ayrshire, did you?'

'Aye, sir, I did, and with good reason,' Craigiehall said. 'This woman, this unscrupulous woman, may strike at any moment.'

'When did you last eat?' said Hercules.

'I had some boiled milk and toast at Peebles.'

'Then you must eat something soon or hunger will damage the clarity of your thinking, hunger coupled to lack of sleep.'

'If,' said Craigiehall, testily, 'I require advice on matters of health then I will consult my doctor. I came to you . . .'

'To do your thinking for you,' said Hercules.

His lordship sighed and, nursing the brandy glass, seated himself on the striped sofa. 'In all my years as a servant of the law,' he said, 'I have never dealt with a case for the breach of a promise of marriage.'

'Few of us have,' said Hercules. Until recently the church courts handled all such petitions. 'Gentlemen of your rank are seldom involved in such petty wrangling. The pangs of love despised seem to be confined to the lower classes or, more often than not, to the sons of merchants and the daughters of clergymen.'

'Have you represented clients in such cases?'

'Several,' said Hercules. 'Well, two to be exact. It has always seemed a marvel to me that a lady—for it is invariably a lady—who claims to harbour a pure and unmercenary love for the fellow who has discarded her will resort to a court of law as possessing the balm of Gilead. Did you promise her marriage?'

'Not in so many words.'

'Did you have connection with the woman?'

'I believe—yes, I may have done.'

'How often?'

'On one occasion only.'

374

'Hmm,' said Hercules. 'An occasion, sir, that somehow or another found itself reported in the *Courant*?"

'And the *Mercury*, and the *Scots Magazine*,' Craigiehall added, gloomily.

'So,' Hercules said, 'the popular perception is that you did have carnal knowledge of Mrs Madelaine Young and any denials you make even under oath will be regarded as perjury.'

'She led me on.'

'No doubt,' said Hercules. 'However—if, and I say again *if*, Mrs Young is foolish enough to hound you into a courtroom then her reputation will be subject to intimate scrutiny. Even if she is as pretty as folk say and simpers sweetly at the jury . . .'

'A jury?' said Craigiehall.

'Unfortunately, she is entitled to call for a jury trial,' said Hercules. 'Have you forgotten all your law, sir?'

'In this aspect, yes, it seems I have,' said Craigiehall.

'If the case were found for her she'd find herself richer by no more than a few hundred pounds for there's no continuation of responsibility, by which is meant no child is involved. After the unfortunate incident on Castle Hill,' Hercules went on, 'did you release yourself from the lady at once?'

'I took her to my home for breakfast.'

'Hmm,' Hercules wheezed again. 'And then you broke with her?'

'In effect,' said Craigiehall, 'I fled. She left for Kingsley with Archie Oliphant and I went home to Ayrshire.'

'How then did you part from her?'

His lordship uttered a despairing groan. 'By

letter.'

'In this letter did you imply that there had been an understanding of marriage between you?'

'I see where this is leading, Mr Mackenzie,' his lordship said. 'I am not so deficient in matrimonial law as all that. I should not have sent the letter. The letter itself is evidence that there was an *understanding* of marriage accepted by both parties, though marriage *per se* is nowhere mentioned.'

'The letter, your letter, is her trump card,' said Hercules.

'As an impartial juryman, I would be more than inclined to regard it in that light,' his lordship admitted. 'The question that's bound to be raised by the lady's attorney is precisely when this understanding was reached and if the plaintiff, Young, would have consented to—ah—to go walking with me on Castle Hill in the wee small hours if I had not promised to marry her.'

'Walking on Castle Hill, even in the wee small hours, is not an offence,' Hercules said. 'You were not "walking" when the city guard discovered you. The guardsmen will be summoned as witnesses against you.'

'Even so, her case is weak, is it not?' Lord Craigiehall said.

'Exceedingly weak,' said Hercules. 'Nonetheless she has one enormous advantage over you.'

'That being?'

'She, from what I hear, has nothing whatsoever to lose.'

'And I have,' Craigiehall said, nodding again.

'Dunbar is already baying for your blood and the honourable gentlemen who prop up our legal system will support him simply to avoid taint,' said Hercules. 'If the woman, Young, so much as threatens to sue you, you will be left without an adequate defence and will be ruined in your career. Obviously, she wants money to keep her mouth shut, more money than she could ever hope to gain in damages through a court.'

'What do you suggest I do?'

'Negotiate.'

'I could, I suppose, make a formal offer of marriage.'

'Good God! Do you really want to marry her?'

Craigiehall shook his head. 'Probably not.'

'Probably not?'

'Certainly not.'

'Then negotiate swiftly through an intermediary.'

'An intermediary?'

'Your son-in-law, perhaps.'

'Grant? Not Grant Peters, no.'

'He is one of the best young advocates in Edinburgh. Surely you can trust Grant Peters to represent you and keep his mouth shut? You are understandably ashamed and embarrassed,' Hercules went on. 'I suggest, however, that you put pride to one side or risk losing not only your high office but your place in society. Is it not better to nibble on humble pie and ask your son-in-law to support you in this crisis than to throw your career on the dung heap?'

'Grant Peters, though, Grant Peters,' his lordship muttered.

'Charge him to talk to the widow.'

'Do I have any other choice?'

'No,' said Hercules, firmly. 'None.'

Once tea had been taken and the order for supper agreed, Charlotte had settled herself comfortably on the carpet and, with her head resting on Grant's knee, had persuaded him to read to her from the late Mr Sterne's curious novel *The Life and Opinions of Tristram Shandy* for Grant had a way of making the salacious humour seem palatable even without much of a story to hold it up. Charlotte was in her usual state of dishabille with her bubbies on display, and Grant was well aware that, Sunday or not, he would soon be called upon to prove himself in a manner more appropriate to Rabelais than to Sterne.

He had just reached the interesting section on 'noses', the length and shape thereof, which Sterne, in Shandy's voice, was at great pains to assure the reader meant simply 'noses' and nothing more and Charlotte, chuckling, had just begun to unbutton the fall of his breeches to allow his 'nose' to sniff the air when Molly knocked upon the door, flung it open and before she could utter a word was rudely pushed aside by John James Templeton.

'Papa!' Charlotte squealed, clutching her breasts.

'Lord Craigiehall!' Grant had enough presence of mind to cover his exposure with the works of Laurence Sterne as he rose, stiffly, to his feet. 'To what do we owe the pleasure of your . . .'

Reaching into his coat pocket, John James whipped out a wad of paper and tossed it at Grant. 'This!' he said. 'This! Now, Peters, clothe yourself, if you please, for I have work for you to do.'

'On Sunday, sir?' said Grant.

'Yes, damned be it,' John James said. 'The devil works on Sundays and so, it seems, must we.'

*   *   *

Valerie Oliphant was sufficiently observant of Sabbath ordinances to keep her cards locked away and to forbid Archie from reading aloud from his blessed epic or rehearsing poor jilted Madelaine before or after the long and tedious trail to St Cuthbert's at the far end of Canal Street. She harboured the somewhat justified fear that she had already burned her boats with the Eternal Father and that He might not be quite so indulgent as her earthly father had been or quite so understanding of her weaknesses as her dear husband. In fact, when visiting preachers to St Cuthbert's thoughtlessly conjured up the stink of sulphur Valerie would resort to prayer and in a convoluted appeal to God would try to convince Him that it was all His fault for saddling her with a mate who had been neutered by an addiction to literature.

Fleur had fully recovered from her brush with smallpox but the disease had aged her or, rather, had made deception impossible. Clearly, she was no longer a child but a slightly built woman whose frilly high-sashed muslin frock and silly giggles now seemed fairly ridiculous.

The Admiral did not seem to mind.

He had passed the summer trolling between Whitehall and Seething Lane, negotiating timber purchases on behalf of the Admiralty. He had spent no more than a week at sea with his official retinue and had had little time to indulge his penchant for the theatre or, for that matter, for small girls before he returned to Scotland to discharge his duties as an inspector of dockyards.

He placed one hand stealthily between Fleur's knees and rubbed his knuckles against the muslin. The girl—the woman—did not flinch. She clenched her knees tightly around his fingers and continued to chat with Valerie as if nothing untoward was happening below the oak.

The three elderly ladies who made up the supper party, together with Sir Archie and Mrs Madelaine Young, were all busy dissecting roast grouse and discussing the imminent arrival of M. Didier's players, a subject on which Archie waxed lyrical but which seemed to engage Madelaine not at all. She was thinking of Gillon Peters upon whom she had not clapped eyes since that hot day in August when Sir Archie had finally returned from his antiquarian tour. There had been no letters from Gillon and even Valerie had been unable to inform her what new adventure had claimed her soldier boy now that he was done with her.

The sour letter from Lord Craigiehall had come as no surprise. Lady Valerie and she together had composed a reply. And then another, and, finally, a third. Valerie had not been dismayed by his lordship's silence and Maddy, bored by Perthshire, by 'Fingal' and the whole silly scheme, could not have cared less. At some indeterminate point in time she had come to realise that she was as much a dupe as his lordship and that behind Valerie Oliphant's mischief-making was a ruthless manipulation of power, wealth and position over lives that her ladyship regarded as of less worth than her own.

She watched a footman cross the floor of the dining-room bearing an ornate silver dish filled with pickled peaches and, behind him, at the door, Bradley peering in. Sir Archie, in full flow, did not notice the butler; then Bradley glided across the room and, covering his mouth with a gloved hand, whispered in Sir Archie's ear.

Sir Archie looked up in surprise. 'Asked for who?'

'Mrs Young, sir, Mrs Madelaine Young.'

Master and servant glowered at Maddy as if she was responsible for the interruption, then, throwing down his cloth, Sir Archie made to rise.

'I'll see him. Fact, I'll see him off,' he said.

Valerie said, 'Who is it, dearest?'

'Peters. Peters wishing to speak with Madelaine.'

'Where is he?'

'Lurking in the drawing-room, apparently,' Archie said.

Madelaine dropped her fork, shot to her feet, and said, 'No, if it's me he wants, it's me he shall have,' and before anyone could stop her rushed headlong from the dining-room.

*　　　*　　　*

He wore a greatcoat and top boots and carried his hat in his hand. He turned when she entered the room. She heard herself say, 'Oh, it's you.'

'I'm sorry to disappoint you,' Grant said.

'Has something happened to Gillon? Is he—is he dead?'

'Dead?' said Grant. 'Heavens, no! To the best of my knowledge he is still alive and, I assume,

381

kicking. My business does not concern Gillon.'

'Where is he? Do you not know?'

Grant shook his head. 'Madam,' he said, 'I have neither seen nor heard from my brother since the courts closed. My guess is that he will have travelled to Newcastle or to York where, in the racing season, good pickings are to be found, if not on the course, in the inns around it.'

Maddy let out her breath and, smoothing her skirts, seated herself, a little shakily, on one of the gilded chairs. She motioned Gillon's brother to another. He folded the skirts of his greatcoat carefully over his knees and placed the hat on the floor beside him. He was, she thought, a methodical man, not easy like Gillon.

She settled herself, and said, 'Now?'

'I am here as a representative of Lord Craigiehall.'

Madelaine fashioned a frown. 'Are you his solicitor, his lawyer?'

'I am his son-in-law.'

'And an advocate?'

'Yes, an advocate.'

'Have you come to read me the law, sir?' Maddy said.

'I am not acting in a professional capacity,' Grant said, adding, 'as yet.'

'Do I detect a certain threat in your tone?' said Maddy.

'You detect, Mrs Young, regret that you have seen fit to misinterpret his lordship's relationship with you as something more than friendship.'

'If John James had been polite enough to reply to my letters you would have no reason to disrupt Lady Oliphant's supper party.'

382

'Your letters,' Grant said, 'did not deserve an answer. You and I both know that your letters were intended to elicit responses that might serve as evidence against his lordship in your suit for breach of promise.'

'I do not require written evidence. My word . . .'

'Your word?' Grant interrupted. 'His lordship has no recollection of promising you anything. You were a willing partner in the summer friendship, until you overstepped the mark.'

'He promised that I would be his wife.'

'Before or after he poled you?'

'Sir!' said Maddy, simulating horror. 'How dare you?'

'Before, after—or not at all?' Grant insisted.

'Are you calling me a liar?'

'I am calling your bluff, Mrs Young. Was it before or after publication of the *Courant* pieces that you recalled that his lordship had proposed marriage? There's no mention of marriage in the newspaper or, indeed, in any of the written evidence.'

'There is Lord Craigiehall's letter of dismissal,' said Madelaine. 'It is that letter that has broken my heart and caused me to seek redress.'

'Broken your heart?' said Grant. 'I see. Is emotional distress the root of your case against his lordship or is it the loss of your reputation?'

'Both.'

'Would both, or either, be cured by marriage?'

'Marriage?' said Madelaine.

'His lordship is under no restraint. He is quite free to marry you,' Grant said. 'Are you free to marry him, Mrs Young?'

'I do not wish to marry him, sir, not after he has

383

made it plain that he does not care for me.'

'Do you still care for him?'

'No, I do not care for him.'

'Yet not much more than seven weeks ago,' Grant said, 'you cared enough to leap at his proposal.'

'I did not leap,' said Maddy.

'No, you lay down under him on Castle Hill and let him pole you.'

'Only because he asked me to be his wife.'

'Where was the proposal made?'

'At the supper table in Fortune's.'

'His lordship has no recollection of making such a proposal,' Grant said.

'He was too drunk to remember.'

'But,' Grant Peters said, softly, 'you were not too drunk to accept.'

'That is correct.'

'If you were a model of sobriety why was his lordship drunk?'

'It hardly matters, does it?'

'On the contrary, it matters very much,' Grant said. 'It will be a point against you if you insist on bringing the affair to court.'

'Lady Valerie Oliphant will speak for me.'

'I have no doubt that she will,' Grant said.

'Sir Archie, too.'

'And my brother, Gillon, perhaps?'

'I am not well acquainted with your brother,' Maddy said.

'You have played whist with him, have you not?'

'One does not necessarily make friends at the card table.'

'Well,' Grant said, 'we will let that matter pass, at least for the time being. I will come directly to

384

the point: how much will it cost Lord Craigiehall for you to drop your threat to sue?'

'My reputation is not a commodity to be bought cheaply.'

'Reputation?' Grant said. 'What reputation?'

'My career as a player.'

'It is not your career but his lordship's that is under threat.'

Maddy tilted her head and smiled. 'Precisely.'

Grant said, 'How much?'

'Ten thousand pounds.'

'Preposterous,' Grant said, flatly. 'Lord Craigiehall is not a wealthy man. His money is invested in land—and he has borrowings.'

'I am well aware of that,' said Madelaine. 'He does not pay his debts even to old friends like Lady Valerie. It is that consideration that obliges me to ask for such a large sum, and take him to court to get it.'

'Taking him to court will serve no purpose at all,' Grant said. 'You may think that because you have shaken his lordship's pedestal he will agree to your demands. Not so, Madam. You are too greedy.'

'What is his offer?'

'Fifteen hundred pounds, in cash, against your binding promise not to communicate with his lordship again.'

'It is not enough, not nearly enough.'

'It's ten times more than you're liable to receive in the unlikely event that a court finds in your favour.'

'It is, however, much less than a court would award me in annuity.'

'Do not be ridiculous. No court in the land will

385

award you annuity.'

'Annuity for my child, that is,' said Madelaine.

'Your child! If you mean that girl, that so-called ward . . .'

Madelaine rose gracefully and laid both hands on her stomach.

'I mean, the child that Lord Craigiehall has placed in my womb.'

'What!' Grant said, rising too. 'Do you tell me that you are pregnant?'

'I have every reason to believe that I am,' said Madelaine.

'How far along are you?'

'Seven weeks.'

'Seven weeks! Phooh!' said Grant. 'It cannot be proved at seven weeks.'

'Then, sir, we will simply have to wait until it *can* be proved.'

'Do you honestly expect me to believe that Craigiehall's the father?'

'Who else could it be?' said Madelaine, and smiled.

CHAPTER TWENTY-TWO

It was barely light when they left Heatherbank. A thick white mist blanketed the meadows. Nicola was glad of her cape for warmth. She sat beside Roderick with the hood pulled forward to cover her face and looked neither to left nor right as the cart trundled out of the yard. At breakfast she had thanked Mother Peters for her hospitality and had kissed Duncan Ralston's hairy cheek, but her anger at Roderick had not waned.

'She will be glad to be rid of me,' Nicola said.

'Who?' said Roderick.

'Marie Hadley. When I am gone she will have you all to herself again.'

Staring ahead, she waited for Roderick to protest, but he did not. They rode in silence as the sun cleared the hilltops and coaxed the castle from the mist.

'Do you have money for the coach fare?' Roderick said, at length. 'I'll give you money if you need it.'

'I have money,' Nicola said. 'Grant gave me money.'

'Nicola.' He brushed back the fold of her hood. 'Nicola, look at me.'

'What?'

'Where will you go? What will you do?'

'To Edinburgh, of course, to look after my sister.'

'And after that?' Roderick said.

'I have given it no thought.'

'You have nowhere to go, do you?'

In Craigiehall she had had a place, an identity. There at least she had belonged. Half a year had passed since she'd lain alone in bed in her room in Craigiehall dreaming of a husband. How childish that dream seemed now.

'You will always be welcome at Heatherbank,' he said. 'There will always be a place for you here.'

'In the byre?' she said, trying to make light of it.

'I'm not looking for another farm servant.'

'No, you have enough of those already.'

'I told you I had secrets I can't share with you.'

'Because Marie Hadley would not forgive you?'

387

Nicola said.

'Marie is not the forgiving sort,' said Roderick.

'No more, I've learned, am I.'

'Then that's a hard lesson, a sad lesson.'

'Perhaps so,' said Nicola, 'but once learned, it cannot be unlearned.'

'Will you not try to forgive me?'

'Forgive you for what, Roderick?'

'Falling in love with you,' he said.

'Love?' she said. 'Is that what you call it? I know that you want me.'

'I can't deny it, Nicola,' Roderick said. 'I do want you.'

'But I do not know the reason.'

'Must there be a reason?'

'I've seen and heard too much these past few months to take you on trust, Roderick. Now give your pony rein and take me to the Kings Park. I have a coach to catch.'

Resigned, he flicked the whip and drove quickly on towards Stirling.

*   *   *

The gentlemen met to discuss strategy at a corner table in Horne's on an unseasonably warm afternoon with no clerks or servants in attendance. It was soon agreed that once Craigiehall's name appeared on the register of causes truth or falsehood, guilt or innocence would count for nothing and the libel alone would be enough to bring the judge to his knees.

John James said, 'I will not pay her ten pennies, let alone ten thousand pounds, until it is confirmed that she is, indeed, with child.'

'It's unlikely,' Grant put in, 'that she'll allow herself to be examined.'

'Of course she will not,' said Hercules. 'She's gambling that his lordship will be sufficiently alarmed to pay her to pack her bags.'

'Oliphant will not release Madelaine from whatever agreement exists between them until she has performed her part in his damned play,' said Grant.

'It is obvious, in hindsight, that you were chosen as a target, sir.'

'Why would Valerie do such a thing?'

'Do you not owe her money?' Grant said.

'A trifling sum,' his father-in-law said. 'A thousand pounds or so.'

'Hardly trifling,' said Hercules. 'Why did you not square with her?'

'She did not press me and I had other matters on my mind,' John James said. 'The harvest is in and my rents are due. I have sold felling rights to a stand of mature timber. I could, at a pinch, pay her off now, I suppose.'

'Can you also afford to pay off Madelaine Young?' said Hercules.

'Yes, but I will go no higher than fifteen hundred pounds.'

'Then,' Hercules rubbed his hands, 'we must at all costs avert a trial.'

'But the child?' John James said. 'What of the child?'

'If there is a child,' said Hercules, 'which I greatly doubt, then it will be incumbent upon Mrs Young to prove that she has had no connection with any other man in the span of time when conception might have taken place.'

389

'Will her word stand up before a jury?' John James said.

'We do not have to prove that connection with another man took place,' said Hercules, 'only that she had opportunity to make such a connection.'

'Sir Archie Oliphant had her to himself all summer,' John James said.

'Sir Archie has long been impotent,' said Hercules.

'What?' said John James. 'How do you know such a thing?'

Hercules tapped the side of his nose. 'Uncommon knowledge, shall we say. I do not imagine that Lady Valerie will be willing to swear on oath that her husband is unable to raise the flag, however, particularly as she will be called to speak on Madelaine Young's behalf. No, there must be another candidate.'

'There is.' John James glanced at his son-in-law. 'There is another.'

'Oh!' said Hercules. 'Who might that be?'

'He means my brother,' said Grant. 'My brother, Gillon.'

*   *   *

The apartment in Graddan's Court was in a state of near uproar when, well after ten o'clock, Nicola finally arrived at the door. Only Molly was there to greet her and, drawing her to one side, told her that her father was in the parlour and that Charlotte and he had been arguing all through supper.

'Is that Grant?' Charlotte called out.

Nicola removed her cape and bonnet and,

390

shaking dust from her skirts, stepped in to the over-heated room.

'No,' she said. 'It's me.'

'Oh!' said Charlotte, without surprise or enthusiasm. 'You're back. I assume you've heard about Papa's latest misfortune?'

'I have heard nothing since the *Courant* piece appeared.'

To Nicola's astonishment her father held out his arms and, when she approached, embraced her. He was seated on one of the chairs at the table, waistcoat unbuttoned, neck-cloth loosened and looked, she thought, haggard beyond belief. He said, 'You will stand by me, my dearest, will you not?'

She was still thinking of Roderick and the summer that had slipped away and, wearied by the journey, found that she had no patience with her father's sentimental gestures. 'Have you been taken to the guardhouse again?'

'Better for all of us if he had not been released in the first place,' said Charlotte. 'He has made fools of us all.'

Charlotte was clad in a loose robe that started at her throat and sloped steeply to her knees. There was a glow about her, though, an unusual air of confidence. She spoke as if her father was not in the room. 'Apparently he decided to marry to keep us from inheriting Craigiehall. He picked the wrong woman to woo, however, and now she claims to be with child and is suing Papa for breach of promise of marriage.'

'Is she with child?' said Nicola.

'That remains a mystery,' said Charlotte.

Nicola seated herself. She could not meet her

father's eye.

'If we hold together then it may not become public,' her father said.

'Why should we hold together?' Charlotte said. 'You so disapproved of my choice of a husband that you would not even turn out to see me married. You tried to sell poor Nicola off to that decaying old man for a few tons of coal. It's as well for you that Grant is not one to harbour grudges or you would be stranded without a friend in the world. I trust that you will not forget that when Grant has pulled you from the mire. If you were so desperate for an heir, another Jamie, you might have paid a little more heed to what was happening to me. My son, your grandson, Papa, born in wedlock and protected by the laws of the land, must surely inherit Craigiehall.'

'Wait,' said Nicola. 'What about me? Papa, who will take care of me?'

'Once I have passed out of this world, Grant Peters will be responsible for your welfare. He's a decent enough fellow, whose value I misjudged. I suppose I was distracted by my concern for Craigiehall's future.' He put a hand to his brow and stroked his thinning hair. 'It was all too easy to trade upon my weakness. The woman, Madelaine, was convincing. I thought at first that she cared for me and would make me a good wife.'

'Infatuation,' said Charlotte, 'is an expensive vice for an old man. We cannot cope with any more silliness on your part, Papa. From what Grant has told me, it will cost you a pretty penny to be rid of her.'

'Where is Grant?' said Nicola.

'He has gone in search of his brother,' said

Charlotte. 'Gillon is the key to Papa's defence, it seems.'

'Gillon?' said Nicola. 'What does Gillon have to do with it?'

'He will swear that he had connection with this woman,' her father said.

'Did he?' said Nicola.

'That hardly matters,' said Charlotte. 'Gillon will be the lynch pin in the case that Grant presents to Mrs Young to deter her from proceeding with her suit against Papa.'

'Will Gillon do it, though?' said Nicola.

'For five hundred pounds,' Charlotte said, 'Gillon will do anything.'

* * *

Gillon had not been seen in any of his usual haunts since early in August but, Grant discovered, he had paid eight weeks' rent on his lodgings in advance which indicated that he intended to return before winter set in. After supping with Somerville at Horne's, Grant dismissed his clerk and made one final tour past Gillon's tenement before he too retired for the night. There, to his astonishment, he saw a candle flickering in the window of the topmost room and, heart racing, bounded upstairs and threw himself against the door.

'Who is it?'

'Me, you scoundrel. Grant.'

'What do you want? I have nothing to say to you.'

'Open the damned door, Gillon, or I will kick it down.'

'Are you alone?'

'Of course, I'm alone,' Grant said. 'What, are you on the run?'

The door opened an inch and Gillon peered out. Grant stuck his boot into the opening and pressed his shoulder against the woodwork. 'What is wrong with you, Gillon?' he hissed. 'Why are you avoiding us? What are you afraid of?'

'Not you,' Gillon said, turning his back on his brother.

Grant pushed into the room which smelled so musty that he almost choked. There was no fire in the grate and only a single candle gave light. On the bed was a knapsack, spilling clothes; on the table a loaf of bread, a wedge of cheese and, wrapped in brown paper, an oozing piece of meat.

'It's icy in here,' Grant said. 'Have you no fuel?'

'I've only just returned,' Gillon said. 'Minutes ago, in fact—and here you are come to badger me. I've been six days on the road, Grant, and I am ready to topple. If you have something to say to me, say it quickly.'

'Where have you been? We'll make a start with that.'

'York—and other places.'

'Following the races?'

'Slap-dash, haphazard things are races these days. I would not wager on a horse even if he was ridden by a Frenchman,' Gillon said. 'If you must know, I went on to London—and a gruelling trip it was.'

'And now you are penniless, I suppose.'

'On the contrary,' Gillon said. 'I did well at the tables. Very well. You see, it does not do to leap to conclusions.'

'If you were doing so well, why did you bother to

394

come home?'

'I have a notion to re-enlist,' Gillon said. 'I have almost enough to purchase a decent commission, and that will do me well enough.'

'Did you not miss your actress, the English widow?'

'So that's it,' Gillon said. 'That's why you're here.' He pushed the knapsack to the floor and seated himself upon the bed. 'Is Maddy returned from Kingsley? Have you seen her?'

'I have.'

'Did she ask after me?' said Gillon, glancing up.

'Her mind is on other things, I fear,' Grant said.

'Has Craigiehall got her after all?'

'Was that the plan?' Grant said. 'To snare Craigiehall?'

'I doubt you will believe me,' Gillon said, 'but I was never too clear *what* the plan was. Has Craigiehall got her?'

'No, his lordship broke with her. It was never a match made in heaven,' Grant said. 'In fact, your Mrs Young is on the point of suing my father-in-law for breach of promise.'

'She'll never get away with it,' said Gillon.

'She might, you know,' said Grant.

'How much is she asking for?'

'Ten thousand.'

Gillon whistled through his teeth. 'Expensive for one night's folly, especially if you were too intoxicated to enjoy it.'

'Or even remember it,' said Grant.

Gillon slapped his knee. 'Good for Madelaine. She'll never persuade the old fool to part with ten thousand, of course, but if she plays the hand properly she may get off with two or even three thousand to make her go away.'

'And the baby, too?' said Grant.

'Baby? Charlotte's baby? What does . . .'

'Madelaine's baby,' Grant said. 'She claims she's with child.'

Gillon blinked. '*Is* she with child?'

'No one knows for sure,' said Grant. 'Time, of course, will tell.'

'Seven weeks,' said Gillon. 'Eight at most.'

'When did you bed her?' said Grant.

'I did not bed her.'

'Were you not paid to bed her?'

'No.'

'Would you be prepared to say otherwise?' Grant said.

Gillon pushed himself to his feet, kicked out a chair and seated himself, horseman style. 'In court?'

'Not in court. I will prepare a deposition, and you will sign it. I will then present the deposition to Mrs Young, together with other salient facts. By proving that Craigiehall may not be the father, her credibility will be destroyed.'

'Will I be named as the father?' said Gillon.

'No, no,' said Grant. 'She will be paid a reasonable sum to take herself out of Edinburgh and that will be an end of it.'

'How much will Maddy be paid to quit Edinburgh?'

Grant shrugged. 'Fifteen hundred pounds, no more. How much will it take to purchase you a commission in the regiment?'

Gillon uttered a little grunt. 'Oh, five hundred will see me back in uniform,' he said. 'Is that fair?'

'Will you do it for five hundred pounds?' said

Grant.

'Yes, I'll do it,' Gillon said, and with just enough weight to be convincing, shook his brother's hand.

*　　　*　　　*

Duncan Ralston had enjoyed having a couple of cultured young ladies in the house. It had tickled him to tease Grant's haughty wife, bring her down a peg or two and perhaps make her appreciate her husband a little more, though Grant, it seemed, was quite capable of keeping the heiress in her place. He was proud of what Grant had made of himself; a King's advocate, wedded to the daughter of a lord and well established in Edinburgh society, albeit a society for which he had never had much regard.

After he finished breakfast and washed the crocks in the last of the water from the kettle, he went out into the yard to fill the kettle at the pump. He could no longer carry the heavy kettle by the handle and toted it in his arms. It was a grey, dry morning with more than a hint of winter in the air. He leaned on the pump, studied the hillside and gathered his strength to grasp the cold iron and begin the process of pumping water from the spring that summer or winter, drought or flood, had never once failed them.

He started when his grandson put a hand on his shoulder. Roderick had the boy with him, holding him not by the hand but by the shoulder too. Duncan looked down at the child, dark eyes sullen and watchful, at the lick of dark hair that marked him as a Peters.

'They are busy over at Hadley's calving the cow,'

Roderick said. 'Will you see to it that the boy gets his dinner?'

'I will,' said Duncan. 'I'll keep an eye on him.'

He lifted the boy, set him on top of the pump and steadied him.

'What can you see, Iain? Tell me, can you see the castle?'

'Nay, Mr Ralston, no castle today.'

'Can you see Cathy's house?'

'Aye.'

'Then that'll have to do us, will it not?'

'It will, Mr Ralston,' the boy said, solemnly.

Tucking his knees to his chest, he let Duncan lift him down again and stood quietly between the men, looking from one to the other.

Duncan said, 'She took the last of the sunshine with her, it seems.'

'I suppose you could say that,' Roderick answered. 'Are you fit enough to carry water?'

'Do you think I've grown soft just because I had a lass to help me for a while?' Duncan said. 'By the by, where's your mother?'

'Gone to the mill for meal,' Roderick said.

Duncan placed the kettle beneath the spout and clacked the handle down to prime the primitive mechanism. Iain moved forward eagerly for Duncan knew that he still regarded the pump as an instrument of magic that could conjure water out of thin air.

'What is it, Roddy?' he said. 'What bothers you? Is it the girl?'

'I can't go on much longer,' Roderick said, 'awaiting Mam's approval.' Duncan thrust down on the pump handle and coaxed a gush of water from the spout. 'I'm thirty years old. What hope have I of finding a woman who'll have me when I'm saddled with . . .'

Duncan put a finger to his lips. 'If the lass from Edinburgh has you so hot and bothered, you should have thought of the consequences before you encouraged her. It wasn't wise to woo a girl who's sister to your brother's wife.'

'He'll have that damned Ayrshire estate yet.'

'Is it the lassie or the land that attracts you?'

'I care not a tinker's curse about Craigiehall's estates.'

'Then,' said Duncan, 'it's the girl.'

'Aye, it's the girl.'

The little boy reached out for Duncan's hand, lifted it to the handle, pressed as hard as he could on Duncan's knuckles and produced a short, sharp jet from the spout. He let out a 'whoo' of delight and pressed again while Duncan, preoccupied, indulged him.

'There have been girls before,' said Duncan, 'an' there will be girls again, Roddy, but your mother won't have you marrying this one.'

'Because of Grant?' said Roderick. 'Do you suppose it will stop him now he has the father swung his way? Mother will soon have what she wants, a son and a grandson linked to the damned gentry.'

'But you'll have Heatherbank,' Duncan reminded him. 'Is that not what you've always wanted? Is that not why you stepped aside?'

'I did not step aside willingly,' Roderick said. 'What choice did I have? Do you think I'm tarred with the same brush as our Gillon? I did not run away from it, from any of it.'

'When Grant has charge of Craigiehall . . .'

399

'When will that be?' said Roderick. 'Ten years, or twenty? You will be gone, and I'll be left here to chew the cud and wonder what became of my life. What about Heatherbank then? Who'll tend this place when I die? Will Grant have it, too, for his sons to play with?'

'By God!' said Duncan. 'You've fallen in love with Nicola Templeton?'

'Aye,' Roderick said. 'I think perhaps I have.'

CHAPTER TWENTY-THREE

Sir Archie Oliphant had no compunction in tampering with the great narratives of Scottish-Irish history. He had been a student of Gaelic poetry for almost as long as James Macpherson and bitterly resented the fame that Macpherson had gathered to himself with the publication of the *Poems of Ossian*, a volume admired by every literate gentleman, and some ladies, the length and breadth of the land, though in Archie's opinion the collection was as spurious an artefact as King Arthur's sword or Wallace's nightshirt, both of which items had lately been put on public display in the College library.

At the mere mention of Macpherson's name Sir Archie would foam at the mouth like one of Cuchullin's stallions and rant about Macpherson's unscrupulous appropriation of source material that Archie considered his by right. Never did it cross the wealthy scholar's mind that his plays were laughed off the stage not because they were inauthentic but for their pretentious metaphors

400

and limping rhymes.

Madelaine had been subjected to Archie's verse all summer long. She knew that whatever Archie's opinion of himself he was no Shakespeare or Marlowe and that his breast-beating speeches and Greek-style choral wailings contained not one drop of originality. Madelaine, of course, kept her views to herself, obediently learned her lines and applied the vocal mannerisms that Archie required. She had even accompanied him to a rock on the hillside above Loch Tummel and had bawled Nu-ala's anguished soliloquies into the wind until her throat ached and every sheep for miles around had galloped off in disgust.

If Sir Archie hoped that M. Didier would lead his 'company' to Edinburgh, then Sir Archie was doomed to disappointment. M. Didier might be French but he wasn't daft and, handshake or no, the little troop that the manager shipped north that October was scraped together from the ranks of the unemployable. It was composed of four untrained kiddies, an actor with shredded vocal chords and a brace of actresses so sumptuously overweight that they could barely waddle let alone 'sway like reeds in the marshes of Morni' or 'gleam like slender wands around the death-bed of Nu-ala.'

Sir Archie was very jolly, though, for here at last were the instruments that would trumpet his genius to the world. He had laid on supper in honour of his guests but after Valerie had stamped her foot and refused to have theatrical riff-raff polluting her bedrooms, had billeted them in Mannering's Hotel which was convenient for the theatre at the tail of Prince's Street and not far from the Oliphants' mansion in whose drawing-room the first rehearsals would take place that evening.

Madelaine did not share Sir Archie's enthusiasm or Fleur's excitement. She was afraid that she might be recognised by one of the London players.

First from the coach were two portly dames, well past their prime. They were followed by a gaunt, rickety-looking man who introduced himself, with a creaky flourish, as Mr Conn Cavendish who M. Didier had put in charge of performance and who would also play the warrior hero. Finally, three youths and a scrawny young girl hopped out, shivering in the chill Scottish air. When they were introduced to Madelaine, however, they stared at her blankly for her name, let alone her reputation, meant nothing to them.

The 'slender wands' headed off in search of a water closet and it was left to Mr Cavendish to greet her with the flattering assurance that although he had frequently heard M. Didier sing her praises he had, alas, never had the pleasure of seeing her perform. Fleur took the scrawny young girl by the arm and led her off to the waiting chaise while a footman unloaded the luggage. The boys, not knowing what else to do, trailed after the girls like lambs to the slaughter.

Sir Archie did not seem dismayed by the tawdry band and as soon as courtesy allowed, thrust into Mr Cavendish's hand a copy of the play script which had come hot from the printer that morning and steered the actor off to the waiting vehicle.

And Madelaine, with a sigh of relief, followed on.

*　　*　　*

Charlotte stopped and, puffing a little, leaned a hand on Nicola's arm; Edinburgh's hills were taking their toll at last. Molly stepped forward and also offered her arm to her mistress but Charlotte shook her off.

'I may be large, but I am not an invalid, thank you,' she said.

'Aye, you're large right enough,' said Molly. 'Large enough to be carryin' a pair, if you ask me.'

In the past few days Charlotte's girth had visibly increased. Her condition was now too obvious to be disguised by cloaks and pelisses and, in Molly's opinion, it was high time the lady affected modesty and confined herself indoors. Charlotte refused to bow to such old-fashioned nonsense, however, and insisted that an afternoon walk was good for her.

Now that young master Peters was clamouring within her, she had purchased several lengths of silk to be sewn into baby frocks. She had bought three sweet little caps from a seamstress in Bridge Street and, rather prematurely, a boned woollen bodice and a pair of boy's shoes to put down in the chest against the day when her son would be short-coated. She was so convinced that the object kicking against her ribs was male that it was all Nicola could do to prevent her sister ordering a painted hobby-horse and a wooden sword on the off chance that the lad would turn out to be a soldier.

'Where, if I might ask, are we goin'?' said Molly.

'Nowhere,' said Charlotte. 'Shopping.'

'Shoppin'?' said Molly. 'There are no booths

here.'

'Well, it makes a change of scene, does it not?' said Charlotte. 'Would you have us go across the bridge to look at the diggings in the New Town again?'

'I've had enough o' that too,' said Molly. 'Besides, the New Town's o'er far for you now, Miss Charlotte, unless you hire a chair.'

'How many times do I have to tell you, Molly, that I'm not an invalid?' Charlotte said. 'Now, step back, if you please, and let us be on our way. It will be dark all too soon and we must take advantage of daylight while we can.'

Molly, muttering, fell into step behind the sisters as Charlotte ploughed on uphill and when the crown of the road was reached swung into a side street lined with ugly tenements.

'Do you intend to drop in on Gillon unannounced?' said Nicola, quietly.

'Oh!' said Charlotte. 'Does Gillon lodge here?'

'Well you know he does,' said Nicola. 'It was unwise of Grant to let it slip, though I don't imagine he thought you'd be silly enough to call on him.'

'I do not intend to call on Gillon,' said Charlotte. 'Under the circumstances it would not be proper.'

'What circumstances?' said Nicola. 'His, or yours?'

'At least we know he is alive and well,' said Charlotte. 'Do you happen to know if this is the street, and what close . . .'

'No, I do not,' Nicola snapped.

'Oh well!' said Charlotte. 'Perhaps we may encounter him by chance.'

404

'Unless,' said Nicola, not seriously, 'he has already rejoined his regiment.'

'Surely, it's too soon,' said Charlotte. 'Such matters take time, do they not? I mean, he wouldn't leave without saying goodbye to me, would he?'

'I have long ago given up speculating on what Gillon might do,' said Nicola, 'what any of Margo Peters' sons might do, in fact.'

'I trust that you do not mean my husband?'

Nicola had no wish to argue. She was not sure why Charlotte had brought them to this low quarter and what Charlotte's intentions towards Gillon Peters might be, or if there was no more to it than whim. In the shabby Edinburgh streets, penned in by tall buildings, she found herself longing to be back at Heatherbank, to watch the white mist rising from the river, cows trailing into the byre and Roderick coming home along the path from the meadow.

She said, 'Is Papa expected for supper tonight?'

'Did I not tell you?' Charlotte said. 'Papa has repaired to Craigiehall. There's no more he can do here and Grant felt it would be better if he were inaccessible for the next few weeks. Grant has everything in hand.'

'Does he?' said Nicola.

'What is wrong with you, Nicola? You've been very sour since you returned from the country.'

'I am concerned about Papa, that's all.'

'Then go to him,' said Charlotte. 'Go home to Craigiehall, if you must.'

'I thought you needed me here,' said Nicola.

'I have Molly to look after me, and Jeannie will be back soon.'

'Are you not still afraid?'

'Afraid? Afraid of what?' said Charlotte. 'I'm in good health and Dr Gaythorn will visit me when required to do so. I have a comfortable house, a loving husband and the best of attention. What, tell me, do I have to fear?'

Nicola shook her head. 'Nothing, I suppose.'

Charlotte's unusual mood of optimism troubled her. She glanced back at the street of tottering old tenements. She felt empty, devoid of substance, like a phantom. She almost wished that Gillon would resume his clumsy courtship, even without a share of Craigiehall to render his wooing worthwhile. Then, before that silly thought could take root, she uttered a little snort of self-disgust and, catching Charlotte's arm, headed towards the High Street, and out of harm's way.

*   *   *

In his haste to convene a company of English actors it had not occurred to Sir Archie that the language appropriate to 'Fingal' might be rendered somewhat less than perfectly by street urchins from Bow or fat ladies from Southwark. He had been spoiled—or deceived, perhaps—by Madelaine's vocal aptitude. She had wit enough to round out vowels, enunciate consonants and add a certain tremble to end lines to make her sound, in Archie's opinion at least, sufficiently like a broken-hearted Orcadian to pass muster with an audience of Lowlanders.

The three boys, Charlie, Tom and Ben, would never pass muster even if Sir Archie rehearsed them from now until doomsday. Their native

406

tongue was Cockney and their theatrical education had stretched no further than learning to walk on stage without tripping over. Ben had taught himself to cart-wheel, though, and exhibited this talent by cartwheeling all over the drawing-room until Mr Cavendish grabbed him and made him stop.

The scrawny girl, Nancy, was so overwhelmed by her surroundings that she could not utter a word at first and when she was finally cajoled into demonstrating a mournful cry, released a series of shrieks so shrill that the silverware tinkled, the crystal sang and Lady Valerie, hands clapped to her ears, dispensed with politeness and fled not only the drawing-room but the house.

The fat ladies, Opal and Pearl—'jewels, we are, sir, rare jewels'—fared little better. They had both acted in the Scotch play and had mastered the Highland dialect well enough to dance round a cauldron and put the fear of God into old Macbeth which, alas, was a far cry from the lyrical chanting required of Melilcoma and Dersagrena, Nu-ala's handmaidens.

On the other hand, Mr Conn Cavendish, who had been too much at the wine, was just sufficiently tipsy to read his role as Fingal with lugubrious enthusiasm and a thick Irish accent cribbed from his dear old Ma who, he said, had been born and raised in Donegal.

All, it seemed, was not quite lost.

Sir Archie retrieved his wig from the floor, smoothed the tufts of hair that he had all but torn out and, before he packed his hirelings off to Mannering's for the night, planted them in gilded chairs to listen to a scene properly played by his star performer, Madelaine Young.

Madelaine retained just enough professional pride to shake off her depression and, summoning Fleur to join her, slipped into the character of the distracted princess. With Fleur kneeling at her feet, she launched into the first of several monologues in which the gullible Nu-ala bemoaned the death of Fingal on the halberds of the Roman emperor, Caraculla, which report was, of course, a calumny put out by the villainous Hidallan, a rival for Nu-ala's hand, for Fingal was no more dead in act seven than he had been in act one.

'How late I thought I saw him beaming on yon distant rock,' Madelaine began, with a suitable gesture in the direction of Prince's Street, 'showered down upon by victory in the shapes of meteors. How e'en now I hear the belling of his horn across the broad, belligerent sea that separates us, as death does, each soul from the other. O that I might lie with him in death on the banks of the Carun, my cold tears melting on his manly cheek, and . . .'

'Madelaine.'

The company from London looked towards the door, wondering, perhaps, if the intrusion was part of the drama.

'Madelaine,' Gillon said. 'I must speak with you at once.'

'What!' Sir Archie shouted. 'Are you drunk, sir, that you would intrude upon our private theatricals? Bradley, Bradley, evict this . . .'

'Aye, sir.' Gillon stepped into the drawing-room. 'I am, I admit, a little the worse for wear, for your lady has broken my heart.'

408

'Valerie? What does Valerie . . .'

'Not Valerie,' said Gillon. 'Madelaine.'

He advanced a step or two towards the woman who, hauling Fleur to her feet, placed the girl behind her as if she feared attack for the dagger in Gillon's hand was no prop.

'What have you done?' Archie cried. 'Have you murdered my butler?'

One of the fat ladies sniggered and the scrawny girl said, 'Oh-ah!'

Gillon said, 'Your butler has gone running out into the street calling for the guard to rescue him. He has no need of rescue, sir. I ask no more than a few minutes of this lady's time, then I will return her to your entertainment.'

'You are an intruder, sir, a ruffian,' Archie said. 'You shall not have her.'

But Madelaine had already drifted towards the lieutenant. She touched Archie's arm and with a shake of her head and a strange little smile soothed him. Then, as lightly as a summer breeze, she floated over to Gillon, placed an arm about his waist, led him out of the drawing-room and closed the door behind her.

For a full minute no one moved, then Ben, leaning across his companions, whispered, 'Know what?'

'What?' said Charlie.

'I fink I'm goin' ter like it 'ere.'

*   *   *

They headed for the staircase like lovers escaping from a masquerade, and tripped down it, arm in arm.

'*Are* you drunk?' Madelaine said.

'No, I'm as sober as you are.'

'Why, then, the dagger?'

'Do you suppose I'd have got past the front door without it?'

She laughed. 'Oh, you're a card, Gillon Peters, a fool. Is it your intention to abduct me?'

'Don't tempt me, Maddy,' Gillon said. 'I'm in enough trouble as it is.'

He paused at the foot of the staircase and wagged the blade in the direction of two young footmen who were lurking in the mouth of the kitchen corridor. 'You may tell your master that Mrs Young will be returned unharmed in a half hour or less,' he said, 'and that it will be better for all concerned if he does not alert the guard.' Then, still arm in arm with Madelaine, he swept her out into the damp night air and into a waiting hack.

*   *   *

Night had fallen long before John James reached home. There had been a great kerfuffle at the horse change at Lanark. He had sent Robertson to sort out the bother with the ostler who, it seemed, had not had his last bill paid and was therefore reluctant to extend credit even to a noble lord. Indeed, the fellow would not budge until he'd had three guineas put into his hand, the payment of which had left John James, and Robertson, penniless.

Cold, hungry and sore in his bones, he slouched to the door and tugged on the bell pull. Behind him he heard Robertson and the coach driver muttering as if the spirit of rebellion had descended upon them. He could hardly blame his servant for being disgruntled. He was, himself, in a very low state, weary of all the jogging up and down, and deeply grateful to his son-in-law for taking the sordid negotiations out of his hands for a spell.

He had just reached for the iron pull again when the door opened and there, in a blaze of candlelight, was his cousin, Isabella.

'You?' he said, stepping in the hall. 'Where the devil have you been?'

'Touring,' she said. 'Here, let me take your greatcoat.'

She moved behind him, helped him slip the heavy garment from his shoulders and handed it to a servant who, accompanied by Mrs McGrouther, had appeared from below stairs. On tip-toe, she removed his hat, gave it a shake and passed it to the footman.

'There!' She brushed his waistcoat with her fingertips. 'That's better,' then, to John James's surprise, put her arms about his waist, hugged him and rested her head upon his chest. 'Poor lamb,' she said. 'Poor lamb.'

Mrs McGrouther cleared her throat and enquired what his lordship would like to eat. That matter settled, John James accompanied Isabella into the little parlour off the hall where a fire had been lighted and glasses set out. He knelt before the fire, warming his hands, while Isa poured brandy.

'How did you know that I would come home?' he said.

'Where else would you go to escape opprobrium?'

411

He sipped from the glass, shuffled round on his heels and looked up at her. She was prettily dressed in an open robe with a pleated bodice and a neat little butterfly cap, all of the garments, he thought, new bought.

'Come,' she said. 'Sit with me, Johnny. I can't bear to look down on you.' She offered him her hand and helped him rise. 'Please be seated, dearest. I have more answers to give than you have questions, and supper will be at least an hour in the making.'

She spoke primly, in a manner that reminded him of Aunt Hankin. He groped behind him, found the armchair and sank into it, crossing his legs and nursing the brandy glass to his chest. Isabella settled herself on an upright wooden chair.

'First,' she said, 'let me tell you where I've been. I've been to London and to Gloucester to visit my children; Ariadne and Willy first and then Olivia, my Duchess daughter. I met my assorted grandchildren, five out of seven of them. Very pretty and polite they are. Ariadne's eldest has already embarked upon the Grand Tour and Willy's lad is preparing to read law in Leiden. How time does fly, does it not?'

'It does, it does,' said John James, indulgently.

'My children were hospitable enough but I embarrassed them rather, I think. They were relieved that I had not come to impose myself upon them, to seek, as it were, refuge in my old age.'

'You are not old enough, dear, to require refuge.'

'I am sixty-three, Johnny,' his cousin said. 'I cannot believe that my daughters are women

412

nearing the middle of life, and my grandchildren, to whom, of course, I am a stranger, are already off making their way in the world. I should never have let them go with Clarence, I suppose, for I have lost them and, heartless as it may sound, I have no particular desire to find them again.'

'Lost children,' said John James, nodding. 'Yes, sad, sad.'

Isabella stared at the toes of her slippers. 'Salton House and all its lands are mine, Johnny. There is no mortgage upon them. Willy, for it is his right to be consulted, has declared no interest in the place and, indeed, has waived his entitlement.'

John James was tempted to ask what this had to do with him but he had endured too many preparatory speeches in and out of court to rush his cousin to the point. Besides, he had a strange, prescient feeling that she was about to tell him something that he did not wish to hear.

Isabella went on, 'Do you know how I learned about the law suit that threatens your position on the bench?'

'Hmm,' John James said, as casually as possible. 'How did you?'

'Lady Valerie Oliphant informed me.'

'Lady Valerie?' He sat upright. 'What does she have to do with you, Isa, or, rather, what do you have to do with her?'

'I'm afraid, my dear, that I am responsible for your predicament.'

'Well, yes, you advised me.'

'I did more than that. I wrote to Lady Valerie on your behalf and asked her to steer you towards a bride.'

'You did *what*?'

'I thought she was your friend.'

'As I did,' said John James. 'We were both deceived, it seems. Go on.'

'I had no means of knowing that Valerie Oliphant would seize upon the opportunity to do us harm.' Isabella lifted her shoulders in a shivering little shrug, like a sparrow on a twig. 'I should not have meddled. Johnny, please say that you forgive me. I fear that all those years alone in Salton House have affected my reason.'

'Are you offering lunacy as a defence, Isabella?'

'Lunacy—or love.'

'Love?'

His cousin sighed. 'I may as well confess, John James, that I have been in love with you since we were both in short-clothes.'

'It does not do to confuse the affection that exists between members of a family with—ah—with love,' John James said. 'Why did you not tell me how you felt towards me?'

'You had the girls,' said Isabella, 'an estate to manage, an exalted position in society. I thought—I thought you were happy.'

'Happy?' his lordship said. 'Good God, Isa! I've not been happy in years.'

'When Charlotte ran off, and Nicola followed,' Isabella said. 'I hoped that I might become your guide, your confidante and confessor, and that when all else failed you would come back to me. You of all people can surely understand what it means to risk everything on chance.'

'Indeed,' John James said, 'but, Isa, it was my happiness that you were gambling with, not just your own.'

'I know it, Johnny. I know it now. If you wish me

414

to leave . . .'

'I do not wish you to leave,' John James said. 'You are not entirely to blame for my misfortune. I was ripe for a fall.' He got up from the armchair and took a tour around the parlour while his cousin watched him apprehensively. 'Why do you think I came to you for advice in the first place? I came to you because I had nowhere else to go. You were my only friend, the only person in the world to whom I could turn, the only person who did not regard me as a starchy, stiff-necked tyrant. You were already my confidante, my confessor.'

'But I betrayed you, I let you down.'

'You did not let me down in any way worse than I let down my daughters. You brought me to my senses and taught me a valuable lesson concerning the density of blood in relationship to water.' He came around behind her and placed a hand upon her shoulder. 'The question is, what can we do between us to salvage what remains of my reputation and my career?'

'Between us? Isabella said.

'As it stands, it appears that both Valerie Oliphant and Madelaine Young will require to be paid off if only to keep them from taking me to court.'

'Then pay them off,' his cousin said.

'I have no money; no ready money, that is.'

He felt rather than heard her laugh, a little tremor of the shoulder beneath his fingers, then she leaped up and, leaning across the chair, clasped both his hands in hers as if she were about to lead him into a gavotte.

'No, dearest, no,' she said, 'but I have. Lots of the stuff, in fact.'

415

'I've borrowed enough from you already, Isa. Even with an easy settlement upon me I doubt if I'll ever be able to repay you.'

'Oh, yes, Johnny,' his cousin said. 'You will, you will,' and, placing one knee carefully upon the chair, raised herself up to kiss him.

*   *   *

The hackney clipped away from the Oliphants' mansion, rounded the corner and drove to that area of dormant ground by the old St Ninian's burial ground where Gillon had had his rendezvous with Lady Valerie. On Gillon's instruction, it drew to a halt by the locked gates. By then Gillon had kissed her not once or twice but a dozen times and Maddy, wild and breathless, would have given herself to him without a qualm if that had been his wish.

As soon as the conveyance stopped, however, Gillon shoved her away.

'No,' he said. 'No.'

'Why?' she said. 'There is no one here to see us and the driver will pay no heed. Do you not want me?'

'Damned be it, Maddy, of course I want you.'

'Where have you been all summer? I looked for you at Kingsley. I thought you'd find an excuse to come to me. Oh, darling, how I've missed you.'

'Missed me, have you?' Gillon said. 'Aye, perhaps you have. But not enough to prevent you going through with your plans.'

'Oh, come now,' Maddy said, with a toss of the head. 'After all the trouble we've been to, do you expect me to give up now? You've been cornered

416

by your brother, I suppose, and have turned honest. No, no, no, darling. I am not going to swallow that.'

'Honesty has nothing to do with it,' Gillon said. 'I advise you to hear what I have to say before you proceed with your suit.'

'If you mean the threats that your advocate brother has concocted, I am reliably informed ...'

'By Valerie Oliphant?'

'By Lady Oliphant, yes—reliably informed that John James will cough up every penny that's asked of him to save what remains of his precious reputation.'

'Ten thousand, Maddy?' Gillon said. 'The old devil is not barefoot, God knows, but he cannot conjure ten thousand out of thin air.'

'He may borrow it.'

'Borrow it? From whom?'

'Sir Archie.'

'What?' said Gillon. 'Sir Archie will lend Craigiehall money to pay you off, you and his wife? Now that's plainly ridiculous. How will Sir Archie secure such a loan?'

'He will acquire a lien on Craigiehall's estate.'

'Sir Archie has no interest in acquiring ground in Ayrshire, has he? The man has more land than he knows what to do with.'

'There is no such thing as too much land for a gentlemen like Archie Oliphant,' Maddy said. 'I have dealt with men like him before, Gillon, men to whom deeds and policies and—what is it?—entails are the very breath of life. Oliphant does not have to attend to his acquisitions. His bankers do that for him. He takes his interest and his commissions ...'

417

'And squanders them on the likes of you.'

She laughed. 'And on you, Gillon Peters. Did you not dip your fingers in that honey pot, lick them clean and ask for more?'

She flinched as Gillon's fist thudded into the worn upholstery. 'I might have known there was more to Valerie's meddling than met the eye,' he snapped. 'Not even Valerie Oliphant would go to such lengths for the sake of a thousand pounds. Presumably Archie was in on it from the first.'

'Presumably,' said Maddy. 'Now I suppose you will run off home and tell your brother?'

'It makes no matter whether I do or not,' Gillon said. 'The Oliphants will not get away with it—nor will you, Maddy.'

'And who will stop me? You?'

'If you take your cause to trial my brother will bring forth evidence that Craigiehall was not your only suitor or your only lover.'

'Then he will have to prove it, will he not?' said Maddy.

'He will also bring Fleur to the stand and wring from her all that he can about your past relationships.'

'Fleur will stand firm,' said Maddy.

'Under gruelling examination by skilled advocates? I doubt it.'

Maddy paused before she spoke again. 'What is his offer?'

'Fifteen hundred pounds.'

'And for my child?'

'A child who will conveniently disappear after you have your settlement, I do not doubt,' said Gillon. 'It will be eight weeks at the very least before a trial can go forward, probably longer. By then there will be no hiding your condition.'

'Delay will be to my advantage,' said Maddy.

'Are you really pregnant, Maddy?'

'Really and truly, yes.'

'Good God in heaven!' said Gillon.

'There! You see!' said Madelaine. 'I may not hold all the cards but I do hold trumps.' She patted her stomach lightly. 'In here.'

'But it isn't—it can't be Craigiehall's child.'

'Who is to say for certain that it is not?'

'It's mine, isn't it?' Gillon said.

'John James does not know that,' said Maddy. 'He may harbour doubts, may even lead out a great trail of servants to prove that you and I had ample opportunity to make a baby between us, but only two people know the truth. I am one and you are the other, Gillon, and you will say nothing.'

'How can you be sure?' said Gillon.

'Because you are part of it, part of the fraud.'

In the faint glow of light from the driver's lantern she looked, he thought, more beautiful than ever. He longed to cradle her in his arms, kiss her, kiss and protect her. He thrust himself back into a corner of the cab, as far from Maddy as the narrow space allowed.

'I will have my money,' Madelaine said. 'I have worked hard for it.'

'I thought—I thought you loved me.'

'You will have your share, Gillon; a reasonable sum for your labours.'

'I don't want my share,' said Gillon.

'Oh, you want it all, do you?'

'I want you.'

'Why?'

'Because we're two of a kind, Maddy, and I love

419

you.'

'But you have no money, Gillon.'

'Look,' he said, 'Craigiehall will pay me five hundred pounds to swear that you and I were lovers. He will pay you fifteen hundred pounds not to bring forward your cause for breach of promise.'

'And square with Valerie Oliphant?'

'Yes, that too, I expect.'

'Two thousand pounds,' said Maddy. 'Even if we round that out in guineas, it will not bankrupt him, will it?'

'I don't know,' said Gillon. 'No, perhaps not.'

'Then I'll have let Sir Archie down.'

'What do you care about Sir Archie?' said Gillon. 'He's not the father of your child.' He paused then said, maliciously. 'Is he, Madelaine?'

'Is that your news?' she said. 'That you will receive five hundred pounds to announce that we were lovers? What if I say otherwise?'

'That would be perjury,' Gillon said. 'Maddy, child or no child, you have no case against Craigiehall. God knows, trials for breach of promise are little more than an entertainment for everyone, including lawyers and judges.'

'For everyone except those involved,' Madelaine said. 'His lordship will pay me to keep my mouth shut and save his posts and his reputation, you know.'

'And will lose his estate.'

'He may, of course, answer to my charges in court, keep his precious estate and lose everything else.'

'Craigiehall is all he has, you know, to pass on to his children.'

'Hoh!' said Madelaine. 'Conscience comes late,

I see.'

'Please, Maddy,' Gillon said. 'Let us cream what we can from this debacle and go off together—with Fleur, of course—out of Edinburgh, out of Scotland.'

'Run off with you, Lieutenant Peters?' Maddy said. 'I think not.'

'Marry me then,' Gillon said. 'Marry me and give our child a name.'

She had the decency to hesitate before, with a shake of the head, she said, 'No, darling, no. Now take me back to Sir Archie's house before he has the town guard and half the regiment turned out to look for me.'

'Maddy . . .'

'I have a performance to give. I must rehearse.'

'Is that your last word, Madelaine?'

'It is,' she said. 'It is,' and holding back her tears, watched him climb from the cab and, with a curt instruction to the driver to take her home, walk out of her life, she thought, forever.

CHAPTER TWENTY-FOUR

Fully half a year had passed since she had first clapped eyes on Gillon Peters, seated then, as he was now, upon the horseman's chair, his chin resting on his hand, those blue, blue eyes still glittering and greedy. It was she, not Gillon, who had changed most in that time. She was no longer dazzled by his gallantry or amused by his flowery compliments. No more was she impressed by Grant's authority; he was too clever and calculating by half. Between them, these men and one other—had taught her that it was not enough for a young woman to be pretty, witty and intelligent if she had nothing to call her own.

Charlotte was munching pickled walnuts from a plate on what remained of her lap. In the cramped little room the smell of brown vinegar mingled unpleasantly with fumes from a cigar that Grant smoked. While Gillon told his tale of mendacity and deceit Charlotte's eyes never left the soldier's face.

There was, Nicola realised, something unwholesome, almost obscene, about her sister's fascination with Gillon Peters, but Grant, if he noticed at all, was unfazed. He was more disturbed by Gillon's account of his meeting with Madelaine Young and the news that Sir Archie Oliphant had stretched out a hand to lay hold on Craigiehall.

'So,' Grant said, 'the woman will not yield to common sense and the offer of a fair price for her silence?'

'Not one inch,' said Gillon. 'Not to me at any rate.'

'I will make her a more formal offer within the next day or two,' Grant said. 'I have your deposition, signed and witnessed, and a draft of how we'll proceed against the issue if she remains adamant.'

'I do not understand,' said Charlotte, wiping her chin on her sleeve. 'Are you saying, Gillon, that you and this woman did in fact—you know.'

'I will swear to it that we did, my dear,' said Gillon, 'if only to save your father's lands for your children.'

'But did you, or did you not?' Charlotte insisted.

'Oh, very well: I did.'

'How could you, Gillon, how could you?'

'With ease, I imagine,' said Grant.

'Did she give you pleasure?' Charlotte asked.

'What if she did, damn it?' Gillon said. 'I'm not a eunuch, Charlotte, nor, thanks be to God, am I your husband. Dwell on this, my sweet, I did what I had to do with Madelaine Young and it was no more difficult than pretending that I worship the ground you tread on.'

Nicola had never seen Gillon so angry. He clutched the edge of the reading desk and for an instant it seemed that he might overturn it. She watched Grant crouch in his chair before, to her relief, both men brought their emotions under control. 'I did not know then,' Gillon said, still seething, 'that Oliphant was after the Ayrshire estate.'

'Are you all in this together?' Nicola heard herself say. 'Has it always been your intention to claim my father's estate for the Peters family? Is that why not one member of your family turned up on your wedding day? Who hatched the idea? Was it you, Grant, or was it your mother, the blessed Margo?'

'Leave my mother out of it, Nicola, if you please,' said Grant.

'Did Mr Mackenzie put you into the way of meeting my father, a gentlemen with lands and good connections and most important of all for your purposes two unmarried daughters and no male heir?' Nicola said. 'And you, Gillon, were you persuaded to woo me just to ensure that the estate was not entirely lost if something went wrong?'

'Courting you was my idea, no one else's,' Gillon

said. 'Grant did not approve, and my dear old mother, bless her, knew nothing of it.'

'Did Roderick?' said Nicola.

'Roderick?' Gillon and Grant said in unison.

'Was he your trump card?'

The brothers glanced at each other and for a split second Nicola was almost convinced that their bewilderment was genuine.

'Did Roderick seduce you?' said Gillon.

Flushing, Nicola answered, 'No.'

'I do not understand,' said Charlotte, suddenly, 'what my sister's chastity has to do with my inheritance, or what part these farmers have to play in it. You are the only cheat here, Gillon Peters. You are the only deceiver.' Her voice rose abruptly. 'Why did you try to ruin us?'

'For money, my dear,' Gillon said. 'For money. Isn't that the magnet behind all that we do, whether we are Margo Peters' sons or Templeton's daughters? We are greedy, Charlotte, greedy beyond reckoning. It would serve us all right if Maddy did marry the old fellow and claim everything for herself.'

'Craigiehall is mine,' Charlotte cried, 'mine by entitlement and I shall have it, all of it, for my children's sake.'

'Of course, you will, my dear.' Grant rose to his feet and crossed to his wife's side. She was perspiring heavily and a little trickle of walnut juice ran down her chin on to her bosom. He took out a handkerchief and gently wiped away the dribbles. 'There will be no estate for you to inherit, dearest,' he said, softly, 'if Oliphant has his way. It matters not to him that Madelaine is expecting a child.'

Charlotte slapped her husband's arm away. 'Papa has given her a child?'

'Papa has done nothing of the sort,' said Gillon. 'The child's mine.'

Nicola said, 'Will you trade away your child to protect Charlotte's legacy, Gillon? Is money all there is for you?'

He swung his leg over the arm of the chair and stood up. He glanced at Nicola but did not answer her. 'I've done what you asked of me, Grant, and I require to be paid. I take it that Craigiehall will honour your promise and a draft will be forthcoming before the month is out.'

'I will see to it that it is,' said Grant. 'Where will you be, meanwhile?'

'At my lodging,' Gillon said, 'until the end of the month.'

'And then where?' said Charlotte.

'Wherever the regiment sends me,' he said and, with a formal bow to his sister-in-law and a nod in Nicola's direction, left the parlour.

And Charlotte, clinging to her husband, burst into tears.

*　　　*　　　*

'Now, now, Margo,' Duncan Ralston said, his voice muffled by a blanket, 'there's no need for you to fret. It's nothin' but a bit o' chill gone into my chest.'

'At your age, Daddy, a bit o' chill's enough to carry you off,' Margo said. 'Stop arguin' an' take a big, deep breath.'

He was clad in a flannel nightshirt and a pair of woollen stockings. A blanket was wrapped over his shoulders and another draped over his head. He leaned over the basin and obediently inhaled while Margo carefully applied another dollop of boiling water to the mixture.

The astringent stench of balsam filled the kitchen.

Nose twitching, one of the dogs rose hurriedly from beneath the table and pattered off into the small parlour. Roderick was tempted to follow and held his sleeve against his nose until the first wave of remedial steam dispersed. He was not inclined to make light of his grandfather's condition, though, for the old man had passed a restless night and had spent the whole day hunched before the fire, shivering and coughing.

'If that's not lifted by tomorrow,' Margo said, 'then I'm sendin' for Dr Petrie whether you like it or not.'

'He'll cost you a pretty penny,' Duncan said.

'Cheaper than a funeral,' Margo said, and plied the kettle once more.

The fire had been built up to keep Duncan warm and sweat out his fever. Sacking had been stuffed along the bottom of the door to prevent draughts and the atmosphere in the kitchen was oppressively hot. Roderick did not look forward to another wakeful night, side by side with his grandfather in the cramped back room, but he knew that if he suggested sleeping in one of the beds in the loft his mother would accuse him of selfishness.

She had a holy horror of her daddy dying alone, of her daddy dying at all, for that matter. When faced with the prospect of the death of her aged parent all her Christian certainties flew away. Old and enfeebled though he might be, he was still the rock to which she clung, the man to whom she answered and whose approval mattered more to her than anything else. It was mainly to prove to her daddy that she, a mere daughter, was twice the man he was that Margo had pushed her sons so hard.

Roderick wondered what would become of his mother when her father had gone. If her elaborate schemes came to nothing would he have to nurse her in her old age? Would he, in due course, be seated where Duncan was now, hunched and shivering? And who would care for him in his dotage; Grant, or Grant's children, or Marie's boy, grown up, or no one at all but a hireling, some greasy girl who couldn't stand the sight of him?

'I've killed a hen,' said Margo. 'You'll have a good plate o' soup to tempt your appetite tomorrow.'

'I had a good plate o' soup today,' Duncan mumbled.

'Och, you ate nothin'. You only picked at the bread.'

'I'll have a dish o' tea before I go to sleep.'

'I'll put some whisky in it,' said Margo.

'It's air I'm needin', not whisky.'

'You do as you're told, Daddy,' Margo administered a soft slap to the side of the blanket. 'Is the steam not loosenin' your tubes yet?'

Duncan coughed by way of answer, a wet rattling sound, and cast off the blanket. He leaned away from his daughter and, cupping his hands to his mouth, spat a string of mucus into the heart of the fire. The effort tired him. He sat back, head resting against the side of the ingle, and dabbed sweat from his brow with the back of his fist.

'Does your chest hurt?' said Margo.

'Nah, nah,' he said. 'It's easier now. I think I'll away to my bed, though. Roderick, will you give me a hand?'

'I will.' Roderick hoisted himself from his chair, put an arm around his grandfather and propped him up. 'Will I carry you?'

'I'm not a babby, son,' Duncan said. 'I'm just needin' your arm.'

The bed had been aired, damp sheets replaced and a clean nightshirt draped over the room's only chair. Roderick fetched a taper and lit the tallow candle while Duncan seated himself on the side of the bed. He lifted his legs to allow Roderick to peel off his stockings then raised his arms while his grandson removed the nightshirt.

Roderick tried not to look at the old man's wrinkled thighs, protruding belly and sunken chest for the crippling ailments of age frightened him. He furled the nightgown over the old man's head and covered his embarrassment. He moved to help his grandfather swing his legs into the bed but Duncan, with a chesty grunt, said, 'I'm not as bad as I look, Roddy. There's still a bit sap left,' got himself under the bedclothes and pulled the blanket up to his throat. 'Now, son, close the door an' sit with me awhile.' He paused, coughed into his fist, then said, 'Have you wrote to the girl yet, to Nicola?'

Roderick shook his head. 'What do I have to say to her?'

'Tell her you love her.'

'The only way I can do that is to break my promise.'

'Then break it,' Duncan said.

'I can't.'

Duncan shifted on to an elbow, grimacing, as if even that small movement caused him pain. 'Have you not done enough for Margo?' he said. 'Do you think Grant has done more, has done better? Would you take a wife like Charlotte Templeton just to please your mother?'

'Nay, not to please anyone.'

'Then take a wife that suits you.'

'There's only one woman . . .' Roderick began.

'An' you are barred from her, or so you think, because of a promise,' the old man said. 'If this business in Edinburgh falls out right for Grant an' Charlotte presents the judge with a grandson, your debt is paid. Tell her, Roddy, tell the lassie the truth, an' see what she makes of it.'

His voice faded and, groping for breath, he rolled over on to his back and let his head fall against the bolster.

'There's something in what you say,' Roderick conceded. 'But what do I have to offer a woman like Nicola Templeton?'

'No less than she has to offer you.'

'And what is that?' said Roddy.

'More than enough to be goin' on with,' Duncan said and with a soft little *tut* at his grandson's bewilderment, closed his eyes and pretended to sleep.

*   *   *

The wind off the Forth had a cutting edge that penetrated the layers of doeskin, nankeen and mixed cloth in which Hercules had wrapped

429

himself. He was not too pleased at being dragged from his crackling fire and well-padded armchair for, as a rule, his clients called upon him or dealt with one of his clerks. It was not to curry favour with Lord Craigiehall or earn a few extra guineas that he had quit the comforts of home but to support his friend, Grant Peters, and, though he would not admit to it, to see for himself the *femme fatale* who had lured Craigiehall into the sort of trap that any hairy-headed young advocate would have seen coming a mile off.

The butler admitted Grant and him to Oliphant's house and a footman ushered them into the library. Sir Archie was on his feet, back to the fireplace. Four other persons were seated about him, listening with somewhat less than rapt attention to the banker-poet rattle on about his blessed play.

Hercules recognised Lady Valerie; her tall coiffure, topped by a bead and gauze ornament, gave her away. The younger woman by her side he took to be the actress, not quite so fresh as he had supposed, but with a beautiful mouth and eyes that aided by a little candlelight and a glass of wine might very well melt a heart of stone. The third female was pretty and fashionably turned out too, though she was, Hercules reckoned, on the far side of sixty.

Then a man rose from the depths of an armchair and Hercules, shedding tact, cried out, 'Dunbar! What, in God's name, are you doing here?'

'I am here to see fair play, sir,' the Lord Advocate told him. 'To protect the interests of my friend.'

'Your friend?' said Hercules. 'What friend?'

430

And Sir Archie, smiling modestly, answered, *'Moi.'*

*   *   *

John James slept late. Isabella had gone to Edinburgh to attend his interests, for being neither quite friend nor quite foe of Lady Valerie Oliphant she was the perfect emissary. He had offered to accompany her but she had insisted that he remain in Ayrshire until the matter was settled and he might return to his court duties if not in triumph at least without fear of being hanged by public opinion and drawn and quartered by his peers. He had sent Robertson with her in lieu of a lady's maid and had given her the run of his town house which, under the circumstances, was the very least that he could do.

The sea was like sheet iron beaten by a stiff off-shore breeze. Great masses of blue-grey cloud moiled over the peaks of Arran. John James knew that it would be cold outside and that he had better wrap himself well in woollens and tweeds before he made his tour of the tenant farms. There had been a time not so long since when he would simply have thrown on a leather vest, jumped into his jackboots and galloped across the fields with his chest bare to the wind but now, well, now he was not so young any more and had lost his love of hard weather and his pride in facing it down.

He topped a second egg, refilled his coffee cup, and gathered himself for the effort of dressing. It had been years since he had dressed himself without Robertson's assistance. He could have sent for a boy to help him but he felt peculiarly

431

independent this morning and the novelty of digging about in chests and closets was quite appealing. He ate the egg and, coffee cup in hand, gazed from the bedroom window, for he was breakfasting informally upstairs which was something he hadn't done since Marion had died.

When a knocking sounded on the door, he called out 'Come,' and, to his surprise, Hugh Littlejohn, hat in hand, entered the room.

'What's the hour?' John James said.

'Ten, sir, a wee bit after.'

'Did I not say that I would meet you at the Kirkton crossroad at eleven?'

'You did, sir, but I have some news I thought you'd be wantin' to hear.'

'News, what news is that, Littlejohn?'

'It's the coal pit, your lordship.'

John James sat up. 'What about the coal pit?'

'There's twenty men on de Morville's patch layin' track.'

'Track?' John James said.

'Wooden rails, sir, from the mouth o' the digging.'

'Twenty men, do you say? Good God! Who's paying for that, I wonder?'

'I thought you'd want to know at once, sir.'

'Oh, I do, I do.' John James pushed back his chair. 'This I must see for myself. Meet me at the stables in half an hour. No, make that twenty minutes.'

'Will it be the chaise for you, your lordship?'

'No, damn it,' said John James, excitedly. 'Have them saddle up the stallion.' Then, caring not that his overseer was still in the room, he threw off his robe and nightshirt and strode, bare-bottomed, to his dressing-room to search for his jackboots and vest.

*   *   *

'Lady Ballentine,' Grant said, 'it's a pleasure to make your acquaintance. I have heard a great deal about you from my wife and her sister.'

'I am not Lady Ballentine,' the woman said, pleasantly enough. 'I am plain Mistress Ballentine; the title died with my husband. I have heard a great deal about you, too, Mr Peters.'

'Not much of it favourable, I imagine,' Grant said.

'No,' the woman admitted, 'not much.'

'May I ask what you are doing here?' Grant said.

'You are very direct, Mr Peters,' Mrs Ballentine said.

'Insultingly so,' said Lady Valerie. 'I am also puzzled by the fact that Lord Craigiehall did not see fit to inform his lawyer that you would represent his lordship as an observer at this morning's meeting.'

'Perhaps,' Isabella said, 'the letter has gone astray.'

'Yes,' said Lady Valerie, thinly, 'that must be it.'

'And you, Hercules,' said Dunbar, 'are you also here as an observer?'

'Well, I am not here for profit,' Hercules said.

'Am I to take it,' Dunbar went on, 'that you had a hand in drafting Craigiehall's offer to this young lady?'

'I had no say in setting the monetary terms, if that's what you mean.' Hercules stepped forward and stood by Madelaine Young's chair until,

433

without reluctance, she offered her hand.

'Madam,' he said. 'I am honoured.'

'Why, sir,' said her ladyship, 'are you honoured when you are here to rob our guest of her entitlement?'

Hercules did not turn a hair. 'I am honoured, Lady Oliphant, to meet a woman of such exquisite beauty, whether she be plaintiff or defendant.'

'She is neither,' Dunbar said, 'yet.'

'Come, come,' Sir Archie interrupted, clapping his hands as if conducting a rehearsal. 'Be seated, gentlemen. Let us proceed with all haste to the substance of our business. I have much to do elsewhere.'

'Very well,' Grant said. 'We will begin with the statement.'

He extracted from his pocket two sheets of foolscap paper and handed them to Madelaine Young. She passed them to Lady Valerie without so much as a glance. Lady Valerie held the sheets at arm's length, scrutinised the minute handwriting, then passed the sheets to Dunbar.

The Lord Advocate crouched over the foolscap as a dog might over a bone, moving his lips a little as he read, then looked up. 'You have given me your case here, Peters. Is that wise?'

'I have not given you my case, sir,' said Grant. 'I have given you an outline of how I might defend my client against a charge of breach of promise of marriage. I have not named witnesses, save one, for that one, surely, is enough to dissuade Mrs Young from proceeding further.'

'Your brother,' Dunbar said. 'What a coincidence.'

'My brother was invited into this venture by

434

Lady Oliphant. In that sense it is not a coincidence. One must put the question whether Lady Oliphant and her husband selected my brother to affect an introduction to Lord Craigiehall because he was my brother or for other, less palatable reasons.'

Dunbar said, 'You are not in the Parliament House now, Peters. There's no need for rhetoric. Your brother makes claim that he and Mrs Young were intimate on several occasions in this very house while Sir Archibald and Lady Oliphant were absent. My client . . .'

'Your client, Dunbar?' Hercules interrupted. 'I find it astonishing that the Lord Advocate of Scotland will stoop to prosecuting a cause for breach of promise. Has the petition gone forward, then?'

Dunbar, scowling, said, 'No, it has not.'

Grant said, 'We are here to prevent it going forward, are we not, sir?'

'On payment of ten thousand pounds,' Sir Archie said, cheerfully. 'Now, gentlemen, why don't we get to the nub of it? Is Craigiehall willing to stump up, or is he not?'

'He is not,' Grant said.

'Oh,' said Isabella Ballentine, 'but he is.'

'Pardon?' Sir Archie said.

'If ten thousand pounds will purchase my cousin's release from all further obligation and ensure that Mrs Young's claim, whether true or false, does not become public,' Isabella Ballentine said, 'I will guarantee payment of ten thousand pounds no later than the first day of November.'

'No, no,' Sir Archie burst out, 'you can't do that.'

435

'Why not, sir? What is to stop me?' said Isabella.

'You do not have ten thousand pounds,' said Lady Valerie.

'Do you, Mrs Ballentine?' Hercules asked.

'Indeed, sir, I do,' Isabella answered. 'I have borrowed against Salton, my estate, for a sum considerably more than that demanded by Mrs Young.'

'Your estate?' said Sir Archie. 'Who in God's name would lend money on that wasteland?'

'You, sir,' Isabella said, 'or, rather, your bank.'

'Hah!' Hercules slapped his fat thigh. 'She's sold you a three-legged donkey, Archie, and you were too blind to see it.'

'I'll put a stop to this,' Sir Archie said. 'By God, I will.'

'It's too late,' Isabella said. 'The documents are sealed. You or, rather, your directors, have granted a lien on my property which will revert into your hands at the time of my death, unless the lien, plus six percent in interest, is paid off before that unhappy event occurs. If it is not paid off then Salton House and all my lands will belong to your bank—and welcome to them.'

'My directors did not lend you money to pay off Craigiehall's debts,' Sir Archie said. 'I mean, good God, why was I not consulted?'

'Because,' Lady Valerie hissed, 'you've had your head stuck so far into Fingal's hindquarters that you haven't attended a directors' meeting in months.'

'Well, well, well,' said Hercules. 'It seems that Lord Craigiehall has found a saviour in this dear lady. If, as she claims, the Salton estates are mortgaged to forfeit and she has the

436

documentation correctly drafted—which I have no doubt she has—then Mrs Young will have her ten thousand pounds. You, Sir Archie, will have acquired another piece of property to add to the bank's hoard although not the property you had set your heart upon—and all smirch and smear will be removed from Lord Craigiehall's name.'

Grant said, 'Mrs Young, are you agreeable to receive payment to the sum of ten thousand pounds on or before the first day of November in exchange for withdrawing the threat of suit, letting the matter of parentage rest and exercising complete and utter discretion in all matters pertaining to Lord Craigiehall's relationship with you?'

Madelaine hesitated, then said, 'I am.'

'I will require you to sign a document to that effect.'

'I will do so.'

'Then it's settled,' Grant said, with a nod.

'Wait,' Dunbar said. 'I am curious as to how Mrs Ballentine presented herself to the directors and how the valuation on the Salton estate was reached. No banker, no money-lender, would advance such a sum to pay off a debt that had not yet been incurred.'

'I have a very shrewd lawyer, sir,' said Isabella. 'As his practice is in the provinces, however, I question if you'll have encountered him.'

Grant put a hand to his brow and closed his eyes.

'Bunting,' he said. 'Walter Bunting.'

Isabella laughed. 'The same.'

'So you are the purchaser of de Morville's coal pit,' said Hercules. 'You acquired Bunting's family

437

business and hid behind the Westmore company name. You even employed me to draft the contract of purchase. But you purchased the pit before Lord Craigiehall had ever clapped eyes upon Mrs Young. Now that is foresight; that is enterprise.'

'Alas, I am no oracle. The coal-workings were intended as a gift.'

'A gift? To whom?' said Lady Valerie.

'My cousin, of course. John James Templeton—my husband to be.'

'Your husband?' said Lady Valerie.

'To be,' Isabella said. 'I have the marriage contract, signed and witnessed, if you wish to see it. We will be wed around the Christmas time.'

'And Charlotte and Nicola, my wife and her sister,' Grant said, 'what will become of them?

'They will have what they deserve,' said Isabella.

CHAPTER TWENTY-FIVE

Charlotte lumbered about the parlour, round by the table and back by the dresser, rattling crockery and bumping into chairs while she waved her arms and ranted. 'Cheated,' she cried. 'Cheated by my own aunt.'

'Isabella is not our aunt,' said Nicola.

'We have always called her aunt.'

'Only for convenience,' said Nicola.

'By our own flesh and blood then. Cheated out of my inheritance by this—this hermit, this crone. How long has she been plotting to catch Papa in her snare? Tell me that, Grant.'

'I have no idea, my dear. I hardly know the

438

woman,' Grant said.

'You should have made it your business to know the woman,' Charlotte said, cuffing him on the shoulder. 'If you had been more diligent in your investigation of the de Morville sale, you might have stopped her from luring Papa into her clutches.'

'I'm not sure that much luring had to be done,' Nicola said. 'Papa has always been fond of Isabella.'

'She set up that other woman, the actress, as a scapegoat,' Charlotte said.

'I think you mean a decoy,' Grant said.

'I know what I mean,' Charlotte snapped.

They followed her with their eyes as they might have followed the feather in a game of shuttlecock, except Charlotte was a good deal heavier than any feather. Molly, Cook and Jeannie, now returned from her convalescence, were prudently hiding in the kitchen.

'Will Isabella have it all?' Charlotte said.

'I have not had an opportunity to examine the marriage agreement,' said Grant. 'As heirs, however, you will have protection. I'd hazard a guess that his lordship has settled a portion of the estate revenue upon her in perpetuity.'

'How much?' said Charlotte. 'Thousands, millions . . .'

'Charlotte,' said Nicola. 'Please sit down. You are making me dizzy.'

'I will sit when I choose to sit,' said Charlotte but nevertheless hurled herself into a chair and planted her elbows upon the tablecloth. 'Is that better?'

'Much,' said Nicola. 'Tell me, Grant, what

happened after Aunt Isabella made her announcement?'

Grant shrugged. 'Hercules and I took our leave. There was no more to be said. Although it was not our doing, the matter had been resolved.'

'But why did Isabella involve the Oliphant woman in the first place? Why did she push Papa into the marriage ring when she wanted him for herself?' said Charlotte. 'Why did she buy de Morville's coal pit as a dowry and then persuade Papa to seek a bride elsewhere?'

'Her actions do, I admit, seem quite lacking in logic,' said Grant.

'She did it to spite us, of course,' said Charlotte. 'She took advantage of your quarrel with father, Nicola. It's all your fault. If you had not run off none of this would have happened.'

'My fault?' said Nicola said. 'You were the one who . . .'

Grant said, 'May I point out that Isabella Ballentine has mortgaged to forfeit her own estate to save your father's reputation and pay off his debts. Whatever she gains from the marriage will not repay her sacrifice.'

'And you are in favour with Papa at last,' said Nicola. 'Is that not enough for you, Charlotte? I am glad it has fallen this way. Papa will be happy with Aunt Isabella and will go to his grave with his reputation intact. Between your mother, Grant, and your brothers and all this grubbing to lay hands on my father's land, I am quite sick of it.'

'My mother? What does my mother have to do with it?' said Grant, in alarm. 'What has been said about me?'

'Nothing,' Nicola told him. 'Oh, the Peters are

good at keeping secrets, so good at pretence, but they—and you—are no better than my Papa.'

'I do not know what you mean,' said Grant.

'They are just as grasping and calculating as any landed gentleman, just as determined to better themselves by marrying above their station.' She got to her feet. 'I am not needed here. I am not needed anywhere now. I have no more to say you, Charlotte, or to you, Grant Peters. I will go home to Craigiehall at the month's end and hope that Aunt Isabella will take me in and make me welcome, for it seems I'm welcome nowhere else.'

'What will I do?' said Charlotte. 'Who will look after me?'

'I will, of course,' Grant said, then leaping to his feet, called out, 'Nicola, Nicola, come back here and explain yourself, please.'

But Nicola had fled to her room.

*   *   *

It had been a long day, a very long day. Sir Archie had insisted on dragging Fleur and her away from the stormy scene in Broughton Gardens to seek refuge behind the stately pillars of the Theatre Royal whose stage he had hired for an afternoon to rehearse his patchwork little company in his patchwork little play.

Six female members of the Edinburgh Choral Society would join the cast later in the month, but the first props had been delivered from Mr Abercrombie's workshop in the Canongate, and Charlie, Tom and Ben had spent a happy half hour leaping over the board-and-canvas rocks and shaking the tottering pine tree. Mr Cavendish, sober and struggling, had endeavoured to find a spot from which he could project his voice with some hope of being heard and Opal and Pearl, like the jewels they were, had practised their entrances.

Over a communal supper in Mannering's—Sir Archie did not dare go home—Fleur and Madelaine had drunk just a little too much claret and, walking back to Broughton Gardens in Sir Archie's wake, had chanted verses from the fourth act of *Fingal* to the tune of 'Cock Up Your Beaver' which rendering had pleased Sir Archie not at all.

Lady Valerie had not been lurking behind the door. According to Bradley she had dined with Lord Dunbar and had then gone out to sup and play cards at Fortune's. Sir Archie had promptly retired to the library to make more revisions to his dramatic narrative, and Madelaine and Fleur had gone to bed.

They lay together, a little tipsy, staring at the patterns of candlelight on the ceiling, then Fleur placed a hand on Madelaine's stomach.

'Is he in there?' she said. 'Can I feel him?'

'Oh, he is in there, darling, but he is too small to be stirring just yet.'

'Are you happy, Aunt Maddy?'

Madelaine sighed. 'I should be happy, I suppose.'

'Ten thousand pounds,' said Fleur. 'We will be rich. Will we go home to London, you and me and baby, and rent a lovely house in the Strand and Mr Billington will come to call?'

'No, I do not think Mr Billington will come to call,' said Maddy.

Fleur placed her head close to her aunt's. 'Why are you not happy? Did we not do well in

442

Edinburgh? Do you not want to have a baby to take home to London?'

'It's not that, Fleur. Go to sleep now, please.'

'Is it me? Are you bored with me? I do not have to go with you, Aunt Maddy. The Admiral has told me that he will keep me in Edinburgh, if I wish it. I will play the piano for him and live in fine rooms with a maid of my own.'

'Until he tires of you, darling.'

'I would make sure that he does not tire of me and when he dies—for he is old, is he not?—then I will have all his money and I will be rich, like you.'

'Fleur . . .'

'I am still pretty, am I not? The pox did not scar me?'

'No, you are still pretty.'

'I think I will come with you to London, however, and look after baby while you are at the theatre. I will be his mama, his sister and his aunt all in one. Will he love me, do you think?'

'I'm sure he will,' said Maddy. 'It may be a girl, of course.'

'Then I will teach her how to play the piano and we will play duets for you when you are old.' She paused. 'Why are you not happy, Aunt Maddy? Are you sad for Lord Craigiehall? Are you sad because he will have that old woman for his wife, not you?'

'She will make him a very good wife,' Maddy said.

'She gave us ten thousand pounds.' Fleur giggled, softly. 'Ten thousand pounds so that he would marry her and not you. How foolish!'

'It's not foolish, Fleur,' said Madelaine. 'She loves him.'

443

'I would not give ten thousand pounds for love of any man,' Fleur declared. 'Would you, Aunt Maddy?'

'Go to sleep now, darling.'

'Would you?'

'Go to sleep, Fleur, please.'

'Have I made you angry?'

'No, I am tired, that's all, very tired.'

'And I am, too,' Fleur said and, kissing her aunt on the cheek, wished her a goodnight and, to Madelaine's relief, wriggled on to her side to sleep.

*   *   *

At first she thought he was dead. He lay sprawled across the desk, face down. His wig had toppled off, one arm hung limply over the side of the desk, the other tucked under his cheek, squashing it, so that she could not see his mouth. His silver hair, cropped short, shone in the light, and his ear stuck up, pink and waxy, like that of a pig or a lamb. She closed the library door and stood for a long moment with her heart in her mouth then, to her disappointment, he snuffled, sighed, and brought up a hand to scratch his nose.

She smoothed down the skirts of her white muslin dress and, in an ugly gesture, tucked a hand between her thighs to mop up the message of love that the young man she had lured out into her carriage had left there. She knew only that his name was Collins, a lawyer up from the country who could not believe his luck, and that he had served her well enough to compensate for her losses at the card table. She smoothed her skirts once more and checked the four cloth buttons of her vest, for young master Collins, once she had loosed his leash, had been rough with her. She unwound her turban and dropped it to the carpet and then, gruffly, barked out her husband's name.

'Archie!' She stepped to the desk, pinched his ear between finger and thumb and gave it a tug. 'Archie, waken up. I wish to have words with you.'

Blearily, the banker-poet opened one eye.

'Uh!'

'Are you intoxicated?'

'Uh! No!' he mumbled

Rubbing his brow, he roused himself enough to identify his wife who, though Valerie could not have known it, was at that moment the ideal representation of Nu-ala. Hair loose about her shoulders, eyes filled with brooding passion, she perfectly personified 'the joy of grief', even if she was a little long in the tooth and—Archie blinked—more than somewhat dishevelled.

'The rehearsal went well, my dear, yes, very well, as well as one could expect given the difficulties,' he said. 'Madelaine has agreed to remain with us until she has performed her part. Is that not the best of news?'

'Is it?' Valerie leaned on the desk and brought her nose into alignment with her husband's. 'Are you still dreaming?'

'I am awake, wide awake, I assure you.' Archie shuffled papers on his desk to prove it. 'Indeed, now that I'm refreshed I must return to . . .'

'Ten thousand pounds for a single performance, Archie?' Valerie said, sarcastically. 'Oh, yes, you have every right to be pleased with yourself. What is this demon that possesses you, causes you to ignore your responsibilities, neglect the business

445

that puts meat in our mouth and leaves me, your wife, abandoned like a gallows-corpse.'

'Well, I wouldn't go so far as to . . .'

'Great God, Archibald!' Valerie said. 'Do you care for nothing but these frightful plays of yours? Has literature stolen away your reason as well as your manhood. I would be willing to forgive you if you desired this English actress and were poling her behind my back.'

'I'm not. I swear, Valerie, I'm not.'

'I know you are not,' said Valerie. 'You care for neither women nor money. I am at a loss to understand what drives you to squander hundreds—nay, thousands—of pounds on these stupid private theatricals.'

'I wish to be recognised,' said Archie.

'You are one of the wealthiest men in Scotland,' Valerie said. 'You are respected for your acumen— though I cannot imagine why—and . . .'

'I am an artist,' Archie interrupted. 'A great artist.'

'Really!' said Valerie.

'In my soul, in my vitals, dearest, I am a true poet.' Archie caught her hand. 'Who in ages to come will remember a mere banker, however wealthy? It's poets, artists whose names are gilded by posterity, who become immortal.'

'Is that what you want, Archie—immortality?'

'Truth to tell, I'd settle for having *Fingal's Return* professionally performed and receive the praise and plaudits of the public at large.'

'That rabble,' said Valerie.

'Rabble or not,' Archie said, 'I am their guiding light. I will lead them to the glories of Old Scotia's ancient past and illuminate the qualities that once made our nation great. In a word, I will enlighten them.'

'Whether,' said Valerie, 'they like it, or not.'

'Aye, you may mock me, Valerie, but one day, one day I will have my audience and will be recognised for what I am.'

'And what is that?'

'A genius,' said Archie, soberly.

'And then will you stop?'

'Yes, dear,' Archie said, 'then I will lay down my quill and be content to wear my laurels in retirement.'

'Do you promise?' Valerie asked. 'Do you swear?'

'I do,' Sir Archie said, sincerely, without a thought for all the trouble that his answer might cause. 'I do, my dear, I swear.'

*   *   *

Nicola was sulking and Charlotte was too stubborn to placate her. She had no idea what had turned Nicola against her and, more particularly, against Grant. A word with Molly would have thrown light on Nicola's unhappiness but Molly had never been Charlotte's confidante and the servant was not brash enough to volunteer the information that Nicola was suffering from a broken heart, an explanation that Charlotte would have treated with scorn, of course.

The sisters encountered each other in the corridor shortly after Grant had left. They exchanged no more than nods by way of 'good morning' before Nicola escaped into the dining-room and Charlotte, still in her dressing-robe, returned to her bedroom and, with a little more force than was necessary, firmly closed the door.

*　　　*　　　*

It was a wild, windy day; no day, in fact, for a slightly built lady of a certain age to be making morning calls. But Isabella Ballentine was used to 'active' weather and thought nothing of toddling down rain-swept Lawnmarket from her cousin's town house in Crowell's Close with only Robertson for support. Climbing the steep stairs was a different story. Isabella was obliged to pause several times on the ascent to catch her breath while Robertson, following on, let her lean against his chest.

'Molly.'

'It's you, is it? Is his lordship back then?'

'Nay,' said Robertson. 'I am serving Mrs Ballentine today.'

'Are you now?' said Molly.

'He is,' said Isabella. 'I have come to speak with my—with the girls.'

'Step in,' said Molly, 'an' I'll see if they wish to speak with you.'

'Oh,' said Isabella. 'I am sure they will,' and ushered along by her temporary manservant, entered the dragon's den.

*　　　*　　　*

Charlotte had sense enough, at first, to be polite to the woman who would soon be her stepmother. She had always enjoyed 'Aunt' Isabella's visits to Craigiehall for the odd, ill-clad little woman had

448

never been stand-offish and had treated Nicola and her as if they shared a secret, though quite what that secret was Charlotte had never discovered. She also recalled how kind Aunt Isabella had been to Papa when Jamie had passed away. After Jamie's death, however, Papa had crept into his shell and Isabella had visited less and less often and it had been four years, or more, since Charlotte and she had last met.

Nicola was summoned from the dining-room, tea ordered and consumed, and general pleasantries about the awful weather and the state of Charlotte's health exchanged before Isabella, with an apologetic smile, said, 'I suppose we had better talk about it.'

'I suppose we had,' said Nicola. 'Indeed, it would perhaps be an opportune moment to offer our congratulations, Aunt Isabella, though your announcement has taken us all by surprise.'

'It was done on the spur of the moment, my dear,' Isabella said. 'I have cherished an affection for your father for many, many years, and now that he's alone . . .'

'He is not alone,' said Charlotte. 'He has us.'

'Now that he is alone,' Isabella pressed on, 'it seemed sensible to remind him that we have always cared for each other and that marriage . . .'

'You bought him,' Charlotte interrupted, 'just as you might buy a pet dog or a pair of slippers. Papa had no choice but to marry you after you put him under such an obligation, so please do not speak to us of love.'

'Do you love him?' Nicola said.

'Of course I do. I have always loved him,' Isabella said.

449

'Why then did you not marry him?' said Charlotte, heating up.

'He chose your mother instead of me.'

'Is this, then, revenge?' said Charlotte.

'Why would I wish to take revenge upon your father?'

'For preferring my mother to you.'

'Charlotte,' Isabella said, 'if you imagine that I have spent my life plotting reprisal then you are much mistaken. I do not grudge your father his years of happiness with Marion. I regret only that they were so few. Lives do not follow precise patterns. Have you not realised that by now? It is not my intention to usurp you or Nicola in your father's affections or steal your inheritance. I am sixty-three years old and under the terms of the marriage agreement that your father drew up I have no claim upon Craigiehall. If John James goes to his Maker before I do then I will return to Salton, to grief and loneliness. I will not impose upon you or upon Nicola, nor will I claim one acre or one penny of your inheritance.'

'Oh!' said Charlotte, chastened. 'Oh! I see. What of the coal workings?'

'They are tied to Craigiehall,' said Isabella. 'However, I have taken the liberty of investing in improvements that will profit us all.'

'Oh!' said Charlotte again. 'Oh, that is generous of you, Aunt Isabella, exceedingly generous. My husband will be pleased.'

Isabella nodded then swivelling in her chair, addressed herself to Nicola. 'Look at you,' she said, 'shrunk away to nothing. Do you suppose I've thrown you to the dogs, my dear? You will have your share of your father's estate, for that, I'm

450

told, is the law.'

'Who told you? Mr Bunting?' said Nicola.

'Mr Bunting,' said Isabella, 'is a thoroughly unpleasant fellow, I agree, but he is possessed of a rustic sort of *savoir faire* that has, and will, prove useful. I am marrying your father for love, that is the truth of it, but I have no intention of throwing my wits into the river along with my bridal flowers. It was Bunting arranged the mortgage to forfeit with Oliphant's bank. He convinced the directors, in Oliphant's absence, that my teetering old house and miles of windswept moor were worth rather more than I asked for them. To put it bluntly, he deceived the valuators.'

'Does my father know what you have done?' said Nicola.

'Not yet. I will choose the proper time to tell him, although by now he will have surveyed the work being done on de Morville's field—our field, my dears, his field—and will no doubt be puzzling over the owner's identity.'

Nicola sat forward. 'Just how did Mr Bunting deceive the valuators and why did you buy the Westmore Coal and Mineral Company? Was it really just to hide behind, Aunt Isabella, and are you now hiding something from us?'

Isabella laughed. 'How clever you are, my dear, how perceptive. You take after your father in that respect. Indeed, if you had been born male or if the Scots lords were enlightened enough to admit women to the bar you'd make a wonderful lawyer.'

'I thank you for the compliment but it does not answer my question.'

'Mr Bunting's seedy little company is the first step, only the first step,' said Isabella, 'a place, you might say, to begin.'

'To begin what?' said Charlotte.

'What Mr Bunting concealed from the valuators,' Isabella said, 'is what lies beneath the ground on Salton moor.'

'And what is that?' Nicola asked.

'Coal,' Isabella answered. 'Coal at no very great depth. All I need is a man to manage the company for me and we will all be rich.'

'A man?' said Charlotte. 'What sort of man do you mean?

'A man like John James,' said Isabella. 'A man just like your papa.'

*   *   *

Jack Cattenach and 'Cyclops', his literary shadow, arrived by hired coach in the Port of Leith well before the appointed hour, with ample time on hand to down three glasses of rum and gnaw on a ham hock. He crouched at a table by the salt-stained window of 'Hackston's Hole' which, as the name implied, was a grog shop so dilapidated and depressing that it had all the appeal of a lazaret. On that rain-lashed forenoon there was no living soul within the place save Hackston, the elderly, half-blind proprietor, and Jack even had his doubts about him.

He rubbed a greasy fist against the bottle-glass and peered out into the twisted little side street that permitted no view of the sea but, ironically, seemed to attract vast quantities of spray from the back end of the harbour wall to add sting to the driving rain. He was surprised that the lady had even heard of Hackston's Hole let alone selected it

452

for a rendezvous, particularly when the famous Nine-Headed Eel was not much more than a hop and a skip around the corner. He had dealt with, and spied upon, too many blue-bloods over the years to be truly amazed, however, and was more intrigued by the motive behind the lady's request for a private meeting than troubled by her choice of location.

He had just taken out his watch for the third time—she was late, of course, but women of her rank were always late—when a conveyance clattered into the side street and drew to a halt by the window. It was not a gilded four-horse carriage nor even a handsome two-horse chaise but one of Edinburgh's hired coaches, identical to the one that had brought him down to the Port from the yard behind the Register Office.

Plastered to his perch by the force of the wind, the driver did not climb down to help his passenger alight. She emerged alone, without footman or maid, and stepped over the puddles outside the 'Hole' with a grace that Jack Cattenach could not but admire. She looked magnificent for a woman no longer quite in her prime, with her black velvet cloak billowing about her and her hood, nipped tight to her throat, hiding all but the tip of her nose. She handed up payment to the driver and, it seemed, gave him instructions, then turned and, without hesitation, entered the tavern.

Jack scrambled to his feet.

'Lady Oliphant,' he said, bowing low. 'It is my pleasure.'

'I'll wager it is,' Lady Valerie said, 'or will be.'

'May I offer you refreshment?'

She looked around the room with her nose in

the air.

Jack said, 'The rum is almost palatable.'

'Rum, then,' her ladyship said.

Still with her cloak around her and her hood clipped tightly to her throat, she seated herself at the table and when the glass appeared before her wiped the rim with her gloves and tossed back the contents in a single swallow, a feat, Jack thought, that would have brought applause from any husky stevedore.

From the corner of his eye he saw the hack reappear, pointing up the side street in the direction of Edinburgh. He watched the driver pull out a feed-bag and strap it to the horse's nose, and was not in the least surprised when her ladyship said, 'I will be with you no longer than it takes to rest the animal for we must not risk being seen together.'

'Of course not, your ladyship,' Jack agreed. 'May I ask . . .'

She glanced across the room at old half-blind Hackston then leaned over the table, so close that Jack could smell the rum on her breath.

'How much fire remains in the Craigiehall scandal?' she said. 'Is it naught now but embers and ash?'

'No, there's still a spark,' Jack said. 'And where there's a spark, your ladyship, there's fire enough to fan a flame.'

'Can you do that? Can you fan a flame?'

'Well,' said Jack, cautiously, 'that depends.'

'Upon what does it depend?' Lady Valerie said.

'On what you have to impart,' Jack Cattenach said. 'Something fresh, something tasty, perhaps?'

'Oh, indeed,' said Lady Valerie, with a little

454

grimace. 'Something very fresh and very tasty. Do you have your pencil and notebook to hand?'

'Indeed, I do,' said the one-eyed giant and with a flourish produced the tools of his invidious trade.

*   *   *

Daniel Horne's salubrious premises in the Old Town of Edinburgh were almost as quiet as the grog shop in Leith. Many members of the legal fraternity were still serving the district courts and the others, Grant assumed, were huddled in their rooms, keeping themselves and their powder dry for the opening of Sessions in a few weeks time. He had more reason than most for defying the foul weather. Charlotte and her sister were at each other's throats and he did not care to be called upon to moderate the quarrel. He was pleased at the outcome of Craigiehall's dalliance with the actress. He did not consider Isabella Ballentine as much of a threat. In fact, he rather admired the woman and saw her as a softening influence on his stiff-necked father-in-law for she was fond of Charlotte and Nicola and would bring a degree of harmony to the family.

Immediately before him was a small matter of forfeiture of tenure on a cottage property, and another even smaller matter of the wounding of a horse by a member of the town guard. Looming larger by the day, though, was a criminal charge involving the stealing of twelve sheep which, come November, would take him to the High Court to plead on behalf of the defendant.

Meanwhile, he was at peace with himself that early afternoon in Horne's, with rain battering on the windows, a bright fire to cheer the empty space and the smell of dinner drifting up from the kitchens. He applied himself to reading preliminary papers while waiting for Somerville to return from the office across town with the day's mail.

It was, of course, too good to last. When Gillon, black with rain and out of breath, stumbled into the room, Grant sighed and said, 'What now?'

'I hoped I might find you here.' Gillon threw off his great coat and hat, scattering water in all directions. 'My next port of call was Graddan's Court. Be that as it may, I've found you, thank God. Have you heard from Roderick?'

Grant frowned. 'No,' he said. 'I have had no letter this week. What's happened? Is it Mother?'

'Grandad.'

'Dead?'

'Not yet, but it seems that his hour is fast approaching.'

Gillon fumbled in his waistcoat and pulled out a letter written in pencil on rough paper which was almost as wet as the bearer. Grant took it gingerly from Gillon's fingers, spread it on the table and pressed it down with his fist.

'It's you,' Gillon said. 'He wants you.'

'Who wrote this?' said Grant.

'Are you blind, man?' said Gillon. 'It's Grandad's hand-writing. His last words, perhaps, his last will.'

'It's not a will,' said Grant. 'It's hardly anything.'

'What do you expect from a dying man,' said Gillon, 'a ten page tract with footnotes in Latin? Damn it, Grant, he wants to see your ugly phiz before he passes on. Can't think why, but he does.'

He poked a finger into the paper, wrinkling it. 'There. See.'

'Yes,' Grant said. 'I see.' He glanced up. 'Why did Grandfather despatch the letter to you and not to me? Roderick has my postal addresses. Come to think of it, why did Roderick not inform me himself?'

'I have no notion,' Gillon said. 'The letter was brought to my door an hour ago, so Grandfather obviously paid for a caddy. He has put no time or date upon it but one would assume it was written and despatched no later than yesterday. For all we know he may be dead already.'

'But why you?' said Grant again. 'Never mind, we had better leave as soon as possible.'

'You won't reach Stirling tonight, not in this weather.'

'Not in any weather,' Grant said. 'We might still catch the afternoon coach to Linlithgow, however, and the Flyer to King's Park first thing in the morning. We can hire horses there.'

'We?' said Gillon. 'He does not ask for me. He asks only for you.'

'You are being fanciful, Gillon. Of course we must go together.'

'No,' Gillon said. 'He has never cared for me. I'm the black sheep in his eyes, which is ironic, do you not think? Even if he had asked for me, I cannot go. I must stay in Edinburgh.'

'Why?'

'To look after Maddy.'

Grant snorted. 'Maddy, I think, can look after herself.'

'She may need me.'

'With ten thousand pounds in her purse, I doubt

457

it,' Grant said.

'Ten thousand pounds.' Gillon's eyes grew wide. 'Good God in heaven, do you tell me that Craigiehall settled out of court?'

'His cousin settled for him. It's long a story, Gillon. Suffice to say that your lady love is now a wealthy woman and has no more need of you.'

'What will become of the baby?'

'That is not my concern, nor should it be yours,' Grant said. 'Settlements have been agreed and you will receive your five hundred pounds, in cash if you wish, very soon.'

'Damn the cash,' said Gillon. 'I don't give a tinker's spit about my fee.'

'Put Maddy out of your mind, Gillon,' Grant said, gently. 'She is not for you. Now that she has money I doubt if you will ever see her again. Come, man, gather your wits and set your priorities in order. I'll have a bag packed and meet you at Mannering's in a half hour. If Grandfather passes away before we get there Mother will need us—both of us—to comfort her.'

Gillon pushed away the chair, grabbed his greatcoat and hat and stood before his brother like the soldier he had once been.

'No, Grant,' he said. 'I've done enough for Mother. I'm no expert in offering comfort. In spite of what you say, I am still needed here. Now, do not let me detain you further.' Then, before Grant could prevent it, he rattled off down stairs, leaving the damp little letter behind.

CHAPTER TWENTY-SIX

A sprinkling of wet snow covered the tops of the hills, an early hint of winter. The track that led across the plain from Stirling was clogged with mud and Grant did not dare drive the hired horse too hard. He held the animal to a trot, nudging it around the deepest ruts and where possible cutting on to grassland to make the going easier. He had been travelling since before dawn, for the 'change coach had left Linlithgow at half past five o'clock and now, at a little after two in the afternoon, he finally had Heatherbank in sight.

He was clad like a coachman in an old greatcoat with two capes and a pair of stout jackboots, his hat tied to his head with a bandana. As he spurred the horse towards the white-washed farmhouse with the wind behind him and flecks of sleet swirling about his face, he prepared himself for the mournful process of seeing his grandfather into the ground and his long life suitably celebrated with a wake. He would only be here for a day or two, however, and would then be gone, for Roderick would look after Mother as Roderick had always done.

He rode into the yard and reined the horse.

A girl he did not recognise peeped at him from the mouth of the byre and a half-grown boy, one of Cathy's brood, was loading a hand-barrow with fresh turnips. There was no sign of Roderick or of his mother. The door of the cottage was closed. No light, save a faint glimmer from the fire, showed in the window. Everything was calm, solemn and

459

calm, and at that moment he knew that his grandfather had passed away.

He dismounted, held the horse by the rein and unstrapped his bag.

'You,' he said to the open-mouthed boy, 'lead him over to Mr McCallum's and see to it that he is rubbed down, watered and fed.' He shook the reins impatiently until the lad obeyed him and then, with his bag slung over his shoulder, stepped to the door of the cottage and, pausing only long enough to suck in one deep breath, thumbed the latch and went in.

'So it's yourself, is it?' Duncan Ralston said. 'You made fair time. I didn't expect you 'til tomorrow.'

The old man was alone in the kitchen. He was not dressed in a nightshirt or, for that matter, a mort-cloth. He wore a thick woollen garment, like chain mail, over a flannel shirt and baggy breeches and seemed to be not only alive but in bounding good health. He was chopping onions at the table, and a huge pan of braised meat, simmering on the side of the fire, filled the room with a savoury smell that made Grant's mouth water.

Grant dropped his bag to the floor and said, wryly, 'Aye, Grandad, you're one up on Banquo's ghost, I see, for he was never considerate enough to cook supper for his guest.'

'Nor Hamlet's father neither,' Duncan said. 'There's bread an' cheese to keep you goin' if you're hungry.'

'I am.' Grant peeled off his coat and cape and draped them on a chair by the hearth. 'There's nothing like a hard ride across the Strath in dismal weather to whet the appetite. Why are you not

460

dead?'

'Margo would not allow it.'

'Were you even ill?'

'Cold in the chest, that's all.'

'Huh!' Grant said. 'I might have guessed you were up to something when the letter was written in your hand. Why did you post it to Gillon and not to me? By the by, he was quite insulted because you didn't invite him to your wake.'

'I posted it to Gillon 'cause I knew he'd get you roused.'

'I take it,' Grant eased off his boots, 'that neither Roderick nor Mother is aware that you've summoned me? What is it? Why do you want to speak with me? Is it the boy?'

'Iain?' Duncan shook his head. 'Nah, nah, the boy's fine. You need have no fear on that score. Marie, though, has been fair hard on poor Roderick since that bonnie wee lass from Edinburgh went off in a sulk.'

'Nicola, you mean?'

'Aye, Nicola,' Duncan Ralston said.

'What do you expect me to do?' Grant said. 'I've no sway over Marie Hadley and I cannot interfere.'

Duncan put a plate before him then a board bearing wedges of new cheese. A butter dish and a half loaf of bread followed and a tea-cup and saucer, knife and a spoon. Grant watched the old man dress the table. He moved slowly but he showed no sign of feebleness in body or mind.

'Where's Roderick?'

'Falkirk,' Duncan told him. 'Sellin' calves.'

'And Mother?'

'In the village visitin' Mrs Bryant. She'll be back e'er long for the milkin', though we only have four

461

cows in yield.'

Grant stretched his legs under the table. 'Damn it all, Grandad, why have you brought me here?'

'I want you to tell her.'

'Tell who?'

'The girl, Nicola.'

'Tell her what?'

'The truth.'

'I see,' Grant said. 'May I ask why, after all these years, you are meddling in something that's over and done with?'

'It's not meddlin', son, an' it's not over an' done with,' Duncan said. 'Roderick has fallen in love wi' your sister-in-law an' she, as far as I can tell, has fallen in love wi' him.'

'Did you fetch me all the way from Edinburgh just to play matchmaker?'

'The lass thinks Marie Hadley's boy is Roddy's son.'

'In that case,' Grant said, 'why not disabuse her?'

'Roddy made you a promise, Grant. He helped preserve your reputation so you might marry your heiress. He's never breathed a word an' won't do so now, even though it'll cost him his one true love.'

'One true love,' said Grant. 'What nonsense! He wants Nicola, that's all. I can't say I blame him. If I were not married I would want her myself. Once he has had her, he will be cured of all notion of love.'

'As you were cured o' Marie Hadley.'

'I was never in love with Marie.'

'You promised her marriage.'

'I was too young to know better. Besides,

462

Mother soon put a stop to it. A farm servant wouldn't do for me, no, not when I was cut out to be a gentleman.'

'Would you have married Marie Hadley if it hadn't been for Margo?'

Grant hesitated, then, with a shake of the head, said, 'No.'

'You've a son, Grant, a fine sturdy wee lad, who doesn't know who his father is. Marie's too frightened o' Margo ever to let it out that it was you, not Roderick, who fathered her bairn.'

'I did what was asked of me,' said Grant, 'what was expected of me.'

'An' what suited you best,' said Duncan.

'What do you want from me?' Grant said. 'Do you want Roderick to marry Nicola Templeton to ensure that Craigiehall falls to the Peters family? Did Mother put you up to this? Is she behind the summons?'

'Nah, nah,' said Duncan. 'It's me you answer to.'

'Precisely what do you want me to do? Make full confession to my wife?'

'I don't want you to tell your wife. I want you to tell Nicola.'

'Do you suppose that she will not tell her sister?'

'If Nicola loves her sister then she'll say nothin'; your secret will be safe.'

'Let Roderick tell her.'

'That he won't do,' said Duncan. 'For Roderick's sake, tell her.'

'To add another suitable wife to the family collection, you mean?'

'Make what you will o' it, son,' said Duncan. 'Will you do it?'

And Grant, after a lengthy pause, said, 'I might.'

463

Only those hardy souls who had urgent business in Ayrshire boarded the Flyer that early morning. The vehicle was built for speed not stability and in the course of a year there had been four serious accidents, two fatalities, and a number of minor incidents involving broken wheels and crippled horses. It was not therefore surprising that there were only two inside passengers and no one at all on the roof, for anyone with an ounce of sense had either deferred their journey or had chosen the long, slow route in one of the big barge-like coaches which were less affected by side-gusts and slippery roads.

It did not take Nicola long to realise that risking life and limb in the light-weight little Flyer in wild autumnal weather was just another adventure for her aunt whose enthusiasm for new experiences had been stoked by too many lonely hours locked away in Salton House. She had also been impressed by Isabella's perspicacity, for the woman had refused Robertson's woebegone offer to accompany them in the knowledge that her cousin's manservant was not the world's best traveller and was liable to spend eight or ten hours retching horribly and praying for death to overtake him.

'I'll have you for company, Nicola,' Isabella had said. 'That will suffice.'

If Nicola was aware of the dangers of travelling in the sort of weather that had driven every yawl and lugger from Yarmouth to Cape Wrath to seek shelter, she gave no hint of it. She was too eager to quit Graddan's Court to refuse her aunt's offer of a trip to Craigiehall to see for herself what changes the vicissitudes of the summer and the prospect of marriage had wrought upon her father. She followed Isabella Ballentine into the conveyance and, clinging to the overhead straps, rode out into the teeth of the gale without a qualm.

It was only after the first swift change of horses at Peebles—ten minutes, no more—that the weather abated a little and the ladies were able to converse without having to shout.

'Tomorrow,' said Isabella, 'will bring better weather, I hope, and we will accompany Johnny out to the coal pit to revel in his surprise when I hand him the title deeds. Do you think he will be pleased?'

'Of course he will,' said Nicola. 'He will be delighted.'

'Men!' said Isabella. 'Land is all they ever think about. Love, even love-making, is set at naught against possession of a few acres of good grazing. If it isn't land, then it is position and the power that goes with position.' She put an arm about Nicola's waist and drew her closer. 'He will, however, be delighted to see you too, my dear.'

'Is that why you invited me to accompany you,' said Nicola, 'to please my father and make him think even more highly of you than he does already?'

'Oh, no,' Isabella said. 'Johnny does not think highly of me at all. He is, I believe, in love with me, after his fashion, but he is wary of me; he knows that I am not dependent upon him.'

'Are you intent on making him dependent upon you?' said Nicola.

Isabella laughed. 'Most certainly, but he will never know it. He will stir himself to manage my coalfields, for authority is something he understands. He will believe that he has "rescued" me from the miseries of living alone in Salton House and will set out to impress me by improving my estate which, as you know, he regards as a squandered asset. Indeed, I believe he regards me as a squandered asset, too.'

'I wonder how he thinks of me,' said Nicola. 'I know he doesn't love me.'

'Of course he does.'

'He expected more of me, and more of Charlotte.'

'You are not his chattel, Nicola. There are new laws, new attitudes that liberate young ladies from the sort of tyranny that my father imposed upon me.'

'I do not feel liberated,' said Nicola. 'I feel . . .'

'What? Tell me.'

'Lost, if you must know.'

'Lost because there is no man for you?' Isabella said. 'There is time, my dear, lots of time for you to give your heart away.'

Nicola paused, then said, 'There is a man, a farmer.'

'Grant Peters' brother?'

'Yes—Roderick.'

'Are you in love with him?'

'Yes.'

'Is he in love with you?' Isabella said.

'He wants me, I know, but . . .'

'Is he married?'

'He has a "wife" of sorts, a farm servant—and a child.'

466

'Ah!' said Isabella, softly.

'You must say nothing to Papa about this. Promise me, please.'

'Not a word will cross my lips,' said Isabella. 'However, do you suppose that fathering a child on a servant girl is an unforgivable sin? Your farmer fellow would not be the first, and will no doubt not be the last, gentleman to sow a wild oat or two. I, for one, would not consider it an impediment to a happy marriage.'

'He will not send her away.'

'Which shows, I believe, a degree of responsibility.'

'He will not admit it.'

'Admit what? That he loves you?'

'No,' said Nicola, a little impatiently. 'He will not admit that he was her lover and that the boy is his. His secret, which is no secret at all, has stifled all feeling between us. How can I forgive him if he refuses to acknowledge that there is anything to forgive?'

'Does he still—um—enjoy her favours?'

'I don't know. No, I do not believe he does. Even so, I do not trust him.'

'Is your farmer fellow dashing?'

'He is, if anything, cautious,' said Nicola. 'Brave, but cautious.'

'Cautious, like your sister's husband?'

'Nothing like Grant, not—not cold.'

'Is that how you see Grant Peters?'

'Cold and calculating, yes.'

Isabella gazed from the window for a moment or two. The glass was streaked with mud and speckled by the last rain shower but, it seemed, she could make out enough of the bleak landscape to hold her attention.

At length, she said, 'There are merits in any marriage that are invisible to everyone but the wife and her husband. Even the children of such unions are often at a loss to understand what holds this sort of man and that sort of woman together. In my opinion, my dear, Grant Peters and Charlotte are just such a pair, imperfect in many respects but, together, perfectly matched. Your father and mother were another such couple, whereas my husband and I were never in harness. Do you see yourself as a farmer's wife, Nicola, married to a fellow who is, by your own admission, considerate, brave and cautious?'

'My father will not approve of Roderick.'

'Johnny has no say in the matter. If you are lost then it is up to you to find yourself, though I would advise you not to tarry quite so long as I did to do it.'

'Or be quite so devious?' Nicola said.

'Or be quite so devious,' Isabella agreed and gave the poor, bewildered, love-struck child another soothing hug.

*   *   *

Grant's excuse for visiting Heatherbank barely held water. He had, he claimed, been concerned about his grandfather's health and had taken the opportunity of riding in from Stirling where he had a small piece of business to conduct. His mother may have swallowed this slightly fishy tale but Roderick most certainly did not and after prayers, after supper, he lost no time in steering Grant into the small back parlour ostensibly to help him with the quarterly tally.

After the door had been closed and a bottle of whisky opened, he rounded on his brother. 'Is it true what you say; is Craigiehall out of the woods?'

'Why would I lie to you?' Grant said.

'I thought perhaps you had made up the story to appease Mother.'

'No, it's the truth, every word. What's more, Mrs Ballentine has promised Charlotte that she will place no claim upon the estate, that when Craigiehall passes on Charlotte and I will inherit.'

'And Nicola?' said Roderick. 'What will she inherit?'

'Her share,' Grant said.

'Half?'

'Well,' said Grant, 'that rather depends on how long his lordship lives and just how many children Charlotte produces. I did not travel from Edinburgh simply to impart news that might have been put in a letter, however. Grandfather sent for me. The old devil told me he was breathing his last.'

'I thought as much,' said Roderick.

'He seems set on marrying you off to Nicola Templeton.'

'Nicola wants nothing to do with me.'

'The evidence suggests otherwise,' Grant said. 'She has been moping about Graddan's Court since she returned, snapping at her sister and generally behaving like a love-struck child.'

'She is not a child, Grant,' said Roderick.

'No,' Grant said, 'I do not suppose that she is. She is ripe for marriage and, I believe, will even settle for a rough-mannered farmer with not much more than a couple of hundred acres to call his

469

own. God knows, Roddy, Nicola is a tasty piece. You would be lucky to have her.'

'I can't have her.'

'Because of your promise to keep my indiscretion secret? Ah, Roddy, you are honourable to the point of stupidity. For God's sake, man, tell Nicola the truth. If she tells Charlotte then I will deal with it.'

'Nicola will not believe me. She thinks we're all born liars, like Gillon.'

'Will she believe me?' said Grant.

Roderick leaned an elbow on the table and toyed with the glass of whisky that Grant had poured for him. He swirled the dark brown liquid about and studied it as intently as a fortune-teller might study a globe.

At length, he said, 'Would you do this for me?'

'Have I not just said as much?' Grant answered. 'Once Nicola knows the truth she will fly into your arms, I'm sure. In any case, I've made my offer. I'll be gone tomorrow, early, for I have several causes on hand and must prepare for the courts opening. I've made my offer and will waste no more time trying to reconcile my past with your future.'

'When will you speak with Nicola?'

'Soon, very soon.'

'And then?' Roderick said.

'And then it's up to you,' said Grant.

*   *   *

Dank brown-paper leaves plastered themselves against the chaise and the dust that rose from the mouth of the pit coagulated in dense clouds, like bloodstains on a blanket. Hugh Littlejohn had arrived early. His horse was tethered to a birch tree on the edge of the wood. At the bottom of the slope a broken dry-stone wall marked the division between Lord Craigiehall's land and that of Sir Charles de Morville. There was no sign of de Morville or his sons, and the gang of labourers shoring the tunnel mouth worked under the supervision of two men in tall hats and mud-stained riding frocks.

Beyond the workings, near the stream, were four dwellings fashioned in the shape of igloos and covered with weather-beaten canvas. Smoke rose from the iron chimneys that poked through the coverings and the smell of frying bacon carried on the remnant of yesterday's gale was strong enough to make John James to wrinkle his nose in disgust.

The chaise was too bulky to thread through the trees and John James, with Isabella on one arm and Nicola on the other, picked his way down the hill to join his overseer.

'What news have you heard of the owners?' John James asked.

'None, sir,' Hugh Littlejohn answered.

'What do you make of it?'

'It's strange, sir, but if you'll take a bearin' on the line o' the track you'll see they're aimed at our field gate.'

Holding his hat with one hand and shading his eyes with the other, his lordship peered in the direction of the one and only gate that his land shared with de Morville's. The gate, he noticed, had not only been opened, it had been removed, and a pile of timber, high as a man's head, unloaded beside it.

He growled and glanced back at Littlejohn.

471

'Did you give permission of access?'

'Nay, your lordship. No application was ever made to me.'

'Then,' John James cried, 'I'll have him, who ever he might be. My land is my land, coal or no damned coal. What sort of man would shear off a piece of another man's estate without arranging compensation?'

'Only a fool or a bully,' Isabella said and nudged Nicola.

'Yes, Papa,' Nicola chimed in, 'or someone ignorant of the law.'

'Ignorant of the law *and* good manners,' said Isabella. 'What a coarse fellow this new owner must be.'

'Well,' John James planted his hands on his hips. 'Well, Littlejohn, now we have our excuse and, by God, I will have my answer without further delay. Shake yourself and follow me. We'll soon find out what oaf with money to burn has appropriated my field gate.'

'Have a care, Papa,' said Nicola.

'Yes, John James,' said Isabella. 'After all, he may be armed.'

'Armed?' His lordship swung round. 'Armed with what?'

'This,' said Isabella, brightly.

She offered him a packet of title deeds, neatly bound with silk ribbon.

Scowling, John James looked from his overseer to his daughter while his cousin, smiling broadly, shook the packet at him. At length, he took it, undid the ribbon and clutching the documents firmly in both hands scanned the florid script for half a minute before, bewildered, he glanced up.

472

'Isa,' he said, 'what on earth is this?'

'My dowry, Johnny,' Isabella said and, giggling like a schoolgirl, threw herself into his arms.

CHAPTER TWENTY-SEVEN

There was more artfulness than artistry in Mr Cattenach's reporting. The journals to which he contributed were not salacious scandal-sheets like *The Rambler's Magazine* or the *Bon Ton*. There were no risqué jokes in *The Edinburgh Courant* and the moral tone of *The Mercury* was considered impeccable. Even so, there were quite enough women immured in country houses or locked away in stifling city mansions yearning for a little scandal to make Mr Cattenach's accounts of dirty doings among the high born well worth the printer's ink.

Thanks to 'Cyclops' the public first learned that Sir Archibald Oliphant had penned another verse-play. Thanks to 'Cyclops' the public were made aware that the 'celebrated London actress' Mrs Madelaine Young would appear in a private performance of the work. Thanks to a delicate hint by 'Cyclops' Madelaine's 'interesting condition' was broadcast to the world, accompanied by a slightly less delicate reminder that a famous jurist had climbed down from the bench long enough to have more than a casual connection with the mother-to-be.

Thus, piece by piece, snippet by snippet, throughout the early days of October, fact and conjecture were rubbed together and the spark of gossip fanned into flame.

'Does he mention *Fingal*, dearest? What does he say about *Fingal*?' Sir Archie reached for the newspaper, which his wife hastily snatched away. 'Has Macpherson published a riposte yet?'

'No, no,' said Valerie. 'So great is the interest in your new work, however, that everyone is clamouring for an invitation. It is, says "Cyclops"— let me quote you his words—"the most eagerly anticipated event of the season". Does that please you, Archie?'

'It does, it does.'

At the dinner table in Horne's there was less enthusiasm.

'Libel,' said Grant. 'Without doubt—libel.'

Hercules shook his head. 'Cattenach is too nimble to fall into that pitfall. He knows we cannot prove him wrong, particularly as he names few names.'

'But surely Madelaine has broken her agreement?'

'Madelaine has given nothing away,' Hercules told his protégé. 'The piece does not cite her. Cattenach's information derives from other sources.'

'Lady Oliphant, do you mean?'

'Of course that's who I mean,' said Hercules.

A little further up the High Street in the Lord Advocate's chambers on the Parliament Square, Dunbar, Buller and Marsh were enjoying a dinner sent in from a chop house, a dinner punctuated by many toasts to the downfall of their lubricous colleague, Craigiehall, and the subsequent elevation to the bench of Lord Buller's son-in-law whose time, all present were agreed, had come.

In Leith, slightly the worse for wear, Gillon was

shaking the newspaper and trying to make Lucky Findlater understand that he, not the illustrious Craigiehall, was the begetter of the actress's child, while two of Edinburgh's disreputable dandies raucously jeered his claim and urged him to come upstairs and play brag before he got too drunk to hold the cards.

At Graddan's Court poor Molly bore the brunt of Charlotte's spleen and bitterly regretted that Nicola had left her behind to attend her sister, while far to the south Nicola and Isabella put their heads together over a dish of roasted cheese and wondered which of them would break the news of the latest slander to Papa who had been out all day overseeing the propping of a shaft.

Fleur was at the piano in the Oliphants' gilded drawing-room practising the chords that would signal the clash between Fingal and the Roman general, played respectively by Conn Cavendish and young Tom. In a corner, invoking the muse, Pearl and Ruby quietly chanted dialogue and Ben—Ossian—stood on his hands and made faces at the villain of the piece, his pal Charlie. By the window Madelaine and Sir Archie were engaged in fierce debate over the latest of Jack Cattenach's revelations.

'The theatre will be filled from pit to gallery,' Sir Archie said. 'I could sell invites at ten guineas apiece and cram the building to the rafters. In fact, I have heard a rumour that the proprietors of the Royal are considering delaying the opening of *Braganza*, with Mrs Buckley and Mrs Yates, to allow us to put on three public performances of my *Fingal*—subject to licence, of course—with you as the leading player. Do you think I'm going to be denied an audience because you have suddenly become bashful?'

'They are coming to gawp at me, sir,' said Madelaine. 'Are you so blind that you cannot see that your play is inconsequential? Would you have me bare my belly so that public curiosity will be satisfied and the hogs will have their tuppence worth?'

'It is my chance to be recognised, Madelaine. I care not a fig why.'

'Because Lady Valerie broke a confidence, that's why,' Maddy said. 'It matters not to her that I will be naked before them, there only to be mocked.'

'What does it matter what brings them flocking? They will be entranced by your performance and by my verse, each in equal measure. Have you not been well enough paid?'

'I have not been paid at all as yet.'

'Mrs Ballentine's bank draft will come forward soon. You have my promise.'

'Your promise—what is that worth?'

'Hush, now, hush! No tears, if you please.'

'Tears, sir?' Maddy tilted her chin and blinked. 'I have shed enough tears to fill a lake. I will shed no more, not for you, nor for *Fingal*. As soon as the performance is over I will take my fee and flee this blighted country.'

'And let down the company?'

'Damn the company,' Madelaine said. 'And damn you too, sir.'

'Madelaine,' Sir Archie cried, 'are you leaving us in the lurch?'

'I am going to make water, if you must know.'

'And then will you return?'

'Yes,' said Maddy, biting on her lip, 'then, like

476

Fingal, I'll return.'

*   *   *

Papa was a deal more sanguine about the 'Cyclops' pieces than either Nicola or Isabella had anticipated. He was so caught up in the study of wresting coal from the ground that he had little time to fret about anything else. He was gone before breakfast and did not return to the house until last light. When the latest of Cattenach's smears appeared in the *Courant*, he merely sighed and said that no matter how the lure was trailed he would not return to Edinburgh one minute before the Lords of Council required it of him, for he had, it seemed, engaged Messrs Gall and Gibson, the gentlemen in frocks and tall hats, to take a crew to Salton to sink a few exploratory shafts before frost and snow set in.

He even brought an Almanac to the supper table and, fork in one hand and book in the other, counted out the days until Christmas, not, alas, in anticipation of becoming a husband or a grandfather but to tally the possibilities of drawing coal in quantity from the Ayrshire field to meet the winter market. He was, Nicola realised, caught in the grip of a new passion but neither she nor Isabella grudged him his zeal for he had shed his reserve and pranced and danced about the drawing-room and stole kisses from his bride-to-be when ever the mood came upon him which, as it happened, was fairly often.

The big house at Craigiehall stood bright and warm in the autumnal gloom for Isabella Ballentine had not forgotten how to manage a

477

household and make it comfortable. She applied herself to revising domestic expenditure and chivvying the servants, including Mrs McGrouther, and soon made a friend of Robertson, who had eventually returned from Edinburgh, by gouging out his lordship's dressing room and sending a great bundle of worn and outmoded garments to the Kirkton workhouse.

In all of this she was assisted by Nicola, for one day, Aunt Isabella said, Nicola would have a household of her own to manage and it would be as well if she learned to do it properly.

Nicola did not disabuse her aunt of the notion that she might marry a gentleman. She did not mention Heatherbank or Roderick Peters, though the place and the person were never far from her thoughts. But she spent more time than Isabella quite approved of with Hugh Littlejohn inspecting stock on the tenant farms and asking questions that were, perhaps, a little too knowledgeable and earthy for the daughter of a laird.

When Grant Peters showed up out of the blue one damp afternoon, Nicola assumed that her brother-in-law had made the journey from Edinburgh to discuss business with her father. She was, therefore, more than a little surprised when he requested Aunt Isabella's permission to speak with Nicola before his lordship returned. It was all oddly formal, Grant's manner stiff and cold. His assurances that Charlotte was in sound health did not allay Nicola's fear that he was the bearer of grim news.

As soon as the door of the parlour off the hall closed behind them, she rounded on him and blurted out, 'Is Roderick ill?'

478

'Ill?' said Grant. 'No, as far as I know he's in perfect health.'

'Is he to marry then? Is that what you've come to tell me?

'He is certainly in need of a wife,' Grant said.

'He is, then, to marry?' Nicola plucked at the lawyer's sleeve. 'Is it her, is it Marie Hadley?'

'No, Nicola, it's no rustic wooing, nor rustic betrothal. I might tell you that I am not here willingly and would not be here at all if an obligation had not been placed upon me.'

'By whom? By Roderick?'

'Sit, please,' Grant said. 'I find it disconcerting to stand here as if we were about to trip into a dance.'

'I will sit,' Nicola said, 'only when you tell me what . . .'

He took her by the shoulders, steered her to a French chair and pushed her down on to it. 'You are,' he said, 'almost as stubborn as your sister. Be still now and listen to what I have to say.'

It was almost dark in the parlour. No fire had been lighted and Nicola could see her breath, and Grant's too, printed in the air. He stood over her, his hands on either side of her, pinning her down.

'I ask you to answer me truthfully and without prevarication,' he said. 'Are you in love with my brother, Roderick?'

'I don't know.'

'No,' said Grant, sternly, 'that will not do.'

'Did you not indicate that the matter concerns you and me, not Roderick?' Nicola said. 'If that is the case, then why . . .'

'God in heaven!' said Grant. 'Do not split hairs. Are you or are you not willing to acknowledge my brother as a suitor?'

'Did Roderick send you? Are you here on his behalf?'

'Nicola, answer me.'

'Yes,' she heard herself say. 'Yes—but not without conditions.'

He took a step back, folded his arms and looked up towards the plaster ceiling, then he said, 'The child is mine, not Roderick's.'

'Marie's child?'

'Yes, Marie's child.'

A little sound, a gasp or a sob, escaped her. 'Why did he not tell me?'

'He did not tell you because of a promise made long ago,' Grant said, 'a promise that is now obsolete.'

'Does Charlotte know what you have done?'

'Certainly not,' Grant said.

'Do you expect me not to tell her?'

'I must take my chance on your discretion.'

'Is he the only one?'

'What?' said Grant, startled. 'If you mean Iain, yes, he's the only one.'

'Did you love her—Marie Hadley, I mean?'

'No.'

'Did you promise her marriage?'

'Not that either,' Grant said. 'I made her no promise; she asked for none. My excuse—my only excuse—is that I was too young and too hot-blooded to consider the consequences.'

'And your mother covered it up?'

'She refused to allow me to squander my opportunity to advance in the world. It was obvious that Marie would not make a suitable wife for an advocate. So, you see, Roderick did not deceive you. I did. He merely colluded.'

'Charlotte knows nothing of all this?' Nicola said.

He shook his head. 'Nothing.'

Nicola got to her feet. 'Is this another of your mother's tricks, Grant? Am I to be snared for the benefit of the Peters family, as Charlotte was snared? I am worth little or nothing, you know. Once your child—your child in wedlock—is born then I will be worth even less.'

'You are worth nothing to *me*, Nicola, that's true,' Grant told her, 'but it appears that my brother has fallen in love with you.'

'Has he?'

'Unfortunately, he has,' Grant said. 'Let me ask you once more—do you love him enough to consider becoming his wife.'

Nicola, with a small tight smile, said, 'If ever Roderick has the gumption to ask me in person then I will give him an answer, but not before, Grant, and certainly not through you.'

'Do you not trust me, Nicola?'

'No more than you trust me,' said Nicola and, hiding her elation, thanked him for his courtesy and hurried him out into the hall.

*   *   *

It was all Isabella could do to prevent John James lighting up a battery of pine-torches and leading his son-in-law out through the darkness to inspect the coal-workings at first hand. The talk at supper was dominated not by Lord Craigiehall's damaged reputation but by coal, coal in the ground, coal in the heap, and the possibility of developing the

481

Westmore Company's miserable little patch on the banks of the Clyde to cope with an increased production.

The purpose of Grant's visit was lost in the general mêlée for, as the evening progressed, Grant soon became involved in his father-in-law's ambitious plans for expansion and pitched himself into a discussion of tonnages and transport and just how best to employ Mr Bunting's father and brother, and if they were employable at all.

When plans, surveys and purchase of new machinery were mentioned, Isabella lost no time in despatching the gentlemen to the library to drink their brandy and pore over papers to their heart's content while she ordered tea to be served in the drawing-room where, at last, she could be alone with Nicola and discover just what Grant had wanted with the girl.

'It is a private matter, Aunt Isabella,' Nicola told her.

'A matter of the heart, my dear?'

'Yes.'

'Does it concern a marriage proposal?'

'It may.'

'You are behaving coyly,' Isabella said, 'and it does not become you.'

'Am I not old enough to have secrets of my own?' said Nicola.

'You are playing a game with me and you are too coy—and too smug—to play it very well. Look at you, flushed with—with what?—not embarrassment, I'll wager. Do you wish me to wring it out of you?'

'Yes,' Nicola said. 'Wring it out of me—if you can.'

Isabella placed a thoughtful finger to her cheek. 'The proposal, if proposal it is, cannot be from Mr Grant Peters who is already married. It must come from someone closely connected to Grant Peters; a relative, perhaps?'

'Perhaps.'

'Gillon? One could do worse than Gillon. He is very handsome and . . .'

'Not Gillon.'

'Then,' Isabella said, 'I can only conclude that your taste runs to the agricultural and that it is the farmer . . .'

'Roderick.'

'Yes, Roderick . . . whose head you have turned.' Isabella paused. 'Be serious with me now, Nicola: has Grant Peters approached you on behalf of his farmer brother?'

'He has,' said Nicola.

'He is not wealthy, this farmer brother.'

'No,' said Nicola, 'but no more is he poor.'

'Your father will not give his approval to such a match, you know.'

'I doubt if Papa will care,' Nicola said. 'You've given Papa what he wants and he has no more need of me. He will, I imagine, be relieved to be rid of me.'

'You are very hard on him, Nicola.'

'With reason, do you not think?' Nicola said. 'Besides, I have not yet received a proposal of marriage from Roderick Peters. Grant is merely sounding the depths. I've told him I will consider such a proposal only if it comes directly from Roderick, if, in effect, he comes to me.'

'Does he know where to find you?' said Isabella.

'If he loves me,' Nicola said, 'he'll find me.'

CHAPTER TWENTY-EIGHT

No stone had been left unturned to make 'Fingal's Return' a success. Sir Archie had commissioned a back-cloth from a reputable painter and a canvas-covered rock and an imitation pine tree to set the scene. He applied the latest innovation in lighting by veiling the all-too-obvious footlights with coloured silk screens and paid close attention to the costumes, for he had no wish to have Macpherson or any other *faux* historian biting his ear on that score. Gowns were carefully trimmed and dyed and the cardboard armour that Tom wore on head and breast was accurately copied from Munro's definitive work on the Roman Empire.

Musically, even Sir Archie had to admit, the play was not quite up to it. He had been unable to purchase a suitable composition for band or orchestra and had settled for an eight-note choral chant, not un-akin to plainsong, and several flurries from an in-the-wings piano that Fleur would render when she was not on stage clinging to Nu-ala's leg. There was also a drum, a very large drum, which Ben—as Ossian—lugged about with him and, as warrior-poets were wont to do, apparently, beat slowly to sound the knell of heroic characters and rapidly to announce their resurrection.

All this theatrical business Sir Archie handled by throwing guineas in all directions. But it was 'Cyclops', in collusion with the indefatigable Lady Valerie, who elevated the verse-epic into a sensation, for never in the history of puffery had a campaign of innuendo worked so well. So well, in fact, that some folk were convinced that Lord Craigiehall would appear on stage to kiss his charming fancy. Others were of the opinion that Oliphant had delivered a satire and that Fingal was intended to represent the Prince of Wales and Mrs Young, God bless her, the infamous Mrs Fitzherbert, whom the Prince had married illicitly and to whom he had returned in secret in defiance of the law and the King's command.

Heated debates on the interpretation of a play that no one had yet seen broke out in the commons of the University and on the Sunday before 'Fingal' opened, the play, and Sir Archie, were roundly denounced as blasphemous by several lesser divines.

The coveted invitations were despatched a week before the performance.

Doyennes of Edinburgh society wept into their teacups when they did not receive one. Dukes and earls, as well as fat merchants and wealthy traders, engaged in shifty negotiations to purchase admission by nefarious means. Gentlemen from country seats, who had no interest at all in drama, devoted themselves to wooing councillors and magistrates who might have influence upon Sir Archie. And Sir Archie's bank was inundated with applications for new accounts in the fond hope that a ticket of entry to the Theatre Royal might be attached to the pay-book.

By a combination of bribery and cajolery, Hercules Mackenzie had succeeded in separating elderly Lady Wyville from her ticket. As the Writer was at pains to point out, she had not risen from her sick bed in six months and could not reasonably expect her litter to be carried up three flights of stairs to the footmen's gallery where she would have to fight for breathing space on a backless wooden bench. Surrendering at last to common sense, the miserable old harridan charged her solicitor twenty guineas in exchange for the printed card and, cackling, sent him away with a curse.

In the depths of the Ayrshire countryside the feverish excitement of Edinburgh's *literati* seemed distant, though neither Nicola nor Isabella was unaware that Lord Craigiehall would have to return to the capital to answer to the Lords of Council for his conduct before the courts opened in November. If the Lords of Council had seen the great Lord Craigiehall when he returned from a day at the coal-workings, however, they might have been concerned more for his sanity than his conduct, for he had shed all pretence at dignity and arrived home caked with mud like a common labourer.

'Hoh, Isa,' he would shout as he bounded through the hall. 'Come fill the cup and bring me wine for I have earned my drink this day, by God I have.'

Bathed and changed, but with energy undimmed, he would next appear in the drawing-room, kiss his intended and his daughter and, glass in hand, relay news of the height of a seam or the depth obtained by his diggers while his ladies listened patiently.

On that particular evening, though, his lordship's vivacity was tainted by anger. He strode into the drawing-room with a card, including its packet, wagging in his fist.

'Gall,' he shouted. 'Gall and impudence!'

'What?' said Isabella, sitting up. 'Have you been dismissed?'

'Dismissed?' John James said. 'Nay, his lordships do not have the power to dismiss me without a hearing, several hearings, in fact. I have not been dismissed. I have been allotted a box at Oliphant's infernal play.'

'Oh!' said Isabella. 'I take it that we will not be going?'

'Going? No, not for a thousand pounds. Do *you* want to go, my dear?'

'It's tempting,' Isabella said, 'but it would not be wise.'

'Who sent the ticket?' said Nicola. 'Was it, by any chance, Mrs Young?'

'Mrs Young?' John James said. 'Hmm, I never thought of that.'

'If you wish to see Mrs Young perform, I'll understand,' Isabella said.

'I do not wish to see Mrs Young perform,' John James said. 'I do not wish to see Madelaine Young ever again. Unless I miss my guess Valerie Oliphant is behind the invitation. What a triumph for her, what an endorsement of her slanders, if I, Lord Craigiehall, were to turn up, slavering like a puppy, in a side box in full view of the audience.'

'Sensation upon sensation, yes,' said Isabella, softly.

'See, here's what I think of Oliphant's invitation,' John James said and tossed the card into the hearth—from which place Isabella discreetly managed to retrieve it just before it went up in smoke.

                    *   *   *

'Marriage,' said Margo, 'isn't a step to be undertook lightly.'

Her father let out a groan. 'Can you not think o' somethin' a bit more original to say to the boy? It was a light enough arrangement you had wi' your man all those years ago.'

'Aye, but I wasn't thirty years old.'

'You were seventeen an' mad in love wi' the chap,' Duncan reminded her. 'If I had stood in your way, you'd just have run off wi' your daft ploughman on the night o' the first full moon. Am I not right?'

Margo had the decency to laugh. 'It's the truth, 'cept I wouldn't have waited for the first full moon.'

'Besides,' Duncan said, 'the lassie hasn't given Roddy the nod just yet.'

'She'll be havin' a long think about it,' Margo suggested. 'Craigiehall will resist handing her over to a farmer, so she'll have to win her daddy round.'

'Nah, nah,' said Duncan. 'That's not the way o' it, Margo. She'll be wantin' our Roderick on his knees.'

'Our Roderick bows the knee to no one,' said Margo.

'Then he'd better learn,' said Duncan. 'It's all very well for us sittin' here snug by the fire. Miss Nicola Templeton may not be so easy pleased. She's the daughter o' a laird, an' has a right to expect more than we can offer her.'

'Is she not in love wi' him, then? Was Marie Hadley only an excuse?'

'There're no certainties in love, dear,' Duncan reminded her. 'Nicola's back wi' her family now, so Grant tells us, an' it would be surprisin' if she wasn't havin' second thoughts.'

'Is Roderick havin' second thoughts?' said Margo.

'He's cautious, that's all, cautious an' frightened.'

'Frightened? Our Roderick?'

'Frightened she'll turn him down,' said Duncan.

'After the all sacrifices Grant's made?'

'It was no sacrifice,' said Duncan. 'Grant was glad enough to get it off his chest. He's under no obligation now, Margo, not to you, nor to me, nor to Roderick. From what he told us in his last letter, he's flyin' under Craigiehall's banner fair an' square an' there will be no stoppin' him. You'll be takin' tea wi' lords an' ladies before you're much older, never fear.'

'That was never my aim,' said Margo. 'I want nothin' for myself.'

'Only for the boys, aye, always the boys,' said Duncan. 'If mother-love isn't selfishness wrote large, Margo, then I don't know what is. Well, you've done the best by them an' most o' your plants are bearin' fruit. You've a right to be pleased wi' yourself, I suppose, an' wallow in pride a bit.'

'An' you, Daddy,' Margo said, 'are you not proud o' me?'

'Since the very minute you were born,' Duncan Ralston said.

*   *   *

489

John James was a trifle shocked when Isabella entered his bedroom. She wore a thin silken robe embroidered with roses and forget-me-nots over a plain linen nightgown, and a dainty little cap, like dandelion seed.

'Ah, you're reading,' she said. 'I saw the light beneath the door and knew you were not asleep.'

She approached the bed, seated herself on the side of the mattress and kicked off her slippers. John James pressed the book—a volume of Mandeville's *Fable of the Bees*—against his chest and slid lower beneath the sheets. His knees stuck up like two great boulders and he felt as awkward as a boy whose voice has not quite broken.

He cleared his throat. 'Isa, what do you want?'

'May I lie with you?'

'I do not think that would be—ah—seemly.'

'I do not mean "lie" with you,' Isabella said. 'I mean, may I lie beside you, Johnny. The bed is high and my feet do not quite reach the carpet.'

'Lie by me then, if you must.' He sighed. 'Are you not cold?'

'No colder than you are.' She swung herself on to the bed and tapped his nose with her forefinger. 'I will thaw you out, my dear, have no fear on that score—but not until we are married.'

John James eased himself against the bolster, put the book to one side and tentatively draped a long arm about his cousin's shoulders. 'I am not so cold as you imagine, Isa, but—my, my, you are really very beautiful, you know.'

'In candlelight, perhaps,' Isabella said, 'but not the light of day.'

He kissed her cheek and drew her closer. 'In any light,' he said then, gruffly, 'Now, what so troubles

490

you that you'd risk entering an old roué's bed chamber in the middle of the night?'

'Old roué, indeed!' She tapped his nose again. 'Nicola will not be coming with us to Edinburgh.'

'Oh! May I ask why?'

'She prefers to wait here in Craigiehall.'

'Wait for what?'

'Her lover.'

'Does Nicola have a lover?' John James said.

'Her beau, then, the man who will make her his wife.'

'The farmer, Grant's brother?'

'Yes.' Isabella peered anxiously at his stern profile. 'Why do I not hear a grouse, a grumble, or a roar of objection?'

'What point would it serve to object?' John James said. 'If Nicola's mind is made up—and you are on her side—then I have no say in the matter. Will he make her a good husband?'

'Nicola seems to think that he will.'

'Then she has my blessing.'

'Is this indifference, John James? Are you dismissing her out of hand?'

'Certainly not.' He shifted position, propped on a hip. 'Tell me, though, why can't she accompany us to Edinburgh, let this farmer fellow propose to her there and we can all pounce upon him at once?'

'For that very reason, my dear,' Isabella said. 'You will have more than enough to cope with in Edinburgh this term as it is.'

'The Council, do you mean?'

'And Charlotte.'

'Ah, yes, and Charlotte,' John James said. 'There's no hope of escape from the responsibilities of fatherhood.'

'None,' Isabella said, slipping from the bed. 'So, may Nicola stay at Craigiehall and wait for her destiny to come to her?'

'Her destiny?' John James said. 'I'm not sure I believe in destiny.'

'You believe in me, do you not?' Isabella asked.

And John James answered, '*Touché.*'

CHAPTER TWENTY-NINE

Riots were common in Glasgow's citadels of culture for the citizens of that town were famed for rough manners as well as critical discernment. It had been some years since violence had broken out on the steps of an Edinburgh theatre, however, for at five shillings for the pit and three shillings for the galleries the coarser elements of society were obliged to find their entertainment elsewhere.

It was not all bows and curtseys in the Theatre Royal, though. Purchase of a ticket did not guarantee a seat and genteel ladies would send their servants to struggle through the crowds to reserve a place for them. Gallants and young gentlemen, advocates and their clerks included, would sometimes split a box or—queues being unknown—attack the doors in the form of a flying wedge and obtain, at no extra cost but curses and an occasional bloody nose, the best seats from which to leer, jeer, and hurl all manner of insults at the stage if the production displeased them which, more often than not, it did.

Maddy was used to hostile receptions;

Londoners were no more refined than their northern cousins and reputation no protection against a faceful of slops. But with an invited audience before her, she was confident that ogling her 'delicate condition', let alone Pearl and Opal's exuberant bubbies, would be enough to defray criticism and get her through the evening unscathed.

At half past three o'clock meat pies were provided in lieu of dinner. By then the commotion outside could be heard on stage. Ben and Charlie raced upstairs, peered from a window and returned with the news that a crowd of several hundred had already assembled in Shakespere Square. In response to this information Sir Archie turned pale. He seated himself on the canvas rock, put his head in his hands and swayed from side to side, moaning quietly. He was well aware that success was as ungovernable as a runaway horse and an official summoning of the town guard would deny him a licence and put paid to his hopes of laying 'Fingal' before the public at large.

Conn and his brandy flask offered comfort and Sir Archie, a true blue trouper, eventually pulled up his stockings, tugged down his waistcoat and took control of himself. He sent the cast off to the dressings rooms and went in search of the manager, Mr Jackson, who, it transpired, had already dispatched a man to the Castle to fetch an armed detail from the 42nd Regiment to restore order and, as it were, put the theatre under military command. Sir Archie wept on Mr Jackson's shoulder, promised undying gratitude and first refusal on any play that he may pen in future, an offer that Mr Jackson accepted without one visible sign of rue.

Major Lomax was just as keen as anyone to view the *fille libre* who had roused old Craigiehall's ardour and, being in possession of a ticket, had cowed the rabble and secured the doors of the Royal before the first carriages arrived around half past five and the great and the good assembled beneath the pillars.

At ten of six, cocky Jack Cattenach, notebook in hand, his current sweetheart, a buxom eighteen-year-old oyster girl, clinging to his arm, marched down the avenue of bayonets and, hailing Lady Valerie Oliphant as if she were a long-lost cousin, followed her party into the theatre, a half hour before the brand-new curtain rose and Sir Archie's play took wing.

*   *   *

Gillon arrived in the Square on foot. The theatre glowed like a great bridal cake, every window lighted. It was a dry night, chilly but windless. He wore his fantail hat and a loose riding frock with broad lapels and deep pockets. When he saw the soldiers guarding the portico he checked for a moment then boldly elbowed through the gawping crowd and presented himself to Sergeant McKellor, to whom he was well known.

'B'God, Lieutenant Peters, is it yersel'?'

'It is, McKellor. Come to see for myself what the fuss is about.'

'No ticket, no admit,' the sergeant said. 'Sorry, but that's the way o' it.'

Gillon produced the card from inside his coat and held it out for the sergeant's inspection.

494

'A reserved box, is it?' the sergeant said. 'Sir, you're very favoured.'

'Friends in high places,' Gillon said

'Make a way, make a way,' the sergeant called out, clearing a path for Gillon with the flat of his sword. 'Enjoy the play, sir.'

'Thank you. I'm sure I will.'

Relieved, Gillon joined the mill-race of lords, ladies and gentlemen that poured through the doors into the vestibule. He was jostled and nudged and even given a tall eye by one or two ladies as he edged across the entrance hall to the staircase that led to the first gallery's semi-circular corridor which, not unexpectedly, was already jammed with a chattering throng. The smell of powder and pomatum, face-paint and perfume was as cloying as candy as he navigated a route though a sea of ruffles, flounces and trains and tried not to meet anyone's eye.

There were several familiar faces in the crowd, not least among them the Admiral who was escorted by three young naval officers armed with cutlasses. Luckily, the Admiral was occupied in admiring the bosom of the Marchioness of Tulibarton's youngest daughter and did not notice Gillon as he slid past. He soon found the curtain at the rear of the reserved box. He opened it cautiously and looked in at the three tiered benches that sloped steeply towards the bow-shaped balcony, below which, almost within touching distance, was the edge of the stage and a row of footlights.

Motionless against the curtain Gillon peered down at the audience moiling in the pit and up at the crowded galleries. He closed the curtain and stepped down, all the way down and, bowing his head as if he were praying, pressed his knees hard against the swell of the balcony and slipped from the belt behind him a flintlock pistol that he placed on the floor at his feet.

Sweating a little, he brought from his side pocket a silly little muff gun, a lady's toy, really, no more than a precaution, but with enough weight in the charge and lead in the ball to take down a man at thirty feet. He put that weapon too on the floor and dug into his pocket for the pouch of black powder and two packets of lead ball, one lot wrapped in paper, the other in cloth. He tucked them against the base of the bench, took off his hat and laid it over the pistols then spread his feet to avoid tramping on the powder. That done, he looked up again to check his position and take his range. He felt as he had felt that night in the barge on the shore of the Acushnet river just before the regiment had attacked the vessels of the privateers in New Plymouth; full of savage excitement and determined to do what had been asked of him, whatever the cost.

Blowing out his breath, he wiped his brow with his handkerchief, rested his elbows on the rim of the balcony, and waited for the play to begin.

*　　*　　*

They came up to the city three days in advance of John James's appearance before the Lords of Council, a week before the opening of the courts. They broke the journey at Salton House where an experienced crew of four diggers had begun work on the western edge of the estate and small

496

clusters of coal bearing rock had already been unearthed. Mr Gall was now convinced that Mrs Ballentine's belief that several untapped seams lay close below the surface was right. Mr Gall, an educated gentleman, supped at Salton that evening and the two men sat up far into the night discussing how the mining might best be funded, while Isabella, who had much to do next day, took herself early to bed.

It was mid-afternoon, cold, dry and windless, when the carriage rolled into Edinburgh and his lordship and his bride-to-be settled into the apartments in Crowell's Close. Nicola, like a maiden in a tower, remained in Ayrshire, but Grant and Charlotte had been invited to supper. Isabella spent some time in the kitchen with the cook while John James, short on sleep, dozed in a chair by the fire in the drawing-room. He was only half awake when Isabella kissed his brow and informed him that she must attend to an urgent piece of business but that she would be back in time to greet their guests.

'Business?' said John James, sitting up. 'What sort of business?'

'It is best if you do not enquire.' Isabella put a finger to his lips. 'There are certain matters that a bride does not wish to discuss with her husband, and first fittings are one of them.'

'First fittings? Ah, I see. Can't the dressmaker come here?'

'And spoil the surprise?' Isabella said. 'I will be, at most, an hour or two.'

'An hour or two,' John James said. 'What time is it now?'

'Just after six,' said Isabella.

'You're not going to drop in on that blessed play, by any chance?'

'I do not have an invitation,' Isabella said.

'That's not an answer.'

'No, dearest,' the woman said. 'I am not going to drop in on that blessed play,' then, before he could quiz her further, left him in his armchair by the fire and, minutes later, set out in a chaise for the New Town.

*   *   *

Conn Cavendish was first on stage. His appearance was announced by a volley of chords from Fleur's piano and an urgent thumping of the drum by Benjamin who, in a hair vest, broad belt and knee-length undershirt, followed the chieftan into view. The audience settled into an expectant hush broken only by the clatter of late-comers crowding the rail at the rear of the pit.

Straining every vocal sinew, Conn embarked on the interminable introduction with which Archie had burdened the tragic tale of Fingal, Nu-ala and the treacherous Hidallan. At first the audience appeared to be entranced by the quality of the verse and weight of narrative but Maddy, watching from the wings, soon realised that Conn's quasi-Irish sing-song was carrying no further than the fourth row and that the play-goers were more mystified than engrossed. She felt her stomach churn and a rush of bile fill her throat. Clutching Opal for support, she turned her head and was violently sick, splashing liquid across the boards and on to Charlie-Hidallan's leggings.

Charlie uttered a muffled oath and jumped back

498

then, with just enough presence of mind to pick up his prompt, leapt on to the stage, yelling, 'Fain, but it is true, my lord. Only in weltering blood does the warrior find repose. Wherein the freedom that we gain is circumscribed by pain as in a keep whose doors and windows are all barr'd and freedom lock'd away like the charred secrets of the heart.' He shook his left leg and then his right to be rid of the remains of Madelaine's dinner and, slapping Conn on the shoulder hard enough to make the old chap stagger, bade Fingal continue 'demarking out his battle plans and all the ruses required to bring down that ruffian Roman, Caracalla, who seeks to bestride the world.'

'*Roman?*' some pedant called from the gallery. '*What's all this about Romans?*' and was instantly punched on the ear and advised to hold his tongue.

Pearl brought water and Opal tore a strip of cloth from her skirt. Sir Archie, red as a rowan berry, clenched his fists and cursed the carping swine who had challenged his research, while the handmaidens mopped Maddy's mouth and gently bathed her brow.

'Are you well enough to go on?' Opal hissed.

'Yes,' Madelaine murmured, shakily. 'Yes, I'll— I'll manage somehow.'

They huddled together, Nu-ala and her plump attendants, and picked up the thread of Fingal's speech and Hidallan's responses and awaited the cue which, when it came, took them by surprise, as it always did.

Fleur covered the hesitation with four doleful chords and Charlie, on stage, loudly repeated his line as if it had been deliberately inserted to heighten tension. 'See, my good lord, here cometh your fiancée, Nu-ala, and her loyal train, battling to greet you through the wind and rain.'

Grey-green scarves billowing, Maddy strode out into the vast, confusing space. From the corner of her eye she glimpsed the sea of faces in the pit and, like a monstrous frozen wave, the faces in the galleries. Gasps and mutterings were punctuated by sporadic cheering, as if she had already won the beast's approval by merely showing up.

She fixed her gaze on Conn and, with Pearl and Opal trotting to keep up, sped across the boards and, demonstrating horror, flung up her hands and cried out, 'How, sir, is this I find you, strapped in leather and gleaming bronze, emblazoned with longing to wage war? Is war to be our love-song's lasting note, wrote bloody on your targe?'

Pearl and Opal moaned in fractured Gaelic and Madelaine, with a wonderful sweep of her tormented togs, swung round to explain Nu-ala's distress to the audience and, at the same time, give the gawping horde a good long look at her belly which, to everyone's disappointment, was as flat as an unleavened loaf.

'*Shame!*' came a piercing cry from the pit. '*Shame on you, you charlatan! Fifteen guineas for this mockery! Where's the daddy? Show us the daddy?*'

The scuffle was far enough to the rear not to break Madelaine's concentration. She raised her voice, closed her eyes and imagined that she was alone on a bleak rock in Perthshire, howling out her lines to sheep and shepherds, and her pleas to Fingal not to abandon her were sufficiently heart-rending to tweak the audience's attention for a little while.

When she or, rather, Nu-ala invoked the gods to soften Fingal's hard warrior heart, Maddy opened her eyes and looked up, first left, then right, as if unsure in which corner of the heavens the gods might be hiding.

She spotted Valerie and the Admiral in a box with three young men in braided uniforms and three young women—Valerie's married daughters—and Bradley, Bradley craning forward with a ghastly leer on his haughty features. She swivelled once more and in the box just above her head caught sight of Gillon, alone and hatless, Gillon, her brave soldier, who, if everything went badly wrong, would surely rescue her.

*   *   *

He had owned the old flintlock with the heart-shaped butt for half a lifetime. He could prime and load it, in the dark if necessary, in twenty seconds. The little weapon, which had cost him eight pounds, took more time for he wasn't used to its size and, being nervous, spilled powder from the priming pan on his first try. He kept his head up and worked with the guns on his lap, close against the swell of the balcony. He knew that he was being observed now, not only by curious folk in the gallery but by Valerie and her party, too.

The fact that he was alone in the box, like some great dignitary, had attracted attention and when the action on stage flagged—Fingal's interminable farewell—rather too many heads were cocked in his direction and rather too much whispering went on, for the *cognoscenti* had already decided that he was occupying the very box that should, or might,

501

have contained Lord Craigiehall if wishful thinking had had its way. Besides, Mrs Madelaine Young, in spite of her professionalism, had gravitated from the centre of the stage and, dragging the cast with her, seemed to be performing for the sole benefit of the handsome, unsmiling stranger.

Sir Archie, peeking from the wings, was livid, of course. At the fall of the curtain at the end of the second act—only the second act, my God!—he grabbed Maddy by the shoulder and would have shaken her like a child if Conn and Tom had not intervened.

'What is that madman doing here?' Sir Archie raged. 'He wasn't invited.'

'He is here to protect me,' Maddy said, very calmly.

'Protect you from what?' said Archie.

'You and your execrable verse for one thing,' Maddy said.

'Who is it?' Fleur piped up. 'Is it Gillon?'

'Yes, my dear, it's Gillon,' Maddy told her.

Fleur clapped her hands and laughed. 'He came. He came. I knew he would not let us down.'

'What are you talking about, Madelaine?' Sir Archie said, then plunged to one side as the curtain cranked upward and almost knocked him flying.

The female choristers trooped out to set the scene for the battle to come, while Nu-ala and Hidallan who, for reasons unexplained, seemed to have missed the boat, prepared for the wooing scene in which Hidallan's dastardly betrayal of his lord, Fingal, would be revealed.

The angel voices from the Choral Union did not fare well with an audience that already felt cheated. Sir Archie's choral set piece was all but lost in a general twittering and an unseemly chanting of cat-calls and coarse comments that raised laughter in the galleries.

'Who are they? Who are these philistines? What is happening to my play?' Sir Archie wailed.

The choristers, several in tears, scampered for the safety of the wings, and Charlie dragged Maddy—Fleur clinging to her skirts—on to the stage just as the first handful of copper coins rained down from the gallery.

Gillon gripped the flintlock tightly, the heart-shaped butt snug in his palm. He pocketed the pouch, the ball-packets and the pretty little muff gun, and eased himself forward until his chest rested on the balcony rail. He felt very calm, even faintly amused, as four or five fans went spinning up from the pit and split the silk screen that backed the footlights. There was a hiss, a frizzle, a flash of flame, and even a moment of panic before the flame vanished in a curl of blue smoke and Hidallan and Nu-ala, coughing, played tug-of-war with little Fleur.

In the box across the breadth of the theatre the Admiral's equerries drew their swords, some skittish young female in the box above Gillon's screamed and half the invited audience of well-bred ladies and gentlemen scrambled for the doors while the other half, less genteel, hurled fans, pennies, cushions, orange peel and apple cores in the direction of the stage.

Gillon climbed on to the rail of the balcony that fronted the box. He held the pistol like a duellist, cocked and angled, then, taking aim at the fringe of the curtain that hung above the proscenium,

503

pulled the trigger.

There was a flash and a short, sharp, snapping sound.

He saw the curtain pock and shiver and, with the pistol raked, jumped down from the box to the stage. He landed awkwardly and buckled on one knee.

People were running in all directions. There were shrieks and shouts and an overall noise like that of a ship breaking up on rocks as benches were uprooted and overturned. Major Lomax was bawling at the pitch of his voice and the Admiral, with Valerie, her daughters and Bradley behind him, was clambering up the tiers to reach the exit. Mr Jackson, stage left, pleaded with Sir Archie to crank down the curtain which, it seemed, had received a mortal wound and remained stuck at half mast.

Maddy offered her hand and hoisted Gillon to his feet.

'Well, Mrs Young,' he said. 'What's it to be?'

'Do you have my money?'

'That I do,' said Gillon.

'Then let's be off,' Maddy said.

'And quick about it, too,' said Fleur and, hand in hand with her auntie, ran like the wind for the prop room and the little door that led out to the street.

*   *   *

Isabella Ballentine held open the door of one of the two conveyances that waited by the gates of St Ninian's burial ground. It was less quiet in the back street than usual for play-goers had spewed

504

out of the theatre without warning, well in advance of curtain time, and there were few carriages in the Square and even fewer servants to tell their masters what to do.

'Here,' she said. 'In here. There are cloaks and blankets to keep you warm and my man, Dougie, has not forgotten how to drive a fresh pair. He will take you to Leith by the coach road and there, on the morning tide, you will board a boat for Hull, and then . . .' She looked at Gillon. 'I take it you have arranged everything as I asked you to do?'

'Yes,' Gillon said. 'Holland, I think, until the hue and cry dies down.'

'Did you shoot someone?' Isabella said.

'No.'

'Then there will be no hue and cry to speak of.'

'My money?' said Maddy.

'Gillon has the banker's drafts,' said Isabella. 'You may present them at the Scotch bank in Amsterdam or, if you choose, in London. They will, I assure you, be honoured without question.'

'Is there money enough for the journey?' Maddy said.

'Gillon has more than enough hard cash for that,' said Isabella. 'Now, please, climb up before we are seen.'

Fleur scrambled up into the chaise and Maddy followed her. She turned, though, before Gillon could join her and said, 'How can I thank you, Mrs Ballentine? I do not know why you did this for me.'

'Not for you, my dear,' Isabella informed her. 'For myself. I prefer you to be as far away from Edinburgh, from Scotland and from my cousin Johnny, as possible. In a word, I want rid of you.'

Maddy laughed. 'Never to be seen again?'

505

'Precisely.'

'Well,' Maddy said, 'I just hope that the old fellow brings you happiness.'

'He would not dare do otherwise,' Gillon said and, when a gaggle of titled ruffians rounded the corner from the Square, kissed Isabella on the cheek, hopped up into the chaise and closed the door.

As Dougie whipped the horses and brought the vehicle clattering round, Gillon leaned from the window and called out, 'Tell Charlotte . . .' but Isabella had already gone.

*　　　*　　　*

'Ah, there you are, dearest,' John James said. 'Did the fitting go well?'

'Very well, thank you,' Isabella said. 'I was only choosing cloth tonight.'

'And what cloth,' said Charlotte, 'did you choose?'

'Now that,' said Isabella, 'would be telling.'

'Surely you can tell me,' Charlotte said. 'Can I not be trusted?'

'Of course you can, my dear,' Grant said and taking his father-in-law by the arm led him away from the fireplace into a corner of the drawing-room to let the ladies trade their silly secrets without being overheard.

'Well?' said Charlotte, all agog.

'Satin,' Isabella whispered.

'White satin?' Charlotte said.

'White and silver as befits my age,' said Isabella then, rather shakily, went in search of brandy to soothe her shattered nerves.

CHAPTER THIRTY

The news that Nicola received from Edinburgh was by no means stale. Frequent letters from Charlotte added background to the colourful articles that Mr Jack Cattenach churned out for the *Courant* in the wake of the great theatrical debacle. 'Cyclops' even had the audacity to present a review of the portion of 'Fingal's Return' that had preceded the attempted assassination of the playwright, Sir Archibald Oliphant, who, Jack reported, had left Edinburgh for his country seat on the morning after the performance and had announced, through his wife, that he intended to pass the winter in Italy examining the life of Lorenzo de' Medici as a source for a future verse drama.

The shot fired in the Theatre Royal had, it seemed, missed the *Courant's* correspondent by the breadth of a hair, though the same claim was made by half the folk present that night. There was considerable disagreement as to whether the person who had discharged the pistol had intended to harm Sir Archibald or had simply been carried away by the play's reception.

The person had soon been identified as a former Lieutenant in the Highland Regiment and a brother of Advocate Grant Peters, who had entered the theatre by invitation not subterfuge. Hints of an abduction at pistol point were swiftly squashed by members of 'Fingal's' cast, prior to departure on the London coach. They were adamant that Madelaine Young and her niece,

Fleur Cadell, had left the theatre willingly, though where the trio had gone was not known to anyone.

Never one to miss an opportunity to milk the public's fascination with the high and mighty, Mr Cattenach did his best to turn a mystery into a conspiracy by linking Craigiehall, the Oliphants and Madelaine Young to Lieutenant Gillon Peters, though the crucial role of Isabella Ballentine in this medley of events eluded him. The plot, as it were, thickened when, less than a week later, a short announcement was put out by the Lord President of the College of Justice that John James Templeton of Craigiehall had requested that he be permitted to retire from the bench before the start of the winter sessions in order to pursue the interests of his estates, a request that the Senators of the College had, with regret, elected to honour.

'The fool,' Charlotte wrote, 'has thrown up thirteen hundred pounds a year to satisfy a whim. Aunt Ballentine is behind it, I'll wager. Papa would not have surrendered his robes for any reason that I or you might have presented to him. What has become of the man? What *will* become of him? Isabella says he is happy as a schoolboy and was wise to take the leap before it was forced upon him. I cannot for the life of me understand how Papa can be undermined in the Parliament House by pipsqueaks like Lord Buller who, so Grant informs me, will soon propose his son-in-law to fill the vacancy left by Papa's shoes. Where, too, is Gillon? Why have we not heard from Gillon?'

Nicola had no answer to give and no particular opinion. She wrote a short reply to each of Charlotte's rants for she was not uninterested in the outcome of her father's decision to retire from the law, though she was not entirely surprised by it. Impulsiveness, like a Christmas rose, had bloomed late in her father's life but his erratic behaviour in recent months explained the streak of wilfulness that ran in Charlotte and her and, in some small measure, excused it. Blood, as Gillon might have put it, will out.

In those short grey days, while autumn drained quietly into winter, she pored over the news-sheets and journals that Charlotte sent, and read and reread all Charlotte's letters. She did not dwell on Gillon, though, or on Grant or much on Papa. As if she had slipped back into an age of witchcraft and might draw him to Craigiehall by mental magnetism, her thoughts were concentrated on Roderick Peters, on willing him to come to her.

'Grant is very busy with his briefs,' Charlotte wrote. 'Grant fears that his practice of law will suffer because of Papa's retirement. Mr Mackenzie assures him that this will not be the case. Papa tells me he will not relinquish his town house yet, for the lease has some years to run. We do not have rooms enough here to accommodate a nurserymaid. I know it's in Grant's mind to take on Crowell's Close, although he is well aware that I would prefer the New Town. I will not, as Papa suggests, take myself to Craigiehall when the courts are not in session, although Grant is eager to learn more about how our estate is managed and how coal is taken from the ground. I have told him, in no uncertain terms, that I will not have our children reared as rustics, which did not benefit us, as I am sure you'll agree. I am well, though large, and Isabella fusses over me as much as Molly will allow.'

Nicola seldom left the vicinity of the house. She talked with Mr Littlejohn about sales of stock and the quality of winter feed on the tenant farms and, taking a leaf from Margo Peters' book, made poor travellers welcome at the kitchen door where, ignoring Mrs McGrouther's tart complaints, she saw them fed and gave them a shilling or two from the domestic purse.

One morning in mid-November she accompanied Hugh Littlejohn to inspect the progress of the work in de Morville's field but even as she conversed with Mr Gibson and peeped down the long low sloping incline to the mouth of the new shaft, she was anxious to be back at the house in case Roderick came striding down the drive from the road end and she was not there to greet him.

'Papa,' Charlotte wrote, 'has taken a boat to Fife Shire to view a novel contraption that is said to shovel coal by a steam-driven engine. To my dismay, Grant has left his petitions in Mr Somerville's hands and has gone with Papa to see this wondrous device for himself. They will be back on Friday if the weather is clement. Isabella is busy with wedding arrangements. It will be a modest ceremony, although Papa wishes it otherwise. It will take place in the New Chapel of St Giles at an early hour of the morning in the first week of December, a Thursday, before Papa and she return to Craigiehall for good. Isabella has indicated that she hopes you will agree to be her bridesmaid and will write to you in this regard very shortly. Mr Mackenzie and Dr Gaythorn will participate as witnesses. Grant will be groomsman. Does it not seem odd that a son-in-law can serve as a groomsman to his wife's father? But there is little of convention about any of this affair and I am at a loss to understand it.'

One day succeeded another. The weather remained calm and cold. Nicola ate breakfast alone, dined early, did not take tea, and supped in the empty dining-room with all the candles lighted and an extra place set just in case Roderick came late, and hungry. She went to bed in the room she had once shared with Charlotte and lay awake beneath the covers, staring into the darkness, trying to hold fast to her conviction that she would not lie alone much longer, that, surely, her will and Roderick's love for her would bring him to her and, now that there were no secrets between them, those sweet summer promises would soon be fulfilled

'Lo and behold!' Charlotte wrote. 'It appears that Gillon is in Amsterdam. He has the woman, Young, with him and the girl child too. The climate and language do not suit them in Holland and they will seek passage to London before long. They have received the sums Isabella promised and suffer no hardship. This astonishing news came to our ears by way of Roderick Peters who received a letter from Gillon and, knowing our concern, took it upon himself to travel to Edinburgh to impart the information to Grant. I am at more of a loss than ever to fathom why Gillon has not written to me. By all appearances he is caught in the actress's web, as Papa was. Now she has a fortune attached to her name I am sure she will wish to be rid of Gillon as soon as she is able to shake him off. What he will do then, I do not dare to imagine. I do hope that he will not take up arms again and be

511

lost to us in a foreign war.'

Nicola's first impulse was to have a bag packed and a carriage summoned and to set out for Edinburgh at once.

Charlotte's letter had been on the road for two days, however, and Roderick would surely have left Graddan's Court by now. Besides, she had steeled herself to make him come to her and it would be foolish to give in to whim. How typical of Charlotte not to impart more information about Roderick but to go on at length about Gillon.

There was, Nicola supposed, an element of romance in what Gillon had done and how he had captured the English actress but she did not envy them their adventures. She longed for engagement of a different sort, not a harum-scarum existence knocking from pillar to post but a settled life with deep roots and quiet satisfying passions in which dry weather and a safe harvest meant more than the foibles of fashion or the opinion of one's peers.

It was mid-afternoon, around half past three o'clock, but dusk was already thick in the air and the candles would soon be lit. She had just taken her papers, pens and inkwell into the drawing-room to write to Charlotte when Hugh Littlejohn appeared at the window.

Puzzled, she looked up at the overseer who rapped upon the glass, beckoned and then, grinning broadly, stepped to one side.

Nicola moved to the window and looked out across the lawns to the drive and the gates, vague in the fading light. It was all so still, so calm, without a breath of wind to stir the leaves that littered the verges or clung to the boughs of the oaks. For a moment she could not believe her eyes

512

for what she saw was exactly what she had imagined; Roderick, with a knapsack slung across his shoulder and his hat tipped back, Roderick striding down the drive towards the house. She lifted a hand and rubbed the glass as if to erase the image and restore reality then, with a little whoop, rushed out of the drawing-room into the hall and threw open the front door.

They met and kissed outdoors, kissed in the hall and again in the drawing-room. Nicola did not care who saw her, how the servants might tattle and Mrs McGrouther growl her disapproval. She was free of Craigiehall at last, free of constraints and pretences. Soon she would be released into a different sort of world, no longer a chattel, a commodity to be bargained for. She would be free to live a life of her choosing with the man who had chosen her.

How prim it seemed, how scrupulous, to sit with him in the drawing-room drinking tea when every word, every gesture was laden with intimacy. She floated in a little bubble of desire, half afraid of her own intemperate longings. She had no fear of Roderick or of what he would do to her. She trusted him as she had trusted no other man. In a month, or less, Roderick and she would be married, not here in Craigiehall but in the church on the hill that overlooked the fertile plain of Stirling and the little piece of land that would become the corner for her romance, her adventure.

If Papa thought her wilful and Charlotte thought her mad what did it matter? Not one jot. And yet there was within her a strange trace of loyalty, not to her father or to Craigiehall but to her own brief history and the histories that had gone before, a debt to the ambitious rogues who had preceded her and who, quite soon, she would leave behind for Grant and Charlotte and their children to puzzle over and excuse.

At length, Roderick put down his teacup and, rising, cleared his throat and said, 'Nicola, now that you know there's no impediment . . .'

She rose too and, going to him, put a finger to his lips.

'No,' she said. 'No, dearest, not here.'

'Where then?' he said.

'Will you indulge me? Will you do as I ask?'

He laughed and shook his head. 'The oak?' he said. 'The famous Templeton oak tree? Do you expect me to follow in Grant's footsteps?'

'I most certainly do not.' Nicola took him by the arm and led him into the hall. 'I do not wish to be chivvied into accepting a proposal delivered at top speed in dead of night. If you love me then you will do it gracefully.'

'According to tradition?'

'Exactly,' Nicola said.

'Allowing you every opportunity to change your mind?' Roderick said.

'Every possible opportunity.'

'Then, dark or not, we must go to the oak at once,' Roderick said, 'for I have waited too long as it is.'

Nicola summoned a footman to fetch a lantern and a shawl then, hand in hand with Roderick, she steered him through the litter of dead wet leaves to the huge tree beneath which three generations of Templetons had forged their pledges. She placed the lantern on the grass among the weeds and acorns and resting her shoulders against the gnarled old trunk, watched Roderick toss aside his hat and kneel at her feet.

'Miss Templeton,' he said, 'Nicola, will you consent to be my wife?'

'I have no dowry and few prospects, sir,' she said.

'Damn it, woman, will you marry me?'

And Nicola, very soberly, answered, 'Yes.'

CHIVERS
LARGE
PRINT
-direct-

If you have enjoyed this Large Print book and would like to build up your own collection of Large Print books, please contact

Chivers Large Print Direct

Chivers Large Print Direct offers you a full service:

• Prompt mail order service

• Easy-to-read type

• The very best authors

• Special low prices

For further details either call
Customer Services on (01225) 336552
or write to us at Chivers Large Print Direct,
FREEPOST, Bath BA1 3ZZ

Telephone Orders:
FREEPHONE 08081 72 74 75

Boys Don't Cry

OPEN UNIVERSITY PRESS
Gender and Education Series

Editors

ROSEMARY DEEM
*Lecturer in the School of Education at the
Open University*

GABY WEINER
*Course Manager in the School of Education at the
Open University*

The series provides compact and clear accounts of relevant research and practice in the field of gender and education. It is aimed at trainee and practising teachers, and parents and others with an educational interest in ending gender inequality. All age-ranges will be included, and there will be an emphasis on ethnicity as well as gender. Series authors are all established educational practitioners or researchers.

TITLES IN THE SERIES

Co-education Reconsidered
Rosemary Deem (ed.)

Just a Bunch of Girls
Gaby Weiner (ed.)

Untying the Apron Strings
Naima Browne and Pauline France (eds.)

Women and Training
Ann Wickham

Boys Don't Cry
Sue Askew and Carol Ross

Boys Don't Cry

BOYS AND SEXISM IN EDUCATION

Sue Askew and Carol Ross

Open University Press
Milton Keynes · Philadelphia

Open University Press
Open University Educational Enterprises Limited
12 Cofferidge Close
Stony Stratford
Milton Keynes MK11 1BY, England

and

242 Cherry Street
Philadelphia, PA 19106, USA

First Published 1988

British Library Cataloguing in Publication Data

Askew, Sue
  Boys don't cry : sexism in boys education. — (Gender and education).
  1. Sex discrimination in education —
  Great Britain   2. Sexism — Great Britain
  I. Title   II. Ross, Carol   III. Series
  370.19'345   LC212.83.G7

  ISBN 0-335-10296-4

Library of Congress Cataloging in Publication Data

Askew, Sue
  Boys don't cry: sexism in boys education
  Bibliography : p.
  Includes index
  1. Sex discrimination in education
  Great Britain   2. Sexism — Great Britain
I. Ross, Carol   II. Title
Library of Congress card number 87-30158

ISBN 0-335-10296-4

Typeset by Burns & Smith, Derby
Printed in Great Britain by J.W. Arrowsmith Ltd., Bristol

Contents

Series Editor's Introduction

Over the past ten years, there has been a variety of publications on issues of gender and education, whether concerned with equal opportunities, anti-sexism, 'girl-friendly' or feminist approaches. In the main these have been publications, some in this series, which have sought to explain, challenge and/or change the position of girls and women in the education system, by deliberately focusing on female educational experiences, as teachers or pupils.

Concern for the needs of boys has been less of an issue because, it is argued, boys appear to receive more attention in 'mainstream' education, though it is also recognised that if the position of girls and women is to improve in education and in society, that of boys and men will have to change too.

This book, the fifth in the *Gender and Education* series, seeks to correct this omission by focusing specifically on boys, but does so from an anti-sexist perspective. It considers how masculinity is constructed in society and reinforced in schools, structurally and in everyday interaction. It refers to the schooling experiences of boys, whether taught in mixed or single-sex schools, and what impact they have on their teachers, particularly if they are women.

And finally, *Boys Don't Cry* provides a whole range of strategies and ideas which have been tried out and tested in schools by the authors in their development of an anti-sexist approach to the schooling of boys. Written in an accessible and lively style, this book will be of interest not only to teachers and researchers working with boys or concerned with reducing sex inequalities in education, but to parents and to the boys themselves.

Gaby Weiner

Introduction

Over the last five years we have been concerned with anti-sexism and education, particularly in relation to boys. For the first two of these years we worked at a secondary boys' school in East London, developing, monitoring and teaching a new anti-sexist course to all first- and second-year boys. Subsequently, we supported anti-sexist initiatives in the Inner London Education Authority (ILEA) boys' schools (including offering support to women teachers) and were involved in developing and making materials for anti-sexist curricular work with boys, working with boys-only groups in mixed schools, as well as in boys' schools. During this time we have visited schools (observing and participating in classrooms, attending meetings of Equal Opportunity Working Parties and Women's Groups, talking to teachers and running workshops); organised and led courses and workshops for teachers throughout ILEA; been invited to organise discussion on anti-sexist work with boys at Equal Opportunity conferences both within and outside ILEA; and discussed this work with teachers and parents throughout Britain.

We have worked in approximately thirty boys' schools and twenty mixed schools in all parts of London. Some of these schools were multi-cultural and multi-racial, some were predominantly white; some were in economically deprived areas and some in 'well-off' areas; some were Church schools. We have also worked in a range of primary schools throughout London. The issues we write about have emerged from these experiences.

This book is primarily about sexism in boys' schools. However, in writing about sexism in boys' schools we explore many issues which apply to all schools, including primary and further education establishments. We look at some of the ways in which boys are socialised; boys' behaviour at school both in the classroom and playground; and the effects of boys' behaviour both on each other and on other people. We explore the school structure as a social institution: the values and attitudes inherent in the organisation and structure of boys' schools; the social divisions built into the system; its underlying definitions of 'masculinity' in relation to 'femininity'. We look at the experiences of women teachers in relation to both the boys they teach and the institutions within which they work. We explore the implications of doing anti-sexist work with boys and with school staff, and look at some concrete strategies for both.

While we have not talked explicitly about gay boys and how they fare in school, we do look in detail at the construction of different masculinities and implicit in this are issues concerning notions of male sexuality. Our work also has implications for issues of heterosexism and is an expression of the homophobia inherent in 'norms' of maleness.

We feel that because of the range of social issues touched on in the book, it will be of interest not only to students and teachers in all phases of education, but also to parents and anyone working with boys, for example, in youth clubs and social work. Furthermore, the socialisation, behaviour and education of boys have implications for girls, and so the book has relevance for people concerned with the education of girls. We believe that sexism in schools is a microcosm of sexism in society. But we feel that sexism in boys' schools is particularly overt. Because it is a more polarised situation it can be easier to recognise how boys' schools operate as sexist institutions. We feel, therefore, that an understanding of sexism in boys' schools can illuminate how it is built into all schools.

We wanted to write this book because we think we have found some gaps in the literature of sexism and education. For example, not very much has been written about women teachers, beyond looking at their position in the school hierarchy; boys have been mainly written about only in so far as their behaviour affects girls. Their behaviour has not been sufficiently looked at in the context of why it occurs and how it is reinforced and perpetuated by the school system itself. We also felt that there has been a lot of interesting research relating to sexism in education which we wanted to draw together in the light of our experience in boys' schools.

Our initial involvement with anti-sexist work with boys did not come from any special commitment to working with boys only. On the contrary, as feminist teachers, we were more concerned with anti-sexist work with girls. However because of our particular employment circumstances we found ourselves working in a boys' school. This put us in a unique position over the last five years which has allowed us to explore the sorts of issue we raise in this book. As a result of this work, we have attempted to confront and examine why many of the approaches we took did not work as well as we had hoped. We were forced to consider a variety of issues surrounding what happens in the classroom. We realised that there were many layers and levels. Each time we identified a particular factor we became aware of other underlying features: dynamics within the classroom; relationships between the pupils; relationships between pupils and teachers; the school structure beyond the classroom; issues of racism and classism.

It may seem a contradiction to talk about addressing sexism in boys' schools. However, boyhood is the induction period into manhood . Boys themselves are victims of their socialisation and experience difficulties from the pressures they are put under to prove their masculinity and hide their vulnerability. As adult men it is true in one sense to say that they are still victims of their socialisation, but they are also perpetuators of sexism, and in a position of power (in a class-related way) over women.

It is not our intention in this book to identify boys as 'the problem': rather our aim is to locate boys' behaviour within the context of the social structure. We feel strongly that unless the social structure itself changes the power relationships between people in terms of race, class and gender will not change. Rehana Minhas (1986) writes:

> If racism and sexism are defined in terms of a problem of individual attitudes and personal prejudices — often unintentional — then we cannot begin to deal effectively with the

varying manifestations of these inequalities. Attitudes and ideas, moreover, do not exist in a vacuum but are rooted in the economic/political/legal and social system.

We believe that anti-sexist work with girls is very important, for example, changes in the organisation and content of certain subjects to allow girls to succeed in male-dominated areas of the curriculum, such as maths and science. It is also important to examine the things that may be negatively affecting girls' education, such as the amount and kind of teacher attention they get in mixed classrooms. But we also feel that the position of girls will not really change fundamentally until the underlying nature of the school as an institution changes.

However, the curriculum is the level which is most accessible for teachers to change. Within the curriculum there are different approaches to equal opportunity work. One is at an explicit level which involves teaching children to be aware of and to negotiate sexism (for example, assertiveness training and self-defence for girls). At an implicit level we can work towards reorganising the way a given school subject itself is constructed as a body of knowledge, the language of the subject, the content and the teaching methodology. The limitation of explicit anti-sexist work is that it puts the onus for changing sexism on the pupils themselves — when actually they are not in a position of power to change the system. The explicit approach may be useful at a personal, individual level, but it is not going to change the ways sexism is structured in an institution. It can affect self-image and confidence, and this may mean that when pupils are adults they will want to fight to change the social system in which they live.

The aims of explicit anti-sexist work with boys and with girls are very different; for example, boys learning to be more co-operative and take on more caring roles; girls being encouraged to enter 'male'-dominated subjects and to be more assertive in their social interaction. However, anti-sexist aims relating to the reorganisation of subject areas apply equally to both girls and boys. This work involves making structural changes to the curriculum which would redress the balance of control by the dominant social group within subject disciplines. Baran (1986) describes the way we have to rethink the science curriculum at the more 'implicit' level:

Encouraging girls to pursue an interest and/or career in Science and Technology cannot be done by a few cosmetic and structural alterations ... It is very important to: challenge stereotypes; develop new images; demonstrate the relationship between interesting career prospects and the need for qualifications; consider the need for girl-only groups or introduce an element of compulsion at the option stage. However, these measures alone will make little impact, particularly in relationship to the majority of working class girls, unless we are prepared to re-think what Science education is, what it is for, and how we are going to teach it.

These are some of the issues we explore in the book. We write this book in the spirit of a 'discussion document' — these are our thoughts arising from our experiences of anti-sexist work with boys. We hope the reader will find it thought-provoking and a useful basis for taking these ideas further.

CHAPTER 1

The Construction of Masculinity

During the last two years we have talked to hundreds of teachers from over one hundred primary, secondary and special schools in one Local Education Authority. All of these teachers contacted us, or attended courses, because they are concerned about the 'problems' associated with boys[1] (Chapter 2 of this book describes these 'problems' in more detail). Such problems include domination in the mixed classroom by boys and boys' use of space, for example in the playground. These descriptions point to the need for girls' education to be reassessed with considerable urgency and many teachers want to work with boys as a way of trying to minimise the 'problems' and because they see much of boys' behaviour as having a detrimental effect on the boys' learning and on the boys themselves. They also see it as a direct outcome of inequalities in school and in wider society.

Talking about boys' behaviour can itself lead to reinforcing gender stereotypes: the number of boys who are a 'problem' might be fairly small in any one class. Not all boys are aggressive, demanding and disruptive. Those that are may be so for a variety of reasons. They may be reacting against inappropriate work; may need extra help in terms of developing particular skills, or may be reacting against a whole number of things in and outside the educational system itself. What is important is that, for whatever reason, it is boys rather than girls who are reacting in ways perceived to be a problem and receiving an unfair share of teacher attention, albeit some of it very negative.

1

A gender focus may help to explain some surprising and worrying facts. For example, the Fish Report (1985) on special needs showed that of all pupils in schools for emotionally disturbed behaviour 86.6 per cent are boys; boys have more problems learning to read.[2] In the old days of the 11 plus it was established that boys did worse than girls and so the pass mark for boys was lower than for girls. There is evidence to suggest that the grading of primary pupils in at least one Education Authority discriminates against girls in the same way (Toynbee 1985). Boys have been shown in recent research (Mahoney 1985) to make life exceedingly irksome, if not unpleasant, for girls. It is not uncommon to hear the comment: 'Boys mature later than girls'. Indeed, we remember thinking as adolescents in co-ed schools that the boys were childish and beneath our notice. But all this is 'common-sense' understanding. It is unproblematic for some people. Our contention is that it *is* problematic and that the way in which masculinity is constructed in our society might provide clarification on it. Our 'common-sense' understandings and the significance we give to particular things themselves arise out of a particular political and social situation. We may not realise the theoretical significance or importance of what has happened to us.

What are the stereotypes of boys/men?

This chapter focuses on how boys learn to be male. How do boys get a sense of themselves as male from which their masculinity is constructed? Boys learn the kind of behaviour by which they can express their masculinity. It seems likely that many different factors contribute to this sense of 'maleness', but here we discuss those aspects which seem to have direct implications for learning and behaviour at school.

There is a *dominant* view of men with which we are bombarded through the press and other media. This view of men represents them as being tough, strong, aggressive, independent, brave, sexually active, rational, intelligent, and so on. The corresponding view of women is that they are vulnerable, weak, non-aggressive, kind, caring, passive, frightened, stupid, dependent and immature.[3] It is interesting that the descriptive words used for women are also those which are used for children.

Lloyd (1985) points out that this also creates a conflict for young men between being young, with all that implies, and being men, with all that implies. The contradiction, he suggests, is both confusing and complicated because all young men are affected by this dominant view of masculinity though mediated by their race and class position. While these stereotypes are obviously damaging and prevent young men from developing their full potential, they are also internalising extremely negative images of girls and women.

Trefor Lloyd writes that upper-middle-class men are expected to be aloof, to rule and to be separate from 'the others'. They are sent to boarding school at an early age, intimidated by older boys, and then offered the opportunity to do the same. It is also interesting to consider how they see women in the cut-off male world of the boarding school and to speculate on the fact that warmth, caring and empathy for others is severely curtailed by this practice of sending very young children away from their parents (see 'Private schools confront boys' hidden emotions', *Times Educational Supplement*, 18 April 1986). Lloyd argues that middle-class men are expected to be good with their brains, to be self-reliant, made to compete, told it is better to think than to do. Working-class images of masculinity, argues Lloyd, are perhaps most pervasive. They are seen as rough, tough, loud, beer-swilling, good at fighting, and more able to 'do' than to think. The idea that black and/or working-class men are more 'macho' and sexist than white middle-class men is another stereotype.

Value ascribed to stereotypical traits

Stereotypical traits are value-laden. Those which are assigned to the men who have power in our society are generally those which are seen as being desirable. A large sample of Americans was asked in the 1970s to list the characteristics, attributes and types of behaviour in which they thought men and women differed. Both men and women expressed a preference for the behaviour they had designated male. For example, traits described as follows were seen as *both* masculine and as desirable: very aggressive, very independent, not at all emotional, almost always hiding emotions, very objective, not at all easily influenced, very dominant, liking maths and science very much, very active, very competitive, very logical, never crying, very ambitious, talking freely with other men about sex, thinking men are always superior to women, and very active. Traits opposed to these were all seen as feminine and less desirable. Out of the forty-one traits that the sample was asked to list, only twelve were seen as feminine *and* desirable. These were: doesn't use harsh language, very talkative, very tactful, very gentle, very aware of feelings of others, very neat in habits, very strong need for security, enjoys art and literature, and easily expresses tender feelings. While indicating that men and women *are* seen differently this study showed that masculine behaviour is *valued* more highly. The qualities ascribed to middle-class masculine behaviour are also those which are implicitly valued in Western society and in its major institutions. Schools are centrally places of 'reason', 'objectivity', 'competitiveness' and 'logic'. Boys and girls are expected to aspire to these ends if they are to 'succeed'.

There are still arguments about whether or not the types of stereotypical trait we have listed are based on observable differences between the sexes. We feel this is not true. Women as a whole are not passive, illogical, unselfconfident, just as men as a whole are not active, adventurous, ambitious and aggressive. Individual women and individual men vary greatly in their characteristics and behaviours. These traits are assigned to men and women by those who hold the dominant positions in society in order to secure and perpetuate the positions of privilege which result from a society based on inequality. Stereotyped traits are extremely dangerous both because they limit expectations and because we internalise the myths to a greater or lesser degree and either limit our own behaviour to fit in with them or else see ourselves as abnormal (of course, others will see us as abnormal as well!).

Apart from denying these stereotypes we are also concerned to challenge the value ascribed to traits considered to be 'masculine'. If young people are taught to be very competitive, to always act as leader, to be very independent and very ambitious, they are being offered a view of the world which reinforces ideas about winners and losers, some being powerful and others being powerless, some being strong and some being weak, some being equal and some inferior. It seems to us that a caring, humanitarian society is one based on equality, compassion, collaboration and interdependence.

Boys learning to be boys

We take it as given that much of the behaviour described as 'masculine' is learned (as opposed to being innate) and reinforced by stereotyped ideas about what it means to be male in this society. Baby boys and girls are treated very differently from birth. They are spoken to differently, dressed differently, played with differently, and there are different expectations for them. Nicholson (1984) writes:

> Take a baby out into the street, stop the first twenty people you meet ... ask them to hold 'Mark' and tell you what sort of baby he is. Repeat the procedure ... this time ask them what they think of 'Mary'. The baby will be the same in both cases ... Whatever the baby's real sex, 'Mark' will be described as bouncing, cheeky, mischievous and strong; while 'Mary' will be seen as lovely, sweet, gorgeous and cute.

An experiment at Sussex University (Smith and Lloyd 1978) invited thirty-two mothers to play with a baby they had never seen before and filmed the results. The same baby was presented to the mothers as either a 'boy' or a 'girl'. As you would guess the toys which the women chose for the baby were very different, depending on whether it was thought the baby was a girl or a boy: a doll for a girl, a hammer for a boy. But, more interestingly, they interpreted the same behaviour differently, depending on whether they thought it was a girl or a boy. When the baby became restless and they thought it was a boy, it was interpreted as a wish to play; so the women played with 'him'. When they thought it was a girl and she started to wriggle, the behaviour was interpreted as an indication that 'she' was upset and she was soothed.

It seems to us that if this is typical it is teaching boys and girls powerful messages about the way they manipulate and control their environment. Boys are being taught to demand attention and to control situations to get what they want; whereas girls are being taught to be passive and wait before reacting. If this is true, it has far-reaching consequences for adult behaviour.

The stereotype of 'active' male and 'passive' female can be applied to many situations: men are expected to be 'better at sport'; women are expected to assume supportive roles. If boys do learn to negotiate their environment more actively then this has enormous implications for learning, particularly for learning which involves experiment and investigation. We do not want to perpetuate any stereotypes about girls as passive recipients of knowledge, and boys as active 'makers' of knowledge, but to ask questions about how far socialisation of boys and girls affects the learning process.

Parents are clearly powerful role models for young children and it is still mothers who do most nurturing. Nicholson (1984) points to evidence which suggests that fathers tend to be more physical when playing (particularly so with boys). If so, that would fit in with a suggestion that boys and men do learn to value action rather than emotional closeness and communication in relationships. He also argues that there is evidence to suggest that men are more concerned than women that their sons should be 'masculine' and their daughters 'feminine'.

The books and other media images which children of all ages read still suggest very stereotyped roles. It seems to us that the majority of television programmes watched by our young children are showing male heroes in a variety of violent postures. Stories abound about baddies and goodies, with very little difference between them, except the goodies have 'right' on their side. Most cartoons for children are a variant of this theme and involve fairly horrific incidents. Recent Home Office research (see *The Sunday Times*, 15 December 1985) has shown that young children do, as parents have always known, copy the heroes they see on television. Female characters, if they are shown at all, are 'helped' out of trouble or stand around admiringly, or are just shown as plain stupid. Recently there have been one or two cartoons with central female characters (for example 'She Ra', 'He Man's' twin sister). These characters are all beautiful in a stereotyped way, but more muscly than usual, and they fight the baddies at their own game and win. Interestingly, one of us has noticed that the two four-year-old girls who live with her have suddenly taken to sword-fighting 'for the honour of Graysculls' (like She Ra) and to joining battle with their boy neighbours in a way which is quite new since these new heroines appeared. Advertisements for toys on television for young children are extremely stereotypical. Girls are always shown playing either with toys which copy adult 'women's' roles, such as toy cookers, toy hoovers, or tea sets, or they are shown with soft cuddly animals. Girls are even encouraged to buy 'My First Sink', and a 'head' on which they can practise putting make-up and putting in curlers. Boys, on the other hand, quite predictably are shown playing with games, cars, mechanical toys or space monsters. Most of these are now toys which are taken straight from the violent cartoons mentioned earlier, and the main aim of playing with the toy is to battle it out with an opponent.

Even when boys and girls are playing with the same toy it appears, from our personal observation, that they are often playing with it very differently. When a little girl plays with a doll she very often plays at being 'mother'. She feeds the doll, takes it for walks, bathes and dresses it. Boys, on the other hand, play very differently with action-man type dolls. They *are* the doll: taking part in an elaborate fantasy about fighting and killing. Girls' play revolves around relating to a second person (the doll); boys are the 'heroes' of their own play. One of us watched her daughter playing with cars. At last she thought she was observing a breakthrough, until she realised that her daughter was also playing 'mummies and daddies' with the cars — mummy car, daddy car and baby car!

Research has shown that an awareness of characteristics which are appropriate for each gender develops very early. Kuhn *et al.* (1978) presented two- to three-year-olds with two paper dolls, Michael and Lisa, and played a game where they asked about the characteristics and gender roles. At two years of age both boys and girls believed that girls would clean the house when they were grown up, and that boys would be the boss and mow the lawn.

The language we use to young children also reinforces the positions, expectations and 'stereotypes' of 'masculine' and 'feminine' behaviour in this society. Browne and France (1985) noted that in observations, tape and video recordings which they made of interactions between adults and children in nurseries that nicknames are gender-related.

> Girls were bombarded with terms of endearment — 'honey', 'sweetie', 'lovey', 'darling', 'treasure', 'precious', 'little charmer' ... whereas boys got terms that reinforce the tough behaviour expected of them — 'buster', 'bruiser', 'toughie', 'big bully', 'wise guy', and so on ... It is comforting for children to receive terms of endearment when they are sincerely meant. In our experience these terms are hardly ever offered to older boys in the nursery — for some reason it is 'unmanly' for them to be given signs of warmth and affection.

Before boys even leave the nursery stereotyped notions of masculinity are already absorbed.

Boys learning to be aggressive

One of the most worrying aspects which we and other teachers have observed about boys' schools is the level of aggression and violence in them. Many of the teachers we have talked to about working in boys' schools have expressed anxiety over this. Teachers in primary and mixed secondary schools have also talked to us about aggressive behaviour in boys. The general belief that men are more aggressive than women is perhaps the most common belief about differences between the sexes. It is probably also the one which is most commonly attributed to biological determinism rather than social construction. In staff-rooms we have commonly heard the opinion that the physicality between boys is not really aggressive but is 'play-fighting'. This seems to us closely related to other statements such as 'boys will be boys', or the unproblematic acceptance of 'Well, that's just how boys are'. The strange thing to us is that there seems to be an acceptance that boys are more aggressive naturally, and therefore it is *all right*. We would argue that *even if* boys were born with a natural inclination towards violence, that does not make it acceptable. After all, social conventions generally mean that many behaviours which by nature we might feel disposed towards are frowned on in society, and we have to restrain ourselves!

The evidence that boys/men do behave more aggressively than girls/women is strong. Bob Connell (1985) writes:

> Almost all the soldiers in the world are men. So are most of the police, most of the prison warders and almost all of the generals, admirals, bureaucrats and politicians who control the apparatuses of coercion and collective violence.
>
> Most murderers are men. Almost all bandits, armed robbers and muggers are men; all rapists, most domestic bashers; and most people involved in street brawls, riots and the like. The same story, then, for both organised and unorganised violence. It seems that there is some connection between being male and being violent ... It is also very important that much of the actual violence is not isolated and individual but it is institutional. Much of the poofter-bashing is done by police; much of the world's rape is done by soldiers in the context of war. These actions grow readily out of the 'legitimate' violence for which police forces and armies are set up.

The majority of reports dealing with aggression in young children have been concerned with nursery schools. They have also largely focused on middle-class boys (Archer and Lloyd 1982). In more than twenty investigations published before 1966, boys were observed to be more aggressive than girls. More recent studies in Britain have had similar results. One study carried out in fifteen different nursery schools and playgroups found that conflicts between boys were more frequent than conflicts between girls or between girls and boys (Smith and Green 1975). In a study of eleven-year-old boys and girls in the classroom, the boys showed more physical aggression than girls of the same age (Archer and Westman 1981).

In a study in California, four-year-old children were invited to play in groups of three — all of the same sex — on a trampoline in a room with a one-way mirror. A clear difference was found in the way the boys and girls played. About a quarter of the boys engaged in fairly extreme types of horseplay, piling on top of each other on the trampoline or rushing into each other. None of the girls played really boisterously. John Nicholson (1984) comments on this study:

> There does seem to be a sex difference in children's games, but
> two points must be borne in mind. The first, that even the most
> exuberant boys in the California study *were only fighting in fun*, so
> it would be rash to treat this as evidence that boys are more
> aggressive than girls (our emphasis).

His second point is that the rough-and-tumble play is actually
due to the behaviour of a small group of untypical boys.

It seems to us that whether or not boys only 'fight in fun' is
rather beside the point. If we accept that much of children's play
is a copy and a practice of adult roles, then this kind of 'play' is
worrying. And, although our classroom observations also
suggest that the number of boys engaged in aggressive
behaviour at any one time is small, it seems to us that a high
proportion of boys we have observed over extended periods of
time have exhibited aggressive behaviour *at some time or other*.
This is not true of the same proportion of girls observed over an
equal period of time. This reminds us of the times we have tried
to set up various role-play situations with groups of boys, and
then tried the same exercise with groups of girls. We have
realised over the years that, if it is at all possible for the role-play
to have a violent outcome that is, in all probability, how many
boys will interpret it. For example, the following situation was
provided for some pupils. Two pupils have had an argument in
the playground over who has the most expensive shoes. Two
volunteers take the role of pupils and the third plays a teacher
trying to calm down the situation and discuss with the pupils
why it should not have happened. What invariably happened
was that the two pupils started fighting and the 'teacher' joined
in! The situation, when presented to girls, never had the same
outcome.

Aggression has also been studied in children through the
questionable method of setting up a situation in the laboratory
where children think they can inflict pain on other children
without any risk of retaliation. In the experiments children have
been given a reason to use this power. In an experiment of this
kind, a group of eight-year-olds was told that a child in the next
room was working on a set of arithmetic problems, and asked to
help by pressing a button every time a wrong answer was given.
The button would mean the child would be hit with a punching-

machine. They were told this would help the child learn. The children were told from time to time that the 'victim' had made a mistake, and pressed buttons which were supposed to deliver blows ranging in power — number one, a soft punch; five, a medium punch; and ten, a hard punch. The boys chose to inflict significantly more pain than the girls on their non-existent victim. (Nicholson, 1984).

Questionnaires have been used with boys and girls to ask what they think about various situations involving violence and aggression; these have also shown that boys appear to be more aggressive than girls. It seems that boys think more aggressively and have a more aggressive image of themselves from these studies. (However, when girls have been rewarded with 'prizes' for beating up a doll, they have beaten it up as aggressively as the boys!)

Nicholson (1984) comments about studies comparing adult male and female levels of aggression.

> What really seems to hold women back is that they feel much more strongly than men that they ought not to behave aggressively, and become much more anxious after behaving aggressively unless they have some justification for their action … the circumstances in which women show aggression are very different; either there is a matter of principle involved, or else they see someone else treated unfairly.

There seem to us strong arguments to point to the social construction of male aggression. Firstly, even *if* a biological explanation is given, for example male levels of testosterone, there is evidence to show that hormones themselves are affected by the environment. For example, Rose *et al.* (1972) have found that when a monkey moves up the hierarchy by winning a fight and gaining in dominance, his testosterone level rises dramatically. The level of testosterone in the defeated monkey drops. It has also been found that emotional stress causes marked reductions in the levels of both male and female hormones in human beings (Archer 1979). Additionally, the greater aggressiveness of boys is observed from a very young age, from as young as two or three, long before the rise in testosterone levels at puberty. As we argued earlier, many of the toys seen as 'boys' toys' encourage physical activity, if not aggression. For example, guns, swords, action men, and the new, very popular, space models. Again, as we mentioned earlier, most of the male heroes in comics and on television (whether goodies or baddies) are violent.

Toughness and aggression are approved of in boys — the argument goes as follows: boys are encouraged to be tough and stick up for themselves. This is not usually meant as an open encouragement for them to be violent, but more of a message that violence is all right if not taken to extremes, that it is an appropriate way of 'looking after yourself' and can, in many circumstances, be a way of improving social status with other boys. Perhaps the most important message that boys learn is that they must at all costs avoid being thought to be afraid to fight. Boys also see members of their own gender engaging in violence, whereas girls generally do not. Boys may be rewarded with parental approval for being rough: 'I like the way he's rough. He's a proper lad', remarked one mother about her four-year-old son (Newson and Newson 1968).

Bob Connell (1985) argues in relation to the social construction of masculinity:

> War, murder, rape and masculinity are *cultural* facts not settled by biology. The patterns we have to deal with as issues of current politics have been produced within human society by the processes of history. It is the shape of social relations, not the shape of genes that is the effective cause. 'Male' and 'masculinity' are very different things. Masculinity is implanted in the male body; it does not grow out of it.

The main point we would like to make here is that aggression, whether 'in fun' or 'for real' *is* associated with masculinity in this society. Aggression in boys is a reflection of attitudes and beliefs about violence generally in society and it is, therefore, related to the nature of wider society and to the power relations between groups in it. Metcalf and Humphries (1985) argue that the popularisation of monetarist politics on both sides of the Atlantic has played upon a particular kind of masculinity:

> In the USA and Britain growing Western militarism has played on the most reactionary ideas of male sexuality ... President Reagan and Mrs Thatcher sell themselves as military leaders, the leaders of fighting men, real men, not wimps or wets.

Bob Connell also argues that:

> This connection between admired masculinity and violent response to threat is a resource that governments can use to mobilise support for war. A cult of masculinity and toughness flourished in the Kennedy and Johnson administrations in the USA and helped commit the country to war in Vietnam. I can remember the process operating on young men of my generation in Australia, whose Conservative government sent troops to support the Americans in Vietnam. Involvement in the war was presented as standing up to a threat, the opponents were smeared as lily-livered effeminates. In the fullness of time support for napalm raids and carpet bombing by B-52s became the test of manliness.

Aggression should not be seen as unproblematic and just a normal part of being male. We should be developing strategies to deal with aggression in school which take into account its gender implications and seek to challenge it in a more positive way (more positive than only reacting to violent incidents, when they occur, by a telling-off, suspension, calling in parents, and so on).[4]

Society encourages boys to behave aggressively. This does not mean that they are not responsible for their actions. The older they get, the less excusable are sexist acts of hostility and aggression which are aimed either towards one another or towards women. Schools should be places which challenge these patterns of aggression. As one male teacher put it: 'It's no good saying society makes men behave like that towards women. Men *allow themselves* to be kept in that role. We shouldn't deny our ability to change this. Male teachers, particularly, need to help boys by offering them another model as a way of being and behaving. Unfortunately, many men in schools do not offer this and do not see any reason for doing so'. In our experience, boys and men sometimes 'blame' women for their own aggressive sexist actions. For example, a woman teacher 'asked for it' or 'really deserved it', so they can be forgiven for 'giving it to them'. They shift responsibility for a sexist action onto others instead of accepting it themselves.

How do men and boys experience the pressures to be 'male'?

Hodson (1984) appears to be arguing that men are oppressed by
sexism and that there is a need for 'male liberation'.

> Men are the super-sensitive sex. They feel threatened and are
> getting hurt, but won't accept it. They are in great need of stable
> relationships, but women are currently criticising, rejecting and
> divorcing them. Men are poor at intimacy. The rules of the power
> game have changed. Women are gaining equality with men.

Metcalf and Humphries (1985) observe that 'traditionally men
have been quite at ease spouting off on any subject under the
sun except one: themselves'. We do not regard men as being
oppressed by sexism, but we do acknowledge that they may be
prevented from reaching their full human potential because of
it.

We are not primarily concerned in this book that because of
socialisation boys and men find it difficult to talk about
themselves. (In fact, we think it is erroneous to assume that girls
and women can talk about themselves. We believe the opposite
— that because of socialisation, girls and women are often very
far removed from recognising their own feelings and needs,
although they may be more tuned in to the feelings and needs of
others.) In the same way, an assumption that women are
gaining equality with men or that 'the rules of the power game
have changed', we also believe to be false. *Some* women may
have gained more equality with *some* men, but for the majority
of women the rules have not changed and the power still resides
very firmly in the hands of white, upper-middle-class males.

We go on to look at ways male socialisation may restrict the
personal development of boys and men. This is very important
because it often results not only in damage to the boys
themselves, but can be even more destructive to the people they
interact with and their relationship with their environment.

Several studies have been published in the last few years
which are concerned with men's experiences and the adverse
effect of male socialisation on men's lives. Morrison and Eardly
(1985) believe that:

> Boys grow up to be wary of each other. We are taught to compete
> with one another at school, and to struggle to prove ourselves

outside it, on the street, the playground and the sportsfield. Later we fight for status over sexual prowess, or money, or physical strength or technical know-how. We fear to admit our weakness to one another, to admit our failures, our vulnerability, and we fear being called a cissy, a wet or a softy. The pressure is on to act tough. We fear humiliation or exclusion, or ultimately the violence of other boys if we fail to conform.

Vic Seidler (1980) supports this:

> As boys, we have to be constantly on the alert to either confront or avoid physical violence. We have to be ready to defend ourselves. We are constantly on our guard ... Masculinity is never something we can feel at ease with. It is always something we have to be ready to prove and defend.

Other similar studies focus on how men experience masculinity and describe the ways that it is problematic for men (Hodson 1984; Metcalf and Humphries 1985; Ingham 1984; Levinson 1978). Morrison and Eardley (1985), for instance, argue that male cameraderie often takes the place of and expresses men's deep desire for genuine friendship with other men; but that this cameraderie occurs in a context that is designed to put men in competition with one another. A contradiction emerges that is at once a reaching out and 'a keeping at bay'. Tolson (1977) reports the difficulty many men expressed over communicating. He found it was difficult for them to discuss any personal feelings with one another.

Boys have expressed similar feelings. Below are edited extracts from an interview originally recorded for *True Romance*. Gary and Dave were in the fifth form of a London comprehensive school at the time. Paul Morrison, who talks to them, describes them as 'exceptions' in terms of being able to find the 'strength to reject much of the power of "boys' world".'

Gary: That's a funny thing, really, because if a boy is close to another boy, it's sort of said: 'No man, this is a funny thing. Them two are too close, you know. They must be gay or something'. When two girls are close, they could walk down the street holding hands, everything's fine.

Dave: But if two boys did the same, their names'd be mud in the school.

Gary: Yeah, because ... If I went into a room, right, the
acceptable way to greet my friend was to punch him on
the shoulder or shake hands, you know. But if a girl went
into a room, they'd kiss each other on the cheek, or
something like that.
...

Gary: If you've got a friend, it doesn't matter how long you've
known him, you keep him at a distance, as a man. But you
let the girl get close to you. I just don't see it as right. The
only way you're meant to relate to a boy is if you're
boasting. 'Cos you come into school and if you wanna say
something to a guy you boast about it. You don't talk
about your failures to him. You're not meant to do that.
Your failures are meant to be kept in yourself.

Dave: You don't talk about your failures or shortcomings with
girls, either. When you're with a girl you're supposed to
be a Superman. Like I know a lot of boys, when they're on
their own they're friendly to you, when they're with a girl
they try to take you on or something — put on a veneer of
super-hardness, try and pick a fight or something.
...

Paul: What is it that blokes don't talk about?

Gary: Their failures. That's basically it. Their failures.

In our work in schools with boys, several have described to us
what it is like for them. Wayne, who is fourteen, and at a
London mixed comprehensive, describes his experiences as
follows:

In school most people are concerned with their image — most
boys are expected to conform, to dress the same. They're
supposed to be interested in football matches and beat up other
people, and that's taken as fun. They especially beat up younger,
smaller people. Anything extraordinary or unusual that you
happen to do is taken as something from another planet. There's
a lot of pressure on boys to be friends with popular boys. If you
don't go around with them then you're treated as a weirdo. It's
'follow the leader'. If you don't see another boy outside school,
you can't get to know what he's really like ...

There's a lot of pressure on kids to be fashionable. It has to be a
certain style. You can only dress casually or trendy or punk if
you're part of those groups ... It's hard if you want to get on in
school because you're expected to participate in the messing
about, especially if you're a boy.

Sean goes to a boys' school. He talks about how his behaviour is guarded in front of other boys:

> You have to be careful about what you let out about yourself. You get picked on for anything around here. You've got to be careful not to let the other kids think you're soft.

In this chapter we have suggested that there are considerable pressures on boys to behave in stereotyped masculine ways. One of the effects of this is that constraints operate in their interpersonal relationships with other boys. We have described some of the possible effects on their socialisation and absorption of stereotyped notions about girls and women. This socialisation process has important implications for the way boys learn, which we look at in the next chapter.

Notes

1 Boys are often perceived as a 'problem' in this sense in terms of discipline. It seems important, though, to ask which boys are thus perceived. If they are largely black, working-class boys then clearly there are classist and racist implications.
2 In one LEA a diagnostic centre for learning difficulties reports that approximately 75 per cent of children referred for problems with reading and writing are boys.
3 The twenty more commonly assigned adjectives characteristic of women found by Bem (1974) included childlike, gullible, shy, yielding, loyal and flatterable.
4 We would like to make a distinction between general aggression and violence which might be destructive to the boys themselves or others and the ability to express anger assertively and positively over a personal or political issue.

CHAPTER 2

Classroom Dynamics

Evidence from extensive classroom observations suggests that girls and boys may be involved in quite different learning processes at school. They may be learning different interests and skills, valuing various activities differently, and even using the same materials or activities in quite different ways. This may occur even when 'equal opportunities' are apparently available to both girls and boys. The evidence suggests that this starts very early.

Learning in primary schools

To explore boys' and girls' learning experiences in infant classes, we began by 'interviewing' infant children in a racially mixed Inner London primary school about their favourite activities. The children were individually presented with photographs of different activities and areas of their classroom as a basis for discussion. They talked about what toys they played with, how often, who else played with them, how they used them, and what they were most interested in. Some striking points arose from these discussions: all the boys were very enthusiastic about the photo of the lego, while only two girls said they played with it, when pressed, and three girls said they didn't like lego at all. Most children described lego as being used to make cars and houses — and said that boys made cars and girls made houses. Most boys described using the home corner in a variety of ways, for example, they pretended to be

18

dogs and jumped on the table and around the room. The girls used the home corner for more conventional domestic activities.

The picture that emerged time and again throughout the classrooms of primary schools we observed was one of boys being primarily involved *in an individualistic way* in processes of 'making', constructive play, physical manipulation and an expansive use of space. Alongside this, we commonly observed girls involved in various forms of social play and restrictive use of space. Girls and boys seemed to approach joint activities in very different ways. Girls tended to talk to each other about their activity as they went along. They would discuss how to organise their work; for example, break it up into different aspects and decide who would do which, or work out what was necessary for preparation. Boys tended to talk together about things not related to the activity they were engaged in, talking about it only when absolutely necessary or when a conflict arose. In fact, conflicts concerning joint work arose very much more frequently with boys than with girls. Here are two 'typical' examples of girls and of boys working together:

Two girls were painting a joint picture (a large snail in the garden). They decided what colours they wanted and shared mixing the paints. They decided who should draw the outline (and why) and they proceeded to divide various aspects of the picture for each to do. There was discussion throughout the session about how the picture was coming on, how things looked, colours, and so on.

Two boys were painting a joint picture (a road with shops behind it). One boy insisted on drawing the outline. Then each boy took charge of painting one half of the picture. When one boy, who was painting the road, came to the middle of the page, he painted a careful vertical line down the middle of the road and stopped. Talk between the boys was about an episode on the playground and the only time they discussed the painting was when one boy didn't like the way the other painted the shops — then conflict arose and the second boy stopped painting.

It is not enough to devise certain learning strategies without also taking into consideration the different ways that boys and girls may engage in them. When setting up our own collaborative learning situations, for instance, we found that boys tended not to collaborate, but to work independently.

A number of interesting studies have highlighted the different ways in which boys and girls approach collaborative tasks. For example, a small-scale research survey undertaken by Davis and Ticher (1986) with a group of reception-aged infants in a school in East London, was primarily set up for the purpose of looking more closely at how groups of reception children use construction materials. Jonathan Ticher, the class teacher, and Jenny Davis, a consultant mathematics teacher, noticed early on that the boys were choosing construction materials, especially lego, more often than girls, and were making more elaborate models with it. In order to look at the processes involved they videotaped a group of four girls and four boys who were given the following problems to solve with large-size lego: (a) how to build a 'house', and (b) how to build a tall structure. The four girls worked together constructing an enclosed space. Two boys, working on a separate wall, decided they would like to join their wall to the girls' house. The boys then assumed control of the building and directed the girls to bring them bricks. The group was then asked to make their structure 'tall' instead. The girls did this by standing on chairs and passing bricks to one another. The boys first copied this, then knocked down the girls' structure and took their bricks. The next week a different group was given the same task. This time the girls began collaboratively to build their house without discussion among themselves, the boys began work on four individual constructions. 'Several wonky piles of bricks resulted', while the girls quickly built a wall that was as tall as themselves and were expanding it vertically and horizontally. When the bricks began to run out the boys started taking bricks from each other's structures until a fight ensued and a teacher intervened. The girls again worked collaboratively on the 'tall' structure. The boys began to lose interest in their task and drifted away. Davis and Ticher comment:

> This re-emphasised for us just how important the feeling of 'being in control' is in the learning process. The children who opted out could have felt inhibited by others who had greater competence than they had. Once another child had taken over, whether pleasantly or by force, the excluded children seemed to lack the will to negotiate their way back into the activity.

Davis and Ticher realised that they were mistaken in assuming a deficit model in relation to girls' constructional abilities. They were interested to see what happened when the girls from the two different groups came together without boys. Immediately there was a noticeable sense of freedom and more talk. After some initial building near the beginning 'an elaborate fantasy play began: one girl became the mother and went to cook in the kitchen. An outside girl was bodily lifted in and her inclusion was reinforced by her being chosen as the cat, given food, stroked and petted in a display of affection and tenderness'. In answer to their initial question, Davis and Ticher wonder whether the difference in use of constructional materials had something to do with both the nature of the materials offered to children and with the different ways those materials are seen. They suggest, for example, that because lego is very small and abundant in most classrooms it tends to encourage small, individual work rather than collaborative work (which girls seem to prefer). This research, although small-scale, reinforces the idea that the gender differences between boys and girls will have serious implications for learning in school and that expectations of gender behaviour will have been internalised at an early age. (One of the interesting things to have emerged from our discussions with teachers is that the differences in behaviour between boys and girls are as noticeable at five as at fifteen.)

The observations which we made of primary school playgrounds were consistent with the sorts of behaviour we were seeing in the classroom. In general, we observed that, for the most part, boys dominated the playground space and were engaged in active, physical pursuits, while girls often occupied the peripheries or the 'quiet' playground space (where provided) together with the smaller children. Many boys were commonly engaged in physically manipulative play which utilised a large area, while many girls played games not requiring much space and talked together constantly as part of their activity. These observations have been corroborated by many discussions with primary teachers.

In both playground and the classroom, competitiveness was another feature which constantly permeated many boys' activities (be it physical sport, whose model went faster, who was further along in their maths book, or who was on a 'higher' level in their work). Even collaborative activities which required team work were organised and approached in such a way that competition became a key feature of the activity. Our observations of the girls usually showed the opposite — almost any activity provided a chance to collaborate, discuss, assist and interact generally.

In one classroom small groups of boys and girls were engaged in an activity making cylinders of various sizes and seeing how much weight they could take. Each group was asked to describe the task to one of us as a newcomer to the classroom. The girls' group described the task in purely descriptive terms, and also described how they had helped each other to make the cylinder, load it with weights and record how much it could take. Without exception, the boys' groups described the task in competitive terms (for example, 'to see who can make the strongest cylinder' or 'to see who can use the most weights').

As we have said, we observed that certain areas of the classroom and playground tended to be dominated by the boys. This territorial attitude extended even to certain classroom activities which were not primarily related to considerations of space. Certain materials, such as lego and other constructional toys, and anything to do with science, seemed to be regarded by the boys as 'theirs'. This was evident not only in the number of boys doing these activities, but also in the ways the boys behaved towards the girls. If, during a class project which involved the use of items such as scales, measures or stop watches, the boys ran out of these materials, they would commonly simply take them from girls, despite the fact that the girls were using them. In the main, the girls we observed who were 'pushed out' or 'taken over' behaved quite deferentially towards these boys. Some girls complained, some would fight back, but we saw the latter less commonly. We wondered if this behaviour, in part, reflected the fact that the girls perceived the boys as having a greater right to use these materials. The question of how definitions or assumptions of what type of knowledge, activity or behaviour belongs to whom has direct implications for what we learn.

It could be that the way many girls accept boys monopolising certain areas of the classroom has to do with their more pressing desire for a 'quiet life' and a peaceful atmosphere. Pat Mahoney (1985) attributes the apparent passivity of some girls towards boys as being a 'strategy' in itself, a way of coping that works best for themselves in that situation. We remember that, as children, many of 'us girls' simply did not take the boys seriously. We disdained their 'showing off' and 'being silly', and were dismissive about their 'immature behaviour'. We wonder if some of what appears as passive accommodation in girls could reflect, in fact, a 'can't be bothered with you' attitude.

It seemed to us that boys have a greater need than girls to identify certain activities as male or female. A consequence of this seemed to be that boys would often not only assume dominance over activities they have identified as 'male', but also avoid those identified as 'female'. Furthermore, not only do many boys bring competition into almost all activities they engage in, but also it is the competition which seems to become the fundamental source of motivation.

It may well be that because of boys' monopoly of classroom activities, girls may not be getting the same grounding in mechanical, physical and three-dimensional skills. Girls score lower on tests measuring spatial reasoning and problem-solving. The Cockcroft Report (1982) shows that boys scored significantly better than girls on tests requiring spatial ability; and on more complex items requiring abstract thought; problem-solving; conceptualisation. (Girls were found to score better on tasks requiring rule-following.) Spatial visualisation in itself is often taken to be particularly crucial to the comprehension of mathematics. However, statistics about sex-related differences in mathematics are themselves contentious, as Walden and Walkerdine (1982) have shown.

It has been claimed that the reasons girls under-achieve in mathematics are social, to do with unequal opportunities at school, low expectations by teachers, and lack of positive role models. All those things are likely to affect girls' interest, confidence and aspirations, especially in combination with the messages of non-entitlement they often receive from boys' domination of these areas in school. But is there not another important factor also affecting girls' and boys' learning? The way that girls, by and large, do not have the same opportunities to develop constructional and manipulative skills because of boys' domination of activities which facilitate this. It is reasonable to suppose therefore, that girls may not be developing the same conceptual framework, and that this in turn puts them at a further disadvantage in certain areas of mathematics and science.

Boys, on the other hand, usually do less well than girls on verbal reasoning tests and, later in their school careers, achieve less well in, and opt less for, English and modern languages. In 1982, 18,000 more boys than girls left school with no qualification in English, 10,000 more girls than boys achieved pass grades in O level English or equivalent.

Generally, boys have limited verbal interaction, and use language less than girls. Similarly, a study of the behaviour of nine-year-old boys and nine-year-old girls at the University of Denver, Colorado reported that:

> In practically every case, the boys ignored each other as people. They displayed no personal curiosity. They did not look at each other's faces. They didn't ask personal questions. They didn't volunteer information about themselves. Conversation was confined to the technical problems of lego-design. In every essential respect, the boys stayed solitary and played by themselves.   (Hodson 1984)

In contrast, the girls revealed three times as much about themselves as did the boys. Afterwards, it was discovered that the girls liked each other more as a result of their greater efforts towards getting to know each other. The boys remained mutually indifferent.

Although we are describing learning differences between girls and boys, we are in no way describing differences in *capacities* for learning. This is an important point; our examination of learning differences is entirely in terms of 'how' and 'why'. We suggest that differences in girls and boys may go deep, and so it is important not only to look at discrepancies in achievement terms, but also to look at the actual processes of mental, emotional and physical development in terms of gender.

Boys do not aspire to 'caring' roles or professions which are traditionally female spheres. Our observations suggest that there is very little time in school when boys are able to 'rehearse' skills of personal interaction, intimate communication and caring or co-operative behaviour, as girls do. They are not developing, in the main, the same skills, interest in or even valuation of these areas. Furthermore, because activities and play related to these activities are identified as 'female', such behaviour may well be avoided or considered not appropriate 'masculine' behaviour.

General issues in relation to gender and learning

In our opinion, early socialisation and sex-stereotyped attitudes about boys and girls have a fundamental effect on the *processes* of education in relation to teaching style and methodology and the way in which learning is negotiated by boys and girls. For instance, we were recently told by the head of a Learning Difficulties Diagnostic Centre that 'somewhere between 70 and 80 per cent of pupils referred to us are boys'. Boys are referred to Diagnostic Centres mainly for problems with reading.

Barrs and Pidgeon (1986) report that gender differences in patterns of reading are of increasing concern to teachers. They argue that there are sharp and observable differences between boys and girls as readers. Both in terms of reading *ability* and in terms of the *amount* of voluntary reading, girls consistently read *better* and *more* than boys. A primary school survey by the Assessment of Performance Unit (1983) noted that 'girls achieved higher mean scores in reading and writing than did boys'. More detailed evidence came from the ILEA Junior Survey (1985), which showed differences between boys and girls in terms of average reading scores both on entry to junior school and in the fourth year. It could be assumed that the sex stereotyped portrayal of the world presented by the great majority of books for young children, would mean that girls would be less successful readers. Barrs and Pidgeon offer compelling reasons why this is not so. Firstly, although boys are shown engaging in many different activities in books, one activity they are not shown doing is reading, nor taking part in any other quiet or thoughtful activity.

In addition, Barrs and Pidgeon suggest that 'girls and boys

must begin to develop views of themselves as potential readers when they are quite small, and the adults around them are likely to be a major influence on the self concepts in this, as in other respects'.

It is interesting to speculate that boys' slower development in reading might also relate to the differences observed between girls and boys in their ways of interacting with others. Girls' greater reliance on verbal skills for social interaction might give them an advantage when they begin to learn to read. It may also mean that girls place a greater value on language-based activity. In addition to difficulties in learning to read, it has been shown that the reading matter of boys and girls is quite different. Surveys (for example, Whitehead's report 'Children and their books', 1977) have consistently shown that boys read more non-fiction than girls. Non-fiction gives access to external knowledge, 'facts', and information, while fiction is concerned with the lives, thoughts and feelings of other people. This choice of reading matter fits well with what is known of early socialisation of boys and girls. And of course, reading of any kind is a passive activity.

Ways in which boys and girls may internalise gender expectations in their learning were highlighted by an experiment by Hargreaves (1983). He showed that males and females may only have to *think* that a task will be performed better by the opposite sex to do badly at it. Hargreaves asked 38 boys and 38 girls to play with a 'wiggly wire'. This is a game sometimes found at school fêtes where the object is to pass a wire loop all the way down a wiggly wire without touching it. If you touch the wire a bell rings. Hargreaves told half the children that this was a test to see how good they would be at mechanics or operating machinery, and the other half that it would test how good they were at needlework, sewing and knitting. Compared to the number of errors the children made when they were given instructions 'appropriate' for their sex, both boys and girls did significantly worse on the task if they thought the game tested a skill that was the 'prerogative' of the opposite sex. 'So apparent sex differences in certain abilities', Hargreaves says, 'may be even less ingrained than people think'.

Teachers' responses to their pupils can also provide strong messages about the type of behaviour and ways of working that are most valued, and these often relate to gender stereotypes. Walden and Walkerdine (1985) looked into the criteria teachers used for entering girls and boys for an O level mathematics course. Although the fourth-year girls outperformed the boys in the test they administered, many more boys than girls were entered. They found that teachers felt that 'male' characteristics such as haphazardness, rule-breaking and challenging the teacher on maths problems accompanied 'flair', 'brilliance' or 'real understanding'. At the same time, 'female' characteristics, such as conscientiousness, neatness and co-operation, led teachers to suspect a lack of 'real understanding' and mere 'rule-following'. Their study begs a closer look at what sorts of trait teachers (unconsciously?) associate as desirable with certain subjects and how these may in fact be stereotyped traits which are gender related.

Just as certain assumptions may be made about a child on the basis of gender, class assumptions may also be made. Ideas about criteria for success are often linked to middle-class traits (such as ways of speaking) so that it is these class traits themselves which become associated as accompanying and necessary for success.

This also operates in racist ways. There is now evidence that teachers perceive the same behaviour in different ways, depending on whether a child is white or black. The Eggleston Report (1986) showed that some white teachers seemed to perceive certain behaviour in black boys as more threatening than the same sort of behaviour in white boys. These teachers responded differently to these boys in their lessons according to their ethnic group.

We are likely to internalise the dominant stereotypes about race, class or gender qualities and characteristics of pupils. We work in institutions which reflect the inequalities in society in terms of the dominance and power of some groups. We need to guard against stereotypical assumptions that affect our expectations of pupils. Steve Goldenberg (1986) writes: 'The term (under-achievement) assumes the existence of equality of opportunity and that all students are striving for the same success, which they can achieve on a purely meritocratic basis whatever their place in the socio-economic structure'. He argues that this does not take into account the way the education system privileges the already privileged and ignores the initial inequalities. Several teachers interviewed by Goldenberg were conscious of a disparity in their attitudes towards the classroom behaviour of middle- and working-class pupils:

> The tutor set think I give more attention (to a group of middle-class girls) in two ways, both in terms of their work and how I treat their behaviour. And I think it does influence me that, because I know they are nice girls, I do let them off the hook sometimes, and I shouldn't.

Expectations about *ability* as construed in terms of behaviour are also apparent in this girl's explanation about why she was in a CSE rather than an O level class:

> It's who she likes. If you are a big mouth who likes to back-chat her, she chucks you in the CSE and if you're a softy, you know, listen and don't talk a lot, she puts you in the 'O' level. You know I think that's how she done it.   (Riley 1985)

Riley writes that most of the black girls she interviewed had been placed in the CSE group. The interrelationship of classist, racist and sexist assumptions and expectations about children in school seems to us highly complex. For example, we cannot talk only about teacher expectations and *sexism* in the system contributing to boys' success in sciences in comparison to girls'. In a school we visited recently the Physics O level class was made up of about 60 per cent white, middle-class boys, and about 30 per cent white, middle-class girls. The CSE science class was made up of mainly black and working-class children. Another example is the high proportion of black boys removed from main stream schools and marginalized into 'special schools'.

Many of the boys we have talked to in schools have expressed unhappiness in relation to the position they find themselves in. Wayne complained, and two others in his class concurred, that

> The boys get in trouble more than the girls. It's the boys that always get told off. The girls get more treats and are asked to go with the register more or do something responsible.

Additionally they all felt that it was the black boys who received most of the negative attention.

Boys in mixed secondary classrooms

There is considerable evidence that boys demand the greater proportion of teacher attention, in both primary and secondary school. Boys' monopoly of physical space, use of facilities and teachers' time in secondary school is well documented and is not essentially different from primary school observations. Carricoates' (1978) interviews with primary school teachers about teaching girls and boys brought consistent comments such as: 'The boys are more difficult to settle down to their work … they don't seem to have the same self-discipline that girls do'. 'It's a bit harder to keep the boys' attention during the lesson'. 'Boys are more difficult to control. It's more important to keep their attention … otherwise they play you up something awful'. Stanworth (1981), Walkerdine (1981) and Fuller (1980) have all pointed to the extent of boys' domination of the mixed classroom in secondary school: their noisiness; their demands that lesson content be interesting and directed at them; the need for discipline. Tingle (1985) writes about his experience as an English teacher of boys being amalgamated into a girls' school:

> The boys plunge into things, interrupt discussion, can't keep still, can't wait. Ten boys in a class of 29 and they demand 50% or more of my time. Yet the work they produce is often shallow, non-reflective and is always messy … The boys, in protective groups, generally resist giving anything of themselves. They hide their feelings, they joke, they are loud, they are very physical.

Margaret Sandra's (1985) research also reveals ways in which boys can cause continual disruption within the classroom. She was principally concerned with why boys consistently under-achieved in English. She observed classes in the ILEA with the intention of exploring whether it was possible to map any differences in girl/boy performance in English. Initially, she taped lessons but it soon became apparent to her that verbal responses were only a tiny fraction of the ways in which pupils are caught into sex-differentiated behaviour affecting learning. She listed all activities she saw pupils engaged in during lessons and used this to create an observation chart. Certain activities could clearly be identified with one sex or the other, the most disruptive behaviour being male. Here are some of them:

Girls	*Boys*
hand-up	pencil tapping
chewing	calling out
reading	bag on table
make-up	shove ha'penny
brushing hair	misusing material
showing work to teacher	

In addition, boys were more likely to arrive late in the classroom and to be poorly equipped.

French (1986) suggests that the way boys disrupt a lesson in which they are not interested might lead teachers to gear lesson content to the boys as a means of imposing discipline. Boys also appear to exert control over the classroom through direct intimidation of the girls. Pat Mahoney (1985) observed classes and interviewed girls and boys in three inner-city secondary schools. She concludes that boys control the mixed classroom by dominating the girls physically as well as verbally. She believes this provides a means of proving masculinity for boys in mixed schools. (This concurs with our observations in primary schools where we have observed a 'low-level', on-going harassment of girls by some boys. This took the form of 'put-downs', comments about girls' work or ability, needling and 'wind-up', tapping, poking, touching with feet when sitting on the floor, knocking down girls' work, taking over equipment girls are using, as well as overt forms of intimidation. 'Blaming' was another often observed behaviour, which seemed to result in some girls adopting a defensive deferential stance in relation to certain boys.)

Teachers said that most girls requiring their assistance will generally sit with their hand up or come over to them (and if the teacher is not free hover nearby, without speaking), while boys often shout out from across the room for assistance. Teachers talked about their own determination not to respond, but nevertheless, they continuously found themselves looking up or answering the 'summons'.

But beyond these overt ways of boys demanding teacher attention or claiming dominance in the classroom, it is also clear that boys claim a great deal of their teachers' time and attention simply as a result of their approach to their schoolwork, and the dynamics between themselves. Because of the preference for 'doing', 'making', 'handling' and 'manipulating' shown by so many boys, there seems to be a real reluctance towards undertaking other sorts of task. For example, after a science activity boys in one classroom we observed made it clear that being told by their teacher to 'put the scales away and write up the experiment' was perceived as a *punishment*. Making sure that boys complete assignments, conclude activities, write up experiments and even see through games that they've started, appears to take a great deal of teacher attention in the form of constant coaxing and cajoling, tempting, insisting and threatening. Additionally, a certain amount of teacher time also seems to be taken up mediating conflict between boys.

Boys-only groups

We have written about the ways in which boys learn to identify certain spheres of activity, knowledge and behaviour as masculine or feminine and value them accordingly. We have also shown why there is every reason to believe this begins long before secondary school. We have discussed evidence which suggests boys may dominate physical space and teacher time and attention, have greater difficulty in collaborating and relating personally; and may measure their own worth or success by direct competition with other boys. Certainly these types of behaviour, already so evident in primary school, seem to continue and polarise in secondary school. The curriculum itself is more clearly polarised into 'male' and 'female' subjects, with option choices and exam results reflecting this. (Of those entered for woodwork and metalwork O level in summer 1980, 99 per cent were boys. The corresponding figures for the other subjects were: physics, 77 per cent; mathematics, 60 per cent; economics, 59 per cent; geography, 56 per cent; art, 44 per cent; French, 41 per cent; biology, 37 per cent; sociology, 27 per cent; needlework, 0 per cent.)

Observing girls and boys in the mixed classroom can illuminate their learning of different skills, their different interests, expectations and behaviour and the different influences in their environments and development. It is also valuable to look at boys in all-boy settings in order further to illuminate the dynamics between them; the ways they may be relating to their school environment; ways they may be internalising the social context they operate within; and the ways boys learn.

Power dynamics and competition among boys in boys' schools

We referred earlier to the research by Pat Mahoney (1985) in which she observed classes and interviewed girls and boys in three inter-city comprehensive schools, and concluded that boys control the mixed classroom by dominating the girls physically as well as verbally. She suggested that this provides a means of proving masculinity for boys in mixed schools. Mahoney argues that as boys' schools lack this opportunity, masculinity has to be proved in another way, usually in terms of physical strength, which results in more physical violence. We agree with this, but our experience also agrees with Spender (1982) who reports some teachers' comments on single-sex boys' classrooms:

> It seems to me that the boys create an inferior or outside group and level the abuse at them that they would otherwise direct at girls. The least 'manly' boys become the target and are used as substitute girls in a way.

> In an all-boys' school a group of 'not real boys' gets created. They are called the poofters and the cissies and are constantly likened to girls. The sexual hierarchy gets set up but some boys have to play the part that the girls would take in a mixed school.

In one boys' school this was very overt. In one class, the boy who took on the role of 'girl' was even known as 'Janice'. All the boys called him 'Janice' most of the time and some teachers were heard to refer to him as 'Janice'. It seems clear that the boys' behaviour in classes we observed, while superficially directed against girls or against the teacher, is in fact directed at each other. They are proving through their behaviour that they are, in fact, 'real men' and very dependent on one another's approval. Pat Mahoney (1985) also wrote about this:

> What seems to emerge from this is that, contrary to popular myth about the independence of boys, they are in fact highly dependent on others. Yet there seem to be two sorts of

dependence at issue — boys' attempts to impress girls are not the
same as their attempts to impress other boys. In the one case,
girls are needed to provide servicing; whereas, in the other, boys
depend on other boys for their identities as men.

Servicing, Mahoney explains, includes such things as girls
providing boys with rulers, pens, and so on, and helping with
homework, sorting out arguments, and generally making them
feel 'nice'.

Boys in boys' schools confirm their identity as males through
physical aggression and violence (or sometimes by their
behaviour to women teachers: see Chapter 4). It appears that
boys' behaviour to girls in mixed schools and much of adult
male behaviour to women (for example, a group of men
whistling at a woman) is a confirmation of their masculinity
aimed at *each other*. The fact that boys themselves would prefer
to go to mixed schools is confirmed in an EOC Report (1982):
'less homosexuality (top of the list), getting on with girls, less
pressure to conform to macho images'. This same report also
said that 'staff would certainly agree that there is less violence'.
Pat Mahoney concludes from this:

> It is perhaps possible to theorise not that boys' schools construct
> masculinity more strongly but that it is reinforced in different
> ways. In mixed schools boys confirm their masculinity to each
> other through their behaviour towards girls, but in the absence of
> girls they may resort to physical violence to achieve their position
> in the male hierarchy ... That boys are so violently homophobic
> perhaps bears witness to the fact that they see each other as
> masculine if their sexuality is being practised on girls.

There follows an analysis of data we have compiled from
classrooms observed in a boys' school over a two-year period;
observations of a variety of lessons in a large number of other
boys-only groups in other schools, extensive discussion with
individual teachers and in-service workshops and conferences
on working with boys. Our research focused on issues to do
with the ways boys interrelate. For example, the things we
concentrated on included both observing and asking about
collaborative learning activities, the ways boys relate to each
other, to men and women teachers, to different subjects and to
different teaching methodologies. The sorts of issue that arose
are central to the teaching of boys and their behaviour at school.

We observed a 'continuous power play' underlying most interactions between boys, an ongoing process of positioning and a continual seeking of status and prestige. This competitive behaviour not only operates at explicit levels, but also implicitly. It not only permeates social interaction but also affects approaches to most school activity. In our study many teachers complained that boys may be preoccupied with each other to the point where it affects practically everything they do, including their concentration and performance in their work and their relationships with the teachers. This seems especially true in the lower school where boys are new to the school or still smaller physically and in a more vulnerable position.

In many classrooms of eleven- and twelve-year-old boys there was continual competitive interaction among many of the boys. This could relate to their work, skill, dress, behaviour or activities, feats or fights outside the classroom. Boys seemed to be constantly attempting to impress each other through various antics in the classroom (which might involve provocative behaviour or rudeness towards the teacher) or generally 'winding' each other up, resulting in physical violence from time to time.

The ways girls and boys learn to develop self-esteem appeared largely to derive from different sources. It is true that there is also a competitive element in some of the ways girls develop self-esteem. From the time they are old enough to view themselves as female objects (and there is evidence to suggest this happens when they are quite young) girls are encouraged to assess and value themselves in terms of their physical appearance. Notions of 'beauty' exist within narrowly defined perimeters, and in direct comparison to other girls. In this sense, girls may learn to derive their self-esteem through a competitive relationship with other girls. But, because of the 'norms' of femininity (such as the 'caring' role), girls also learn to derive their self-esteem in ways to do with how supportive and helpful they are to others, in other words, not only through comparison in directly competitive terms, but also in a 'complementary' role to others. However, after observing and working with boys we suggest that, for boys, this sort of competitive basis to self-esteem goes very much deeper, starting much earlier, and is bound up with not only their appearance but their general performance throughout their lives. In our belief it relates, in some way, to the concept of the 'hero', reflecting the notion of a 'superior' male. In order to be 'the hero' of their own fantasy play or, indeed, a worthy male in their own lives, they must not merely possess certain qualities (for example, honour, bravery, strength) but must be superior in these to other boys. It is in this sense that the competitive dynamic among boys involves the development of masculine identity. Social divisions are being played out at a variety of different levels and of course gender is just one of them. School reflects this in its hierarchical organisation, its structures, its values and beliefs. (Chapter 3 deals with this in more detail.)

Modes of communication among boys

The boys in our study (who were from a variety of cultural, ethnic and class backgrounds) seemed largely to depend upon rigid, stylised and competitive ways of relating to one another within the classroom. Alongside the ongoing 'power-play' (and as a result of it?) most of the boys we observed demonstrated a general lack of trust and support towards each other. Unless they had been in classes where teachers had spent a long time deliberately developing relationships among the pupils, they, unlike girls, were unwilling to say things in front of each other which were personal or left them at all vulnerable. They were, for the most part, guarded towards each other and their talk revolved around impersonal subject matter. While boys would willingly and enthusiastically discuss the rights or wrongs of a particular political issue (for example, nuclear war) they were overwhelmingly unwilling to discuss their own behaviour, feelings or lives with each other. Furthermore, even when working together on a shared or collaborative task, talk was often restricted to either a minimal utilitarian exchange or else about something totally external and unrelated. It seemed as though they were unable or unwilling to use talk as a way of sharing experiences. Teachers we interviewed concurred with our observation: 'I've sometimes tried to do the same kind of discussion work in boy-only and girl-only groups with very different results. The girls always seem far more comfortable when discussing their own experiences'. 'I used to work in a girls' school. I've noticed at this boys' school that collaborative activities that worked with the girls don't work with the boys'.

There was considerable non-verbal, aggressive or physical communication among boys. 'Body language', such as stance or tone of voice, played a large part in interaction. Physicality was not only used as a means of intimidation between the boys, but also as a way of making social contact. It was not unusual to see a boy, walking past another, reach out and deliver a little 'punch' as a way of saying 'hello'. Conflicts, such as whose turn it was to use some materials, or how to go about a joint task, would often be expressed and decided in physical terms (for example, by a 'push' and 'shove'). Demands for teacher attention or classroom disruptions (intended or unintentional) were often in physical terms (such as tapping, banging or other noise-making tactics). A good deal of talk among boys in the classroom was to do with issuing challenges or 'put-downs' to each other.

We also repeatedly observed how difficult many boys seemed to find listening to one another. They would meet each other's statements with contradiction, comparison, derision or direct challenge. More often, they would simply not bother to listen, especially if they had something they themselves wished to say.

These observations clearly relate to our earlier findings, from our primary school observations, and other research about communications and gender. In our view, it has much to do with the pressures to erect and then protect a 'masculine' façade of hardness, toughness, imperviousness to pain and 'objective' unemotionality.

It probably also involves the rigorous denial of anything identified as 'female' within themselves (and this may well include certain types of social and verbal interaction). However, in terms of the dynamics between boys which result from these pressures, it seems to acquire a 'life of its own'. The more boys present this exterior, the more impossible it must become for them to relate to each other in other ways. The more boys take every opportunity to demonstrate their own superior 'masculine' qualities, by pouncing on another boy's weakness, the more dangerous it becomes to express any vulnerability in front of each other. Boys 'need' to keep their emotional distance from each other, perhaps because they are afraid of each other and of their own emotionality — lest they appear soft!

Bullying and aggression

Much that we have described so far comes under the heading of non-explicit aggressive behaviour. However, there is also a great deal of explicitly aggressive behaviour among boys at schools. Our observations in a variety of schools indicate that boys from all social classes and ethnic groups are involved in bullying or aggressive behaviour. Additionally, there was much racist bullying specifically affecting children from black and ethnic minority groups.

Apart from physical bullying we have heard a great amount of verbal abuse so common as to become part of 'normal' speech. Clearly much of the verbal abuse was homophobic, since much was done and said by boys which seemed to be based on the need to prove that they were not homosexual and that they despised homosexuality. If a boy physically touched another boy in any way other than aggressively he was likely to be called a 'poof' or 'queer'. In discussion with a first-year class of boys we asked whether they had wanted to come to a boys' school. Every boy in the class said 'no'. When asked why, one boy said he was worried his friends would think he was 'queer'. Another actually said he was worried that he would *become* 'queer' at the school. This attitude and the subsequent behaviour reinforces oppression of gay people and especially gay boys and pupils in the school. It also ensures the continuation of an aggressive social relationship, reinforces 'norms' of 'masculinity' and reflects the degree and urgency with which boys must actively defend this masculine identity. It seemed as though one of the most virulent insults that could be directed at most boys (judging by the strength of their reaction) was to be called 'soft' or 'wimp' or 'poof', 'coward' or something to that effect. This sort of insult usually resulted in the 'necessity' to retaliate aggressively in order to demonstrate the untruth of the accusation. Indeed, the insult itself often seemed to be issued as provocation or as a 'signal' for aggression.

Equally common was abuse describing female sex organs, 'cunt' being the most common. Curiously this seemed acceptable to most boys and did not cause any particular retaliation. An exception was when this form of abuse was used against mothers. This led to the boy defending his mother's honour and, by inference, his own, and sometimes to physical violence.

Bullying among boys at school, both within and outside the classroom, appeared to be chronic. Almost all the teachers we met complained about it. Pupils, too, frequently mentioned bullying:

Paul: There are some boys in the class who are always proving how hard they are. I haven't had a fight for a while, but if any one does bother me I'm ready to beat them up although I don't like fighting.

Derek: I keep a low profile, keep myself to myself really. There's always some kind of trouble going on, but I keep out of it if I can.

We suggest that to some extent it is bound up with 'acting out' the power structures within the school itself (and in wider society). One dimension of bullying has to do with the way physical power and strength are part of stereotyped male attributes. Bullying is a major way in which boys are able to demonstrate their manliness. Even though a boy might be physically weaker than another, to be able to 'take it like a man' is usually considered to be a good second-best masculine quality. In this sense, bullying can be seen as a manifestation of pressures put on boys to conform to male stereotypes. While we acknowledge that bullying also takes place among girls, we do not regard it as a gender issue in the same way. It conflicts with, rather than reinforces, stereotyped notions of 'femininity'.

Bullying is also a gender issue because of its implications for the ways in which males may relate to each other and to women in particular. The status given to the strong and the lack of status given to the weak creates power structures which are also reflected in male–female relationships. Stereotyped 'norms' encourage a dominant male role. (For example, the 'hen-pecked' husband is the butt of much humour.) Bullying becomes one way of gaining or expressing power and dominance over women.

In a boys' school there may be an increase in the extent of bullying among boys because it is an all-male environment. If it is true that weaker boys 'take the place' of girls at boys' schools by providing a 'butt' for proving masculinity, then perhaps bullying should not be regarded as essentially different from sexual harassment. It may be that it is simply a different expression of a power-play underlining both. The need to confirm aspects of 'masculinity' which involve competitive definitions of strength and power (perhaps especially exacerbated in the strong male ethos of the boys' schools) must be recognised as an element involved in attempts to explain the extent of violence by boys in school. Additionally, Suleiman and Suleiman (1985) argue that boys' response to competitive situations in the school may be with racist and sexist abuse, threats and physical violence.

Strangely, there seems to have been little research into the gender implications of bullying and violence in schools.[1] The fact that there is a need for research which will add to our understanding of bullying and violence in schools *is* supported by the findings of some small-scale surveys that have been conducted by LEAs. While not looking into the *type* of bullying, these have shown, for example, that in ILEA 22 per cent of the parents of eleven-year-olds identify bullying as a problem for their children. John and Elizabeth Newson (1984) also found bullying a problem in their account of the upbringing of 700 Nottingham children. Over one quarter of the parents of eleven-year-olds they interviewed knew their children were being bullied. Olweus (1978) found that bullying is two to three times more common among boys than girls. Many more boys than the 22 per cent reported in the ILEA study may be affected by bullying at school. When observing classes where bullying was actually taking place, we noticed that even if children were not directly affected (as the bully or the bullied) the fact that bullying was going on was very clearly recognised by all the boys in the class, and this put many constraints on everyone's behaviour — they had to 'watch their step' constantly in case they were the next victim, as our interviews with boys show. In addition, as parents, we both know of various occasions where our own children have been seriously bullied in school. Although we both initially reported incidents to the respective schools, neither of us liked the way it was handled and have not reported some subsequent incidents.

Boys' attitudes to teaching methods

In our own experience and the experience of the many teachers we have conferred with, certain teaching methods have fairly predictable outcomes in boys' classrooms. Some types of discussion and collaborative teaching methods are particularly difficult with boys. The difficulties relate to the sorts of observation we have made concerning ways in which boys communicate their competitive behaviour, the types of activity they identify as 'male' or 'female' and related valuation of these. Boys' expectations and perceptions of what is 'appropriate' education derive from the 'norms' and values of the school itself. These are discussed in Chapter 3.

There is a strong notion among many boys of what constitutes 'real work' and what does not. 'Real work' is usually written work. It is *product*-orientated. It is instantly recognisable as being about a particular subject, especially if it is a 'real' subject such as science or mathematics. Furthermore, most boys do not seem to regard talk-related activities as 'real' work.

While girls may also have a low opinion of the 'worth' of these activities in terms of school achievement, they will probably also value them as appropriate 'female' activities. This results in not only different attitudes towards various subjects, but also very different attitudes to different ways of organising work within a given subject, particularly as relates to talk or interactive activities.

Discussion methods are a good example of the sort of activity generally devalued among boys. There are other reasons why boys may find discussion difficult which relate to the ways they are less able to behave supportively towards each other. The degree of their competitiveness, inability to listen to one another, and lack of skill at verbal interaction (confined to a fundamental devaluing of discussion as a worthwhile process) can make it extremely difficult to have productive class discussions. Having said so, however, it is important to point out that this is very much affected by what sort of discussion is being set up. In classes where discussion is used regularly as a valued and established activity, boys may participate enthusiastically. Discussions about sharing personal experience sometimes seemed to result in boys talking in extremely generalised or stereotyped terms, not listening to each other and complaining that they were wasting time. Interestingly, this was not the case in the first weeks after transferring from primary school. But the school setting soon 'taught' them not to 'open up' in front of classmates.

As already discussed these observations also relate to collaborative tasks. Boys often do not communicate sufficiently to plan or organise what they intend to do, and may end up each doing his own separate work, or else with one boy taking total responsibility while the others opt out completely.

As we will argue in the next chapter, school itself fosters an individualistic and competitive approach to learning, with children being measured and assessed against each other. These are characteristics regarded as 'typically' 'male' (while supportive, co-operative behaviour is 'typically' 'female', as women take the 'caring' supportive role in society). From our observations, it does seem that many boys and girls are set on to these paths, and do develop along these lines. A co-operative approach to collaborative activities is often fairly alien to many boys.

Notes

1 We made a search of the *British Humanities Index, British Education Index, London Bibliography of the Social Sciences, Register of the Educational Research in the UK., Index to Theses* (Universities of Great Britain and Northern Ireland), and the *Journal of Educational Research* (USA), and could not find anything about bullying and violence among boys at school or about social interaction among boys.

CHAPTER 3

Sexism in the School Structure and Organisation

So far we have discussed ways in which boys' behaviour in school may be problematic. However, we now go on to argue that in exploring the roots of the problem we must not only focus on the boys themselves but on the structure and organisation of the school system. We have become increasingly aware that there are almost infinite layers and levels which have to be considered if strategies adopted in the classroom with boys are to be more than merely cosmetic. Segregated boys' schools are one mechanism by which sex roles are reinforced. This is not to say that we think that boys' schools are more 'sexist' institutions, but that since they are predominantly all-male institutions, the sexism in them is very overt. The same structures and organisation will also perpetuate sexual divisions in mixed and girls' schools, but perhaps not be so easily recognisable. In our view the study of boys' schools provides an important model for the analysis of sexism in all schools.

In our society institutions are organised in such a way that power and success are derived from competitive, divisive and hierarchical structures. The only way we can achieve power and success within society (unless we are born in a rich or powerful position) is to conform to the rules of the institution. The continued dominance of some groups in society is dependent on their internalising and perpetuating establishment values. The result of this association between 'success' in a patriarchal capitalist system and those who hold the power in it is the identification of the system's characteristics with 'male' characteristics: such behaviour as competitiveness, aggressiveness and ambitiousness are seen as 'masculine' behaviours. Schools, as social institutions, are established as 'masculine' structures in which boys and girls need to operate in 'masculine' terms in order to succeed. This is particularly evident in all-boys' schools, where the expression of 'masculine' structures may be exaggerated.

In our report (Askew and Ross 1984) of work in one boys' school we tentatively suggested a direct association between the school organisation, policies on discipline and teaching methods, and the gender behaviour and relations we observed: 'We believe that boys' schools are usually built on values of competition, strength and power; bullying and "running down" become norms of gaining status'. This belief has been reinforced by our subsequent work in other boys' schools. Other research has made similar associations. Davison (1985) writes about being struck by what he considers the 'charged, hard-edged nature of life in a boys' school'. He argues that: 'The many elements that comprise the ethos of the school can perpetuate and, indeed, create the aggression a school seeks to control'. He states that there is a clear need for research in boys' schools into such things as the forms and manner of discipline; teaching styles; teacher expectations of pupil behaviour and the organisational structure of the school. The rest of this chapter is concerned with our research into these issues.

Discipline and authority in boys' schools

Discipline in boys' schools is often characterized by authoritarian power and control through strength. Whether or not male teachers actually use violence against pupils (and we have known cases where they have), boys we interviewed revealed that they *think* that violence will be used against them if they step out of line with a male teacher.

> John: I'm dead sure that if we acted up with Mr.—— he'd clobber us.
> Luke: He tells us he'll string us up against the wall if we don't shut up!

While such threats may be made with little intention of enforcement, nevertheless they encourage and reinforce the idea that discipline can only be attained and maintained by the 'strong' male teacher! Such attitudes make the discipline difficult for non-authoritarian teachers.

Teachers have discussed ways in which the aggression among boys is a reflection of the authoritarian structures within the school. For example, a male Head of Year in a boys' school which has made considerable strides towards analysing the issues and developing strategies to deal with them, reports to us in an interview:

> I think that bullying is often an acting out of the power structures of the school itself rather than the fault of individual boys. This discussion has come up very often in the last couple of weeks where we've been talking about the fact that, although we're shifting now, it has very much been a male structure and it might be more useful to look at a responsibility structure. The whole way of relating to boys in this school seems to come from a punitive approach and a blaming approach. There's a deficiency model and it's very aggressive. So you can imagine someone, kind of ticking along saying: 'Don't you dare bully this boy' and it's a kind of contradiction in terms where the actual process is in direct conflict with what's actually being said. I think one of the most important things is for people to become aware of how they deal with an issue like bullying. So it's not just a curricular thing, it's a school structure as well. Women are notable by their absence within our hierarchical structures so, although it's male-orientated, aggressive style if you like and a dominant style of dealing with someone who's gone against the rules or their behaviour is deficient in some way, the message is: 'This is how you get what you want', and I think they go: 'Ah ha', you know, 'This is the way'. So there's a modelling thing going on as well and it's very much a male modelling thing.
>
> I think there's probably a whole ethos where there's bullying as a way of going on. So I can see that bullying is, apart from obvious specific issues, a thread running through the way boys relate to one another. They see it as a competitive thing rather than a collaborative thing. That's how you establish yourself.

Another teacher talked to us about how he believes the means of controlling the boys within the structure of his school set up destructive power relationships:

> People don't have to feel it's a control issue and a power issue. I'm not saying that you don't need certain dynamics going on in

the classroom in order for people to pay attention, take information in. I think that's essential. It's a case of how that particular classroom climate comes about and whether you're there to educate or control, and the sorts of methods by which control is achieved seem to me too often to rely on an aggressive style and a controlling style. I think you can see a shift in our school to sharing the power with the class so that they engage much more in their own learning. A negotiated position that has real meaning for them means that you don't fall into the power thing again afterwards or they see the negotiation as a totally empty gesture. I think this power model is fundamentally a male model. I base this on my observation of how men behave. Also because it's by and large men who inhabit those regions. Also, for women to get into that structure they have to play out the man's game. It's sort of in order to establish credibility or some kind of equality in the situation they feel they need to be seen in those positions of power. I feel it's more useful to question the structure than to get into what's already there. I think it is a male structure because I think women are much more ready to be supportive to one another. I don't know why. It might be that the factor of oppression *caused* women to be more supportive because they had to. I think it's a much more useful way of working. I don't think men have that ability as much.

Apart from the maintenance of discipline and authority in boys' schools by actual and threatened physical punishment, there are other ways in which boys are kept 'in check' which also rely on power and strength, for instance, loud shouting at the boys to 'shut up'. When a boy *has* misbehaved it is usually dealt with in an individual and 'crisis-orientated' way. The individual boy is sent to see the (usually) male Head of House, Year or Department. Undisciplined behaviour is most usually an outcome of social relationships and is quite often something which involves *all* the boys in a class, not just one. For instance, it is fairly accepted that when the one pupil who is the 'bane' of the teacher's life ('if only he wasn't there the teaching would be easy') is removed, another invariably takes his place. There is constant peer-group pressure on individual boys to take the role of the joker or the class bully, or the disruptive pupil. The only way, we feel, to deal with this is to make bad behaviour in the class a subject for discussion. The Head of House who comes into the classroom to reprimand the class and warn them, is reinforcing the idea that the responsibility for behaviour lies solely with the teacher who is big enough and loud enough to enforce it. This attitude denies the possibility of pupils being self-disciplined or being able to co-operate for their own self-interest and out of consideration for others. Our evidence suggests that instead it is based on fear and power of the big over the small, the man over the boy and the adult over the child. It perpetuates the notion that pupils behave better with 'tough' and 'strict' teachers and undermines teachers who prefer not to rely on these methods of discipline. We have frequently heard some men and women teachers described as 'too soft'. Implicit in this description is the idea that the 'soft' teacher is a *bad* teacher.

The fact that the 'hard' teacher is setting impossible (even undesirable) norms and expectations is never raised. Although negotiated methods of discipline and authority *can* work within a school where norms are different, an incredible amount of work is needed to reach that point and often the strengths of 'soft' teachers go unrecognised. For instance, one of the hardest-working, creative and 'soft' teachers in a particular school, who did not work in an authoritarian way, was congratulated not on her hard work and skill but on her *luck* in having such a nice class of boys. These kinds of assumption, too, affect the ways in which some teachers respond to complaints about bad behaviour: 'He's not like that with me' suggests that the teacher is at *fault*, rather than that bad behaviour is unacceptable *whoever* the teacher.

In addition, there may be other consequences of discipline gained through aggressive methods. O'Hagan and Edmunds (1982) interviewed pupils to find their response to the different ways in which teachers respond to disruptive behaviour. They interviewed sixty girls and sixty boys aged thirteen and fourteen years. The result of the research showed that aggressive teaching strategies, which may appear initially to be effective in controlling misbehaviour, could well have deleterious consequences in other ways — such as the increased likelihood of truancy.

The pastoral system

The pastoral system in boys' schools is clearly directly related to discipline structures within the school. It usually takes the form of a House system rather than a year system. This means that some pupils in each year of the school belong to the same 'House'. Although in theory there are advantages to the system (such as boys getting a sense of and feeling part of the whole school, breaking down boundaries between peer-groups, allowing house tutors to get to know whole families) in practice it is often rooted in competition — one 'House' against the other. The following is typical of comments made to us: 'There's no kind of pastoral programme in my school. It's thought this would take time away from more important things. Pastoral care is simply seen in terms of dealing with individual ''problems'' '. Teachers in boy's schools have complained to us that the pastoral system in their schools is more concerned with the social control of boys rather than with developing an overview of pupils' achievement and progress or social well-being. Much of what seems to go under the heading of 'pastoral care' therefore appears to be somewhat negative. Pastoral care is identified in some boys' schools with 'problems', for example, truancy and bad behaviour. The positive aspects are very often lost: for example, ensuring a point of continued personal contact, offering guidance on personal or educational issues, or career development. This has contributed to a split between the academic and the pastoral. In many of the schools in which we have worked, if discipline deteriorated it was the responsibility of the Head of House (pastoral) rather than the Head of Department (academic). This invested certain members of staff with an aura of power in the eyes of the pupils. Why not share that responsibility by sending for the teacher next door or form tutor?

The social control element of the pastoral care system also results in and perhaps intensifies the 'labelling' process which occurs in schools. Because pupils tend to remain in the same house, with the same Head of House from the first to the fifth year, once they are labelled 'disruptive' they cannot easily lose that label. If the responsibility for discipline problems were spread more widely this might not happen so readily.

Competition

Most learning in schools, as we have observed, is based on
competition. Children learn very early to see themselves as
better or worse at writing, reading, running, drawing, than
other children. The measure is how well they compare with
every one else, not whether they are making progress. This
approach to learning is reinforced by systems of stars, marks,
tests and teachers comparing pupils. The examination system is
a competitive system, with marks graded so that only a certain
percentage can attain high grades each year. In all these ways,
boys' schools are similar to other schools.

However, we feel that in boys' schools this competitiveness is
more overt. In this society a high value is placed on
competitiveness and it has become one of the stereotypical traits
associated with masculinity. In mixed or girls' schools the
competitiveness at the basis of all education in the system has
been blurred, due to the presence of girls and a larger number of
female staff. This is not to say that women and girls are not
competitive or that competition isn't inherent in mixed and
girls' schools. The point is the manifestation of competition will
be less extreme and therefore less visible. Whether or not to
encourage competition in girls has become a controversial issue.
Some argue that we are all 'naturally' competitive and point to
the way in which even small children boast 'I'm better than you,
na na na-na na'. (However, it seems to us hardly surprising that
this should be so given the kinds of comparisons which adults
make so frequently.) Other people argue that, given the system
as it is, the best we can do is instil in our pupils as great a
competitive spirit as possible so that they will struggle more
determinedly for success. This view sometimes concurs with
calls for fewer 'progressive' teaching methods, and perhaps
even a feeling that the 'good old days' of selection and grammar
school education should be brought back. Given the lack of
power which most of us feel in terms of actually changing the
present system, it is tempting to opt for this view. One teacher
put the dilemma as follows:

It comes right down to what school is about. Some people argue
that school has to reflect how society is, so after all it is a

competitive world and if kids are going to fit into it you have to make them competitive. Or whether schools can be an agent of change and it doesn't have to be dog eat dog.

Whether or not schools can be agents of change, we think that a competitive ethos does not aid learning. We think that more is likely to be learned *and* remembered if pupils work in a way which motivates and engages them in classroom activities. Reducing stress levels and improving social relationships is also particularly important.

Hierarchies in school

In the thirty or so boys' schools that we have visited, we have found it rare for women to be in senior management positions. Women are in the minority. Where women have posts of responsibility they tend to be in the humanities, languages or special needs departments. Decision-making in boys' schools tends to reflect the male authoritarian make-up of the school. There may on the surface appear to be a democratic decision-making structure. For example, we observed staff meetings where all staff were invited to 'air' their opinions. However, these meetings were often run on hierarchical lines, with the Head or senior management in the chair, and members of staff sitting in rows listening. One male member of staff talked to us about the problem of a hierarchical structure as follows:

> There seems to be a really deep kind of hierarchical structure and it seems to be that, in order to be successful, you have to rise up through the ranks and each stage you go up you seem to be removed further from colleagues down there somewhere. There's a kind of psychological distance, and to me it seems like a communication distance as well. The power seems to be in terms of you can tell people what to do — you have this duty. I think, because of the psychological distance, it doesn't allow for any support to go on. I don't think that people, therefore, can feel any ownership in their work situation and it's very stressful or potentially very stressful. I think when people are involved and engaged their motivation is there. And also, if there is a consultative structure or a very flat hierachy, then it's possible to

set up situations where people are able to consult perhaps in smaller groups and still have the links between the groups. It's possible for people to relate on a much more equal footing, and I think you make much better use of expertise. I think if people are experiencing difficulty or are feeling dissatisfied with anything that's going on, then rather than perhaps store it inside or resent their job or feel angry with other people, it can be aired. Or, if people need support or are having a terrible time — you know, it's OK to be vulnerable. The other model suggests that any sign of vulnerability is not fitting with this model, which, I think, is essentially a male model. The responsibility model is a support model. You may have responsibility for a particular area of work, but you have a more humane thread running through it.

In terms of the way in which pupils view teachers, there is a need to combat hierarchism. It may convey strong messages about who is to be granted respect in the institution and ideas about inferiority and superiority in relation to gender, race and class. Ways in which that power could be more equally shared include involving junior colleagues in decisions on discipline. Senior colleagues asking junior colleagues' opinions both in meetings and in front of pupils, junior colleagues being seen in a position where they are expert, knowledgeable or have particular skills outside their own classroom situation, for example, by taking assemblies.

The 'male' curriculum

The curriculum in boys' schools may also reinforce traditional male roles. We observed a heavy emphasis on competitive sport and on traditional 'male' subjects such as design and technology and science, while traditionally 'female' subjects such as home economics and child development were not on offer. Within the subjects, study centres on white male achievement in a predominantly Eurocentric way, for example, in science and in history. We also saw in the sixth form little provision for the arts and humanities. Many materials and resources used as part of these courses had a racist/sexist and class bias. For example, positive images of black girls and boys and of white girls were absent; in history, the struggles and resistance of black people were often invisible, as was the contribution made by women of all ethnic groups to historical developments. In school libraries the books on the shelves also reflected this bias. In our experience boys' schools are no worse than mixed or girls' schools in relation to this, and many individual teachers in these schools are struggling to make changes and write their own materials. But in boys' schools many teachers we spoke to do not see the point of addressing gender issues. For example, one teacher said: 'Why bother so much about whether or not there are pictures of girls when it doesn't matter so much because there aren't any here?' In our view, it is important to present positive images to girls with which they can identify, but also to present to boys alternatives to the predominantly white, middle-class, male view of the world. In any consideration of the curriculum questions should be asked about *who* controls what knowledge should be made available to children..

Attitudes towards boys as a reflection of the school ethos

We have argued that 'strength' plays an important part in the control of boys in schools. It is not surprising, therefore, that there tends to be a fairly uncritical view within the schools towards some forms of boys' aggressive behaviour. For example, frequent comments such as 'Boys will be boys' or 'That's just like a boy' are made with reference to aggressive behaviour by boys to each other. Indeed, the expectations that boys will be aggressive towards each other are often reflected in some teachers' beliefs about boys. Comments such as 'He's a cissy', or 'He's got to learn to take it like a man', carry implicit assumptions about 'normal' behaviour in boys. In our experience, a pervasive 'masculine' ethos is inherent in boys' schools — a kind of 'all boys together' feeling which reflects uncritically aggressive 'male' stereotypes. A woman teacher commented to us:

> Many of the men like and care about the kids very much. But they often show it by fighting! It's joke fighting of course, and both the boys and the men think it a lot of fun, but women would rarely relate to the boys like that.

This relates to what Davison (1985) has called 'the common culture of maleness': 'Male teachers in an all-boys classroom have access to this shared culture from which female teachers are debarred'. Margaret Sandra (1982) also found that 'all boys' or 'all girls' situations 'engender a particular atmosphere which has sufficient degree or consensus that conflict between pupils and pupils and teachers ... is much reduced and disruptive behaviour is confined'. This may reinforce the particular expectations of boys and girls in this society and perpetuate sexist assumptions.

The very reasons why some parents have stated they sent their sons to boys' schools are to do with this 'masculine' ethos. The following comments were made to us by parents we talked to: 'He's a bit "soft". I thought coming here would toughen him up. He's got to learn to stand up for himself'. 'I've sent my boy here because I want him to have more discipline. I like the fact that there's a cadet corps here'.

Teaching styles and school values

We have suggested that certain activities and teaching methods reflect 'norms' and values of the school (which we asserted are 'male' qualities and values) and thereby reinforce stereotypical 'masculine' behaviour in the boys. We also implied that this might explain the resistance and difficulty that many boys display when confronted with collaborative work, or non-product-orientated activities.

From primary school, activities are credited with being either 'work' or 'play' — 'If you do your maths and writing work you may do art work or look at books during your free time'. Notions of 'real work' and 'non-work' are clearly built into school life, and schools tend to value activities with visible end-products over activities with none. This is true also in general societal terms. 'What did you do today?' 'Nothing. I just visited a friend!', or 'I just read; I didn't do anything'. Generally speaking, what is valued in society (and school) relates to the stereotypical 'male role' of 'make' and 'do'. Interactive activities which relate to the 'female role' of social intercourse (and generally do not result in an end product) are not afforded the same status or recognised as 'real' or worthwhile activities, and are devalued accordingly.

While all school children work within this value system and will internalise it to some extent, our evidence shows that boys are more likely to do it to a far greater extent. In our view this is because it reflects and reinforces the qualities considered 'male' which boys have learned not only to develop in themselves, but to define the boundaries of behaviour. In this way, certain activities may be seen as a 'threat' to their masculinity.

Authoritarian teaching styles, where teachers place themselves in a dominant role in terms of both knowledge and control of behaviour, tend to reinforce power structures of 'weak' and 'strong', as well as 'right' and 'wrong' (in the sense of what is valuable to know). We feel this results in yet another way that status is achieved in terms of a power relationship. This is not to say that teachers should relinquish their role of creating a structure in which pupils can feel safe and secure and know what is expected of them.

Some teachers, we observed, worked towards maintaining class discipline through alternative methods, drawing their status from mutual respect established within the classroom. Methods they used included attempting to develop genuine relationships with the boys; helping the boys talk about their behaviour; breaking down the 'macho' approach to discipline; helping to develop collective responsibility as opposed to individual responsibility as a way of working toward collaboration rather than competition; and generally helping to develop pupil autonomy through facilitation and guidance; working towards developing a supportive atmosphere where boys no longer feel under as much pressure to 'take it like a man'. Two important results of adopting alternative teaching styles might be to provide a model and validation of behaviour and interaction which does not rely on power and strength.

We have argued that the value system implicit in schools will reflect that of the white, middle-class male value system in wider society. It follows that the status and value ascribed to teachers will reflect this to some extent. It may be, therefore, that any teacher who is not white, male or middle-class starts from a position of automatic disadvantage in many respects. Boys clearly seem to have different expectations of their male and female teachers. They expect dominant, authoritarian behaviour from some male teachers (at least initially). Not only do boys expect male teachers to be authoritarian figures but, when they are, it confirms boys' expectations and provides a role model of masculinity in terms of superior power or strength. The boys' deference to these male teachers is in terms of power relationships rather than drawing respect from other criteria. There are various important ways that men and women teachers occupy different social positions within the classroom, and we discuss these in the next chapter.

CHAPTER 4

Women Teachers' Experiences

Women teaching in boys' schools often find themselves in a particularly difficult position. Although women's individual social position, circumstances, backgrounds and attitudes may vary considerably, we noted certain common experiences. These related to the ways women teachers are perceived, undermined and sexually harassed. The issues we shall discuss in this chapter have been raised by women teachers while working within schools, in schools' women's groups, in workshop situations and at several conferences (both mixed and women only).

A recent ILEA Report (1985) stated that the main difficulties women face in boys' schools are: isolation, sexual harassment and an undervaluing of their contribution to school responsibilities. Among problems mentioned were hostility of male staff and discrimination by management and governors over appointments, including direct discrimination at the short-listing stage, unacceptable questions being asked at interviews, and general pressure or intimidation to prevent women seeking promotion. The extent of such incidents has led us to focus on the common context of women's experience in school, and to ask questions about its essential nature. The pattern which emerged clearly indicated that these difficulties and observations occurred directly in relation to institutional elements.

This, for us and for many women teachers, has been a crucial recognition. It has meant that, instead of identifying ourselves as failing or deficient, we now are beginning to examine what it

55

is about the school as an institution that creates these situations. Being able to locate the source of our difficulties in the structure and organisation of the school itself begins to give us some defence against the way schools usually locate the problems in us, the women teachers (for example, 'not being able to cope', being 'too soft'). By sharing our experiences in the school situation we can effectively identify the underlying sexism of the institution.

Some of the comments that women make in this chapter are specific to boys' schools. However, the issues we look at will be useful to those interested in exploring the more subtle forces at work within mixed schools which affect women's position, roles and status.

Teaching styles and boys' attitudes

As we argued in the last chapter, women are at an automatic disadvantage in schools run on authoritarian lines. When a school is run on the basis of 'authority equals strength and power' and discipline is seen in terms of control, women may find it extremely difficult to operate. When there is this sort of prevailing 'macho' atmosphere in the school, there is intense pressure for teachers to adopt authoritarian teaching styles or be seen as incompetent. Many women can find they are unable to work along these lines. They have described how they feel that whatever alternative strategies they try they are inevitably understood in terms of the 'norms' of the school. Women teachers who attempt to establish discipline through developing relationships with pupils and reasoning with them, rather than dictating to them, will probably be seen as 'soft' teachers who are taken less seriously than 'hard' teachers. One woman described this to us as follows: 'I hate the way that bullying passes for teaching and discipline in lessons and in the corridors. It makes my way of working with pupils seem weak to them'. This is not to imply that all women are unable or unwilling to work in authoritarian ways. But there are various reasons why women teachers may not wish to, or might find it difficult. Often it can simply be a matter of smaller stature and a higher voice that makes authority through physical (or vocal) threat difficult. There is also the expectation that women, just because they are women, will take on a 'mothering' role. 'Women teachers are more understanding', a male pupil told us. 'I suppose a lot of women can adopt a much more friendly, caring approach', a male teacher said. In an authoritarian institution, measures of success are inextricably bound up with 'good discipline'. A good teacher is seen as one who can 'control' the class. As one woman teacher explained: 'It doesn't matter what I try to do in my lessons, or how creatively or conscientiously I prepare them — most male colleagues see me as a "useless" teacher because my lessons are noisy'.

In this atmosphere, many women have described to us the necessity to abandon teaching styles based on equality and mutual respect, and attempt (however unsuccessfully) to conform to the norms of the system:

> I feel when I teach boys I have to be much more authoritarian and aggressive than I want to be, otherwise they take absolutely no notice.

> I have had to prove myself as a strict, tough teacher ... but there are still some boys who don't rate me at all as an authority — and sometimes they'll laugh at me.

> Authority in my school is in terms of bullying or intimidation. Some women yell wildly because they can't use muscle mass as a threat or are so frustrated. I personally have little problem since I teach small groups in a team situation with a woman Head of Department who has learned to threaten like the men.

> I feel in a dilemma as a woman teacher. Whatever I do, I feel I end up reinforcing the norms of how teachers should behave in a boys' school ... By adopting a more authoritarian style, I feel I'm validating this way of teaching and invalidating alternative methods. Yet if I take a more creative approach, I'm 'acting like a woman'.

Clearly, not all men are able or even want to teach in heavy-handed authoritarian ways. Some will face their own version of disciplinary problems or ridicule for failing to conform to stereotyped expectations. None the less, because the threat of physical power is central to an authoritarian structure many men teachers need not overtly express their physical authority — it is implicit in the ethos of the school itself. This compounds the situation, since it means that there will be some men who will be able to teach in less overtly authoritarian ways without 'discipline problems'. Therefore, it appears that it is the incompetence of women that causes their own problems with pupil control, rather than anything about the school itself. The fact is that generally men, by virtue of being men, are backed up by the system, while women are undermined by it.

This may seem to lead to a conclusion that women have no place teaching boys, particularly in a boys' school. But there is more involved than the ability to maintain control. The ways that women suffer or have difficulty within an authoritarian system highlight the norms of that system. The implications for the ways boys will develop and the values they will hold within a system that equates physical power with strength and 'might with right' are very frightening. Some of its effects are evident in women teachers' experience of boys' attitudes towards them. These observations clearly underline the values and behaviour that the boys are being taught by the school to validate and emulate. These women teachers made the following comments to us:

> Some boys in my class are always doing things that are intended to demonstrate that I have no power over them. Often it's very subtle — maybe just the way they look at me or their tone of voice. Of course, sometimes, it's very out-front and unbelievably rude, sexist comments, answering back or direct challenges.

> Several boys in the class have told me I should try to 'teach more like a man'.

> Boys have told me outright that they would never behave in a man teacher's class the way they do in mine.

> My experience of teaching boys is that the style of presentation must always be tough and no-nonsense or they disregard it. You must always be 100% on top of activities involving things like video operation or they delight that you don't understand equipment.

> In a boys' school, because of the lack of girls, the boys tend to notice the female staff and they often make unpleasant remarks and speak of them in a sexist way. Mind you, in a mixed school I guess the girls get it.

Boys we talked to said of their women teachers in interviews: 'She should act more like a man teacher', or 'She's a soft woman teacher'. Some women said they adopt more authoritarian methods simply to survive: 'I feel when I teach boys I have to be much more authoritarian and aggressive than I want to be, otherwise they take absolutely no notice'. And another woman: 'As a woman teacher in an all-boys school I feel almost "invisible" sometimes. I think there is a male culture in the classroom that I can never enter into'.

Michelle Stanworth (1981) found that: 'Both boys and girls feel more at ease, more attentive and more able to participate in classroom activity when they are taught by teachers of their own sex'. When one of us first began teaching in an all-boys school she was struck by the initial lack of friendliness from the boys. Early on, she heard one boy greet a woman teacher in a friendly way when he passed her in the playground. Another boy, overhearing, said to him: 'You big poof'. In her experience of teaching in mixed schools there didn't seem to be this pressure on boys not to be friendly to women teachers. Boys' schools, on the whole, do not seem to encourage close, non-aggressive friendly relations between either the boys themselves or the boys and staff. Jon Davison (1985) investigated boys' attitudes to women teachers. He says that a typical comment from a fourth-year boy was:

> At an all-boys school, boys are more liable to respect a male teacher than a female one. The female teacher would be more vulnerable to mickey-taking, lip and cheek. Whereas if a man was teaching, the boys might think twice.

Other remarks he mentions included: 'Women have to put up with abuse, dirty remarks'. 'You get away with murder with women teachers'. 'When men teachers shout, you shut up. When women shout you take no notice'. 'Women ain't strict ... they're fools'. Such remarks, in our opinion, reflect the overall position of women in the school and the general structure of power and control and attitudes to discipline cited in the previous chapter.

Carabis and Dodds (1984) also found that boys behave differently towards women teachers — that boys 'tried it on more'. They summed up boys' behaviour as including, in addition to explicit sexual harassment, looks, body language, verbal abuse and demeaning attitudes towards women.

They suggest that language can include a judgement of women based on their sexuality rather than ability to do the job.

Evidently most boys respect women teachers less than men as teachers and believe they learn more from men teachers. They often like and feel liked more by women, find them more understanding and their lessons more interesting and enjoyable. For example, a boy has said to us:

> You learn more in Mr ——'s class and Mr ——'s class because they really know how to control us. Lots of the women are a bit 'soft'. But you can talk to some of them. I like Ms ——'s class because it's the most interesting.

This quote indicates a confusion of values in the boys in that the qualities that bring them more warmth, understanding and pleasures are not worthy of respect. The boys not only learn that 'hard' behaviour is appropriate 'male' behaviour and 'soft' caring behaviour is female; but also that 'hard' is superior to 'soft', so they develop a disdain for what they identify as female behaviour, to be deplored and avoided at all costs.

Women teachers undermined

The undermining of women teachers may occur out of the 'best intentions', but reflects the assumptions and attitudes about women held by some male staff members. Women have described being undermined or being 'rescued' by men in several ways, including the following:

> I find myself being undermined by male colleagues — sometimes when they think they are 'protecting' me. For example, there's a man who teaches in the room across from me. Whenever the noise level in my lessons reaches a certain point, he'll burst into the room to quieten down the class or tell them off. It makes me feel totally stripped of authority in front of the boys.

> I sent a boy to the Head of Department (a man) over an episode where he spoke to me with abusive language. The Head of Department told the boy he 'shouldn't talk like that in front of Miss ——' — meaning the issue was that he had sworn in front of a woman.

I found a degree of protectiveness from the mainly male staff towards the small number of women staff. Soon after I arrived there was an incident between a boy and myself ... It was observed from the staffroom window by a male teacher who wanted to punish the boy. I reported that the matter was solved as far as I was concerned, but my male colleague was very rejected at not being able to leap to my defence.

On one occasion, when teaching a very difficult class of fourth years, bottom stream, who had responded well to me and were very attentive, I was interrupted by a man entering my room and, without any introduction, threatening any boy with a beating who caused me bother.

The point about 'rescuing' (however 'well meant') is that it expresses a fundamental belief that women are essentially less competent or weaker or less able to cope than men, and conveys these messages to boys. In a mixed school it also conveys messages to girls who are, in a sense, being 'told' what it means to be a female. This kind of subtle sexism is invisible yet likely to be internalised by all, boys, girls, men and women. This kind of 'protective' attitude to some women teachers is a result of assumptions made by some men based on the kind of stereotypes about women discussed in Chapter 1. The result for women may be an internalisation of their 'inferiority' and feelings of powerlessness and not being able to cope.

The way in which male colleagues react towards their female colleagues will reflect the stereotypes about women in relation to gender, race, class and sexuality. For example, some women teachers may not be patronised in a 'protective' way, but in other ways which are equally or more damaging. Older women may also suffer from being patronised in ways that are not specifically protective but give the message that they are generally useless and ineffectual.

Often women teachers who are having trouble with discipline in the school are themselves seen as the 'problem'. For example, one experienced woman teacher who came on a weekend course we ran for women teachers who worked with boys, came because both she and her Head had presumed that the course would 'help me learn how to handle the boys'. Another woman told us that when she reported to her Head of Department that she felt she was having discipline problems because the boys were not taking her seriously as a woman teacher, his response was: 'How about spending a couple of lessons observing John — I'm sure you'll learn a lot from him'. John was a very big man with a loud voice who, needless to say, had very few problems with discipline. This kind of comment indicates that the women teachers are very often identified as the 'problem', rather than the disciplinary structures in the school. Both men and women teachers who either do not want to, or cannot, fit into this aggressive style are labelled as 'unable to cope'.

There is a category of undermining behaviour towards women from some men that, we believe, is directly misogynistic and fully intended. Although many men do not behave in this way to women, it none the less appears to occur, can be very damaging, and can also be very subtle. Women have described to us incidents with male staff which they believed were deliberately aimed at making them feel belittled or humiliated:

> I was sitting in the staffroom at 5 pm when a male staff member asked me: 'Haven't you got a home to go to and a husband to cook for?'

> I've heard from pupils that some male teachers make sexist or racist jokes and comments to pupils as a regular part of their lessons.

> Some boys in my form have repeated some of the 'jokes' their (male) C.D.T. teacher has told them. I have to say I was shocked. They were really disgusting — the usual sexist jokes about women.

> I was told by a male Inspector, after a request to retrain in C.D. & T., that I did not look right for the part and maybe Home Economics would be more my line; and 'Why don't you go home and talk to your husband about your career prospects?'

> I sent a note to a male science teacher with my form when they were going to his lesson, asking him if he could complete and return their reports. He read it and then said aloud, in a fury and in front of my whole form: 'I'm not having any bitch tell me what to do'.

> After I'd dealt with an incident between two boys, a male colleague came up, asked for an account of what happened, and what I'd done, and then told the boys they were lucky it wasn't

him who'd seen them first — the implication being that I was a push-over.

I get comments about the way I dress, sometimes with direct sexual innuendo, from some men on the staff — sometimes right in front of the boys, too.

I feel I am dismissed and invisible in all sorts of ways by several men on the staff. I have to sustain a personal determination not to be discounted, but I would prefer not to have to resort to such tactics.

I was told by a senior member of staff, after an absence of three days, 'If the climate does not suit you, girl, why don't you go back home?'

What's a little girl like you doing with such a big red apple? (said to a 50-year-old woman teacher).

I was shown a newspaper clipping 'French women are dirty, they only change their knickers once a week' — and then he said to me 'You're French, you ought to know'.

Women who complain about this kind of treatment tend not to be treated seriously. They are quite likely to become the 'joke' feminist. If they complain they are likely to be labelled as 'nag', 'aggressive' or 'one-track-minded'. The woman is seen as wrong and unnatural, not 'feminine'. The common use of the term 'girl' when applied to women teachers is in itself disrespectful and undermining. Such behaviour makes it difficult for women teachers to criticise some male colleagues for their attitudes and behaviour.

Many women have complained to us that their observations, particular incidents and general difficulties are often not taken seriously by some male colleagues. They are made to feel foolish, told they are being 'hysterical' or 'neurotic', or else (most commonly) that they 'don't have a sense of humour' or are 'taking it too seriously'. The message, once again, is that the problems lie within the women themselves, are not real issues, and are not important: 'Whenever I complain of a sexist incident, the general male reaction is "Here she goes again" '. 'I can't tell you how many times I've been told "don't be hysterical" by male staff. They act like I'm imagining the whole problem — or else that *I* am the problem'.

Staff meetings

Women teachers are often subjected to undermining attitudes and behaviour at staff meetings. Dissatisfaction is usually focused on the way meetings are organised, or the way contributions from women are dismissed as of no value:

> Staff meetings are mostly a monologue from the Head, with contributions from senior staff (all male).

> When I do make a point, there is silence for a minute, then they continue as though I hadn't said anything. But often later on a man will repeat the point I made, and then it will be taken up.

It is evident that the organisation of staff meetings directly affects the position of women attending them. There is an unspoken, implicit value system in any method of organisation. When the organisation is in terms of a hierarchical structure, we believe this carries 'encoded' messages about power, status and value. And, of course, there is also the issue of who, within such a context, is 'worth' listening to. It is a structure loaded with values ascribed by the dominant groups within it: anyone not part of the dominant culture is likely to be dismissed — in some sense excluded before they begin.

Sexual harassment

Most points raised in this section can be subsumed under the heading 'implicit sexual harassment'. We interpret the term in its broadest sense; that is, all the ways that women are negatively affected by their position of social subordination. In the male institution of a boys' school sexual harassment may be 'invisible' because it is so 'normal' within the establishment.

In its broadest sense, sexual harassment (although varying in context, manifestation and degree) is a constant feature of women's lives. It usually has, on some level, an implied threat of violence. We define sexual harassment as any behaviour, however subtle, that identifies or responds to women as less than equal to, or primarily existing for, men. It expresses itself in all the ways women are physically or verbally assaulted, undermined, excluded, denied power, made invisible, expected to defer, held down and generally 'kept in their place' both by individual men and by male institutions.

Benn (1985) writes about sexual harassment in terms of the construction of masculinity:-

> The description 'sexual harassment' itself rings wrong. To me it conjures up images of 'moments', episodes of coercion, bad times ... but there is also something overwhelmingly ordinary, tedious and day-to-day about it. The point is, isn't sexual harassment really about masculinity? But shouldn't any campaign against it contain some recognition of, and commitment to change, masculinity — rather than simply to amend 'unacceptable', 'individual' 'male behaviour'?

Male domination depends upon the subordination of women. 'Femininity' is developed in relation to 'masculinity'. In one sense, everything which expresses the subordination of women is an expression of masculinity. The term 'masculinity' has become synonymous with power, and especially power over women.

The implications of defining sexual harassment in this way are enormous in the context of school, and boys' schools in particular. Schools are, after all, based on power relationships, for example, who has knowledge and who doesn't, adult and child. Sexual harassment is, in a sense, an expression of masculinity and this suggests that in an institution that is organised in overtly 'masculine' terms, values and attitudes which promote the subjugation of women must be absolutely implicit in its very structure. We have suggested that in boys' schools the curriculum, discipline, teaching, methodology and most interactions are displays of masculinity. One of the ways that boys are learning to define their own masculinity and notions about women is by this example of 'masculinity' and masculine behaviour.

Pat Mahoney (1985) has shown how girls are continually sexually harassed in mixed schools. In boys' schools that harassment is directed at the women staff. Below are some examples of the kinds of harassment women have talked to us about. Some of it is physical, for example:

> Every time I turned my back on a first-year class of boys, one of

them touched my bum. When I turned around they sat 'innocently'. I felt completely humiliated. How could they take me seriously as a teacher when they were touching my bum?

Some of it is sexual innuendo: 'I went in to cover a class of fifth-year boys I didn't know. As I walked in one of them said, "I wouldn't come in here if I was you, you might get raped"'. 'Sometimes it's something said that is supposed to be a joke but it leaves me feeling sick inside'. Some of it is about physical appearance: 'A male colleague said to me: "I'll bet you don't have any trouble with the sixth form boys when you wear that!"' Some of it is written: 'I'm forever finding obscene graffiti in our text books'. 'I've had some absolutely disgusting notes from pupils. I felt so ashamed of one that I never told anyone about it'. Some of it is belittling:

> I find boys especially difficult if I take them after they've had a lesson with a man teacher who's particularly 'big' and 'strong' in his approach to the class. Somehow, this always results in the boys laughing at me and joking about me really a lot.

Some of it is verbal abuse: 'I've been called an "old bag", a "slag", and a "whore" by some first-year boys'. None of these examples are about extreme, overt, violent sexual harassment. This is not because we have not heard about this sort of episode — we know it to exist. However, as physical attacks may be the only form of sexual harassment officially recognised, we are focusing on descriptions of less acknowledged forms of abusive behaviour towards women.

One disturbing aspect of sexual harassment in schools is the attitudes towards it expressed by male pupils. Carabis and Dodds (1984) write about the results of their interviews with boys on this subject: 'Boys we interviewed expressed surprise that women should object to this treatment as they consider it natural'. 'Part of the problem is that what we believe is sexual harassment is regarded as "natural" male behaviour'. Indeed, we believe it is this 'normality' of sexual harassment, its acceptance by our society, especially in male establishments, that renders it invisible and unrecognised except for the most extreme cases. So, in most institutions, there are rarely satisfactory channels for complaint by women who have been sexually harassed. Few schools have established effective procedures for dealing with sexual abuse.

The idea that women 'exaggerate' the problem, or get 'too het up' about it, is clear from descriptions given to us about the way many men in the senior hierarchy deal with it. Women have said that they are often asked to 'prove' the incident in a way which would be quite unheard of if a male member of staff were to accuse a boy of hitting him. The implication is that women are not to be believed. This, of course, further undermines a woman teacher if she has been sexually harassed. One Head of a boys' school even said to a group of women who went to him to discuss incidents of harassment in the school: 'We didn't have any problems with sexual harassment in the school until the Women's Group was formed'. This Head saw the women's group as encouraging their 'neuroses' rather than as giving women confidence and an understanding that their situation was not unique.

Many of the behavioural problems women teachers face from boys in their classrooms are directly related to issues of sexual harassment. Women often have difficulty in asserting authority because of not being taken seriously as women. This extends to the attitude that it is a woman's own fault if she has been heckled or sexually harassed in some way — it is a sign of her own incompetence as a teacher. Most women are therefore unable to make sexual harassment public without putting themselves in a vulnerable and even more difficult position.

The version of masculinity rooted in power and control is dependent upon a view of women as wishing to be overpowered and creating circumstances where they will be controlled. It assumes everything women do is with men in mind and will be motivated in some way to gain or reject male attention. In this way, women are also blamed for the more overt forms of sexual harassment, both in school and in society at large.

As we have intimated, one of the greatest difficulties about all but the most brutal forms of sexual harassment is making it visible and having it taken seriously. It is rarely censured because most of it is considered an expression of 'normal', 'healthy' masculinity. It is often described as 'harmless', 'innocent', or 'natural'. We believe that because dominant groups in society generally presume to 'know' what subordinate groups are like and what they want, they are generally surprised and disbelieving if they are told anything else. They reject anything else as atypical. We have seen women who refuse to behave in the role assigned to them being labelled as, at best, unusual, or as 'frustrated', 'aggressive' or 'abnormal'.

We have also heard male teachers suggest that women themselves collude in their own sexual harassment. By this they appear to mean that a woman teacher's behaviour is sometimes flirtatious or her dress is attractive. We disagree with this argument for several reasons:

1 the removal of moral responsibility for the harassment from the perpetrator to the 'victim';

2 the suggestion that because someone looks 'nice' it is all right to be rude to them, or even to attack them;

3 the reinforcement of the idea that women are sexual objects and should be reacted to as such, rather than out of respect for them as teachers.

In our experience there are some men in senior management who have difficulty with the idea that women, rather than senior management, should be involved with dealing with incidents of sexual harassment. In one school we visited, however, the male senior management do not deal with incidents of sexual harassment directly. In cases of sexual harassment boys are suspended and their parents are invited to a meeting with a member of the senior management and the woman involved or her woman representative. Before the boy is allowed back into school he is 'counselled' by two women on the staff who explain why his behaviour has caused offence (if he doesn't know), and it is carefully explained what the consequences of his actions will be in case of future incidents of this nature.

Below are some ideas on dealing with sexual harassment which came out of a weekend conference we organised for women teachers:

1 There needs to be a structure for dealing with sexual harassment — a consistent approach to the problem.

2 Sexual harassment must be made recognisable and visible.

3 It needs to be easily apparent that women are in an official position to respond to and deal with sexual harassment.

4 Women must have the option to have cases of sexual harassment dealt with by women only.

5 Women dealing with cases of sexual harassment should not be asked to break confidentiality. To spread details of incidents is to compound sexual harassment.

6 Sexual harassment must be put on the agenda for discussion in schools. It needs to be clearly defined in order to make it clear what it is and that it is not the 'fault' of individual women or girls.

7 A record of incidents should be kept to monitor the scope of the problem.

8 Sexual harassment undermines the woman teacher's authority — it should be made clear that sexual harassment does not occur because she cannot control the class.

The Women's Groups within the school

In a number of boys' schools a women's group has been formed to respond to and combat sexism. This can give women the opportunity to share experiences, support each other, identify issues of sexism within the school, and thus politicise themselves and begin to devise strategies for change.

Women's groups have been perceived as threatening, faced overt or open hostility and have been attacked as 'sexist' because of their exclusion of men. The idea that women-only meetings are 'sexist' indicates the misunderstanding which many people have about the term. Sexism stems from prejudiced and discriminatory attitudes together with the *power* to act on these assumptions. To argue that it is 'sexist not to allow men into women's groups' is to ignore the fact that in education, as in other areas, women are both stereotyped as inferior in many ways *and* that the control of the institution rests, to a large extent, in the hands of men. There are strong arguments for Womens' Groups. People who join together in order to confront and combat their victimisation are not *creating* the problem — they are *responding* to it.

Women's groups have found it productive to set particular objectives at a practical level as well as operating as a support and consciousness raising group. For instance women have reported that their group works best when they have a clear focus or task in mind. The women in a women's group may have very differing political perspectives and needs, and therefore the uniting feature may be the fact that they all work together towards a particular goal. For example, women's groups have organised conferences on sexism for their male colleagues; organised new courses on particular aspects of the curriculum; produced 'anti-sexist' posters and other materials; produced policies on such issues as sexual harassment.

Each school situation is different, will have different 'immovable' forces and different potential for change. Women's groups have started by looking for 'chinks' in their own school situations where inroads would be made.

We include here a set of suggestions for the type of activity which may be undertaken in Women's Groups which was drawn up at a conference for Women Teachers.

- Trying to make some specific objectives.
- Trying to include all the women in the school, where possible, not only teachers.
- Initiating things in other groups (Don't isolate yourselves).
- Consciousness raising.
- Giving one another support.
- Dealing with sexual harassment.
- Looking at the position of women teachers in the school and making suggestions.
- Taking on the planning of an anti-sexist conference or whole school meeting, etc.
- Practising difficult situations.
- Dealing with hostilities toward the women's group.
- Dealing with divisions within the group.
- Looking at curricula imbalance and content, including resources.
- Producing documents and written statements.
- Fighting invisibility in school meetings.
- Looking at sexist issues in relation to race and class issues.
- Producing own resources.
- Thinking about ways of working with the union.
- Assertion training.

A list of general problems at school with sexist implications was also drawn up. The areas pin-pointed by the women at the conference underscored the kinds of issues raised in our own experience and research, and reflect many points we raise in this book. The list includes:

- Curriculum imbalance.
- Forming a women's group (also dealing with divisions within it and hostilities towards it).
- Sexual harassment.
- Numbers of women teachers within the school: scales, position in hierarchy.
- Women's lack of access to effective discussion; structure of staff meetings; other meetings.
- Pressures on pupils from stereotyping.
- Parental contact; helping parents find ways of stating their criticism; positive involvement.
- Disseminating and implementing anti-sexist initiatives:
  (a) in the classroom (or as a specific course).
  (b) at a whole school level.
  (c) in terms of individual efforts.
  (d) resistance to change from other staff members.
- Curriculum content, materials used, etc. (as existing).
- Discipline.
- Amount and use of pastoral time.

This chapter has concentrated on some sexist experiences women have described in school, and some ways they are responding to this generally. In the next chapter we go on to look at specific anti-sexist strategies with boys in the classroom.

CHAPTER 5

Strategies for Working with Boys

Much of this chapter and the opinions expressed in it are built on our experience in one boys' school over a period of two years teaching and monitoring a course specifically set up to tackle issues of sexism and provide equal curricular opportunities. During the last three years we have both continued to work alongside teachers in the classroom and to develop materials for anti-sexist work with boys tried out in a wide range of different schools. (We include some examples of these materials in the text.)

It has been argued that anti-sexist work in school must be 'girl-centred education' (Weiner 1985). We accept that it is girls who are directly oppressed by sexism in school, as in many other areas of their lives, and that it is true that most education in schools is already 'boy-centred' in the sense that it is the achievement and experience of men which forms the greater part of the curriculum content. Boys, as we showed in Chapter 2, have also been labelled a 'problem' in the classroom — in relation to being more demanding and disruptive and therefore negatively affecting girls' experience of education in the mixed classroom.

Many teachers, however, are also concerned about the problems for the boys themselves. As we have argued, while girls and women are exploited and oppressed by sexism, boys are under unnecessary pressure in school to conform to masculine stereotypes which result in damaging expectations from both teachers and other boys, and stereotyped views of girls being reinforced. As we have shown earlier, boys are taught to compete with one another, to struggle to prove themselves physically, and quite literally to fight for status. Some may argue that working with boys on these issues is not in itself 'anti-sexist'. Trefor Lloyd (1985), a youth trainer who has done much work with boys on issues of manhood, masculinity and sexism, writes that:

> Boys' work, as I see it, *is not* anti-sexist work. Its focus is clearly with boys' needs and any work that is anti-sexist must, in my view, be primarily focused on young women (as the main 'victims' of sexism). However, I believe the *effects* of boys' work *are* anti-sexist. In doing this work the results appear to be an undermining of the young men's institutional sexism. As the young men's awareness of themselves grows, their need to participate and support abuse and containment of young women reduces.

We do not want to make a distinction between actually doing work with the boys and the effects of any such work. We argue, in fact, that it is the *intentions* which matter, and we intend that our work with boys challenges oppression and therefore includes an anti-sexist dimension.

We argued in the introduction to this book that for any school to tackle issues of power and inequality requires a fundamental reorganisation of the whole curriculum in terms of both the content and teaching methods (particularly with reference to which knowledge it is thought necessary to transmit). Such fundamental rethinking would have to be within the framework of challenging dominant and ethnocentric forms of knowledge. Such a new curriculum would be anti-sexist, as well as anti-racist and anti-classist, and equally accessible to *all* pupils. Change can happen at various levels. It can involve these kinds of fundamental change which challenge sexism at a structural level within the institution, or it can involve exploring attitudes and assumptions of teachers and pupils. This chapter describes work of the latter kind done with boys. We feel this is an important part of all pupils' education as it gives them awareness and understanding of sexist issues while, at the same time, offering them some strategies for coping. However, we recognise that the pupils themselves are not in a position to change the nature of oppression, whether in or out of school, and in different ways and to different degrees, are victims of it.

While girls are the chief victims of sexual oppression and therefore more resources need to be allocated to meeting the particular problems for girls, boys also need 'anti-sexist' education as a way of both undermining the brutalising effects of the construction of masculinity in this society and, by implication, challenging the effects of male sexism on girls. Most of our experience of anti-sexist work with boys has either been in setting up special courses to this end, or in developing 'topics' or units on particular issues of sexism within existing subjects.

Specific 'anti-sexist' courses for boys

Courses have been set up, both in boys' and mixed schools to focus especially on sexism and equal opportunities for boys. In mixed schools separate-sex work has been undertaken mainly in the pastoral curriculum. Because the socialisation processes for girls and boys are so different, as are our images of ourselves and our experiences, explicit anti-sexist courses for girls and boys also have to be very different. Explicit anti-sexist courses for girls have focused on sharing experiences of sexism, making its patterns visible, and equipping them with positive ways of offsetting it. With boys, teachers have worked on areas such as domestic role imbalances; unequal access to job opportunities; and stereotypes in the media and in books. Discussion around the more fundamental gender issues as they affect boys has been built into some anti-sexist courses — exploring with boys the kinds of pressure they are under, for instance, to act tough and not to show or talk about their feelings. The ways in which boys relate to one another have been addressed using themes like 'friendship' or 'bullying'. The aim has been to create a supportive classroom atmosphere which will encourage stereotyped 'norms' of masculinity to be challenged.

There are few such courses for boys in existence, and these often have a twofold approach which includes both the intention of fighting sexism and also offering boys access to those areas of the curriculum which have traditionally been viewed as 'female' areas. The course we were originally involved in developing had the following aims. First, to provide equal curriculum opportunities (including childcare studies and domestic crafts) to help boys to learn to take domestic responsibility and not to regard this as a women's realm. Second, to combat sexism by:

1 Helping boys to learn to express themselves and relate to others in ways traditionally considered to be within the female realm and not masculine attributes; developing behaviour which is often repressed in boys and men (this includes communicating in intimate ways; co-operation rather than competition; being supportive to each other; feeling responsible for the emotional well-being of each other).
2 Exploring explicit gender issues. In this context the following aims will be worked towards:
   (i) an examination of male and female stereotypical roles, attitudes and values;
   (ii) an awareness of the ways in which sex-role stereotyping imposes limits on the behaviour of both men/boys and women/girls;
   (iii) an exploration of positive alternatives to sex-role stereotypical behaviour.

We have found that provision of equal curricular opportunities, though very important in itself, does not automatically challenge sexist attitudes and behaviour in schools. Learning to cook, or learning about children, does not necessarily change boys' stereotyped notions about roles in the home. We have often heard comments such as: 'It's useful for when my wife goes into hospital' or 'It's a good idea because I might be on my own for a while before I get married'. In certain schools 'equal opportunities' work has been used as a foil for tackling some of the fundamental issues. For example, boys worked together in a small group making a meal and then eating it (often with a guest), as an opportunity to develop their ability to work collaboratively as well as develop a sense of responsibility for another person's well-being. The assessment built into the work allowed the boys to reflect, not on how good their finished food was but on how well they have worked together. The making and eating of a meal together in groups provided a valuable opportunity to develop social skills. We have often used practical work as a means of enabling discussion and thought about the topic rather than as an end in itself. For example, we used toy-making and book-making to allow the boys to think about the needs of young children and sex-role stereotyping.

Work on early childhood is incorporated into several 'anti-sexist' courses in boys' schools. The aims of this work have included: to extend equal opportunities by offering boys the chance to learn about young children; to encourage boys to regard child-care as the concern of males as well as females; to challenge role-stereotyped images of men and women; to examine how children are socialised into gender stereotypes; and to help boys to share their experiences and relate on a more personal level.

In two schools where we have worked, the boys had an additional sense of purpose when working on a child-development course by organising their own visits to the infant or nursery class of their old primary school. These visits were very successful and resulted, in some cases, in the boys being invited back to do such things as cooking with younger children or helping with teaching English as a second language.

We found it useful, when encouraging boys to share their own experiences, to relate our own memories of childhood and wrote stories to this end.

We have found that it was often less threatening to examine how younger children are socialised into gender stereotypes. For example, we discussed the toys we had played with and books we had read as young children (see Figures 1 and 2 — we designed these as posters to initiate discussion). We found that, because these stereotypes are so 'normalised', it was useful to examine them in conjunction with contrasting positive images. So we brought in a selection of children's books, some of which showed various stereotypes including gender, and some which presented alternative images. Our discussion led to the boys making their own 'non-stereotyped' children's books and toys.

A rather different 'course' on which one of us worked was a half-term project on developing work in single-sex groups in a junior school. This school (like many mixed schools attempting single-sex work) had a severe imbalance of girls and boys, with boys outnumbering girls by about 2½:1. The aims of this project were to:

1 give both girls and boys the experience of working in a single sex group;
2 give girls increased access/opportunity to certain non-stereotypical activities and teacher time;
3 encourage greater assertiveness in the girls;
4 give boys the opportunity to reflect upon and share their feelings with other boys and, at the same time, to develop listening and discussion skills; and
5 encourage boys to examine the expectations stereotypically put upon boys and the influence this has on their behaviour towards girls, and to offer alternatives to these.

In addition it was hoped to:

1 enable the mixed groups to operate more collaboratively and fairly;
2 encourage teachers to examine their own attitudes which might reinforce stereotypes; and
3 formulate some future strategies for these particular groups, teachers and the school as a whole that challenge sexist behaviour, opportunities and expectations.

This work was carried out with two first-year junior classes with children aged seven and eight, their two female class teachers and the male Head teacher. The boys in both classes doubled up to work with the Head and one class teacher, while the other class teacher took all the girls. The work took place over six afternoon sessions.

The original idea for carrying out the work arose from concern over the way in which the boys dominated the classroom and the playground, and the amount of aggression among them (this seems to be one of the major concerns behind similar work in secondary schools). It was therefore decided that the work with the boys should focus particularly on the ways boys relate to one another. In describing this work we concentrate primarily on the work with the boys because of the emphasis in this book.[1]

It was decided to try focusing on 'active tutorial' work with

Figure 1

Figure 2

the boys (although there are certain problems with this kind of work and we are far from uncritical of it[2]). The rationale behind active tutorial work or developmental work in tutor groups emphasises the development of such elements as supportive atmosphere, trust within the tutorial group, communication skills, the ability to project consequences for one's actions, and decision-making skills. The boys were brought together to sit in a circle in the hall and told that it had been decided to try some work on friendship and relating to one another. Each week they followed the same lesson structure. This was:

1 *An introductory activity* in the circle. For example, we played name games or clapping games.
2 *Discussion in pairs*. Each week we introduced this by an example from the teachers. The subject for discussion was kept very simple — 'Things that frighten me', 'Things I like about school'.
3 *Discussion in fours*. Each person related to the group what their partner had said in the pair discussion.
4 *Task*. Staying in small groups, the pupils carried out a task and shared the results: for example, putting some photographs in order to 'tell a story', writing a group collaborative poem.
5 *Physical activity*. This was an exercise to develop closeness between the boys, for example, 'trust walk', rocking one another.

The six-week project revealed some interesting issues. Each week at the beginning of the session the boys were restless, obviously felt unsure of what was happening and rather tense. They said things like: 'This is boring. Why can't we play with the computer toys?' They found the work difficult, but each week at the end (and progressively more so during the six weeks) they were clearly relaxed and enjoying themselves — sitting leaning against one another and the teachers in a relaxed atmosphere.

We felt that the plan to stick with the same lesson outline each week was crucial so that the boys began to understand what to expect. The intention of sticking to the same plan wavered after the first couple of weeks. However it was decided, because this was obviously something the boys found difficult, that we must give them more practice. This simple realisation was quite important — because at the beginning of lessons things didn't go as well as we'd hoped, we were tempted to abandon our plan. But giving the boys practice did pay off.

After six weeks, we felt that the boys were talking much more openly and listening much more carefully to one another. The Head and class teacher also felt that this *did* affect relationships positively back in the mixed class.

Although there seemed to be some positive feedback and this type of work may be a very useful starting point, we feel that it has its limitations. We do not feel that it can *fundamentally* affect the relationships between boys and girls.

Comments on specific anti-sexist courses

We believe that explicit anti-sexist courses such as we have been describing should not be offered as a solution to fundamental problems within the education system as a whole. In our view such courses as we have described are excellent and have a great deal to offer pupils, but they can only 'work' in a limited way because of the particular realities of the situation they were set up to combat. These 'structural' realities do not disappear by working with the pupils.

A course on anti-sexism puts the onus for change on the pupils. However, their behaviour is, in part at least, an outcome of the structure they operate within. This was particularly striking on one course we taught in a secondary school. During the initial few weeks of the course, taught to every first-year class (eight classes), almost every boy joined in the discussions enthusiastically, openly and with a great deal of empathy for other class members. However, over the following few weeks the boys began to be much less communicative about themselves; they became guarded; bullying seemed to be in evidence; and they began to question the validity of the work. Discussion became more difficult, and sometimes had to be abandoned in favour of more concrete activities. However, those classes whose teachers in other subjects were working in similar ways (for example, allowing for negotiation between teacher and pupil and including discussion work) continued to be able to discuss issues sensitively and with a great deal of obvious interest and involvement.

The whole school 'ethos' is vital in consideration of what

kinds of classroom method and teaching style can be implemented. In a school where the majority of classes are very formal, where the pupils are mainly passive learners, and where teaching methods are didactic and discussion kept to a minimum, it will be more difficult to teach in more informal ways. Pupil expectations of teacher roles may also be more rigidly stylised in keeping with the norms in the school. Additionally, teachers can find themselves in a dilemma when doing this kind of work. As one teacher said: 'It's difficult to get the balance right in this kind of work as far as pupil–teacher relationships are concerned. There's a thin line between being matey and sitting down chatting and being authoritarian'. The teacher wanting to create an atmosphere in which discussion can take place needs to develop a relationship with the pupils based on mutual regard and respect rather than authoritarian power. In many ways a classroom style which demands almost complete silence and obedience from pupils can be easier to attempt because the rules are much simpler. Moreover, the kind of relationship necessary for anti-sexist work with boys is extremely difficult to establish if there is only limited contact time, as is the case with many specific anti-sexist courses.

Another point which we found to be crucial concerns the way in which the needs for the course have been identified. While an anti-sexist focus may be helpful in identifying useful strategies and finding out what works well, we have realised that this has to be done in the broader context of looking at race and class oppression.

In secondary school, issues of equality of opportunity permeate every area of the curriculum; given this, they cannot be properly tackled as part of a separate course. Indeed, we found that this could be quite dangerous if it gives the illusion that they need not be tackled in other areas of school life. There are a great many important issues (for example, teacher expectations, teachers as role models) which have to be addressed if anti-sexist work is to be meaningful. If these are not taken into account across the curriculum, it is possible that the meanings and messages of an 'anti-sexist' course will be undermined or contradicted in other areas of the curriculum.

The advantage of 'a course' is that it will probably be taught by committed and enthusiastic teachers — if it is seen to be successful by other members of staff it may have a 'knock-on' effect within the school. This is particularly true where there is a policy of team teaching or an 'open door' policy where other members of staff are very actively encouraged to observe or join in lessons where possible. In this way we have seen some courses act as a spur to the development of a whole school approach to a policy within the curriculum.

Units of 'anti-sexist' work within the curriculum generally

Most teachers are either not in a position to or do not think it is desirable to set up a separate course in which to address issues of sexism. We have done 'support teaching' with many teachers in boys' schools to develop units of work which might be used elsewhere: for example, within English, humanities, home economics, social education, art or pastoral courses. All the materials which we produced are aimed at boys at top junior or lower secondary school levels (that is, ages nine to thirteen). Although some of the units could be suitable for girls as well as boys, they were specifically developed with boys in mind. If they were to be used with girls in mixed classrooms it would be necessary to rethink the context within which they are presented. As we have already stressed, certain styles and teaching methods are helpful in facilitating discussion of issues: method and style can be itself implicitly anti-sexist by challenging the stereotypes about how boys/men and women teachers should behave. For example, various teachers have become aware of themselves as 'role' models in terms of challenging sexist assumptions. Several men teachers talked to us about the dilemma of trying to get the boys to question male stereotypes of power and strength, on the one hand, yet found themselves relating to the boys in those terms on the other.

Didactic teaching methods seem to us inappropriate. So also do methods which try to lead the boys to a 'right' answer. We found, for example, that if we asked questions which sounded as though there was a 'right' answer, this inhibited real exploration. Where we asked for the pupil's own experience and gave ours, this seemed to generate a more lively and genuine discussion. It also enabled pupils to relate the issues

BRAVE MEN
on television and in films
are {Tough} and {Hard}
BUT
How Would They Get On In Real Life?

Would the Things They Do Be
BRAVE OR STUPID?

Muck Tray Chordates

→ What would you think of someone who—
→ Was always looking for a fight?
→ Was never scared or sad?
→ Was always trying to impress people
   by acting tough?

CAROL ROSS

Worksheet A

Worksheet B

more directly to themselves. Because of the nature of anti-sexist work, where children are being asked to reappraise the 'norms' of the world around them, it is important that scope is given for them to internalise the issues and relate them to their own experiences. If we are encouraging boys to explore their own experiences, it now seems to us vital that this includes space for them to reappraise the norms of a variety of circumstances surrounding their lives.

The remainder of this section gives examples of some of the anti-sexist units we have developed for use with boys. One unit of work was called 'Heroes and Stereotypes'. We wanted the boys to examine and question stereotypes of masculinity; reappraise a value system which prizes physical strength and aggression in males above all else; explore what we mean by the concept of a 'hero'; look critically at the images of masculinity presented by television, books, comics, magazines and cinema; and offer alternative images of masculinity.

When we used these materials some issues repeatedly arose. The central one was the problem of how to encourage pupils to re-evaluate the stereotypes involved in the concept of a 'hero', without either reinforcing those stereotypes or directly attacking pupils' sub-culture and, therefore, pupils themselves. We found that one way round this was to introduce humour into the materials as a way of involving the boys in their own gentle mockery of the concept of the television 'hero'. For example, the poster 'Brave Men' (Worksheet A) was used as a follow-on from some project work investigating various aspects of the television hero — for instance, violent images of men, and effects of violence on small children. This poster was intended to ask questions about how and why action is interpreted as brave or stupid. We found it useful also in moving the discussion from the subject of heroes to the question of bravery. The poster also stimulated discussion about different contexts in which the same action could be considered either brave or stupid. 'Ridiculous Heroes' (Worksheet B) was similarly used as a way of introducing humour.

Some teachers working on this topic felt initially that their approach led to resistance in the pupils. They felt that this was because they were trying to steer pupils to reach certain conclusions without being open about it. We found it more successful when we introduced the topic of 'heroes' with a clear hypothesis. For example: 'Television heroes encourage violence in young children'. The class then investigated this hypothesis.

Some teachers found that the point got muddled when they tried to develop the idea of an alternative 'hero'. They found it was better to talk about the concept of 'bravery'. We found it impossible to develop discussion in a non-stereotyped way because implicit in the concept of a 'hero' are qualities such as superior strength, intellect or skills. Furthermore, heroes are constantly superior rather than simply rising to the occasion.

Another 'unit' of work we have developed is called 'Talking Personally'. This was an attempt to provide materials aimed at challenging stereotypes of tough and competitive behaviour as 'masculine' and 'caring and gentle' behaviour as 'feminine'; attacking the idea that certain emotions are not 'masculine'; and helping the boys to express their more vulnerable feelings; and promoting understanding and trust within the group.

Materials in this unit included posters, role-play situations, poems, stories and photographs. For example, the poster 'I feel I'm 4 different people' (Worksheet C) was intended to explore how people get trapped in certain roles and images. It raises the different ways people experience themselves often in relation to the expectations others have of them. It was found to follow on well from bullying and was used to lead into gender stereotypes. All the materials in the units were produced with the intention of giving teachers something to trigger ideas. The materials were certainly never envisaged as perfected, finished products — many teachers have adapted them to suit their own situations. Worksheet C, for example, was used by one teacher in the following ways. In small groups the boys discussed what they thought was happening in the poster — how the boy was behaving in each picture. The teacher then gave some examples of different roles she took in her life, both now and as a child, for example 'When I'm a teacher I'm like this ... As a parent I'm like this ...'. The boys then made their own list of the roles they took in their lives (pupil, friend, Saturday job, brother, and so on). They talked and wrote about the way they behave in each role. This was followed by discussion about how they thought other people saw them in each role and expected them to behave. The discussion continued by focusing on which roles individual

Worksheet C

boys liked themselves most and least in. The boys discussed whether people find it hard to change the way they behave in each role — did people expect them to behave in certain ways? Some groups developed role play based on the ideas in the poster.

A second example from this unit was a prioritising exercise called 'How do boys feel in school?' (Worksheet D) which was used with small groups of boys as a starting point for discussing their experiences as first-year pupils in a large boys' inner-city comprehensive school. We found that this usually promoted a great deal of discussion and exchange of ideas which again was useful in breaking down some of the stereotypes of masculinity.

Comments on units of anti-sexist work within the curriculum generally

There are problems in attempting work on gender within existing curriculum areas. Much of the work we have been involved in has been concerned with developing an understanding of how 'stereotypes' operate, and why they are 'untrue'. We have found that introducing the concept of stereotypes is itself problematic. As we noted in relation to 'Heroes', lessons on stereotypes can actually reinforce stereotypes among some children. This can happen because of the apparent 'normality' of the stereotypes discussed. Thus, pointing out to pupils that stereotypes exist does not necessarily make them problematic for the children and encourage them to question them. We once observed a teacher who by pointing out stereotypes led the children to believe he was giving his own opinion about groups of people.

Another aspect of the problem is that so many stereotypes are offensive and emotive. In our experience, for some children to recognise a stereotype as destructive rather than as a description of reality, requires that the pupils have already gained the framework to understand it as such. We have tried to deal with this by discussing innocuous or silly statements — such as 'all children love baked beans', 'all boys are good at football', 'all teachers are unfair' — and ask pupils to talk about how people could get the idea that these statements were always true. We talked about images of children at school, on television, exaggerated stories from friends and advertisements. This led to

Worksheet D

How Do Boys Feel In School?

Boys behave differently when there are no girls around.	Teachers don't care what boys feel.
Most of the time at school, boys have to hide what they really feel.	It's harder to make real friends in secondary school than in primary school.
Being at an all-boys' school makes boys act more tough than they'd like to.	

1 Separate the cards into two piles: Agree and Disagree.
2 If there is more than 1 card in the Agree pile, put them in order from the one you most strongly agree with to the one you least strongly agree with.
3 If there is more than 1 card in the Disagree pile, put them in order from the one you most strongly disagree with to the one you least strongly disagree with.
4 Compare your piles with the people you're sitting next to.
5 Explain why you decided to put your cards in this order.
6 Think of some things *you* feel strongly about. Write them down as statements for discussion.

discourse about assumptions people make about others — because they are young or old; girls or boys; black or white.

Other issues include difficulty in identifying sexist patterns in society without directly criticising the boys themselves (or their families). Examining how sexism operates to oppress girls and women can be threatening and meaningless because it is difficult for boys to relate the issues directly to their lives and internalise them. 'Gender work is *against* boys — everyone's trying to tell me I'm wrong' is typical of the comments we have heard. In addition, the more explicit gender issues are difficult to discuss in a meaningful way because of the underlying relationships between boys themselves which we have described. As we have argued, there are pressures on boys in a boys' school to appear 'invulnerable', and until this dynamic is itself the object of discussion the outcome might be the creation of general unease, and perhaps more bullying.

These issues have led us to believe that anti-sexist work with boys must *start* with the boys' own interests, experiences and opinions. In Freire's (1972) terms, through re-thinking assumptions, actions may change:

> Students, as they are increasingly faced with problems relating to themselves in the world and with the world, will feel increasingly challenged and obliged to respond to that challenge. Because they apprehend the challenge as inter-related to other problems within a total context, not as a theoretical question, the resulting comprehension tends to be increasingly critical and thus constantly less alienated.

We have said throughout the book that we do not just view boys as 'the problem' in relation to sexism, but that institutional/ structural sexism also exists. We feel that any work done with pupils should be part of a process, therefore, which also challenges the values and assumptions on which the school as an institution is built.

Notes

1 The girls did some work with the computer, big tracks and robot (computer toys). They also carried out simple science experiments

around a theme (mechanics). Each week there was talk about what influence the presence of boys would have on their activity, and the ways they maintain their integrity and control in a mixed group. Both girls and class teacher said they looked forward to and enjoyed these sessions very much.

2 While the aims of active tutorial work are important, in our view they cannot be developed out of the context of the situations within which people live. Active tutorial type work may not take into account the social divisions within the group. Additionally, these aims need to be developed within all areas of the curriculum. We feel doubtful about whether they can be taught in one area of the curriculum and then 'internalised' and transferred to all other areas of school and life.

CHAPTER 6

In-Service Work with Teachers

In this chapter we will outline some of the workshops which we have developed and tried out with teachers. All of these workshops were produced in response to requests from individual schools or teachers' centres and were used as a way of exploring some issues relating to sexism in the school structure and anti-sexist work with boys. We will also touch on some issues which arose in relation to them. We think that, just as children need to use active learning methods in order to develop skills in questioning, evaluating and coming to decisions, participatory methods are equally helpful for teachers' understanding. In our work with teachers we have, therefore, tried to develop materials and ways of working which encourage this. The materials are presented as they were actually used in workshops with teachers and may provide a useful basis for adaptation to the needs of both other school situations and other groups, for example, parents. We have selected a small number of workshops as illustrations of the kinds of materials developed. These do not provide a comprehensive coverage of all the issues relating to anti-sexist work in boys' schools or with boys, nor are they offered as 'models' of good practice — we merely hope they may 'spark off' ideas. When the materials were used with teachers, several points were considered, for example, what kind of need has been identified and by whom? who are the participants (within one department, whole school, women's group, equal opportunities working party, parents)? is the workshop a 'one-off' or part of a developing series? is it aimed at mixed groups of men and women, women only or men only? how many people are taking part? how much time is there for the workshop?

Workshops addressing sexism in the school structure

We have argued in this book that issues relating to inequality are not just curriculum issues and need to be addressed by the whole staff with regard to both the curriculum and the school organisation and structure. We began our anti-sexist work with a focus on working with teachers to develop curricular initiatives. However, we became increasingly aware of the need to put curricular development into a broader school context. Many teachers we have worked with expressed a wish to find a way to raise consciousness in their school and gain support for curricular work from colleagues. Many of the teachers felt that their schools needed to confront the way that sexism is institutionalised in the basic school structure. They felt that anti-sexist curricular initiatives alone put all the onus for change on the boys and resulted in a one-dimensional approach to equal opportunity work in school.

Prioritising exercises

We have often been asked to work with the Equal Opportunities Working Party in a particular school. In some boys' schools this kind of working party exists alongside the Women's Group. In other schools, the Women's Group has developed into a mixed working party to promote equal opportunities. One of the difficulties at the outset of the formation of a Working Party (as with the Women's Group) may be identifying where best to put energies in a situation where so much needs to be done. We have found it a useful exercise to sort and prioritise tasks: for example, members of the Working Party ranking their priorities according to statements on cards (Worksheet E) (some cards can be left blank so that participants add their own — if they wish they can also be asked to change the wording). This task is followed by comparing, in small groups, individual priorities and attempting to reach a consensus on which priorities it is most feasible to act on.

Worksheet E

Identifying possible action and prioritising tasks in a boys' school	
Look at bias in materials and investigate alternatives (start small).	Choose an area of the curriculum where a small initiative could be made: develop and monitor it.
Investigate harassment in the school and make recommendations for dealing with it.	Look at how bullying and violence operate within the school and make recommendations for dealing with it.
Act as a consciousness-raising group.	Initiate in-service work with colleagues.
Act as a support group, e.g. for teachers who may have been harassed or for teachers trying to promote curricular initiatives.	Look at how the structure and organisation of the school may contribute to inequality and oppression.
Examine ways in which a separate focus on sexism, racism and classism could be contributing to work in each area being less effective and develop strategies for changing the situation.	Produce a school policy.
Look at ways of informing and involving parents.	Please write your own.

Some of the boys' schools in which we have worked have begun by developing a whole school policy. We ourselves have mixed views about this. On the one hand, we feel that a policy is useful in that it acts as a reference point for future action and behaviour, and legitimises work in this area. In theory, the whole school is then committed to the implementation of the policy: if something is out of line with the policy it is possible to refer to it in support of change or challenge. It is a *starting point*, but no more than this. The policy itself is not a solution, but a programme for change. However, we have seen situations where the production of the policy is itself seen as an end. The ways in which the policy are implemented, monitored and adapted to meet the changing needs and situation of the school are all crucial.

Discussion 'openers'

We have attempted to explore some of the fundamental ways in which sexism is part of the school structure. Looking back, we feel that starting by trying to involve all staff in these discussions can be pretty disastrous. For example, one of us was asked to 'talk' to a large staff group about anti-sexist work in boys' schools. The school was closed early for this purpose. However, the group was much too large to develop any real discussion, and there were several members of staff who clearly did not want to be there. We now feel it is much better to start on a small scale, with a few committed and interested people who can slowly make progress towards involving others. We have often been told by frustrated teachers who feel isolated in the school that there are 'so many teachers who just don't feel it's important, or who make fun of, or sabotage attempts to tackle inequalities'.

Teachers who are alone in feeling that change needs to be made need support and the chance to discover that their experiences are shared by others. We have run several courses and weekend workshops which have aimed to enable teachers in boys' schools to share their experiences of how sexism operates within their institutions. One useful starting point for discussion is to use quotes from former discussions as 'openers' (see, for example, Worksheet F).

The quotes used in this worksheet are from teachers discussing sexism in boys' schools. They touch on teaching styles: discipline; bullying; pastoral care; staff meetings; school hierarchy; sexual harassment; competition.

Worksheet F

1 *Individually*. Pick out about three cards which you feel express something about which you feel strongly.
2 *In small groups*. Compare and discuss why you have chosen these cards. Write your own statements if you feel strongly about some aspect of sexism not expressed by any of the statements.
3 *In whole group*. Feedback from the small groups of most important points made in discussions.
4 Start thinking about strategies for action. You may like to follow this up by writing some kind of statement/s from the group.

'I feel a dilemma about my teaching — if I try to teach in a non-authoritarian way I am stereotyped as a soft teacher. But if I try to be more authoritarian I feel I am both reinforcing a system I hate and undermining other ways of working'.	'I feel that bullying among the boys is an acting out of the power structures of the school itself. I think it's too simple to say it's the fault of individual boys'.
'I think it's important when we are looking at sexism in school to see it as part of a more fundamental oppression affecting black, gay and working-class children'.	'Discipline is the responsibility of the Head of House. Kids who misbehave are taken off to see him. There is little consultation with the form tutor and never any negotiation between the boy involved, the form tutor and the class'.
'Our staff meetings reflect the hierarchical organisation of the school. They are didactic and many people feel too intimidated to give their opinions'.	'It's not that sexual harassment isn't taken seriously in my school, it's that it's not even recognised when it happens. There's no policy structure for dealing with it'.

'Not many women are a part of the hierarchy in my school, and if they are it's in the subjects people feel are 'female' like languages, English or special needs'.	'When I first started teaching in a boys' school I felt completely deskilled like a probationary teacher all over again. I felt incompetent. But now I think that a lot of what I felt to be my being ineffectual is a direct result of in-built sexism in the structure. I think this exists in a mixed school, too, of course, but exaggerated vastly in all boys' schools'.
Please write your own	

Sexism exercise

Another approach which we have found helpful involves looking at how we internalise sexist assumptions and stereotypes and, in turn, how these affect our attitudes towards men and women teachers and the boys we teach. An extension of this involves looking at the similarities between assumptions about women and those about other oppressed groups. For example, we might begin by asking the course participants to 'brainstorm' their responses to the word 'sexism'. From this, we ask people to work in small groups to develop a definition of sexism. We then ask the group to pick a statement. These statements vary depending on the situation we are working in, but might be something like this:

1 It is absolutely natural for boys to behave in aggressive, 'macho' ways and for girls to be quiet and passive. Men and women are supposed to complement one another and we should not try to change that fact. It is all down to our genes!
2 If women teachers have trouble with discipline in boys' schools that is their problem. They should leave.
3 Women teachers who are harassed bring it on themselves. They should dress and behave differently.

4 Sexism isn't an issue in a boys-only school. It's important only in work with girls — after all they're the ones whose education will be affected if boys muck around in the lessons.
5 Sexism operates within all social institutions and affects all those working within them. As such, the education system ought to ensure that its effects are reduced to a minimum wherever possible.
6 Don't misunderstand me. I'm against sexism like the next person. But I think discussion about sexism in school takes time away from the really important thing — and that's getting kids through the exams, isn't it?

The groups are asked to discuss the statement in relation to the following questions:

1 What are the values and assumptions implicit in the statement?
2 What kinds of power relations are at work here?
3 What are the implications for practice?

Practice situations

In our own experience it is much easier to run workshops and courses at schools and centres other than those in which we have been permanently working. Teachers on these courses have talked of their own lack of confidence in setting up workshops in their own school situations for colleagues. We feel that this relates to how authority and status are conferred in schools; unless we hold a high-status post it can be very hard to be recognised as having particular skills to offer in the school. Many teachers found it helpful to work in small groups on a 'practice' situation. For example, at one weekend conference, the participants divided into four groups of about six people. The groups were given a task — in each case two of the groups had the same task. These tasks were to devise a workshop on one of the following themes:

1 Boys' behaviour in the classroom.
2 Possible aims for anti-sexist work with boys.

Each group spent a session planning the workshop, for example, deciding how it should be organised and who should lead it. Two groups which had worked on different themes were then 'paired up' and ran their workshops for each other. At the end of each session the groups gave one another feedback on the workshop. A third session allowed each group independently to assess how well their work had gone, how it might be changed or adapted, and whether it would be a suitable session to organise in school. This was one way in which we felt that some new and exciting ways of organising discussion and action were being generated in a 'safe' environment and, at the same time, there was an increased understanding of the issues involved for those involved in the 'practice'. An example of how this can work in school is that of a women's group in a boys' school taking on the planning and running of a staff conference. In this particular case, the number of staff was fairly small (under 50) and the women divided into small groups of three or four to work together on planning and running workshops with different themes — they practised these workshops on each other before running the sessions with other staff. Where these kinds of initiative have been taken they have generated a sense of excitement because they allow everyone to participate directly in bringing about change at a structural level.

Exploring issues in anti-sexist work with boys

We have run many workshops aimed at exploring strategies for working with boys and some issues involved in such work. One way in which we have found it helpful to start discussion about this work is by using a questionnaire, such as Worksheet G. This is filled in by workshop participants individually and then can be discussed in pairs — looking particularly at statements over which people disagree and exploring why this disagreement occurs. This exercise can be used as a very general 'way in' to some of the issues and can be followed by a focus on any one of the statements in ensuing workshops.

Worksheet G

	Agree	Disagree	Don't know
The only way we can do useful anti-sexist work with boys is within an overall school policy which seeks to change the structure and organisation of the school.			
Anti-sexist work cannot be just a part of one course — it must be part of a general change in the curriculum.			
Teachers are role models for children and therefore it is essential that they look at their own sexist attitudes and assumptions first before trying to change their pupils.			
Boys are not the 'problem' in relation to sexism. Their behaviour is a reflection of the way in which masculinity is constructed in this society.			
Anti-sexist work with boys must be done as part of a wider examination of inequality generally.			
Anti-sexist work with boys should be concerned with 'what's in it for them' rather than with just challenging their sexism.			

Aims of anti-sexist work with boys

We have found considerable disagreement over what the aims of anti-sexist work with boys might be. As a way of reaching some consensus we produced a list of possible aims which can be practised as a 'diamond nine' exercise (see Worksheet H). In this exercise participants, working in pairs, arrange the statements in a 'diamond' shape (the cards can be added to and altered as required). When the cards are prioritised small groups of people compare their priorities, trying to reach a consensus and discussing ways in which the aims can be put into practice.

Worksheet H

To teach boys home economics and child care (how to look after children).	To help boys communicate on a more personal level.
To help boys empathise with other people.	To help boys understand that there are ways of behaving other than 'macho'.
To promote collaborative rather than competitive work.	To gain an understanding of how oppression and exploitation operate.
To explore with boys ways in which people are sex-role stereotyped.	To look at sexist images in the media and in books.
To help boys learn to take responsibility for other people.	To help boys listen to other people.
Please write your own.	

Problems and issues in addressing sexism with boys

As we suggested in Chapter 5, various problems have emerged in attempting anti-sexist work with boys. Several teachers have talked about experiencing similar problems and we have found it helpful to share these experiences as a way of working towards finding solutions. We have also developed workshops with teachers who are just starting anti-sexist work with boys which aim to anticipate and, hopefully, avoid some of the 'pitfalls'. Where this is attempted quotations such as those from teachers on Worksheet I can be used. These may be considered in relation to anti-sexist curricular initiatives being taken within particular schools, with a focus on those which seem particularly relevant. We feel it is important for workshops to end on a positive note rather than focus only on 'problems'! With this in mind, a workshop focusing on problems can include time being given to a compilation of strategies for overcoming them.

Worksheet I

'Lots of classroom practice in boys' schools can be implicitly non-sexist such as presenting a balanced curriculum, providing resources which reflect women's achievements as well as men. When explicit anti-sexist work is being attempted this must determine the content of the lesson and include looking at the power structures and oppression involved. It must also occur within a context which recognises that the victims of sexism are girls and women although boys and men are also affected by it'.

'Presenting work which directly deals with exploring stereotypes is extremely difficult. It is easy to end up reinforcing stereotyped norms. Pointing out a stereotype doesn't necessarily make it problematic. It isn't self-evident that stereotypes are damaging unless you are already looking at them from a particular position'.

'It can be difficult to identify things as sexist in society without putting the kids down for how they live or what they like. For example, domestic roles at home; macho 'heroes' in comic books or on television'.

'Equal opportunities work with boys isn't necessarily anti-sexist. It doesn't necessarily challenge sex roles and assumptions. For example, some boys doing cooking said it would be useful "in case my wife is in hospital".'

'The dynamics of the classroom can undermine the anti-sexist content of the lesson. For example, the way the boys relate to a woman teacher; the way the boys relate to each other; the way a woman and a man teacher teaching relate to each other and the boys, e.g. who takes charge of discipline'.

'Focusing on sexism in isolation from other forms of oppression can inadvertently be racist or classist'.

'It's difficult to make issues of gender meaningful and related to the boys' lives, but if they are not able to internalise them, the anti-sexist work is meaningless'.

'Anti-sexist work with boys is in itself a contradiction. What do you say to boys in my class who said: "Gender work is *against* boys"? Particularly when the boys themselves are oppressed in so many other ways'.

Currently teachers in many schools are besieged with different demands and requirements from the education authority, from industry and from parents. They often have to prioritise issues which all seem equally important. Teachers are also under pressure from the media in relation to such things as discipline. It is not surprising, therefore, that many teachers in boys' schools do not see gender issues as an urgent priority. One important strategy for working in boys' schools is to show the ways in which anti-sexist work is good educational practice. Also anti-sexist strategies are often in line with recommendations made in other reports with a different focus. For example, and anti-sexist strategy stressing the importance of collaborative activities for boys would be in line with suggestions made about collaboration in reference to mixed ability teaching or the educational needs of bi-lingual pupils in the main-stream classroom. In this chapter we have looked briefly at some of the ways teachers can take on for themselves issues to do with examining sexism in school. It is important to recognise that there are limitations of the sorts of changes that can be made in schools without social change. We sometimes tend to look on schools as a vehicle for changing society. There may indeed be this potential but it is important at the same time to recognise them as perpetuating society. The next chapter briefly places schools as an institution within their broader social context.

CHAPTER 7

Conclusions

In this book we have focused on sexism in schools, primarily in boys' schools. We have addressed the issue of how boys relate to each other, to male and female teachers, to the position of women in the school, and to sexism in the curriculum, structure and organisation of the school.

We have tried to address the issue of sexism from two perspectives. These relate to approaches taken to exploring the issue more generally in wider society. One is concerned with looking at individual experiences of sexism and sexual inequalities, focusing on the socialisation of women and men, the dynamics between them, and on developing various personal strategies for change. The other is related to the political context, and involves examining sexism as a reflection of the socio-economic system, analysing social relations in terms of dominant power structures and institutions. We have tried throughout this book not only to describe various manifestations of sexism at an individual level, but to relate these to the power and value structures of the institution.

Schools are society in microcosm. Their purpose is to perpetuate the values and ideologies dominant in society, and they are organised so as to achieve this. These values and ideologies are those of the white, middle-class male. Boys learn to identify with the dominant group and its belief system which rewards achievement in competitive and individualistic, rather than collaborative, collective, terms. Success for one group means failure for another. This has clear implications for the socialisation and education of boys. We saw in earlier chapters how boys interrelate, approach their work, working in a more individualistic, competitive and aggressive way than did girls, and how the school system itself reinforces this, especially in boys-only schools.

We have argued that the most socially valued spheres are the domain of men. These are areas which relate to science and technology, the centre of economic and political power in our industrialised, technological society. We have also argued that women's roles exist essentially in relation to supporting and facilitating work done by men. According to Overfield (1982) 'the male (white, middle-class, heterosexual) is taken as the norm against which everything else is measured', and

> if the male, or masculine, is the baseline from which everything else is measured, anything else tends automatically to be defined as deviant, prohibited, or an expression of 'otherness' .... Conversely, it is seen as an achievement to *reach* male standards, to become *equal* on male terms, to attain accredited status.

She describes two fundamental results:

(1) Women are defined not on their own terms, not even from their own point of view, but in relation to the male — to men's wants, prejudices and fears;

(2) The male/female distinction is the first of a long line of divisions: masculine/feminine; subject/object; good/bad; logical/emotional — and the whole point of having categories means that entire populations are placed according to certain 'features'.

This has implications for the ways boys are socialised and develop. In Chapter 1 we looked at some socialising factors in the construction of masculinity, for instance, expectations of boys and the pressure on them to adopt masculine 'values' and behaviour. In our society any behaviour which falls outside of these 'norms' is 'unacceptable'. Thus in schools, and particularly in boys' schools, boys are at great pains to dissociate themselves from any traits regarded as female. We have discussed how this affects the ways they express themselves and relate to others.

Most of us generally accept what is called 'knowledge', especially 'scientific knowledge', as being unquestionable and unassailable 'truth'. Yet what is regarded as 'knowledge' is as socially constructed as is the use to which it is put. Western science has been developed within the tradition of 'objective' thought; the whole basis on which 'scientific truths' are established is supposed to be 'detached' and therefore beyond question. Furthermore, the discipline reflects 'male' qualities and these reinforce each other to promote an image of 'male rationality' which is supposed to be superior to any other form of consciousness. The whole notion of male rationality in this culture affects boys by teaching them to regard emotionality with suspicion and to avoid expressing their emotions (with the exception of anger) at all costs. It leads to the sorts of rigid and restricted way of boys interrelating which we describe in Chapters 1 and 2.

In our view, therefore, any meaningful anti-sexist work must involve changes in the curriculum which revise our concepts of knowledge and education. In Chapter 5 we talked about specific anti-sexist strategies with boys which could be used within the existing curriculum. This is, clearly, the area to which teachers have individual access with regard to implementing change. What types of change should be implemented is a contentious issue. It has been tempting to make those subjects which are not seen as 'boys' subjects more 'objective' and 'rational' in order to attract boys to them. For example, one recent approach to attracting more boys into Home Economics has been to try to reconstruct it as a more 'scientific' subject. This may attract boys initially but it does nothing to break down barriers between what is 'male' and what is 'female', what is 'affective' and what is 'objective'.

It is vital to understand the ways our social system is reflected and reproduced in our school system. We have suggested that, in society, the roles and 'characteristics' claimed by the dominant groups will determine the roles and 'characteristics' assigned to subordinate groups. It is therefore possible to learn a great deal about the position of subordinate groups through examining the dominant groups. In this book we look mainly at issues surrounding the education of boys because we believe this will help to illuminate prevailing structures in all educational systems. Within this, more explicitly, we believe that the ways boys are socialised and educated have direct implications for girls' education. In an important sense, 'masculinity' exists in direct contrast to femininity; what is 'feminine' is defined by what is 'masculine', and 'women's roles' are defined as complementary (and supportive) to 'men's roles'. We have looked at various 'male' attributes and examined the implications of how and what boys develop (or don't develop). Working with boys and coming to understand some of the ways they are socialised and educated has given us a clearer understanding about the position of girls.

Bibliography

Archer, J. (1979), *Animals under Stress*, Edward Arnold.

Archer, J. and Lloyd, B. (1982), *Sex and Gender*, Penguin Books, p. 105.

Archer, J. and Westerman, K. (1981), 'Sex differences in the aggressive behaviour of school children', *Brit. J. of Social and Clinical Psychology*.

Askew, S. and Ross, C. (1984), *Anti-sexist Work with Boys*, ILEA.

Assessment and Performance Unit (1983), *Language Performance in Schools*, Primary Survey Report No. 2, HMSO.

Baran, Graz (1986), 'Re-thinking the science curriculum', in *Secondary Issues: Some Approaches to Equal Opportunities in Secondary Schools*, ILEA.

Barrs, M. and Pidgeon, S. (1986), 'Gender and Reading', in *Language Matters*, ILEA, Centre for Language in Primary Education.

Bem, S.L. (1974), 'The measurement of psychological androgyny', *J. of Consulting and Clinical Psychology*, 42, pp. 155–62.

Benn, M. (1985), 'Isn't sexual harassment really about masculinity?', *Spare Rib, 156*, July.

Browne, N. and France, P. (1985), 'Only cissies wear dresses: a look at sexist talk in the nursery', in Gaby Weiner (ed.), *Just a Bunch of Girls*, Open University Press, p. 150.

Carabis, E. and Dodds, V. (1984), 'All in a day's work', unpublished paper, London University, p. 5.

Carricoates, K. (1978), 'Dinosaurs in the classroom: a re-examination of some aspects of the hidden curriculum in primary schools', *Women's Studies International Quarterly*, 1 (4), pp. 353–64.

Cockroft Report (1982), *Mathematics Counts: Report of the Committee of Inquiry into the Teaching of Mathematics in Schools*, HMSO.

Connell, B. (1985), 'A New Man', in *The English Curriculum*, ILEA, English Centre Publication.

Davis, J. and Tichner, J. (1986), 'Can girls build — or do they choose not to? A study of girls and boys using construction materials', in *Primary Teaching Studies*, Vol. No. 1, Polytechnic of North London.

110

Davison, J. (1985), 'Boys will be ...?', in *The English Curriculum: Gender*, ILEA, English Centre Publication.

Eggleston Report (1986), *Education for Some: The Educational and Vocational Experience of 15–18-year-old Members of Ethnic Minority Groups*, Trenthan Books.

EOC Report (1982), *What's in it for boys?*

Fish Report (1985), *Educational Opportunities for All*, ILEA.

Freire, P. (1972), *Pedagogy of the Oppressed*, Penguin.

French, J. (1986), 'Gender and the classroom', *New Society*, 7 March.

Fuller, M. (1980), 'Black girls in a London comprehensive school', in R. Deem (ed.), *Schooling for Women's Work*, Routledge and Kegan Paul.

Goldenberg, S. (1986), 'Race, sex and the missing link', *Teaching London Kids*, 23, p. 22.

Hargreaves, D. (1983), article in *New Society*, 10 March.

Hodson, P. (1984), *Men: an Investigation into the Emotional Male*, Ariel Books.

ILEA (1985), Report of the work of the working party on single sex and co-education, unpublished.

ILEA (1985), Junior survey. Referred to by Barrs, M and Pidgeon, S. (1986), in 'Gender and Reading', *Language Matters*. No. 1

Ingham, M (1984), *Men*, Century Publishing Company.

Kuhn, D., Nash, S.C. and Bruchan, L. (1978), 'Sex-role concepts of two- and three-year-olds', *Child Development*, 49, pp 445–51.

Levinson, D. (1978), *The Seasons of a Man's Life*, New York, Knopf.

Lloyd, T. (1985), *Working with Boys*, National Youth Bureau.

Lloyd, T. (1986), 'Boyswork: Discussion Paper No.1', unpublished.

Mahoney, P. (1985) *Schools for the Boys*, Hutchinson.

Metcalf, A. and Humphries, M. (1985), *The Sexuality of Men*, Pluto Press.

Minhas, R. (1986), 'Race, gender and class — making the connections', in *Secondary Issues: Some Approaches to Equal Opportunities in Secondary Schools*, ILEA.

Morrison, P. and Eardley, T. (1985), *About Men*, Channel 4 film.

Newson, J. and Newson, E. (1968), *Four Years Old in an Urban Community*, London, Allen and Unwin.

Newson, J. and Newson, E. (1984), 'Parents' perspectives on children's behaviour at school', in N. Frude and H. Gault (eds.), *'Disruptive Behaviour in Schools'*, John Wiley.

Nicholson, J. (1984), *Men and Women: How Different Are They?*, Oxford University Press.

O'Hagan, F.J. and Edmunds, G. (1982), 'Pupils' attitudes towards teachers: strategies for controlling disruptive behaviour', *Brit. J. of Ed. Psychology 52* (3), November, pp. 331–40.

Olweus, D. (1978), *Aggression in the Schools: Bullies and Whipping Boys*, John Wiley.

Overfield, K. (1982), 'The packaging of women: science and our sexuality', in *On the Problems of Men*, eds. S. Friedman and E. Sarah, The Women's Press, pp. 67–70.

Riley, K. (1985), 'Black girls speak for themselves', in Gaby Weiner (ed.), *Just a Bunch of Girls*, Open University Press.

Rose, R.M., Gordon T.P. and Bernstein, I.S. (1972), 'Plasma testosterone levels in male rhesus monkeys: influences of sexual and social stimuli', *Science, 178*, pp. 643–5.

Sandra, M. (1982), 'A Study of the experience of girls and boys in the Secondary mixed ability classroom in one school'. M.A. dissertation, Institute of Education, University of London.

Sandra, M. (1985), 'Ruler Banging and Other Noises', in *The English Curriculum: Gender*, ILEA, English Centre Publication.

Seidler, V. (1980), 'Raging Bull', in *Achilles' Heel*, No. 5, p. 9.

Smith, P.K. and Green, M. (1975), 'Aggressive behaviour in English nurseries and playgroups: sex differences and responses to adults', *Child Development, 46*, pp. 211–14.

Smith, C. and Lloyd, B.B. (1978), 'Maternal behaviour and perceived sex of infant', *Child Development, 49*, pp. 1263–5.

Spender, Dale (1982), *Invisible Women*, Writers and Readers, London.

Stanworth, M. (1981), *Gender and Schooling*, Hutchinson.

Suleiman, L. and Suleiman, S. (1985), 'An education in racism and sexism', in Gaby Weiner (ed.), *Just a Bunch of Girls*, Open University Press.

Tingle, S. (1985), 'Going mixed', in *The English Curriculum: Gender*, ILEA, English Centre Publication.

Tolson, A. (1977), *The Limits of Masculinity*, Tavistock.

Toynbee, P. (1985), 'So many bright little girls — and so many humble young women', in *The English Curriculum: Gender*, ILEA, English Centre Publication.

Walden, R. and Walkerdine, V. (1982), *Girls and Mathematics: The Early Years*, Bedford Way Papers, No. 8, University of London, Institute of Education.

Walden, R. and Walkerdine, V. (1985), *Girls and Mathematics: From Primary to Secondary Schooling*, Bedford Way Papers, No. 24, University of London, Institute of Education.

Walker, S. and Barton, L. (1983), *Gender, Class and Education*, The Falmer Press, p. 3.

Walkerdine, V. (1981), 'Sex, power and pedagogy', in *Science Education, 38*, Spring.

Weiner, G. (ed.), *Just a Bunch of Girls*, Open University Press.

Whitehead, F. *et al.* (1977) Children and their books', in *Schools Council Research Studies*, Macmillan Education.

Index

113